STRANGER WITH A STAR

A JACK SAGE WESTERN - BOOK 1

DONALD L. ROBERTSON

COPYRIGHT

1

June 2, 1870

The three shots jerked Jack Sage's attention from the water bottle pressed against his lips.

He slapped the cork stopper back into the bottle and dropped it. The short line, looped around the bottle's neck and secured to the saddle horn, saved it from crashing to the rocky ground.

A normally cautious man, Jack waited and listened. The shots had echoed from at least a mile down the road. Far enough to mute any spoken words or hoofbeats. Loosening his revolver in its holster, he pulled his .56-56 Spencer from the boot. Astride Smokey, his big grulla gelding, he urged him into a walk. The mule he was leading stood firm, ears forward, eyes wide, peering down the road, reluctant to continue.

"Come on, Stonewall. Don't fight me now, or I'll sell you the first chance I get."

The mule's big brown eyes gazed up at Jack. As if considering the possibility, the animal stood a moment longer, then reluctantly stepped forward and shook his head, indicating his displeasure with being forced to advance toward the shots.

Jack gave the lead rope a sharp tug as he bumped Smokey into a fast walk. The rope tightened and then slackened, the mule giving in to a man he trusted—most of the time.

As he rode along the dusty Texas track, Jack cautiously scanned the mesquite and scrub oak. He leaned forward and spoke softly to the black-maned grulla he rode. "Smokey, I figure someone's in the dirt up ahead, so you keep a good lookout. You don't want me to be number two."

If a man had a mind to, the gorges and ridges covered with oak thickets, thorny mesquites, and prickly pear offered plenty of spots from which to ambush an innocent traveler. Jack was a careful man, but he didn't shy from trouble, and he wanted to get to whoever might be shot as rapidly and as safely as possible. The wars he had fought in had taught him to stay alert. He couldn't help a wounded man if he was shot.

Nearing where he suspected the shooting might have occurred, he removed his hat, dropped it over the saddle horn, and eased Smokey to the crest of the hill. Gradually, his line of vision lifted above the ridge. He pulled the horse to a stop.

He was looking into and across a shallow valley. A creek meandered along the grassy bottom. Tall pecan trees lined the water, and a wagon had been halted at the crossing. It was pulled by a two-horse team with a prime-looking thoroughbred tied to the rear. A man sat slumped over the wagon seat.

Jack saw no other activity. Whoever else had been here was long gone. Clucking, he started Smokey and Stonewall over the hill and into the valley. The thoroughbred spotted them, pulled at the lead rope as its head jerked up, and neighed. At the sound, the man in the wagon jerked himself erect, twisted his wounded body around, and pointed a big .44-caliber Walker Colt at Jack.

"Easy, mister," Jack said. "Ain't no call to get riled with me. I heard the shooting and came to help."

The man watched him as he rode nearer. The man's strength

must have given out, for the Walker dropped to his side, clunked on the dried wood of the seat.

The familiar smell of blood and death joined that of the honeysuckle.

"Thank God. I thought it might be the bandits coming back after their partner." With a weak hand he could barely lift, he pointed toward a thicket to his left.

Jack could just make out a booted leg thrusting from the brush. He swung down from Smokey, looped the reins around the saddle horn and secured Stonewall's lead rope across the mule's pack frame. Slapping him on the rump, he said, "Go get a drink, boys. I'll be with you in a minute."

His animals, who had been eyeing the water, made their way to the creek, while he lowered the hammer on the Spencer, placing it in the wagon bed. His right hand grasped the .36-caliber Remington New Model Police and, in one fluid motion, slipped it from its holster. With the Remington ready, he carefully moved toward the boot.

"I am quite sure he's dead," the man in the wagon said. "I do not miss at that range."

Jack nodded, his face impassive. Many a fellow had been killed by a supposedly dead man. He slowly stepped around the bush, bringing the man into full view.

He was tall and young, his youth emphasized by the surprised look still on his face, like that of a boy when his mother catches him stealing a cookie from a cookie jar. His gun was still clenched in his left hand. His eyes stared sightless into the dark tops of the pecan trees, and a bullet hole was centered in the middle of his forehead.

"Yep, you're right on both counts, mister. You don't miss, and he's danged sure dead."

Jack turned back toward the wagon, dropping his Remington into its holster. "Now, let's have a look at you."

He climbed into the wagon, could see the blood on the right

side of the man's chest, and continued to look him over. "You hit anywhere else?"

The man shook his head, turned it quickly over the side of the wagon, and threw up. He extracted a handkerchief from inside his vest with his left hand and wiped his mouth. "Sorry, it has been a long time since I shot a man, especially anyone that young."

"No need to apologize. Unfortunately, they don't realize it, but if they're old enough to point a gun at someone, they're old enough to die. Can you stand?"

"I think so." He stood on shaky legs.

"Let's get you into the wagon bed, and you can stretch out." Jack helped the man over the seat and lowered him gently. He leaned him against one of the large canvas-wrapped packets and eased off the man's coat. "You got a name?"

"My name is Bartholomew Stanton Lawrence the third, but you can call me Bart."

"That's a good thing, Bart. Don't know if I could get my tongue wrapped around all of that." Jack removed Bart's vest and examined the bloody shirt. "Hate to do it. That don't appear to be a cheap shirt, but I'm gonna have to cut it off you. It'd take too much movement to take it off, and that bullet may have broken bones."

While he was talking, Jack reached into his pocket and pulled out his Barlow. He opened it and pulled the shirt away from the wound. The Barlow's blade sliced through the shirt like slicing butter. Once Bart's shoulder was exposed, Jack examined the entry hole. Bart winced but said nothing as Jack's fingers pressed around the wound. He leaned the wounded man forward and examined his back. There was a bulge under the skin where the bullet remained.

"Bart, I've got some good news for you. It appears nothing's broken."

The wounded man examined Jack's face. "I'd say there is a but in there."

"Yep. But the bullet didn't make it all the way through your shoulder. The skin above the wound is bulging. Also, it took some of your shirt with it when it went in. You don't want to poison up, so all the cloth and the bullet need to come out."

Bart nodded. "I understand. I have spent time in the army. I know the importance of preventing infection."

Jack heard Smokey and Stonewall and turned to see them walking toward a patch of grass. *They'll be there for a while,* he thought and turned back to Bart. "We've got a couple of problems. One, it's important we get that gunshot taken care of, but it's also important we clear out of here as soon as possible. Those gents could be coming back, and they just might be bringing friends."

"I was returning to Cherry Creek when I was attacked. It is less than five miles down the road. They have a doctor, whom I think I would rather have digging on me instead of you. No offense meant, I assure you."

"None taken." Using the remains of Bart's shirt, he bandaged the wounded shoulder, looked at his handiwork, and gave a satisfied nod. "I think that'll hold you. Let me tie my animals beside that fine-looking thoroughbred, and we'll be on our way."

He jumped down from the wagon and gathered Smokey and Stonewall. Once they were tied, he walked over to the dead man, dragged him to the back of the wagon, and heaved him in. The man's body flopped next to Bart. Climbing back in, Jack looked first at the dead man and then at Bart, who had calmly lifted the dead man's arm and tossed it from across his body. "I'll tell you, this wagon ain't gonna be a fun ride with that shoulder."

"I am well aware of what lies ahead, Mister—?"

"Folks call me Jack, Jack Sage." He looked at the seat and then at the wagon bed. "This seat has a spring. You'd be a mite more comfortable on it than stretched out back there. That is, if you can sit up." He paused for a moment, staring at the dead body. "Plus it'll be a lot less crowded."

"Good idea, Jack," Bart said coolly. "I believe I can. If you would be so kind as to give me a hand, I do believe I shall be able to move back to the seat."

After Bart was positioned on the seat next to him, and his Spencer leaned between his leg and the wagon wall, he clucked at the team. With a jerk, the wagon bounced forward across the rocky creek.

Bart, his face pale from pain, threw Jack a weak grin.

Jack jerked his head toward the bed of the wagon. "It'd be a lot worse ride back there, and you'd have company."

Reaching the more level ground on the opposite side of the creek, Jack noticed his passenger relax some. "This ain't much of a road, but it's smoother than what we just came out of."

"You are correct, my friend."

They rode in silence, Jack continuously scanning the red rock and green-tinted orange boulders scattered among the oak and mesquite thickets. Finally he turned to Bart. "Sure thought I heard three shots."

Bart nodded. "You did. There were five of them. I had just pulled up to water the stock when they appeared out of the brush, all on foot. They told me to step down, or they'd kill me where I sat."

The front wagon wheel on Bart's side dropped into a deep hole, jerking him to the edge of the wagon. Jack grabbed him before he fell out. His big hand clutched the man's left arm, yanking him upright. Bart gasped, but held on. The front wheel jerked up and out of the hole, and moments later the back wheel went through the same jolt, but this time tossing the heavy packaged equipment around the bed, metal clanging on metal.

The wheels cleared the hole, leaving one of the heavy packages resting on the legs of the dead man. After glancing back and then returning his gaze to the team, Jack said, "Don't think he'll mind a little weight on his legs. You were telling me about the three shots."

"Yes, as I was saying, there were five of them, all on foot. One of them, I assume the leader, told me to step down, but then, for no reason I could see, he shot me. At that point, I drew my weapon and shot him in the belly. That's when he"—Bart nodded back toward the dead man—"thumbed back the hammer on the six-gun he was holding on me. I had to protect myself, so I shot him in the head. It all happened in a very short span of time. When the boy started to fall, the others took off back through the brush. Moments later I heard their horses racing away."

Bart shook his head. "The funny thing is, there were three others. Any one of them could have killed me before I fired another shot, but they all ran."

"Cowards. All they could think about was you killing them like you did their two partners. They figured they had themselves an easy dude from the east, but instead they found a fellow with the bark on. They may still be running. I figure the one you shot in the belly'll die. I'm surprised they didn't leave him, too."

Bart winced with another sharp jerk of the wagon. "The man I shot in the stomach wheeled around as soon as he was hit and disappeared into the brush."

"Most likely why he wasn't left to bleed out and die, but he'll be dead by now. That big Walker would've blown a hole big enough for most everything to leak out."

The two men rode in silence, Jack trying to miss the larger holes and rocks. Still, the wagon occasionally jerked hard enough to cause Bart's face to tighten and his eyes to squint, almost closing, with pain.

After another rather severe jolt, Jack asked, "You gonna make it?"

"Yes. It's not much farther. In fact, when we reach the top of this next rise, you'll be able to see it."

Topping out, the town came into view. *Bigger than I expected,* Jack thought. *There's even a bank.*

"The doc's office is the rock house on this end of the street."

Jack nodded, thinking the horses would enjoy the shade cast by a massive red oak standing next to the house. He stopped the horses beneath the oak, swung down, and moved to the other side of the wagon to help Bart.

He heard the door open behind him, footsteps, and a man of similar age to Jack hurried from the house. The man was shorter than Jack, but that wasn't unusual. He had thick black hair graying at the sideburns and piercing blue eyes. He wore an open vest over a brilliantly clean white shirt. With no concern for blood on his shirt, he stepped to Bart's right side and placed his arm around the wounded man's waist. "Let me help." He nodded to Jack and started toward the front door. "I'm Dr. Alexander Cook." Then to Bart, as if he were speaking to a child, he said, "Bartholomew, you've lost a lot of blood. Let's get you inside, where I can examine your wound."

Jack had placed his foot on the first step leading up to the front porch when a striking young woman stepped through the door. Her blonde hair was pulled back from her face, and she was wiping her hands on a towel. Her dark blue eyes were the color of the Atlantic off the Georgia coast. Flour graced her forehead where she must have pushed her unruly blonde curls from her face with one of her slim hands. A smooth forehead was now creased with lines of worry. "Oh, Bartholomew, what happened? Have you been shot?"

Blue eyes wide with questions, she looked first to Bart, then Dr. Cook.

Before either answered, she backed into the house. "Come in. Hurry."

Stepping inside the home, Jack assessed the interior. To his left was a parlor containing a green sofa, two high-backed chairs, and an oak table. On a smaller table, at the end of the sofa, sat a simple porcelain tea set and a porcelain hooded lamp. A hall continued to what Jack figured were the bedrooms and kitchen. To the right stood an open door.

With a long delicate finger, the blonde pointed toward the door. The doctor stepped ahead and into the room, leaving Jack to help the wounded man through the narrow doorway.

Light coursed into the large room from the windows on the side and front. The antiseptic smell of the room brought back painful thoughts to Jack, but he didn't pause. He moved Bart toward the high, narrow examination table in the middle of the room. It was covered with a pad, white sheets, and a pillow. "Here," the doctor said, indicating the table. Jack helped Bart sit.

Dr. Cook looked at the blonde. "Nancy, please get hot water started, and bring my tray." He gently began removing the bandage Jack had made out of Bart's shirt, and glanced at Jack. "I don't think you mentioned your name."

Jack shook his head. "Didn't, but it's Sage, Jack Sage."

The doctor, completing the removal of the bandage, paused for a moment, the corners of his eyes and brow wrinkling in concentration. He looked up at Jack. "I've heard that name before."

Jack said nothing.

With Bart's bandage clear, Dr. Cook began examining the wound, first the entrance and then Bart's back, which now had a bluish-purple circle around the obvious bump that was the bullet pushing against the skin. Shooting an accusing look at Jack, he started to speak, but Bart jumped in first.

"Don't get huffy, Alex. I was shot at the creek crossing. Since you were so close, I figured it would be better for you to do the cutting and cleaning than for Mr. Sage to take on the job. You have the expertise and the equipment." He paused for a moment. "Plus you have Nancy."

Nancy walked back into the room carrying a basin of steaming water, which she placed on a wide cabinet at the head of the exam table. "Did I hear my name?" She bent, opened a door in the cabinet, and removed a towel-covered tray. Turning, she placed it on the stand next to the exam table.

"You did," Dr. Cook said. "Would you take Mr. Sage into the parlor. Perhaps he would like a cup of coffee. Then you can return and give me a hand with Bart."

She cast a worried look toward Bart and said, "Certainly, Alex. I'll be glad to," and turned back to Jack. "Mr. Sage, would you follow me?"

"Sure."

Before he could leave, Bart's left hand shot out and grasped Jack's arm. "Thank you for helping me, Mr. Sage. I would have been in extremis had you not arrived and volunteered your aid."

Jack nodded. "Think nothing of it. Right place, right time."

Nancy had paused, waiting. Now she motioned. "This way, Mr. Sage."

They walked into the parlor, and Nancy turned to look up at him. "I hope you won't think me forward, but you are a big man. May I ask your height?"

He grinned down at the lovely blonde. "Yes, ma'am. You sure can. The last time anybody checked was when I joined the army during the war. At that time, I was six feet and three and a half inches tall. They weighed me, too. I weighed two hundred and five pounds. I think I've lost some weight since then, but I'm still a load for that grulla." He tossed a thumb toward the animals tied up in front.

"Well, since I'm being so inquisitive, would you mind one more question?"

"No, ma'am, I wouldn't mind at all."

"I don't think I've ever seen a horse that color. You called it a grulla?"

"I did. Some folks call it a gray dun, but down Laredo way, they call it a grulla. It's because of its coloration. It's gray with a black mane and tail, legs too. When you get up close, you can see a few stripes in the black on his legs, and a black stripe down the middle of his back. He's also got a white face. Mighty fine horse."

"He is certainly big."

Jack grinned. "He has to be to carry me."

She smiled and said, "I can see that. Please have a seat," indicating the sofa. On the wall, across from the sofa, hung an oval mirror. Jack couldn't help but notice his reflection in the mirror and the black stubble on his wide face. Above a straight nose that had never been broken, gray eyes stared back at him. With a big hand he reached up and rubbed the stubble. Streaks of dust across his broad forehead mixed with the sweat caused by the Texas summer heat.

"Ma'am, I've been on the trail for quite a few days, and I'm mighty dirty and dusty. I'd rather not mess up your sofa." He couldn't help noticing the striking deep blue of her eyes framed in golden hair and the wide red lips when she tilted her head back to look up at him.

"Nonsense. Alex gets cowhands in here much dirtier than you could ever hope to be. Now sit, and I'll bring you a cup of coffee, or would you prefer tea?"

"Coffee's fine, ma'am."

"I'll be right back."

She whirled away from him and hurried down the hall. He couldn't help but notice her slim stature swelling out in all the right places. He looked away. It wouldn't do to be getting feelings for a married woman.

2

She was back in no time, carrying a tray with a porcelain pot, a cup, and a saucer of cookies.

He rose to his feet as she entered. "Ma'am, we haven't been rightly introduced. My name is Sage, Jack Sage."

She extended a delicate white hand. Small and soft, it disappeared in his calloused paw, but the shake was firm. "How do you do, Mr. Sage. My name is Nancy Cook. Please call me Nancy. Now sit down and enjoy your coffee. I brought some sugar cookies I made this morning. I hope you enjoy them."

"Thank you, Nancy."

Dr. Cook's voice rose from the other room. "Nancy! I need your help."

She gave Jack a quick smile and hurried to assist the doctor, closing the door.

He poured himself a cup of coffee. The welcome aroma of the fresh brew enveloped him, his mouth watering. Normally he drank it black, but he couldn't resist the fresh cream. After pouring in a substantial amount of cream, he picked up the spoon and thought, *What the heck,* and shoveled two rounded spoons of sugar into the coffee. He carefully stirred the concoction. The cup was too full to lift to his mouth. The last thing he wanted was to spill coffee on what looked like an expensive rug. He leaned over and slurped it from the cup and gave a sigh of contentment.

The brew was delicious. He hadn't tasted anything like that for quite a while. His coffee had to be strained through his teeth, and this, with the cream and sugar, was like a big dessert. When he thought of dessert, he remembered the cookies and picked one up, squeezing it between his big fingers. It was soft in the middle, just like his ma used to make. He took a bite. The crispy edges gave it a crunchy feel while the soft center was chewy. The cookie disappeared in two bites.

After several slurps of coffee, the level was low enough to bring the cup to his lips. He lifted it and cautiously took a long sip of the hot liquid just as several distant shots rang out. He jerked, his hand reaching for his holstered weapon.

After hearing no other disturbance, he relaxed. *Could be cowhands letting off steam,* he thought. He took another sip, still thinking, *Anyway, this isn't my town. I'm just passing through.* He relaxed back into the sofa.

Moments later, he heard running footsteps, pounding on the door, and someone calling, "Doc!" Whoever it was, they didn't wait. A portly, white-haired man charged into the house, halting suddenly upon seeing Jack. The tall man behind him ran into him and would have knocked the older man down if Jack hadn't reached out an arm and steadied him. Flustered, and examining Jack, the portly man pulled at the bottom of his vest self-consciously and nodded. "Thank you."

He would have said more, but the examination room door flew open, and Nancy stood in the doorway. She looked first at the portly man and then the tall one. "Mr. Franklin, Mr. Pierce, what has happened?"

The tall man, Mr. Pierce, received a scowl from the other man when he spoke first. "Man's been shot, Nancy. Right there in my store. He weren't doing a thing. One of them lowdown Lazy T hands drew on him and shot him. Right there in front of his wife and kids. I don't think the man even had a gun."

The portly man finally got a word in. "I know he didn't. He's homesteading on the land over on Cherry Creek. Name's Tobias Carter. Came into the bank today. I just gave him a loan." The banker shook his head. "I should've known better. They're good people, people we need in this country, but they don't have a chance."

Dr. Cook pushed past Nancy, a bag in his hand. "Where is he?"

"He's in my store, next to the candy counter. He was getting hard candy for his kids when Blaisdale shot him. Laughed at him, said, 'I can't stand sodbusters or their vermin,' and shot him. I was afraid he was going to shoot the whole family, but he turned and walked out, whistling."

"Show me," the doc said, and charged around the two men. Over his shoulder he called to Nancy, "Take care of Bart and sterilize the instruments. I may be back with Mr. Carter."

Nancy looked over at Jack.

He held up the china cup. "Mighty fine coffee, ma'am. Those cookies are right tasty, too." He took another sip of coffee.

She stared at the low-slung gun on his hip, then looked up into his gray eyes. "Aren't you going to help?"

"Not much I can do, Nancy. I'm not from around here. I'm not big on taking sides in something I'm not familiar with."

"You heard Mr. Franklin. Both he and Mr. Pierce said the poor man was unarmed. This Blaisdale shot him down in cold blood."

"That may or may not be true, ma'am. Anyway, this is something for your marshal to take care of, not me."

Jack watched those eyes, which had been so soft and blue and kind before, turn rock hard. She glared at him. Ice dripped from her every word. "Mr. Sage, you are obviously familiar with the use of a gun, and you could be a great help to that family. I would think you would at least look into it. Those poor people need your help, and, for your information, we have no marshal. He was ambushed and killed over two weeks ago, and no one will take the job."

Jack looked at the cup, still half full of cream and sugar and coffee. He looked down at the almost full plate of cookies. *Only one,* he thought, *and it was mighty good. I shoulda eaten faster.* He gave a big sigh, took one last sip of coffee, and set the cup on the serving platter.

"Well, ma'am, it's been nice meeting you. There's a dead body in the wagon, and those horses need some watering, so I'll head on into town. Maybe I'll stop by the store."

"You can leave the body at the barber's," Bart, in a weak voice, called from the examining room. "He takes care of any burying needed here. Johnson's Stables is the place to leave my horses and wagon. He's old and cranky, but the best in town. Just leave my things in the wagon. And Jack?"

"Yeah?"

"Be careful. Blaisdale is fast."

"Thanks, Bart. Reckon I'm not lookin' for any trouble with this Blaisdale. I'll take care of your stuff and probably be on my way." He picked his hat up from the sofa and nodded to Nancy. "Thank you, ma'am. Those cookies were mighty good. So was that coffee."

She eyed him coolly. "You're welcome, Mr. Sage. I'd suggest you do as Bartholomew said and be careful."

He looked at her long and hard. "Truth is, ma'am, I wouldn't be needin' to be careful if you hadn't prodded me into going."

Nancy's face flushed, and one hand flew to her cheek. "I . . ."

Jack put his gray, sweat-stained Stetson on his head. Using both hands, right at the front of the hat and left at the back, he straightened it until it was level, just the way he liked it, and raised his right hand to touch a finger to the brim. "Ma'am."

Stepping onto the porch, he looked to both sides of the house, then widened his scan until he was comfortable there was no threat near. Moving quickly, he reached the wagon, untied the horses, stepped onto the wheel and into the wagon. Glancing at the wagon bed, he confirmed what he had suspected. The Texas heat was swelling the dead body, and it was beginning to stink. Turning the horses toward the town, he snapped the reins, and they stepped out at a trot.

It wasn't a big town, but it wasn't small either. There was a bank, a general store, three saloons, the barber, whose window advertisement let everyone know he was also a dentist and an undertaker, a gunsmith, and two liveries. Several homes extended up and down the street. The livery on the left was the one he needed. The bank sat across the street from the general store.

In front of the store sat a wagon drawn by a single horse. It was loaded, waiting for its owner.

Jack, he thought, nearing the store, *you can drive right on by. You owe no one in this town a thing. You've had some good coffee and a cookie. You promised yourself you would never again get involved with other people's problems. You've done it too many times.* He thought he was going to make it. He thought he had his mind made up. He thought wrong.

Jack brought the wagon to a halt in front of the store, looked at the open door, and listened to the sound of crying coming from inside. Resigned, he climbed down from the wagon, slipped the leather thong from the hammer of his Remington, and checked it was loose in the holster.

From down the street, he could hear laughter and a tinny-sounding piano banging away. He walked into the store, dry boards creaking under his weight. As he stepped over the threshold, it was like he could feel and hear the heavy steel door of a bank vault slamming shut. It was his mind. He had decided, and he wasn't much for changing direction.

Inside, the crying was louder. He followed the sound. Dr. Cook was bent over a slim man of about thirty. The woman next to him was near the same age. She looked up, and seeing his gun, her eyes widened with fear.

Jack held his palms toward her as the children pressed against her. "I mean you no harm, ma'am."

The doctor glanced around and nodded his head in assurance. "He's fine, Mrs. Carter—a friend."

The doctor's turning had given Jack a better view. The wounded man had a big hole in his belly the doctor was trying to clean. There was only a little bleeding. Jack knew no bleeding from a belly wound meant the injured man was probably bleeding inside.

The wounded man gasped out, "Am I gonna make it, Doc? My family." His mouth pulled down, and his face scrunched up like a dried-up grape while a wave of pain washed over him.

Dr. Cook looked up at Mrs. Carter and shook his head. The woman's brown eyes were red from crying. Channels had been cut in the dust on her cheeks as the tears flowed to her chin, only to drip off, leaving spots on her dusty dress. But at the doctor's headshake, she stopped crying, pulled a handkerchief from her pocket, wiped her eyes, and blew her nose. Jack stepped away to give them some privacy.

Women always amazed him. Where did they get their inner strength? His ma would have said God. He watched the lady gather her children and softly explain what was happening. He heard her tell them to tell their pa goodbye.

There were five. The youngest no more than three years old. He didn't understand what was happening, but his older brothers and sisters were crying, so he cried, too. He lay down beside his father, put his chubby little arms around the man's neck, and squeezed him tight. His little face buried in his pa's hair. Jack could faintly hear the boy say, "I wuv you. Goodbye, Pa. Jesus is waiting for you."

Jack was a hard man. In his thirty-five years he had fought in three wars. He had been wounded. He had killed other men and watched others die. But this was one of the most heartbreaking scenes he had ever endured. He turned and stood in the doorway, looking toward the saloons. He was unable to make out what the other children said, just their little voices murmuring, and their continued sobbing.

A lady, probably Mrs. Pierce, led the children to a back room. Jack watched them, the younger ones still crying, but going with her and disappearing behind a curtain. The older boy's face also had tear channels cut through the dust, but he was no longer crying. The young man, he looked to be twelve or thirteen, walked with a set chin and muscles working in his jaws. Jack had seen the look before and understood. After the children were gone, Jack looked back up the street at the saloons. Blaisdale was in one of them. His time was short.

Dr. Cook and Mrs. Carter stood. She shook his hand, looked momentarily at Jack, and joined Mrs. Pierce and the children in the back. Crying grew more intense and then quieted down. The doctor, wiping his hands on a bloody cloth, walked toward Jack. He was followed by Mr. Franklin and Mr. Pierce.

Jack looked his question at the doctor. Cook shook his head. "He's gone. He was lucky. The bullet must have clipped the liver, and he bled out quickly. Otherwise, he would have died, but it would have been a long and painful death."

Jack shook his head. "Too bad. Sometimes a man is just in the wrong place at the wrong time."

"Tell him," the banker, Franklin, said.

Dr. Cook looked up at Jack. "How tall are you?"

The question surprised him. "When I stopped growing, I was six feet, three and a half inches, but that's been a long time ago. I'm gettin' older, and I've ridden a mile or two. May have shortened up some."

The doctor looked at him. "Not by much if at all. I remembered where I knew your name from."

"Thought you might, eventually."

"You were marshal in Laredo shortly after the war. You cleaned the place up. Threw a bunch of folks in jail, though they were eventually released by a biased court. As I remember it, you also killed a few."

"I wasn't alone. I had help."

The banker spoke up. "Funny you should mention that word, Mr. Sage. We need *your* help."

"Who's we?"

The storekeeper, Lewis Pierce, spoke up. "The town. About six months ago a Mr. Scott Mather came to town, looking for a ranch to buy. The Lazy T was having a hard time, so I recommended it to Mather."

Jack frowned. "Why were they having a hard time? Grass is good. You can make enough to save or build a ranch on one cattle drive if you're successful."

"That was one of the problems. They tried a cattle drive and lost everything in a storm along the Red River. Stock drowned, got caught in quicksand, and was scattered by Indians. On top of all of that, homesteaders have started moving in and claiming much of the water. Makes it hard for the cattlemen to water their cattle. The Lazy T folks didn't have much fight left in them, so they sold out to Mather."

"That's right," the banker said. "Once he had the ranch, he started bringing in some mighty hard-bitten riders, gunmen I think."

Pierce nodded his head.

Franklin continued, "After that, homesteaders started disappearing, and the toughs started hurrahing our town. Our last marshal was bushwhacked only a couple of weeks ago. He was the third one we've hired. The other two quit."

Jack looked at the doctor, then at Pierce and Franklin. "You sure aren't making this job look very attractive. I can put on your badge and take my choice, either get run out of town or get shot.

You must be paying a mighty hefty wage. It'd take that for anyone but a fool to take the job."

The doctor looked directly at Jack. "A fool or a man who believed in justice."

The banker spoke up. "The town is small. It's growing, but we don't have a lot of money. We need the cowboys calmed down. Now that Mather has started it, a couple of the other ranches have joined in. The town and the homesteaders need protection."

"Whoa," Jack said. "That's not what a town marshal does. His jurisdiction goes only to the borders of your town. What about the sheriff?"

Dr. Cook looked at the other two. "We never see him, maybe once every two months." He gave the banker and Pierce a conspiratorial glance. "I'm sure the sheriff would be willing to deputize you when he found out who you are, especially if he didn't have to pay you."

Franklin frowned. "Whoa, who's going to pay Mr. Sage as deputy if the sheriff doesn't?"

"We are, Joseph," the doctor said. "We have to get this place under control, or we'll never survive. We have a newspaper about to start, when the owner recovers from his gunshot wound. We are growing. We need to protect the homesteaders and decent ranchers alike. I think Mr. Sage can do this."

The doctor gave the other two a questioning look. Pierce nodded enthusiastically, followed with a hesitant nod from Franklin. Dr. Cook, said, "Mr. Sage, we are prepared to pay you one hundred and fifty dollars a month as our marshal. Your juris-diction would include this part of the county where our home-steaders and ranchers are located."

"Now wait, Doc," Franklin said, "we haven't considered an amount that large. That is a lot of money."

Impatient with the banker's interruption, the doctor shook his head. "I'm not through." He turned back to Jack. "You will be provided a room at the hotel and three free meals a day either at the hotel or Ma McGinty's, whichever you desire. Also, your animals will be stabled and fed at Johnson's stable."

Franklin glared at Cook. "Is that all, Dr. Cook?"

The doctor smiled back at the banker. "Yes, Joseph, I believe it is."

Jack had made up his mind when he first stepped over the threshold of Pierce's store. He was in this until the bitter end. "First, do the three of you make up the city council?"

"No," Franklin said, "there are three others, but they will go along with whatever we decide, especially after today."

"Then I'll accept the job, but I will consult with no one about my actions. The city council has the power to hire me or fire me, but they will not"—he looked at each one—"you and you and you, plus those who are not here, will not tell me how to do my job. Is that understood?"

Both Dr. Cook and Mr. Pierce were nodding their heads, but Franklin's head was shaking. "Mr. Sage," he began, "we have the right—"

3

Jack bent, stepped through the door, and straightened his hat, ensuring it was level on his head. "This is not open for discussion. Good day, gentlemen." He strode toward the wagon.

"Wait, wait, wait, Mr. Sage," Franklin said. "It only seems fair that we have the right to oversee your work. You would be our employee."

Jack said nothing.

Reaching the horses, Jack flipped their lead loose from the hitching rail, fastened it to the harness, and walked around the animals to climb into the wagon. At the wagon's wheel he paused. Dr. Cook and Pierce were in a heated argument with Franklin. He stepped up and into the wagon and picked up the reins.

"Wait, Mr. Sage," Dr. Cook called.

Jack, reins in hand, turned his head toward the doctor.

"We gladly go along with your terms."

"Do you gladly go along with my terms, Mr. Franklin?"

The banker gave a slow nod. "Yes."

"Good. Then I want a document drawn up. I'm sure you have

an attorney in this town. I want it written with my requirements as I have stated them and signed by every councilman."

"And councilwoman," Pierce added.

"I beg your pardon?" Jack said.

The storekeeper gave Jack a half-smile. "I said 'and woman.'"

Jack looked at Dr. Cook.

"She's the owner of the Cherry Creek Saloon. Her name is Gabriella Campbell. She runs a reputable place. A cowhand or drifter or doctor"—at the last he shrugged—"gets an honest drink and a fair chance at cards or roulette. More than I can say for the Gilded Lily. Since that place opened, my business has increased, plus the jail's occupancy rate was up until the last marshal was shot."

"You have a badge?"

Franklin reached into his vest pocket and started to bring out a tin star.

Jack shook his head. "Hang on to it." He motioned with his head toward the dead man lying in the wagon. "He's gettin' ripe. I'll drop him off at the undertaker and take this wagon and horses to the stable. By that time, you should have our contract drawn up. By the way, feel free to include a termination clause in it. You can fire me at any time, but upon termination I will be paid an additional full two months' salary."

Franklin started to say something, but Cook flashed him a warning glance. "We'll have it drawn up by the time you're finished," Cook said. "Meet you at the marshal's office?"

Jack nodded and clucked to the horses. The wagon lurched forward. *After Laredo, I promised myself no more badges. I'll be lucky to get out of this with my skin intact, but those kids need to know their father can't be laughed at and shot without justice.*

Rolling by, he examined his new office on the left. It didn't look like much from the outside, just a shotgun building with a front entrance and a side exit partway back into an alley. Across the alley, the jail faced a two-story structure. The taller building had an outside stairway leading up to the second floor. In the front, a sign hung above the entrance, Val Jessup, Attorney at Law.

A gunsmith had a storefront to Jack's right, adjacent to Pierce's store. The Cherry Creek Saloon sat next to the attorney's office, and the Gilded Lily faced the Cherry Creek from across the street. Laughter and the tinny piano could be heard inside the tavern. Jack pulled the horses up in front of the next building on his right.

A red, white, and blue barber pole stood next to the large front window. Clearly visible through the window was an empty barber's or dentist's chair. He tied the horses, mounted the board-walk, and by the time he had made his two steps across the rough planking to the door, it swung open.

A man dressed in black trousers, a dingy white shirt, and a black vest waited inside the door, smiling. His smile exposed two gold teeth. "Come in, sir, come in. I am Reginald Farnsworth, dentist, barber, and final caretaker of the misfortunate. A very pleasant day to you. Are you here to have a tooth pulled or a haircut?"

"How about a burial."

The man looked Jack up and down, rubbing his bony hands together. "Well, sir, you look mighty healthy to me, but if you're sick and planning ahead, I can fix you right up. Yessirree, I certainly can. For a man of your size, and you are extremely large, if I do say so myself, it will be a bit more expensive."

"Not for me." Jack tossed a thumb toward the wagon. "Gent in the wagon—regular size, economy."

"Well, let me see. How did you say he died?"

"I didn't, but *you* could say lead poisoning."

Farnsworth nodded, eyes slightly hooded. "I see. Were you involved in his ... er ... demise?"

"No. Look. The man has been dead several hours. He's swelling and beginning to smell. All I want is to get him buried cheap and quick."

"Yes, yes of course, Mister . . .?"

"Sage, Jack Sage. Just call me Jack. How much?"

"Let's see." Farnsworth's brow wrinkled, and he started counting out on his long bony fingers. "The economy package is thirty-five dollars. Embalming adds another twenty-five, and a nice, basic casket will only add another fifteen. Mourners, of course, will take another seven dollars—"

"Look, *Mr.* Farnsworth. I'm not interested in any of that. This fella is a bushwhacker. All I want is for someone besides me to put him in the ground. If you can't do it, I'll haul him outside of town, find a ravine I can toss him into, and leave him for the skunks and coyotes."

"Well, if you want the dear departed to just be dropped in a hole, I can do that for twelve dollars."

"Make it ten and you've got a deal."

Farnsworth said nothing, just held out his open hand.

Jack fished out two half eagles and dropped them into the upturned palm. "Come on. Help me get him out of the wagon."

While they were haggling, several cowhands had gathered around the wagon. Jack walked out, followed by Farnsworth. The cowboys saw the big man coming toward the back of the wagon and moved aside.

One of them, a ruddy-complected cowhand with hair and eyebrows the color of sandstone, watched Jack approach. He nodded to the body. "You kill Junior?"

Jack walked to the back of the wagon, dropped the gate, and grabbed the dead man by the ankles. "Grab his arms," he said to Farnsworth, and yanked the man out of the wagon. The man's head and shoulders bounced over the floorboards of the wagon and dropped off the back.

The undertaker jumped forward just in time to catch his arms before the body crashed onto the ground. He started backing toward the door.

"Hey, big man. I'm talking to you."

The body drooped between Jack and Farnsworth, its butt banging on the edge of the boardwalk as Farnsworth backed up the steps.

The cowhands jumped back when Junior hit the boardwalk. "Careful," the cowhand who seemed to be in charge said, "that's Junior Blaisdale. His brother's not gonna be too happy with you, mister. Was I you, I'd handle him mighty careful like." He turned to a younger cowhand. "Toby, run over to the Lily and tell Flint his brother's body is at Farnsworth's."

The young cowhand turned and started to swagger toward the Gilded Lily.

"Run, I said!" the ruddy-complected cowboy yelled.

The boy broke into a run, spurs jingling as his boots thumped on the boardwalk.

Jack kicked the door closed behind him.

Farnsworth, carrying his end of the body, walked past the chair used for both the cutting of hair and pulling of teeth. "Bring him on back here." He continued through another door opening into a room with equipment Jack had no desire to learn about. The room had no windows, and the only light came through the door they had just entered. There was a kerosene lamp sitting on a stand next to a table, but it was unlit. The room had an exit at the back. "Put him on the table."

They dropped the man on the table, and Farnsworth let out a long breath. "Mr. Sage, I don't know how you're mixed up in this, but, should you desire, feel free to make use of my back door. In fact, I'd recommend it. You're a mighty big man, but Blaisdale is mean and fast with a gun. I have heard he thought quite highly of his brother."

Farnsworth indicated the body. "Though I'm not familiar with him, it seems that the cowhand out front is, and if this is, in fact, Junior Blaisdale, you are in deep trouble."

The front door clanged, and the sound of boots and spurs

filled the room. Farnsworth shook his head. "I'm afraid it's too late. Like I said, I can fix you up with a very nice burial."

Jack eased to one side of the door. On the one hand, he hated to have anything start before the town council signed his contract, but on the other, he could still hear the crying children and see the brown eyes of their mother filled with despair. He thought of the principle he had been taught as a button. Pa had always said, "If you're going up against a gang, get the leader first." It had always worked for him, even at seven years old, and he saw no reason to change now.

Blaisdale stepped through the door, followed by five cowboys, the sandy-haired one in the lead. In the dim light, Blaisdale saw his brother stretched out on the embalming table and headed straight for him. Jack could see the bullet hole in Junior's forehead had turned a nasty-looking black, and felt sure that was all Blaisdale was seeing.

The gunman must have sensed Jack's bulk and began to turn toward him. Before he could speak, Jack, using his left hand, hit him just in front of his ear with a massive fist. It sounded like a sledgehammer hitting a watermelon. Blaisdale's knees buckled, and he collapsed to the floor.

Eyes wide, the remaining cowhands stared at their unconscious leader piled on the floor at their feet. Then, in unison, their heads turned to Jack and the .36-caliber Remington New Model Police, dwarfed in his big right hand, the muzzle steady toward them.

Jack waggled the muzzle toward Blaisdale. "Pick him up, and take him to the jail. I'll be right behind you."

Still the spokesman of the bunch, the red-faced cowhand's eyes moved from the Remington to Jack's face. "What? Why?"

Jack leveled the Remington at the man's chest. "What's your name?"

"Red. Everybody calls me Red."

"Alright, Red, you boys pick up Blaisdale and do like I said."

Jack watched Red's face. The surprised look faded, and a stubborn frown took its place.

Red looked at the other four men. "Boys, he may be big, but he's just one man. There's five of us."

"Four," Jack said.

Puzzled, Red looked back at the men as if he was counting. "No there ain't. There's five."

Jack wiggled the muzzle of the Remington. "Red, if any one of your bunch makes a move, you're dead, so that makes four." He ran his gaze over the other four. "And boys, I've never seen the day I couldn't put down four men, especially this close." Jack's tone was cool, conversational. "This is the last time I'm saying this. Pick up Blaisdale and take him across the street to the jail."

Red seemed to have thought out the problem and arrived at the only sane conclusion. He moved to Blaisdale's arms, grabbed them, and looked up at the men. "Well, don't just stand there. Somebody grab his feet."

Two of the cowhands jumped forward. Each reached down and picked up a foot. Jack had been watching one of the men who had not moved. His hand was hanging loose by his low-slung revolver.

Jack swung the Remington to cover him. "You're welcome to try, young fella. I'm sure Mr. Farnsworth will welcome more business. You may think you're fast. You may even be the fastest man in town, but I've never seen a man outdraw a drawn weapon. To keep you from winding up a customer here, why don't you unbuckle that gun belt and hand it to Mr. Farnsworth."

The young man watched Jack's expressionless face only for a second, then slowly unbuckled his belt and handed it to Farnsworth.

"Good. You"—Jack pointed to the remaining cowhand with his Remington—"take an arm from Red." The man moved to take one of Blaisdale's arms.

. . .

THE FOUR ARMED men were now carrying Blaisdale, and the fifth was unarmed. "Get the door," Jack said to the unarmed cowhand.

"What about his hat?" the man said, pointing at Blaisdale's hat lying on the floor.

"Pick it up if you've a mind to, then get the door."

The cowhand scooped up Blaisdale's hat and headed for the front door. Jack followed the procession. They went through the door and down the boardwalk back the way Jack had just driven the wagon. In no time, they were surrounded by spectators.

As they stepped into the dusty street, to cross over to the jail, Jack said, still in a conversational tone, "Alright, folks, give us room." The spectators moved back. Blaisdale was still out, his head lolling from side to side.

Jack continuously scanned the buildings, rooftops, corners, and windows for anyone who might be hostile. He was relieved there were none, yet. They had been taken by surprise.

As they neared the marshal's office, he saw the door open and a striking woman step outside followed by Dr. Cook, who had a document in his hand. Jack nodded to the woman as he passed, catching the brilliant gold of her eyes, and followed the cowhands into the office. Inside was crowded with people. Ignoring them, Jack ordered, "Drop him." The two cowboys released his feet. Boots and spurs banged and jingled on the floor. The remaining cowhands lowered his arms slowly, allowing his head to gently rest on the floor.

Jack looked around the room and saw what he was looking for. Stepping over to a pitcher sitting next to a washbasin on a cabinet, he picked it up and shook it. Sure enough, there was water in it. He stepped back to Blaisdale and carefully poured the water onto the man's face so that it struck his upper lip, splashing and running into his nose. It took only a second before Blaisdale started gagging and coughing.

When the man began to shake his head and his eyes blinked, Jack handed the pitcher to the beautiful woman standing next to him. He reached down with one hand and yanked him to his feet. At the same time he jerked Blaisdale's revolver from its holster.

Blaisdale, now fully conscious, jerked his head back and forth, confused and surprised at the crowd around him. His eyes centered on the man holding his shirt collar so tight he was having a tough time breathing.

Jack could see the recognition fill the dark eyes. The man's hand flashed to his holster—empty. Jack slapped him. It was an openhanded slap, a slap of disdain, and a hard slap. The crack resonated throughout the room. There had been a low rumble of talk, but the slap silenced it, and everyone stared at this big stranger and the deadly gunman in his grasp.

Jack, still holding Blaisdale, looked at the doctor. "Is that my contract?"

Cook nodded.

"Did everyone sign it?"

Again Cook nodded.

"It has all of my requirements, including the termination?"

Again Cook nodded.

"Do you have a badge with you?"

Cook held it up.

Jack raised and opened his big right hand while holding Blaisdale with the left.

Cook tossed it to him. He caught it, and he shoved the pin into his vest. "You need to swear me in."

Another man stepped up. "I'm Val Jessup. I drew up the contract."

Jack looked at the man, firm chin, steady eyes. Good. "You're the attorney."

"Yes. Raise your right hand."

Jack raised his hand, keeping his cold gaze on Blaisdale. Hate-filled eyes stared back at him.

Jessup said, "Do you swear to uphold the law to the best of your ability?"

"Yep."

"You are now the marshal of Cherry Creek."

"Good." He looked around the room, making eye contact with most of the occupants. "Folks, as you can see, I'm a mite busy. If you'll head on out of here, I'm sure we'll have a chance to meet later. Doc, would you stay?"

The cowhands started easing toward the door. "Whoa up," Jack said. "You boys don't go anywhere yet." He had holstered the Remington. He stepped over to the gun rack and examined the assortment of long guns. He selected a double-barrel shotgun, broke it open. It had two shells in the chambers. Satisfied, he clicked it shut and turned back to the only remaining men in the room, besides Cook.

He looked at Blaisdale. "Move over to the desk, and empty your pockets." He could see the hate and anger filling Blaisdale.

The man stared at him. "Why?"

"The first reason is because I'm now the marshal. I'm the law here, and I say to."

Blaisdale gave a short laugh that sounded like a bark. "What's the second reason?"

Jack lifted the muzzles of the shotgun and pointed them at Blaisdale's belly. The ominous clicks of the hammers being eared back to full cock filled the room. "The second reason, *Mr. Blaisdale*, is that I'm holding this ten-gauge shotgun, and from this distance the buckshot won't spread more than about three, maybe four inches. They'll be all bunched up when I shoot you in the belly like you did Mr. Carter.

"He didn't bleed much, because the hole from your .44 wasn't big enough in his belly, and most of the blood stayed inside. But the buckshot from this here shotgun is going to leave a hole about twice the width of these muzzles, and I'm going to be sure to shoot you right in the middle, so your backbone will be taken out, not that you have much anyway. Do you think that's a good enough reason to empty your pockets?"

4

Blaisdale held Jack's stare for the count of three. Then he moved to the desk and dumped out the contents of his pockets. Once he was done, Jack motioned for the doctor to come close and handed him the shotgun. "Keep these boys calm while I stow Blaisdale." Then he stepped behind the doc to the desk and separated the money Blaisdale had dropped from the other items, opened a desk drawer, and slid the money into the drawer, leaving a long streak on the dust-covered desk.

"Hey, that's my money."

"Not any longer. You just donated it to the family of the man you killed." Jack motioned to the cowboys. "You too. Drop your donations on the desk. I'll see she gets it."

"That ain't fair. I wasn't even there," the young cowhand who had contemplated drawing against Jack said.

"What's your name?" Jack asked.

"Casey."

"What?"

"Casey Miller."

"Casey Miller, do you think it's fair that Mrs. Carter no longer has a husband to provide for her family?"

"I had nothing to do with that."

"You think that makes any difference to me? You're with Blaisdale, aren't you. My pa always said, 'You lie down with dogs, you get up with fleas.' In this case you lose your money. Put it on the table, and do it now."

Miller joined the other cowhands and dumped his money on the table alongside theirs.

"Thank you, boys." Jack bent and swept the money into the desk. He didn't expect much from cowhands or gunmen or whatever they were, but he'd soon be gathering more. "This won't bring Tobias Carter back, but I'm sure it'll help the family." He turned back to the doctor. "You good?"

Dr. Cook nodded, slowly swinging the shotgun back and forth to cover the five cowhands. Jack stepped behind Cook to make sure he didn't interfere with the man's line of fire, grabbed Blaisdale by the shirt collar, and threw him toward the back room. The man banged up against the wall.

"Stand there—or not. I'd just as soon you try to escape. I'd like nothing better than to shoot you down like you did Tobias Carter."

Blaisdale had regained his composure. "You know I'm going to kill you. First chance I git, I'm gonna shoot you in the belly like that worthless squatter. Then I'll gut you like a hog. You'll be wishin' you were Carter."

Jack gave him a slow smile with all the warmth of a Texas norther and said nothing, unlocking the heavy door separating the office and jail. He shoved Blaisdale through the door and against the first cell. There were two cells, both made with crisscrossed iron bars set in the heavy rock wall. Jack swung the cell door open and shoved Blaisdale into the bare room. The sole furnishings consisted of a wooden bunk bed and a slop jar. The jail had been built with rock and joined to the framed front office. The view from the cell was restricted through the single small window with two vertical and two horizontal iron bars.

Blaisdale sat on the bottom bunk in his cell. "I won't be here long."

"No longer than it takes a judge to get here. We've got enough witnesses. Once he arrives, you should be out of here in no time."

"Did you shoot my brother?"

"No, but if I'd been there, I would have. I woulda shot your other men, too."

Jack locked the cell door and turned to leave.

Blaisdale called, "I need out for my brother's funeral."

"No funeral. He'll just be dumped in a hole. That's more than he deserves."

"I said I need to be out for his funeral. I mean it."

"The next time you walk out of that cell will be for your trial and hanging."

Blaisdale jumped up and gripped the bars. "Mr. Mather will have me out of here in no time."

Jack said nothing.

"You'll be dead before sunrise," Blaisdale yelled. Jack stepped through the open door into the office, turned, and closed and locked the door.

Jack looked around the room at the cowhands. He held his hand out to Doc Cook and took the shotgun. He gave the cowhands one more glance. Then he lowered the hammers of the shotgun, broke the action, and removed the shells. While he was unloading the weapon, he said, "My name is Jack Sage, and I am now the law in this town. I want to make that clear. I won't brook any type of gunplay in town. Also, no horse racing within the city limits. Either offense means jail time. Every person in town, including you, will be treated with respect until you break the law. I have nothing against you men having fun, but if you step over the line, I'll be there. Am I making myself clear?" He walked to the gun rack and placed the shotgun in the rack.

Red spoke up. "This ain't gonna fly with Mr. Mather or the

owner of the 7 Bar. You may try to enforce those rules, but you're just one man, no matter how big you are."

Jack turned back to the cowhands. "Anyone else have something to say? Now's the time to get it off your chest."

The men looked at each other, but remained quiet.

Jack picked up Miller's gun belt and tossed it to him. He caught it, strapped it on, and positioned it.

Red gestured toward the jail cells. "What about Flint?"

"He stays. Any other questions?"

Red looked at the other men, then back at Jack. "Mr. Mather depends on Flint. He ain't gonna like this. He'll be coming back."

"I'm willing to talk to anyone who wants to talk. But Blaisdale killed an honest man in cold blood. As far as he's concerned, there is nothing to talk about. You give your Mr. Mather that piece of information. It might save him a wasted trip into town. Anything else?"

Jack waited only for a few seconds. "All right, you boys are free to go. Spread the word around. From here on out, this will be a peaceable town. Now get out of here."

The cowhands filed out of the office and headed for their horses. Moments later they raced down the street past the marshal's office.

Cook watched them until they were out of sight. "Certainly doesn't appear they listened to you as far as the racing on town streets is concerned."

Jack chuckled. "They don't know me yet." He went back to the gun rack, removed the shotgun, and reloaded it. "They have a lot to learn, and so do I, about them."

Puzzled, Cook watched him reload the shotgun and return it to the gun rack. "You just unloaded it."

Jack pulled out one of the drawers beneath the rack. There were several boxes of double-aught buckshot. He removed one, opened it, and dropped two shells in each of his lower vest pockets. Then he opened a desk drawer and dumped in the remaining shells. "That was all show, Doc. I gave them a little more time to relax while I showed them I felt they were no threat. Plus if they or anyone else they tell decides to ambush me in the office, they'll expect the shotgun to be unloaded."

"Are you expecting trouble?"

"Oh yeah. It'll definitely get worse around here before it gets better. I didn't mention a deputy, but I'll need one. Do you know anyone around here who might be up to the job? It's gonna be dangerous. Whoever takes it could take a bullet. They'll get seventy-five a month. The town pays fifty, and I pay twenty-five."

The doc considered Jack's proposal. "Franklin will squawk, but everyone will go along with it, including him. As far as someone I could recommend, I don't really know of anyone." He paused, stepped to the door, and looked across the street. "Unless . . . You might consider the gunsmith, across the street. He was in here when you brought in Blaisdale. He's one of the town council. You might have noticed him. In his thirties, taller than most, but not as tall as you. Upper part of his left ear is missing. It was shot off in the war. His name is Wade Garrett."

"Thanks for your help, Doc. I think I'll go across and talk to him. I'm sure Mather will be showing up later today."

"I've got to go check on Bart and grab a bite. After I get that done, I'll talk to the rest of the council about a deputy. Oh, by the way, there's a deputy badge in the bottom drawer of your desk."

Jack opened the bottom drawer, pulled out the deputy marshal badge, and dropped it into his pocket. He closed the drawer and moved to the door. They stepped outside. The doc turned right, while Jack waited for a wagon to pass. There was only a slight breeze, but it was blowing directly toward the wagon's travel, so the dust kicked up by the wagon seemed to follow it and the driver like a whopping brown bubble. He strode across the street toward the gun shop and saw the wagon and Bart's and his animals still hitched to the rail in front of the barber's place.

Not normally a man for swearing, Jack swore at himself. *I've got to get them fed and watered.* He looked up and down the street. People were going and coming, but a young man was sweeping the boardwalk in front of Pierce's store just next door to the gun shop. He turned and walked over to him.

"Morning."

The boy looked up. Jack figured he was about fifteen, his sleeves rolled back from his forearms, showing thick ribbons of muscle running to his wrist. "Morning, Marshal Sage."

"What's your name?"

The boy stopped sweeping and leaned on his broom, both hands gripping the shaft near the top. He pushed back the flop hat he wore, releasing a thick mass of pitch-black hair. "I'm Nathan Pierce. Everyone calls me Nate."

Jack looked inside, saw Lewis Pierce watching them through the window, and waved. Pierce returned the wave and went back to work. Jack looked down again at Nate. "Nate, I've got a problem I'm hoping you can help me with." He turned and pointed toward the wagon and horses. "You see the mule and horses with that wagon."

Nate looked and said, "Yes, sir."

"I've still got a lot to do to get ready for what's probably going to happen this evening, but I need to get that wagon to the livery and the horses rubbed down and fed and watered. Do you think your pa would mind you doing that for me?"

"No, sir, I don't think he'd mind at all."

"Could you get away right now?"

"Yes, sir. I just need to tell Ma or Pa, and I can do it." Nate grinned. "I like animals."

"Good. Why don't you run in and tell your pa and come right back. I'll wait here."

"Yes, sir," Nate said, spun, and dashed into the store.

Jack watched the boy run up to his pa and quickly explain. Lewis Pierce stopped what he was doing, put his hand on his son's shoulder, and walked with him back to the store entrance. He leaned through the open door, looking at Jack. "Howdy, Marshal. I suppose this is nothing dangerous you're askin' him to do?"

Jack shook his head. "No, sir. As I'm sure you're well aware, we will be having visitors later this afternoon or evening. I've got a lot to do, and would prefer not to take the time to put up that wagon and those animals." He motioned toward the wagon. "I was wondering if Nate could do it for me."

Pierce nodded and gave his son a pat on the shoulder. "Of course he can. Good luck." He turned and went back into his store.

The boy dashed toward the wagon. Jack grabbed him by the arm as he passed. "Whoa, young fella. Don't you want to get paid?"

The boy's eyes widened. "You're gonna pay me, Marshal?"

"Of course I am." His big fingers reached into an upper vest pocket, and he pulled out a silver fifty-cent piece. "Hold out your hand."

Nate held his calloused right hand out, palm up, and Jack dropped the four-bit silver piece into the boy's palm. It was all he could do to keep from laughing. Nate's eyes had grown bigger than the half-dollar he held.

"All this is for me?"

"You bet it is, and you're worth every penny. Like I said, I have a lot to do and not much time to do it in. You're freeing me up. Just take good care of those animals. Don't you want to know where they go?"

"Don't need to. That's Mr. Lawrence's wagon. He keeps it at Mr. Johnson's stables. That's the best in town anyway."

The boy stood, waiting. Jack laughed. "What're you waiting on?"

Nate spun and took off. Jack could hear him say, "Yes, sir," as he dashed down the street. He watched him until he was driving off in the wagon, nodded in satisfaction, and turned back to the gunsmith's shop.

A bell rang as he ducked, pushing through the door, and the man working at the counter looked up, watching Jack bend over to ensure his hat and head cleared the door.

"Must be tough being that tall."

Jack looked Garrett over and nodded. "Sometimes it does present a problem, but I've learned to live with it." He liked the look of the man. Doc was right. Wade Garrett was a big man. Clear brown eyes appraised him right back. Jack saw wide shoulders and bulging sleeves, legs that lifted the gunsmith to a little over six feet. *I bet he'd be tough in a knuckle and skull set-to,* Jack thought.

Jack noticed the man look down at the gun in his holster. "The name's Jack Sage."

The man laid his tools on the counter and extended his hand. "I know, I was in your office when you manhandled Blaisdale. That was late in coming, if you ask me. Name's Wade Garrett." The gunsmith eyed Jack. "You're about to have a problem."

"Mather? I know."

"Mather's bad enough alright, but I'm here to tell you 7 Bar's owner is hell on wheels. He's dead set on driving the homesteaders out of here, and, in my opinion, once they're gone, he'll run Mather out. He's a bad one, for sure."

"I think I've only heard the 7 Bar mentioned once. It's all been Mather."

"Like I said, Mather's bad, but he mostly has other people, like the Blaisdale brothers . . ." Wade chuckled. "I guess you and Bart threw a loop around those two, but he doesn't get his hands dirty. Birch of the 7 Bar doesn't mind getting down in the mud with anyone, and most of the time, he's the one crawling out."

"Sounds like I bit off a mighty big chew."

"That you did. But if you're the Jack Sage from Laredo, you just might be able to handle it."

"I could use some help doing it. Seventy-five a month and all the lead you can throw."

Wade laughed. "If you'd offered me that a couple of years ago, I'd a jumped on it, but not today. Got me a girl. We're not hitched yet, but she'd string me up by my thumbs if I even thought about it."

Jack rubbed the stubble on his chin. "Doc recommended you. I was sure hoping. Is there anyone else around here who might have a hankering to get shot?"

"I know a man. Fought alongside him in the war. When we were younger, I even fought him a few times with my fists until I learned better, but he doesn't live in town."

"If he's not in town, how could he be a help? I need someone now. I might be big, but I haven't yet learned how to stay awake twenty-four hours a day, day after day."

"He's close. He's one of the homesteaders on Cherry Creek. His wife died of pneumonia shortly after they moved onto the creek, no kids. He's a real fighter, and I'm thinkin' he's in the mood to tangle with either or both of those big ranchers."

Jack shook his head. "I'm not looking for a man after blood. I need a cool head who can follow the law."

"He can do that. He's a good man, but he's also a heck of a fighter. You're going to need both."

"So how far is his place?"

"About six miles."

Jack shook his head. "Too far. Mather could be in town before I get back."

Wade grinned. "Well, Marshal, today may be your lucky day. I just saw him ride in while we were talking. His horse is tied up across the street, and I'm bettin' he's in the Cherry Creek Saloon. He likes looking at the owner, Miss Gabriella. She is fine to look at, but don't tell my girl I said that."

"Our secret. You thirsty?"

"Now that you mention it, I am. Let me hang out my closed sign, and we'll be on our way."

Wade reached under the counter, brought out his sign, and headed for the door. He opened it, allowing Jack to bow his way through the door, and followed.

Walking across the street, Wade asked, "How long you been shooting those little peashooters?"

"You mean my fine .36-caliber Remingtons?"

"Girl's weapon. Why, I bet with those big hands, those little police models disappear. I'm surprised you haven't blown a finger off."

Jack shook his head. "They're light, and with my hands and the low recoil, I have almost no muzzle jump. That lets me get back onto my target double quick. Don't know that I'll ever part with them."

"Humph," was all Wade said, and pushed the swinging doors out of the way as they stepped into the Cherry Creek Saloon.

It's surprisingly crowded for a midafternoon, Jack thought. The layout was pretty standard for a saloon. The bar was to the right of the entrance. It was a heavy bar, pecan or maybe cypress, extending for about thirty feet. A six-foot-high mirror ran the full length of the bar behind shelves displaying a variety of liquor bottles. Several cowhands leaned against the bar, examining him and his badge. At the end of the bar and against the wall, a staircase rose to a second floor. At the top, a hallway ran across the width of the building, allowing access to four rooms.

On the ground floor, six tables were arranged in the remainder of the space in front of the bar. A door between the staircase and the end of the bar opened to another room. *Probably a kitchen,* Jack thought. Past the bar and front tables was the gambling paraphernalia, the roulette wheel, craps table, and a faro table plus a couple of other tables where card games were being played. Spittoons were scattered around the saloon, but there was an obvious lack of accuracy around each one.

As his eyes adjusted to the dusky light, he made out the saloon's main attraction weaving her way toward him. Her wide, green, silk skirt brushed against tables, chairs, and customers who laughed or smiled but watched her movements as she, in passing, touched their heads or shoulders. She was a tall woman, maybe seven inches above five feet, and dressed more conservatively than most women Jack had seen in a saloon.

His eyes seemed to have a mind of their own and tracked her as she neared. *She has a figure any woman would envy,* he thought, *but it's her eyes that capture you.* He had seen her at the front of his office. She had been striking, but at that time he'd had little time to look. She smiled and approached him.

5

"How do you do, Wade, Marshal?"

Jack removed his Stetson. "Mighty fine, ma'am, and you?"

She extended her hand to him, and Jack took it in his, careful not to squeeze too hard, but received a surprisingly firm handshake from a wonderfully soft, cool hand.

"Marshal, I am doing quite well. Let me introduce myself. I am Gabriella Campbell. Most of my customers call me Miss Gabriella." She paused, her head bent well back to look into his eyes, causing her black hair to fall over her shoulders. "You, however, may call me Gabby. My mother gave me my nickname because I talked so much. You'll find I can be quite a conversationalist. Now let's find you two a table."

Wade had been watching and listening. He pointed to a table. "Miss Gabriella, we're gonna join Clint, but you'd sure be welcome."

"Why, thank you, Wade. You men go ahead and talk your business. I'll be over in a few minutes."

She turned those beautiful eyes on him again. They were like gold, set inside a bronze ring, and they were as deep as forever. "Marshal, I'll be back to see *you*."

"Looking forward to it, Gabby."

He followed Wade to the table where a wide-shouldered man sat alone, drinking a sarsaparilla. The man's sun- and wind-burned face broke into a wide grin when he saw Wade. "Howdy, Wade." He let his head slowly rise to take in Jack's full height, his eyes stopping momentarily at the marshal's badge on Jack's vest. "Your ma must've fed you right well, Marshal." He stuck out a hard calloused hand to Jack.

Jack took it. "Never missed a meal when I was growing up. She saw to it. You must be Clint Paget. Jack Sage."

"When are you gonna grow up and drink a man's drink, Clint?" Wade asked, pulling out a chair and plopping down.

Releasing Jack's hand, Clint looked at his friend. "I grew up a long time ago. That's why I don't waste my money on liquor. I'll have a big ranch of my own, and you'll still be tinkering with your toys."

Wade laughed. "You're probably right."

Clint turned back to Jack. "I hear you've already made some pretty big waves, Marshal, but you have a hefty job ahead of you."

A young woman walked up to take their order. Wade ordered two beers, but Jack stopped him and pointed at Clint's drink. "I'll have one of those."

She nodded and headed for the bar.

Jack turned back to Clint. "That's why I'm talking to you. Wade tells me you fought in the war with him."

Clint nodded and took a sip of his sarsaparilla, his eyes drifting toward Gabriella.

"He also tells me that you don't mind a fight. Clint, I'll get to the point. I want you as my deputy. It'll be seventy-five dollars a month and all the lead you can duck. It's gonna be dangerous, even could be deadly, but I'm not stopping till this place is cleaned up."

Clint looked at Wade. "Is this your doing?"

Wade nodded. "Seventy-five a month, Clint. I know the money would be handy, and you don't back down from a fight. I thought it might be just what you're looking for. What do you think?"

Clint shoved a hand across to Jack. "If you want me, I'm your man."

Jack pulled the badge out of his pocket and slapped it into the man's open hand. The homesteader looked at it only for a moment. His big thumb rubbed across the face of the metal, and he stuck it into his homespun shirt.

"Raise your right hand."

Clint lifted his hand.

"You swear to do your best at upholding the law?"

"I dang sure do."

"Good. I need to get something to eat."

"Food's good in here, Marshal," Clint said.

"Then I'll eat here. I didn't tell you, but your meals and lodging are also covered, plus ammunition."

The girl brought the drinks back.

"Ma'am," Jack said, "what would you recommend to eat? I'm almighty hungry."

She smiled at Jack and in a melodious voice said, "Marshal, the cook has whipped up the best stew I've ever tasted. We've got fresh biscuits and a big piece of peach cobbler to go along with it."

Jack nodded and looked at his companions. They both nodded. "All around, please."

Jack took a long draw of his drink. It was wet and sweet and tangy. Just what he needed. He liked the lean, good-natured look of Clint. The man had no trouble looking him in the eyes. He had never trusted a man who wouldn't meet his eyes. Clint was tall. Not quite six feet, but close. He had wide shoulders and the build of a working cowhand. It puzzled him that Clint was homesteading instead of ranching, but that was for another time. They needed to prepare for tonight.

He leaned forward to Clint. "I hope you have everything with you that you'll need for a while. We may be locked down in town for a few days."

Clint thought for a moment. "The animals need to be fed, and someone needs to milk the cow, but my neighbor's in town. I'll ask him to take care of my place for a few days. You have any plans?"

Before Jack could respond, the waitress returned with their food. She placed the three large bowls on the table along with a plate stacked high with biscuits.

"I'll be back with your cobbler."

The three men nodded and picked up the large spoons she had brought with the stew. Jack lifted his spoon, full and steaming, to his mouth. It was a beef stew. There were big chunks of beef, falling apart, floating in a mix of vegetables. He took a mouthful and sighed. It tasted delicious. He reached for a biscuit and broke it open. Steam and the aroma of hot bread rose from the center. He tore the biscuit apart, dropping chunks into the stew, stirred for a moment, and resumed eating. With all that had happened today, he hadn't realized how hungry he was. The last thing he had eaten was a cookie and a cup of coffee at the doc's place.

The only table in the saloon a person might be heard belonged to the three men as they ate. Not a word was spoken, but their silence was made up for by the men surrounding them. Laughter, calls for drinks, and men raising their voices to be heard above others filled the room. A pall of smoke hung from the ceiling. The smell of working men filled the saloon, with the occasional whiff of sweet perfume when a saloon girl walked by. The Cherry Creek Saloon was a bustling place.

Finishing off his pie, Jack leaned back. "Clint, Mather will be coming into town this afternoon or tonight. I'm sure he's planning on running roughshod over the new marshal, but we're going to change his mind. There are two Henry rifles in the gun cabinet, a Spencer, and two shotguns. Cartridges are in the cabinet beneath."

Clint nodded at Jack's vest pockets. "Not all of 'em."

Jack pulled one of the brass shotgun shells from his pocket, held it up, and leaned forward to be heard over the piano that had started up in the back. "I'll be carrying a shotgun. There's plenty more of these in the office.

"When we see them coming in, I'd like for you to head over to Wade's Gun Shop and get to a window upstairs." He turned to Wade. "Is that alright with you?"

"Sure, I'll even help out."

"You don't have to. That's what we're getting paid for."

Wade shook his head. "My town, too."

"Alright," Jack continued. "Don't shoot unless you have to. I'd like to take care of this without any more bloodshed."

Both Clint and Wade snorted.

"I know. But we're not going to start a war if we can help it. Not in town. We want to keep the townsfolk as safe as possible."

Clint leaned toward Jack. "The only way we prevent any shooting is you giving them Blaisdale."

"That won't happen. Blaisdale stays in jail until the judge gets to town."

Clint nodded. "So where will you be?"

"In the office. When Mather's bunch shows up, I'll invite Mather in for a little talk. We'll see how it goes."

Wade spoke up. "You know, Mather also has some support in town."

"I expected it," Jack said. "The Gilded Lily?"

"Yep, and Bryant Livery. They both opened up about the time Mather first arrived. They were dead set against hiring an outside marshal. Mather wanted Korkeran to be hired as marshal. Thankfully the council voted against it. Korkeran is the owner of the Gilded Lily, not a very pleasant gent. Rumor has it he's mighty fast with a gun. He's supposedly killed several men before coming here. His bartender is also an unlikeable sort. Bull's his name. Fits him well. I've never heard his last name. He can be pretty tough on drifters. Likes to bait 'em into a fistfight and then tromps 'em. Korkeran's tried to buy Miss Gabriella out, but she told him to forget it."

"Did I hear my name?"

The green silk dress brushed against Jack's arm, and he stood. Clint jumped to his feet, and Wade followed. Clint pulled out the chair between him and Jack. "Have a seat, Miss Gabriella."

"Thank you, Clint." She placed a soft hand on his arm as she sat and gave him a broad smile.

Clint turned red. "Shucks, ma'am, it ain't nothing." He sat and shot a frown toward Wade's grinning face.

Gabriella turned to Jack. "How did you like your stew, Marshal?"

He took in her lovely face. It had a light olive hue to it. Like the sun had touched it for the perfect amount of time. Her wide-set eyes, the corners now crinkled with a hint of humor, were complemented by well-defined cheekbones. Add the full lips above a strong shapely chin and the sum equaled a striking beauty. *Keep your mind on your work,* Jack told himself. To her he said, "It hit the spot, Gabby. You've got quite a cook there."

"Yes, she is quite good. I'll tell her you liked it." She placed her hand on his arm. "Marshal, I'm afraid you have a very big job on your hands. Scott Mather is a hard and dangerous man. He doesn't appreciate anyone getting in his way."

"Ma'am, his men can't kill people in cold blood and get away with it. It's time he learned the law protects folks, even home-steaders. There's a poor woman alone with her children thanks to one of his men. No matter how big he thinks he is, he's not above the law. His man gets punished. When he comes in, I'll try to talk some sense into him. Whether or not he elects to listen is his choice. If he doesn't, he'll face the consequences."

He thought he saw sympathy in the golden eyes.

Her face was somber. She turned to Clint. "Should you get mixed up in this? You know how dangerous Mather can be."

Clint grinned back at her. "I'm already mixed up in it, ma'am. It's just a matter of time before Mather and his bunch, or the 7 Bar crew, show up and burn me out. This way, I might be able to throw a little hitch in their get-along."

The bartender waved, getting Gabby's attention. She stood, looking first at Clint and then Jack. "Sorry, business calls. Both of you be careful. You're dealing with dangerous men." She moved swiftly to the bar, with all heads turning to follow her.

Jack stood. "Time to get to work. Clint, come with me to the office, and you can look it over. We each have a free room at the hotel and can eat there or at Ma McGinty's, no charge. They bill the town. Until Blaisdale is tried and hanged, we'll take turns spending our nights at the jail."

"Sounds good to me, Marshal. I'm right behind you."

The three men stood and strode from the saloon. Wade momentarily raised a hand, index finger extended in a short wave, and headed across the street to his gun shop. Jack made a right turn out of the Cherry Creek on his way to the jail.

"Marshal, I need to get Betty to the stable. I'm sure she's thirsty and hungry, and I don't want her out here should shooting start."

Jack stopped and looked back. Wade was untying a red roan mule, patting its cheek before swinging into the saddle.

"Go ahead. I'll meet you there." He walked on, checking windows, doors, and alleys, just in case some of Mather's men had remained in town. There was always a possibility one of the cowhands might want to prove something to his boss, especially that Miller kid. Jack had the would-be gunman on his mind. *You never know when a youngster like that might explode. There's always one around. Good enough to beat his friends, but not good enough to keep from getting killed, and it looked like he really admired Blaisdale.* He shook his head, opened the office door, ducked, and stepped inside.

It wasn't long before he heard boots on the boardwalk, the door opened, and Clint filled the doorway. He stepped through carrying his saddlebags, closed the door behind him, looked around the room, and nodded. "Marshal."

"Call me Jack, Clint. I was just thinking about Casey Miller. Be careful with him. He's looking for a reputation."

"I know him. He's been by my place with Blaisdale."

Surprised his deputy was still alive, Jack said, "Really. What happened?"

"Nothing, other than some big talk. They didn't seem to want to argue with my ten gauge."

"Yeah, those two big holes staring at a man can really take the steam out of him."

"Too bad Tobias Carter didn't have one with him. He didn't deserve to be gunned down in front of his family, especially by the likes of Blaisdale."

Jack nodded and pointed to the gun case. "Blaisdale will pay. Help yourself."

"Mind if I take two?"

"I don't, but I'm curious. What do you have in mind?"

Clint pulled a .44-caliber Henry from the gun case. He glanced at the loading tube, saw that it was empty, grasped the spring lever, and moved it up near the muzzle. Once reaching the stop, he rotated the lever away from the tube mouth. It locked, and he began to drop rounds down the throat of the tube.

Jack, curious how Clint would handle the weapon, watched

closely. He approved of the shallow angle Clint held the rifle while loading, allowing the rounds to slide slowly into place. Since the cartridges sat one on top of the other, it always made him a little nervous when the Henry was held vertical and the rounds were allowed to drop onto the point of the previous bullet. He'd never seen one fire accidentally, but there was always talk of that happening.

Clint rotated the spring-loaded lever back to the closed position, laid the rifle on the desk, and pulled a shotgun from the rack. He opened it, found two rounds already in the chambers, closed it, and laid it next to the Henry. "I figure to use the rifle initially, if need be. That way I'll only plug the man I'm aiming for. If it seems the shotgun may be needed later, for some close-up work, I'll switch."

Jack nodded. "Good thinking."

Clint pulled a box of shotgun shells from the case and dropped it plus the one full and the partial box of forty-fours into his saddlebags. "Guess I'm ready. If it's all right with you, I'll head on over to Wade's and get myself into position."

"Sounds good. Follow my lead."

Clint nodded his agreement and departed out the door and turned and headed across the street. Clint had happened to grab the shotgun Jack had loaded, so he picked up the other. He threw it to his shoulder a couple of times to get the feel of it. The short barrels reduced the weight of the shotgun, and it snapped to his shoulder, fitting nicely. He lowered the scattergun, broke it open and, from his desk, picked up and dropped a shell into each chamber and snapped the weapon closed. As the action snapped together, the door opened, and a young lady stepped in carrying a tray.

She jumped from the sound of the metal snapping together and the sight of the shotgun. "Oh my."

"Come on in. Just checking the guns. Is that for me?"

"Oh, no, Marshal. I'm Amy from the hotel. This is for the prisoner."

Jake lifted the cloth covering the food. Cornbread, beans, onion, and a steak. Alongside the food sat a small pitcher of coffee and a cup.

"Looks like if you want a good meal, all you need to do is get thrown in jail."

The girl flushed. "My boss says if we're going to get paid for feeding the prisoners, it's our responsibility to feed them well."

Jack pulled out his keys and unlocked the door. "Looks like he lives what he preaches." Once the door was open, he stepped in, followed by Amy.

Blaisdale leered at the girl. "Well now, ain't this sweet. And the food looks good, too. You go with the meal, girl?"

Amy flushed again.

Jack's brows wrinkled in a frown. "Tell you what, miss. Why don't you turn around and take that tray back to my desk."

It was Blaisdale's turn to frown. "Wait, you can't do that. I'm hungry. It's past time to eat, and that smells good."

"It does, doesn't it. Too bad you're not getting any of it." Jack followed Amy out the door, turned and began closing it.

"Wait, Sage. Wait just a minute. All right, maybe I shouldn't have said anything to the girl. I won't from now on. Just bring that cornbread back in here. Man, I told you, I'm hungry."

"You're right. You should've kept your mouth shut. She was doing you a kindly service. I know your ma taught you better. Maybe sleeping on an empty stomach will help you remember to keep a civil tongue in your mouth, especially around ladies."

He pushed the jail door closed to alternating curses and pleadings from Blaisdale and turned to the girl.

"Amy, why don't you give that to someone who'll appreciate it. Next time you bring Blaisdale food, I feel sure he'll be a little more pleasant."

She turned an open face up to him. "Thank you, Marshal.

That was mighty nice, but I do hate to see a man go hungry, no matter how bad he is. Maybe I could leave it for him later?"

"No, you do with it as I said. Now run along, and thanks for bringing it. Tell your manager exactly what happened and what I said. If he has any problem with it, he can talk to me."

He opened the door for her as she left.

6

Shadows had grown long in the street. Bustling had ceased. He hadn't heard a soul pass on the boardwalk for more than an hour.

"I'm hungry, Sage," Blaisdale called through the six-by-six-inch opening in the locked jail door.

Jack ignored him. He was as comfortable as he could get without lying down on the bunk across the room. His office chair was tilted back, and he had his feet on the desk, the ten gauge lying across his thighs. From what Clint had told him, Mather's party should be arriving any time. Clint was on the second floor of Wade's Gun Shop, across the street, and they were as ready as they were going to get.

"I'm hungry, Sage," came a more insistent demand from the back.

It was the fifth time Blaisdale had yelled at him, and he was tired of it. He dropped his feet to the floor, walked to the jail door, and unlocked it, swinging it wide open.

Blaisdale was standing at the cell door, his hands gripping the bars.

"I've told you to shut up and drink some water. You're a grown man. You've been hungry before."

"Before don't count. I'm in jail, and I'm supposed to get fed. I'm hungry."

Jack could feel his anger rising. This obnoxious excuse for a man had killed an innocent father and husband and felt no remorse. Now he was whining about being hungry.

"Is the big, bad marshal getting upset?" Blaisdale sneered at Jack. "Now go get me some f—"

Jack reached down, his big hand wrapping around the bail of the bucket he had set by the jail door earlier. Blaisdale had been offered several chances to shut up, and he wouldn't. He lifted the bucket, took a step into the jail, and hurled the water at the man. "You needed a bath anyway."

Blaisdale tried to jump back, but there was no room. His feet tangled in his spurs. He crashed to the floor and lay there looking up at Jack as he closed the door. He was drenched and hungry. He broke in to a long stream of curses.

Jack relocked the door. He picked up the shotgun and stepped to the front door to take one last look around before dark. Before he could pull it open, he felt the vibrations of hooves and then heard them. Not as many as he had expected, but they were coming.

Before he stepped outside, he heard Blaisdale yell again.

"Now your time's up. That's Mr. Mather to get me out. You're gonna be sorry. You hear me, Sage?"

Jack said, just loud enough for Blaisdale to hear him, "I've got another bucket out here. I think you'll get tired of getting a bath long before I get tired of drawing buckets."

Silence was Blaisdale's only response. Jack stepped through the door as six horsemen pulled up.

The man in the lead rode erect, back straight, on a beautiful long-maned palomino. A gray, almost white, Confederate Cavalry hat sat on his head, canted slightly to the right. His longish dark hair, graying at the temples, pushed out from beneath the hat to cover his ears. The carefully tanned buckskin jacket, matching the golden hue of the palomino, draped his thick shoulders and hung to his thighs. It was pulled back around his right hip, exposing the butt of a holstered Colt. Jack watched him.

A handsome man, probably late forties, arrogant and used to getting his way. He spoke, his voice brusque and matching his posture. "You have my man in your jail."

It wasn't a question.

Jack nodded. "I do. Another of your men, his brother, is laid out for burial at the undertaker. He was shot attempting to ambush Mr. Lawrence, who is even now lying with a bullet in his shoulder at the doctor's."

The man didn't flinch. "You know my name?"

Jack shook his head. "Can't say as I do, since we haven't met. I'm Jack Sage, but you can call me Marshal."

Even though the light was dimming, Jack could see the man's face turn red.

The young would-be gunfighter to the man's left fidgeted in his saddle and spoke up, his voice loud in the quiet town. "Mr. Mather, how 'bout I shoot this smart mouth down where he stands."

Mather's head snapped to his left. "Shut up, Casey. I'll deal with this."

Two of the hard-bitten riders looked at each other. Jack saw the corners of their mouths move up, only slightly, but they said nothing. Casey Miller looked crestfallen, like a dog scolded by its master.

Jack waited.

Mather turned back to Jack. "I know nothing about Blaisdale's brother, but I do know it's in your best interest to release my man, now."

Jack's stance had been the same since Mather's crew had pulled up. He stood relaxed, the shotgun held by its grip in his left hand, muzzle toward the ground, nonchalant, nonthreatening. "Well, why don't you come inside, and we can talk about it."

He could see the satisfaction in Mather's eyes. The ranch owner stepped down from his mount, tossed his reins to Casey, and walked toward the door, straightening his coat. Jack opened the door for him, and Mather strode into the office. Jack followed, closing the door behind him. He motioned to a chair against the wall and laid the shotgun on the desk.

"I'll stand," Mather said, stretching to his full height, but was a good four inches shorter than Jack. Mather said, "Now, Marshal, I'm sure we can come to an agreement. There's a lot of money to be made in cattle and land since the Indians have been driven out. What are you looking for? A nice little spread? Maybe a nest egg for your older years."

While the man was talking, Jack had opened the drawer where the cowhands' money had been stored. He took it out and started counting, then laid it onto the desk's surface. "That's mighty nice of you. I appreciate it when someone considers my future like that."

Mather frowned. The tinge of sarcasm to Jack's words was subtle, but there. "Now, you wait, Marshal," Mather said, his face starting to turn red again.

Jack's face and voice grew hard. "No, Mather. I know what you're trying to do to those homesteaders. I know what your men tried to do to Bartholomew Lawrence. I know what Blaisdale, your man, did to Tobias Carter in the General Store, right in front of Carter's wife and kids. I know a lot about you."

Mather's cheeks had turned a brilliant pink, his eyes the color of hard gray granite. "No man talks to me like that and lives."

Jack nodded toward Mather's gun. "You're wearing one. We can end this right now. You just shuck that iron and drill me right here." Jack poked his finger against his forehead. "Go ahead, take care of your own business. You don't need the likes of that"—he tossed a thumb toward the jail—"to do your dirty work."

Jack waited and thought, *You'd love to, but you know I'd fill you so full of holes you'd leak for a week. No, you hire gunmen to do your dirty work.*

Mather held his hands out wide from his waist. "I'm not drawing against you, Marshal. You're the law in this town. I won't do it."

Jack snorted. "I'm sure it's out of respect for the law." He looked the man over from toe to head. "I'm giving you an opportunity. See this money on the desk?" Jack reached down and fingered it. "It comes to thirty-seven dollars and forty-two cents. That's what your cowhands and Blaisdale donated, out of the kindness of their tender hearts, to poor Mrs. Carter and her children. That's a mighty paltry sum, isn't it?"

Mather said nothing, just stared at the change and small bills.

"I asked you a question," Jack said, placing his fists on the desk and leaning toward Mather. He knew his size could be intimidating. Mather was six feet, but Jack towered above him.

"Yes, that's a small amount."

Conversationally, Jack said, "Now, isn't that funny. That's exactly what I thought. In fact, I thought, 'I bet Scott Mather could help. I bet he'd want to help.' Do you want to help, Mr. Mather?"

Mather glared at Jack.

Outside, one of the riders called, "You all right, Mr. Mather?"

Jack stared at Mather.

"Yeah, you boys relax. I'll be out in a minute."

"How much money do you have on you, Mather? Do like your cowhands did this morning. Empty your pockets."

Mather emptied the pockets of the vest he was wearing under the buckskin coat. He pulled out two half-eagles, five-dollar gold pieces, and two eagles, ten-dollar ones, and one double eagle, a twenty-dollar gold piece, dropping it all on the desk. But when he pushed the coat back to get at the vest pockets, Jack noticed a section of the coat stayed unnaturally flat.

"Empty the rest."

"What?"

I said, "Empty the other pocket. The one with your wallet in it."

"I was taking that money to the bank."

"Well, isn't it fortunate that you stopped here first."

Mather's anger became more desperate. "You can't do this. It's robbery. I'll have you arrested."

Jack grinned and said nothing.

Mather's face became so red Jack was concerned the man might have an attack of apoplexy. His hand shaking, Mather pulled a folded leather wallet from the inside pocket of his jacket. Keeping it as closed as possible, he extracted a one-hundred-dollar banknote, dropping it on the desk. Jack could see the wallet was still bulging nicely.

Jack held his hand out. Mather looked at it, and with his jaws clenched tight, he handed it over. Jack looked in and counted. All banknotes, and all made on the Austin Cattlemen's Bank. Two of the notes were for five hundred dollars, and six were for one hundred dollars.

Jack pulled three more of the one-hundred-dollar notes from the wallet, dropped them on the table, and handed the wallet back to Mather. "It's little enough to pay a family for the loss of their provider, but I'm thinking Mrs. Carter will be mighty thankful for your generosity."

Mather took the wallet back and returned it to his pocket. He had regained control of his emotions. His color was receding to a more normal shade. "You'll pay for this, Sage."

"Marshal Sage to you."

"I still want my man."

Jack picked up the shotgun and, using the barrels, scraped the money, with its new additions, back into the drawer, and shoved the drawer closed with the muzzles. "Mather, I'm telling you like

I've told Blaisdale. He's not coming out of this jail until he walks to court. That's something you can bank on."

He nodded toward the door. "Before we walk out there, I want you aware of what you're up against. Right now there are two Henrys leveled on your men, and you don't have the faintest idea where they're located. When we get outside, if you get a crazy idea to open this dance, it won't be long in lasting."

He noted the momentary surprise in Mather's face.

"Fine. But you need to understand, *Marshal Sage,* my man won't sit in that jail till the judge gets here. He'll come out, one way or the other. The next time I come into town, it won't be with six men."

"That's your mistake to make. Now get on your horses and ride nice and easy out of town. Don't make a ruckus on your way out, and you'd best keep a leash on your boy out there. I'd hate to have to kill a pup his age."

"You don't give him credit, Marshal. He's faster than you think."

"No, Mather, he thinks he's faster than he is, and if he isn't careful, he'll find out the hard way."

Jack gave Mather a push toward the door. The man stumbled forward, caught himself, straightened his coat, and opened the door. He walked to his horse, took the reins from Miller, and swung into the saddle.

In the saddle, surrounded by his men, and looking down on Jack, Mather's voice was cold and confident. "This isn't over, Marshal. I'll see you again."

Jack said nothing.

Mather yanked the palomino's head toward the street and kicked him viciously in the flanks. The horse leaped forward, leading the gunfighters back the way they had come. Casey Miller turned, made a pistol of his hand, and pointed it toward Jack.

He watched as the group galloped past the bank, Pierce's

store, and Dr. Cook's house, disappearing behind the big oak. When he was sure they were gone, he stepped onto the boardwalk. Before he could open the door to his office, the town came alive. People were crossing the street and walking along the boardwalk. Pianos tinkled from all three of the saloons. Life returned to Cherry Creek. It was as if the town had been holding its breath. He glanced to his right and could see the young woman from the hotel hurrying toward him with her tray.

Blaisdale hadn't said a word when Mather was in the office. Since his bath, he had remained silent. Jack thought, *Maybe the man's learning a little self-discipline. Too late for him, but it'll sure make my life easier. At least I won't have to listen to him.*

"Hello, Amy." He opened the door and stepped back so the girl could enter ahead of him.

"Thank you, Marshal Sage. Since he didn't get dinner, I suspect Mr. Blaisdale will be real hungry for supper."

Jack grinned. "I suspect you're right." He unlocked the jail door and stepped in.

Blaisdale sat slumped on his bunk, his head staring down at the rock floor, his clothes no longer dripping but still wet. He looked up as Jack entered. Jack completely blocked the small form of Amy behind him. When he stepped aside, Blaisdale spotted Amy and the tray of food. His eyes grew wide, and his mouth spread in a grin.

"You let her bring me something to eat, Marshal?"

"All her own doing. As soon as your boss left, she came walking down the boardwalk with this tray in hand. I couldn't let her make the trip for nothing."

Blaisdale looked up at Jack. Jack could almost see gratitude in the killer's face. The man turned his gaze back to the tray. "Thank you, ma'am. I surely appreciate your efforts. I'm mighty hungry."

Amy smiled. "Then I think you'll find this pleasing. There's fried chicken, mashed potatoes, and gravy with biscuits, and some fresh collard greens." When she removed the towel from the food, a separate dish was uncovered. "This here is some fresh blackberry cobbler, and I brought you another pot of coffee."

There was a space in the bars where trays or plates could be passed through. However, the space wasn't high enough for a coffee pot to pass. "Take the tray, Blaisdale, and hold it there while she pours you a cup of coffee.

"Amy, once it's poured, just set the pot on the floor next to the cell door. That way, if he wants more coffee, he can pour it himself."

He watched as Amy followed his directions. She straightened, pulled at her skirts, and walked out the jail door. Jack followed. He grasped the door to pull it closed.

Past a mouthful of food, Blaisdale said, "Marshal."

Jack looked at Blaisdale. The man nodded, which Jack returned before pulling the door to and locking it. Turning to the girl, he touched his hat. "Have a nice night, Amy."

She looked at the jail door and then the front door of the office. "Marshal, I'm supposed to bring the dishes back. I'll get in trouble if I don't."

"Don't you worry about the tray. Tell your manager I'll make sure it gets back to the hotel. Now you go along."

She nodded. "Good night, Marshal." She was gone.

The door closed and opened again. Clint and Wade walked in.

"You are a surprising gent. I expected there to be blood in the street, and I don't think I was the only one thinking along those lines. The town was like a ghost town. I can't say I've ever seen it that quiet here. How'd you do it?"

Jack pulled the money from the desk drawer. "We just had a little heart-to-heart. Mr. Scott Mather made a nice donation to Mrs. Carter."

Clint set the rifle and shotgun in the gun case, leaned over, slid the bills apart, and let out a long whistle. "Yes, sir, I'd say that's a mighty fine donation. That'll really help her make a new start. I don't have much, but you can tell her since they've proved their claim, I'll buy her place for two hundred dollars, if she's a mind. If she has a hankerin' to stay and make a go of it, we'll all help her out."

Wade looked at Jack. "How?"

"Oh, he didn't like it, but he understood I wasn't alone, and we weren't going to back down. He made the threat that the next time he comes into town, he'll be bringing more men with him."

"Not just a threat," Wade said. He looked at the unlit potbelly stove and sniffed. "I smell coffee."

Jack tossed a thumb to the back. "Hotel brought it for the prisoner."

Wade shook his head. "You're telling me your prisoner has coffee and you don't?"

"Yep."

"That's wrong. No matter how you look at it. That's just wrong. So what are you gonna do next?"

"First thing I'm going to do is get something to eat. After that, I'll take a swing around town, get the lay of the land, and introduce myself to those folks who are still open."

Clint gave his head a shake. "Watch yourself at the Gilded Lily. Korkeran is slick, and Bull, the bartender, is tough. You want me to go with you?"

Jack confirmed he had four shotgun shells in his vest pocket. "No. This needs to be on me. I don't figure there'll be any trouble tonight." He pulled the Remington from his holster and checked the loads. They looked fine. He looked back at Clint. "I imagine you're feeling a little hungry yourself."

"That's a fact. Where you planning on eating?"

"I figured I'd try Ma McGinty's tonight."

"Good, send a plate of whatever she's fixin' over to me. You'll like her, and you can't go wrong with her cooking. A pot of coffee would be good, too. I'll look around for a pot and a can of coffee. I know the last marshal had one, but I'll wait to fire up the stove till in the morning. Keep it a little cooler."

Jack nodded. "You all right with staying the night here?"

"Yep," Clint said. "Just get that food and coffee here, and I'll be fine."

Wade spoke up. "I'll head over there with you, Marshal. My belly's doing a little grumbling. I'm thinkin' a supper at Ma's will take care of it, and if she can't break anyone away to send Clint's supper over, I'll bring it."

The two men stepped out the door, and Jack pulled it closed behind him.

7

After eating and leaving Wade waiting on Clint's tray, Jack began making his rounds. It brought back not too far distant memories of Laredo.

Darkness had settled on the town. The only light available was that streaming into the street from the several businesses still open. The skies were dark except for the few stars that could be made out behind the fast-moving clouds. He carried the shotgun with the stock resting in the crook of his right arm. He knew it wouldn't hamper his draw, for his left hand would either pluck the shotgun out of his way or grab the forearm, whipping it up to his shoulder. Either way, he would be in action fast.

He yawned. Today had brought action and surprise. Before finding Bart, he had been on his way west. He was thinking of finding himself a little place away from people. He'd always felt he'd been born too late. He would've made a good mountain man, but those times were past. However, it wasn't too late to head west and find himself a little place up in the mountains of New Mexico or Colorado, maybe even Northern Arizona. He'd heard a lot about the White Mountains. But today a man had needed his help, and here he was.

He remembered his great-grandmother. She had lived to be ninety-six. She was holding him by the shoulders and telling him that he was going to be a big man, and he should always use his size and strength to help people. He couldn't have been more than six or seven, but he remembered her as clear as if it had been this morning. Though he didn't consider himself much of a joiner, he seemed to follow her advice. It wasn't that he didn't like people, he just never felt a personal need to be around them.

He stepped into the Rusty Bucket. Another saloon. They were all the same, some nicer, some worse, but all the same. Talking and laughter died down when he stepped in. It didn't stop but took on a more muted note. Heads turned, following him as he strolled toward an empty space at the bar.

The bartender, who Wade had told him was the owner, wore a bowler hat and a long apron hung around his neck and tied at his waist. He was a chunky man. Not tall, but wide with thick forearms much like fence posts.

"It's welcome you are, Marshal. First drink in the Rusty Bucket is on the house. It is Brian Sullivan my dear ma named me, and my friends call me Brian. Now what would you like to rinse away the Texas dust?"

"I appreciate your hospitality, Mr. Sullivan. I'll take a sarsaparilla." Jack dropped a nickel on the bar. "Time will tell whether or not we are friends. When that time comes, I'll let you buy me a drink. For now, I'll take care of my own."

Brian Sullivan turned his head slightly away from Jack, and his thick black eyebrows pulled together as he gave Jack a sideways glance. "Sounds like you're giving me the truth of it. I suspect I'll be buying that drink before long."

Turning to the back of the bar, he picked up a mug, moved to a five-gallon barrel, and opened the spigot at the bottom. Golden liquid flowed from the barrel. When the mug was filled, Sullivan closed the spigot, turned and slammed the mug on the bar, bits of foam flying in all directions. "There you be, Marshal. The best-tasting sarsaparilla you'll find west of the Mississippi. It's my own I brew right back there." Making a big fist, he pointed with his thumb to the back room behind the bar.

Jack laid the shotgun across the bar, grasped the handle of the mug, lifted it to his mouth, and took a long draw. He was pleasantly surprised. The sweet taste was offset by what he would call a welcome bite. He put the mug down and wiped the foam from his mouth. "Mighty good, Mr. Sullivan."

He turned from the bar and looked around the saloon. As clean as the Cherry Creek, and a similar layout. Several girls worked the room, taking and delivering drinks, laughing and flirting with the customers. Some of the customers were cowhands, but he would peg others to be settlers. Both groups seemed to be getting along.

The gambling tables were in the back, and all were busy. The bustle had returned after the observers had figured out there would be no shootings, no fights, and no entertainment. Jack picked up his mug, took another sip, and pointed it toward the back. "You run an honest place, Mr. Sullivan?"

The Irishman leaned one elbow on the bar. "Aye, I'm telling you, I do. Not knowing me, and with the name of my fine place, you might think me prone to lie and cheat, but my wee mother would roll over in her grave knowing her son was doing such a thing."

Jack looked at the man. The blue steady eyes returning his gaze showed no challenge, no deception. He had been at this business long enough to know an honest man when he met one. His life depended on it. He believed Brian Sullivan to be an honest man.

"Then, Brian, I thank you for your hospitality, and the next time I'm in, I'll be pleased to let you buy me a drink, and maybe you can tell me how you came up with your saloon's name."

"Aye, Marshal, come back anytime, and I'll explain the name."

Jack drained the mug and set it back on the bar. "I'll be

looking forward to it. You have any problems, send someone to let me know." He headed for the door. Next he wanted to talk to the liveries. As he stepped outside the saloon, he could see lights in both of them.

His head moved constantly, prying deep into the shadows of the night. Making rounds like this was nothing new for him. His time in Laredo wasn't that far past. He rubbed the scar tissue just above his left hip. The bullet had been close. *I'm glad he wasn't using a shotgun, or I would've been a dead man.* As it was, he was lucky. No bones were broken, no internal organs were ruptured. If it had been daylight, that bullet wouldn't have missed. Though it was scary for some people, he liked it. The night gave him concealment and protection.

He stepped into the barn of Johnson's Stables. He had been warned the old man who owned it was a little crusty, but he was an honest man, and everyone Jack had talked to recommended this place. He walked in through the wide-open stable doors. Smokey and Stonewall stood together in the first stall. It was oversized, giving them plenty of room. Stonewall's side was touching Smokey, but his head was twisted around watching Jack.

"Hello, Stonewall, Smokey." He stepped close, leaned the shotgun in the corner of the stall within handy reach, and started scratching both animals' ears. Smokey nuzzled his pocket while Stonewall tilted his head sideways, as if he were trying to get Jack's fingers in exactly the right place. In the lantern light of the stable, Jack could see both animals had gotten a good rubdown and plenty of feed. Neither acted thirsty.

"Seems they've taken a shine to you," an old man's scratchy voice said from outside the tack room.

Jack kept working on the ears. "Seems so. I'm afraid I've doted on these two way more than they deserve."

"Heh-heh-heh. Yessirree, a good animal will surely get under a man's hide, no matter how tough it is."

Jack looked over Smokey's back and could see the man sitting in a rocking chair, the rocker going back and forth. He looked ancient. "You Mr. Johnson?"

"No, young feller, not to you. To you, I'm just plain Sully. Any man what likes his animals as much as you do can call me by my first name. Other folks call me Mr. Johnson. You that new marshal?"

"Yes, sir, that's me. Just started today."

"Yep. I heard about you. You've caused quite a stir. I reckon that there Blaisdale ain't too happy about cooling his heels in yore jail."

Jack grinned into the dark, walked past his animals, stepped over to the old gentleman, and extended his hand. "You have no idea. Nice to meet you, Sully."

The old man's hand was calloused and wrinkled, but Jack felt the strength still residing there.

"You got your work cut out for you, boy. That Mather bunch is pure bad. They've played the devil with those sodbusters on the crick." The man pointed toward another rocking chair sitting against a tall pile of straw. "Pull up a chair, and rest them legs. They must be tired from holding up all that meat."

Jack walked to the chair, picked it up, and brought it close to Sully. He set the chair down and carefully lowered himself into it. The rocker creaked at his weight but held strong.

"Heh. It's old like me, but still strong."

It did feel good to relax for a minute. He couldn't stay long, but a few minutes off his feet was priceless. "You been here long, Sully?"

"Son, I was here afore this town ever started. I hunted and trapped all up and down that creek, shot Apaches along it fore the Comanches run 'em off, then shot Comanches. They shot me up some, too. This was fine country until the white man decided he needed it." He spit a long stream of tobacco juice, wiped his mouth on his sleeve, and continued, "But I guess that's what they call progress, and now here you come, about to get stuck between

Mather and the squatters." He shook his head. "Not a good place to be, no sir." His voice trailed off. "Not a good place to be."

Jack had been rocking and listening. "Understand this Gideon Birch, the owner of the 7 Bar, is also making trouble."

"Pshaw. According to the city folks he is. Even the homesteaders say they've heard he is, but you can't find a one who's actually seen him hurtin' or chasin' any of the squatters." He stopped his rocking and pointed a long bony finger, a cracked and broken fingernail on the end, at Jack. "You listen to me good, boy. That Gideon Birch don't back down from any man, and he don't ask any man to do his fightin'." He paused for a moment to release a long spit of tobacco juice, wiped off his chin and continued, "But he's about as honest as the day is long. He ain't happy about these squatters, but he's also a law-abiding feller."

"Have you told anyone this?"

The old man shook his head.

"Why not?"

Sully stopped rocking and rotated his upper body toward Jack. He rested his forearm on the arm of the rocker and thrust his wrinkled stubborn face at Jack. "Boy, you think any uppity banker or store owner's gonna get down off his high horse to ask an old stablehand like me about what's going on in this country? And if'n they ain't askin', I ain't tellin'."

"Why'd you tell me?"

"'Cause you take care of yore animals. That's why." He gave a slow wink at Jack and tapped the side of his head. "I ain't stupid. There might come a day I need help from a big young fella like you. Heh-heh-heh. It don't hurt that you're wearing a badge either."

"Sully, you've got my help anytime you need it. I'll be needing to check the country around here, but when I'm here, you just call." He stood. "I've got to finish with my rounds. Still some folks to talk to. What do I owe you for Smokey and Stonewall?"

"Nothin'. Town council's payin'."

"Thanks. If you'd have Smokey ready early, I'll be riding out in the morning to take a look around."

"He'll be all set, Jack, boy. See you in the morning."

Guitar music came from inside Carmen's Cantina, and a woman with a beautiful voice sang a song of love and loss. The cantina was located only a short distance from Johnson's Stables. Tables and chairs were scattered outside on a covered veranda. All were occupied. Hanging lanterns provided light to Carmen's guests.

By the time Jack reached the entrance to the veranda, the music and conversation had died, and all eyes were on him. He stepped through the entrance, swept his hat off, and said, "*Buenas noches señores y señoritas*," and immediately began speaking fluent Spanish he had learned years ago and had used so much in Laredo.

He strode to the bar. Took his Stetson off and laid it next to him. "Good evening."

The bartender nodded, his eyes glued to the tin badge on Jack's vest.

A silky voice from his left said, "Good evening, Marshal."

His turn brought smiling lips and sparkling eyes into his vision. She had jet-black hair, pulled up and wrapped at the back, exposing delicate ears. "Evening, ma'am. I'm Jack Sage."

She laid a slim arm on the bar. "What is it you would like, Marshal Sage?"

"Is this your place, ma'am?"

"Yes, I am Belinda. My mother was Carmen. She has passed."

"I am sorry."

"Thank you, Marshal. As I asked earlier, what is it you would like?"

"Miss Belinda, I am making the rounds tonight in an effort to meet some of the business owners. I'm here to let you know I expect only one thing, an honest business. No cheating of the customers and no watering down of the drinks. As long as that happens, I will be your friend, and I am available should you have need of the law."

Cool eyes appraised him. "And, Marshal Sage, does this rule apply equally to the white businesses as well as the Mexican ones?"

"Yes, of course it does. I'm making the rounds to all of the businesses. Those I don't talk to tonight, I'll speak to tomorrow."

"Do you also plan for this law to apply to the bank and the general store?"

Jack was getting irritated. This little woman was pushing, without letting up. "Yes, Miss Belinda, it applies to the bank and to Mr. Pierce's store."

"Ahhh." She nodded her head. "Then do you know of what *Mr. Pierce* and *Mr. Franklin* are doing?"

Surprised, thin frown wrinkles appeared across Jack's forehead. "Ma'am, I just started today. I can't know everything. Perhaps instead of questioning me like a lawyer, you can tell me what your point is."

Her face softened, and she laid a small soft hand on Jack's sleeve. "I am sorry, Marshal. It is just that I am angry at the gringo, sorry, the Anglo businessmen. They are taking great advantage of my people. So much so, that many come to me for help. I lend to those I can afford to." She shook her head, and sad brown eyes met his. "However, there are others I cannot help."

He could feel the warmth of her hand through his sleeve. It had been a long while since he had known a woman's touch like this. *You've seen a lot of pretty faces today. Keep your mind on your job.* "Ma'am, can you be a little more specific?"

Her tone hardened. "You want specific, Marshal? How about the banker and the general store owner cheating my people. Is that specific enough?"

"No, ma'am, it's not. Do you have specific examples?"

She removed her hand. "Yes, Marshal, I have specific examples. There are those of my people Mr. Pierce has overcharged in his store, again and again. And the banker."

Amazed, Jack watched as the lovely woman leaned over and, with ferocity, spit on the floor. Then her little shoe slammed into the spittle and ground it into the packed-dirt floor until it was gone.

"He has stolen my people's land. Smiling and patting them on the back, he gives them a loan, telling them not to worry about it. When they can't pay it, he suggests they put up a little more land as"—she had a difficult time with the word—"collateral. Then one day he says the loan has come due, and if they don't have the money to pay it in full, they must move off the land. The land that has been handed down from their ancestors. Tell me, Marshal Sage, is that fair?"

"Ma'am, I can't say it's fair, but if a man takes out a loan, he's responsible for it. All I can tell you is I'll look into it."

She gave a sharp nod. "Yes, that is what the last marshal said, and the one before him. They seem to leave or get killed before anything can be done."

"I promise you I'll look into it. However, right now I've just about got a war on my hands. That comes first, but if you have any problems out here, let me know."

She took a deep breath, smiled at him, and extended her hand. It disappeared in his as he shook it gently.

"Good night, Belinda."

"Thank you for listening, Marshal."

He turned and strode into the night.

Jack headed across the street to the Bryant Livery, his mind filled with the myriad of problems that had just been added to his plate. His job was becoming much more complicated than he had first thought. Arriving at Bryant Livery, he gave it a close once-over. Similar to Sully's place, it was bigger and closed. On the one hand he was disappointed, but fatigue was working on him.

Though he had hoped to meet the owner, he was more than willing to let it wait.

The only thing that still showed any life on this side of the street was the Gilded Lily, his last stop tonight. He was anxious to head over to the hotel and get some well-deserved rest. He'd wanted to check on Bart, at Doc Cook's, but that would have to wait. Taking a deep breath, he rechecked the shotgun, straightened, and walked to the Lily. He would see Korkeran and meet this guy called Bull. They both sounded like trouble, and it was time to find out for sure.

8

Jack had been walking down the middle of the street. His steps were quieter in the soft dirt, and it gave him better angles to see both sides of the street, the alleys, the building corners. Laughter, yelling, and the continuous plinking of the piano from the Lily competed with the Cherry Creek Saloon across the street. He checked his revolver rode loose in the holster, and carrying the shotgun by the forearm in his left hand, he stepped to the boardwalk. Reaching it, the sound of his boots on the echoing boards was washed away by the torrent of sound coming from the Lily. He moved to the batwing doors and pushed in.

The Lily was laid out differently from the other saloons. The bar was in the same place, to the right, but at the end of it there was no stairway. Past the bar, a door opened into a room. Jack figured it for an office since the door was open, and he could see a desk and several chairs. The office wall extended into the saloon and ran from the door to the back of the building. Jack figured Korkeran had a living space behind his office, probably also an entrance from the back.

The bar looked the same as the Cherry Creek, about thirty

feet, brass foot rail. A working area provided space behind the
bar and, behind that, shelves of liquor backed by a huge mirror in
a gold-colored frame. Between the bar and the office stood a door
that opened through the back wall. *Kitchen probably,* Jack
thought. It was immediately confirmed when a woman stepped
out carrying a tray of food.

Like the Cherry Creek, fronting the bar were several tables.
Men were gambling as well as drinking at these tables. Halfway
toward the back, against the opposite wall, ran a set of stairs up
the wall to the second level. A landing at the top fronted five
rooms. While he was watching, a woman wearing a low-cut gown
came out laughing, with a cowhand behind her. He swatted her
bottom playfully as they walked to the stairway. Laughing harder,
she slapped half-heartedly at his hand and proceeded down the
stairs.

Jack let his gaze drift across the tables and to the back of the
saloon where the roulette wheel was spinning. A crap table was
surrounded, and cowhands and city folk gathered at both of the
faro tables. Most of the faces who met his eyes looked away, but
there were several who held his gaze for a couple of beats longer
before going back to their game or conversation. A challenge?
Maybe.

He turned right and headed for the crowded bar. The
bartender was huge. He wasn't quite the height of Jack, but he
was wide and thick. His chest pressed against his silk shirt, threatening to rip it apart, likewise his arms. The garters stretched tight
over his biceps appeared they would snap apart at any moment.
Jack looked the man over. *The shirt has to be custom made,* he
thought. *Nowhere could that man buy a shirt off the rack. If he found
one that would fit his neck, it would drape over him like a blanket.* The
man's face and hands told stories. His face had scars across the
forehead and along the cheekbones. His massive hands, like
sledgehammers, carried souvenirs of fights across the knuckles
and fingers.

Jack reached the bar. Before he could speak, a man stepped from the office. *This has to be Korkeran,* he thought. Korkeran was not quite six feet. He was dressed like a gambler, expensive black suit and white shirt with ruffled cuffs extending beyond the coat sleeves. He was overdressed for this part of the country, but the cut of his mouth and eyes would prevent anyone from calling him a dude. He wore a wide green and black cravat with a large diamond stickpin in its center. Over the shirt was a matching green and black brocade vest. But it wasn't the suit, the diamond stick pin, or his chiseled features that drew Jack's attention. It was the pair of ivory-handled Colt .44s on his hips, slung as if he knew how to use them and had.

Korkeran extended his hand as he approached Jack. "So you are the famous Marshal Sage who arrested Flint Blaisdale. My, you are a tall fellow. I am Roman Korkeran of Virginia. I am most pleased to meet you, sir. I had hoped that you might come around today, though you have certainly been busy."

"Thanks. Jack Sage."

"Step up to the bar, Marshal. Let me buy you a glass of my finest. It is straight from Kentucky. Only the best for our new marshal."

Jack was looking at Korkeran, but his peripheral vision caught Bull's sneer. He could recognize trouble when he saw it. "No, thanks, Mr. Korkeran. I'm not much of a drinker." He turned to the bartender. "What's your name?"

"Bull."

"Bull? Is that all?"

Bull stiffened and placed his massive fists on the bar. "Bull. That's what I said."

"Umm, interesting. How did you get the name? Did you cause your ma so much pain coming into this world she automatically gave you the name Bull and nothing else?"

Bull clinched his fists.

Jack could almost see the big man thinking. Maybe trying to

figure out if the marshal was making fun of him or asking a legitimate question.

Korkeran stepped in. "Marshal Sage, Bull has worked for me for several years, and that's all I have ever known him as. You know how it is out here. We leave our past in the past. Sometimes folks change their names. This is the west."

"Yep," Jack said. "Just asking." Ignoring Bull, Jack turned back to Korkeran. "You serve pure liquor and run honest games in here, Mr. Korkeran?" The only difference Jack could see in the man was a slight tightening of his jaws.

"Of course I do. I must say, that is a bit insulting. If anyone else asked me that question, I might be offended."

"I guess it's a good thing I asked it. I'm telling you like I've told all of the other saloon owners, as long as I don't hear about watered-down drinks or customers getting cheated, you'll be in business."

The jaws got tighter.

"So, Marshal Sage, you're telling me you would shut me down on a single rumor?"

"No, Mr. Korkeran. I'm telling you I would investigate that rumor. If I found it unfounded, nothing would be done. However, if I found evidence of watered-down drinks or cheating, yes, I'd shut you down in a heartbeat and run you out of town."

A slow, deep, rumbling voice came from behind the bar. "Boss, let me send this marshal running with his tail between his legs."

Jack turned to see Bull leaning over the bar toward him.

"I'd recommend you call off your dog, Mr. Korkeran, or I might start getting suspicious and look under your roulette table."

"Easy, Bull," Korkeran said. "The marshal wasn't suggesting that we run crooked games. He was just telling us what would happen to anyone who might run those types of games."

Jack stared at the huge bartender. "You heard him. Easy, Bull. Don't saddle a bronc you can't ride."

"Need a drink," someone called down the bar.

Bull held Jack's gaze for a moment longer, then turned and moved away.

"My man is very protective."

Jack nodded. "That can be very good and very bad. Keep him reined in."

"I will certainly do as you ask. Are you sure you wouldn't like a drink before bed?"

"No, thanks. Have a good evening." Jack, still at the bar, turned to leave as the batwing doors swung open and Casey Miller stepped through the door. *I don't want to hurt this boy*, Jack thought and headed for the door.

When Casey came through the door, he was looking at the roulette table. At Jack's movement, his head turned toward the bar. He held out a hand. "Hold up there, Marshal. Don't you move a step closer. You've been making fun of me all day long. You made me look like a kid in front of Mr. Mather and those other hands. I almost killed my horse gettin' back here to teach you a lesson."

Jack shook his head. "Casey, why don't you come on over here, and I'll buy you a drink. You need to calm down. You don't want to get hurt or hurt someone else. Being a gunman isn't what you think it is. People don't look up to you, they're afraid of you. They won't let their daughters talk to you or dance with you. If they let you into the dance, no one will talk to you. You'll always be on the run, lonely and afraid."

The young man stood at the door, shaking his head. He stood in a slight squat, his body thrust forward and his right hand hovering over his six-gun. "I seen Flint. Everybody looks up to him. He's a gunman, and he ain't afraid of nobody."

"That's not right, boy. He's afraid of his shadow. Where does he sit when he comes into a room? Is there anyone he can put his trust in? Has he ever let you ride behind him when you're riding together, or anyone else? Think about it."

Jack watched the boy slowly straightening up.

"He ain't never let me ride behind him." He thought a moment longer. "But that don't mean he's scared. It just means he's cautious."

"What does he do when a man walks into the room unexpectedly? Does he jump? Does he reach for his gun? What does he do, Casey?"

The boy straightened more.

Good, Jack thought, *the boy's thinking. If I can just keep him talking and thinking, we'll both be home free.*

Casey looked at the floor and then looked up at Jack. "He does jump. I've seen that. Sometimes he just keeps watching a stranger. I've seen him almost draw his gun."

"That's right," Jack said. "You don't want to live like that. You want to meet a nice girl, get married, and grow old with her. So let's just walk out of here and get you started on a new way of life."

"Maybe you're right, Marshal." He straightened fully and began to relax.

A big cowhand who had been watching the whole thing spit his plug of tobacco into a spittoon. It clunked and could be heard throughout the silent saloon.

Casey turned to look at the man.

The two were looking each other in the eyes when the cowhand said in disgust, "Dang, boy, you ain't nothin' but a coward."

Jack could hear his mind screaming, *No, no, no, no . . .* as the boy turned back to him. Casey's face was full of fear and pain and confusion.

He screamed, "I ain't no coward, Marshal!" His hand went down to his old Colt and started drawing it out.

Jack waited, hoping the boy would stop. He wasn't fast, but he kept drawing. When he had the Colt out of his holster and was starting to bring it up level, Jack drew.

His hand was a flash. The .36-caliber Remington bucked once. He went against all of his instincts and training. He knew to keep shooting until the man was down and his gun hand relaxed, but he stopped shooting. The single round ball hit the boy to the left of his heart, where Jack had aimed. He could see the blood begin to flow, the surprise on Casey's young face, and the big Colt start to lower. Jack felt a momentary flash of relief. The doc was good. He could probably save the boy's life.

But the big Colt stopped dropping and started rising again. Casey was determined. Jack waited. He shouted, "Don't do it, boy!" But the .44 kept rising. Jack's face turned hard. He had no more options. He fired again.

There would be no more chances. He had been hoping, but hope was gone. He fired a third time, and Casey crumpled in a small pile on the floor. Jack knew he was dead. He shoved the Remington back into his holster, but he didn't walk to Casey. Through the smoke-filled room, his eyes came to rest on the cowhand who had provoked the boy.

Jack was almost four inches over six feet. His stride when he was stepping out was close to five feet, so he reached the cowhand in four strides.

The man saw him coming and held out his hands, palms forward. "Now wait, Marshal. I didn't—"

Jack grabbed the man's left wrist with his right hand and squeezed it hard. He had broken men's wrists with his grip before. He could feel the bones grind together, and the man yelled. His yell was cut short when the muzzle of the shotgun drove into his belly. The cowhand tried to double over, but Jack didn't let him. He yanked him off his feet and dragged him, the cowhand's head and body hitting empty chairs and tables patrons had evacuated. Reaching Casey, he turned loose of the man's wrist and grabbed him by the back of the neck, thrusting him down toward Casey's bloody chest. "See what you did. You should be the one lying on the floor with blood spurting out of you, not him." He thrust the man down until his face was almost touching the boy's chest and held him there.

In a quivering voice, the cowhand said, "I'm sorry, Marshal. I didn't think he'd draw."

"You didn't think." Jack lifted the man by the back of his neck and threw him through the batwing doors, past Casey's body and into the street. The cowhand sprawled in the dirt and slowly stood, cradling his wrist.

Jack's breathing was slowing. He felt the rage subsiding. He knew the sadness would be coming and didn't look forward to it. He took another deep breath and let it out. "Where's your horse, cowboy?"

The cowhand's eyes opened wider, and a look of hope spread across his face. He pointed to a bay standing in front of the Lily.

"You work for a ranch around here?"

He rubbed his wrist. "Just driftin'."

"Then get on your horse and keep drifting. Find a job somewhere far away, because I don't ever want to see your face again. You made me kill a boy tonight who could have had a good life with half a chance. You remember that." Jack pointed to the man's horse. "Now git!"

The man staggered to his horse, pulled himself into the saddle, and turned the animal out of town. Jack watched him disappear into the darkness. The saloons had emptied, and people were standing on both boardwalks and in the street. Jack turned to one of the men who had been in the Lily. "You know where the undertaker lives?"

He pointed to the second story over the barbershop. "Right there. Hearing the shots, he's probably getting dressed right now."

Jack nodded and pointed to a man standing next to the one

he had just spoken to. "You two take Miller's body to the undertaker. Tell him I said the city will pay for his burial."

"Sure thing, Marshal."

He felt the light weight of a hand on his arm. "Are you all right, Jack?"

Looking down, he saw Gabby next to him, her eyes flashing in the scattered light of the saloons. "Yeah, as good as possible. I just killed a boy who could have had a decent life if he'd had half a chance."

"I'm sorry, Jack. You want to come back to my place and talk about it?"

"Thanks. I'm fine. What I need most of all is to get some sleep. I'm heading over to the hotel and get some shuteye, but thanks again for the offer." *She is a beautiful woman,* he thought.

She gazed up at him for a moment. "Anytime. I mean that." Turning, she walked back to the Cherry Creek Saloon.

People remained in the street talking.

Jack raised his voice. "It's over, folks. Go on home." He looked back at the Lily. Korkeran was still standing outside watching him. Their eyes locked. Korkeran shrugged and went back into the Lily.

Moments later Jack heard Bull yell, "Belly up to the bar, boys. Drinks are on the house."

He turned and headed for the hotel.

The clerk was a slim, bookish man. He stood behind the check-in desk with a pen in his hand. "Come in, Marshal. I've already got you set up. Mr. Pierce came by and made the arrangements. You'll be in one of our fine suites, second floor, room two ten. It's up the stair and at the far end of the hall. If you'll sign our register, you can go right up. Your gear is in your room."

Jack had taken the pen and was writing his name. At the last statement, he looked up. "Who brought my things up?"

"Why, Nate Pierce. Wasn't he supposed to?"

Jack recovered quickly, remembering the boy he had given

the quarter eagle to. "Yes, he was. I forgot. It's been an eventful day."

The clerk nodded. "I should say so, Marshal. But you'd better watch out. That Mather is not one to give up easily. If he ties up with Birch of the 7 Bar, you could have your hands real full."

"Thanks for letting me know," Jack said, remembering what Sully had told him about Birch. He took the key the clerk handed him and started up the stairs. *Was it just this morning I found Bart? It feels like I tried to cram two weeks into one day.* Reaching the top of the stairs, he looked back at the hotel's empty lobby. He could see through the front windows. The crowd had disappeared. It was late, and most people had to work in the morning if they wanted food on the table.

He walked down the dimly lit hallway. Coming to his room number, he shoved the key in the lock, turned it, and the door unlocked. He glanced to his right at the end of the building. *Probably an exit*, he thought, and, as tired as he was, decided to have a look. He walked to the exit, opened the door, and leaned out. A small landing quickly gave way to a stairway leading to ground level. The stairway was butted against the back wall of the hotel on the same side as his room. Above the stairway, he noticed hotel windows. Filing away the information, he closed the door, went back to his room, and stepped inside.

After entering, he locked the door and slid the back of a chair under the knob. He knew it wouldn't stop someone from breaking in, but it would sure stop them from entering quietly. He looked around the room. The clerk was right. This wasn't a room, it was a suite. The room was a combination office and sitting room. He had a couch and a couple of wingback chairs. In addition to the office chair he had slid under the doorknob, its twin sat at the desk. A mirror was on the wall behind the desk, giving the desk an additional function as a dresser.

He walked into the bedroom, ducking at the last minute. The door frame brushed his hat to the back of his head. He took it off and tossed it onto the back post of the nearest chair. A cabinet held a basin and pitcher. He checked the pitcher. Full. Moving to the bed, he turned and lowered himself to the mattress and let out a long breath.

Jack leaned his shotgun against the wall where it would be handy, between the side table and the bed. Awkwardly, he removed his gun belt, refastened the buckle, and looped it over the headboard, the butt of the revolver handy. He crossed his right leg over his left, grasped his boot, and pulled. Tight. He relaxed. It didn't surprise him. He'd had them on all day, and it had been a long day.

This time he grabbed the back of a heel in one hand and the toe in the other. Biceps straining, he alternated pressure, rocking the boot until it loosened and slid from his foot. He wiggled his toes, and his foot and calf all but cheered at the freedom. He did the same with the other. After removing everything from his vest pockets, he undressed, laying his clothes across the back of a chair. He needed to check his bags to make sure everything was there, but his back ached, his feet and legs were tired, and he couldn't get Casey Miller's face off his mind.

He pulled down the cover and stretched his full length on the bed. His feet hung over the end, just as he had expected. He was used to it. The last thought he remembered was the picture of Casey, determined and scared, pulling his revolver and screaming, "I ain't no coward, Marshal." And then he died.

9

J ack opened his eyes and examined the barely perceptible light showing around the window curtains. He stretched his long arms and felt tight muscles lengthen and strain. It felt good. This was the first bed he had slept in for a long while. He yawned. Except for the faint glow creeping around the edge of the drapes, darkness filled the room. It was still early. He pulled a pocket watch from his vest's upper pocket and held the face toward the window to take advantage of the dim light. He could barely make out the time, four fifty. Dropping the watch back into the vest pocket, he stood and stretched again.

He had wanted to get an early start, but getting up this late would make it almost impossible. A lamp sat on the cabinet next to the pitcher and basin. He took a match from the small bowl next to the lamp, bent, and lifted the chimney. Striking the match across the brass handle of the cabinet, he placed the flaming tip near the wick. The wick flamed high, and Jack reduced the exposed tip of the wick by rotating the tiny knob at the edge of the lamp. He lowered the chimney and continued to adjust the wick until the brightness suited him. After shaking out the match, he stuck the head in the water and dropped it in the small bowl provided.

He looked at his reflection in the mirror. Those gray eyes had stared out at him from many a mirror, most not as nice as this one. Tousled thick brown hair hung over his ears and down his forehead. He poured water into the basin, wet his hands, and brushed his hair straight back.

The heavy dark stubble still covered his face from high cheekbones to scarred chin. It seemed that his chin took the brunt of most of his fights. *I don't know if it's the closest target or too big,* he thought. Whatever it was, several scars sliced through the dark whiskers.

He rubbed his hands across the stubble, thinking about shaving. "I need more than a shave. I need a bath," he said to his reflection in the mirror. He looked around the bedroom. Nowhere had he seen his Spencer, saddlebags, or supplies. A wardrobe stood against the end wall of the bedroom. He stepped to it, opened the door, and there lay everything. He pulled the drawers open to find his clothes neatly laid out in one drawer. In the other drawer, his remaining Remington, loaded cylinders, powder, the sack of balls he had previously molded, and the mold were placed in an orderly manner. "That boy earned his money," he said to the room.

Disbelief flooded his mind at the sight of his other Remington Police. It reminded him that he had failed to reload last night. He shook his head at the thought. *Forgetting such things will get me killed.* He opened one of the drapes to let light into the room. Daylight was coming fast.

Jack moved his cleaning kit to the small dresser in the bedroom, laid it out, and grabbed both Remingtons, one from his holster, the other from the drawer. He went to work. In less than ten minutes he had them both cleaned and fully loaded.

He checked the loads again, slipped one of the revolvers back into the holster, and laid the other on the bed. He got dressed.

Before pulling his boots on, he lifted each and shook it out. The last thing he wanted was to shove his foot down on top of an angry scorpion. He'd had enough scorpion bites to last him for the rest of his life. Finding the boots were clear, he pulled on first the left and then the right.

Jack looked around the room. If he was going to get cleaned up and eat before hitting the saddle, he'd best get moving. He quickly packed his saddlebags and shoved the remaining Remington behind his gun belt. He picked up the shotgun, checked the loads, grabbed his saddlebags and threw them over his shoulder. On the way to the door he picked up his Spencer.

Jack stepped into the hallway and elected to go out the back door of the hotel. *Never become habitual,* he thought. *Next time I'll go out the front.* When he hit the bottom of the stairs, he stepped clear and turned down the alley toward the main street. The sun was not yet up, but there was already traffic in the street. Farmers and ranchers were early risers, so the town businesses also began their day early.

He headed across the street to the barber, hoping the man would have some baths set up. Nate was in front of his father's general store, washing the windows. The boy waved to him. Though he was in a hurry, Jack changed direction and headed for Nate.

The young fella stopped washing as Jack approached. "Howdy, Marshal Sage. Morning to you."

"Morning, Nate. I just wanted to thank you for moving all my things to the hotel. That was mighty nice of you."

The boy's face turned red. "Oh, shoot, Marshal. It weren't nothing. I was glad to do it, and I felt like it was the least I could do since you gave me all that money. Who-whee, that's a bunch of money, thanks again."

"You earned it." Jack looked through the window and didn't see either of the Pierces. "You think your pa would mind if you took my shotgun across the street to the office?"

"Naw, Marshal. He wouldn't mind a bit."

"Would you take it to Clint? I've got a lot I need to do."

"Shoot yeah, Marshal. I'd be glad to." Before Jack could hand the boy the shotgun, Nate said, "I'm sure sorry about Casey."

Jack sobered. "Did you know him?"

"Kinda. He drifted in a couple of years ago looking for work. He always thought he was fast with a gun. It's a durned shame."

"I didn't want to shoot him."

"I know. Shoot, the whole town knows you tried to talk him out of it. It's just a shame he got all mixed up with them Lazy T riders. They're all no good." He looked up at Jack. "But Casey was always good to me. He liked hard candy, never had much money. Sometimes I'd sneak out a handful and act like I had too much and needed to get rid of it. He wouldn't take it otherwise. He had pride."

"Yes, the boy had pride." *Too much,* Jack thought.

He held the shotgun out for Nate. "It's loaded."

"Wouldn't be much good if it weren't, would it, Marshal."

"No. It sure wouldn't." He dug out the extra shells from his vest and dropped them into the boy's extended hand. "Thanks, Nate. Tell Clint I'll stop by to see him on the way out of town."

"Yes, sir. I sure will." Nate stuck the shells in a pocket and carried the shotgun through the crook of his right arm.

Jack turned and headed back up the boardwalk to the barbershop. He passed Wade's Gun Shop, thought about stopping in, and changed his mind. He needed to be riding. He glanced into the Gilded Lily to see a few people around the roulette wheel and shook his head. *I just can't figure people out, being so anxious to get rid of their hard-earned money.* He stepped clear of the boardwalk to allow a lady to pass and raised his hat. "Morning, ma'am."

The woman smiled, lowered her head, and replied, "Good morning, Marshal." She continued her course down the boardwalk.

Reaching the barbershop, he pushed the door open. The bell

tinkled, and Reginald Farnsworth stepped in from the back room. "Good morning, Marshal. What brings you to my establishment so early."

"I need a bath and a shave."

"You have come to the appropriate facility, Marshal. It just so happens you are early, and being early means you will be the first of the day. Step to the back, please."

Jack knew what he meant, "first of the day." Many bathhouses used the water several times. The later in the day you were, the dirtier the water. Of course, if you were picky, you could pay extra for clean water. He stepped through the back room, where one casket, if you could call it that, had been nailed shut, and Casey Miller lay in the other. He continued past the two of them and through the back door. Behind the barbershop was a lean-to with a partial fence around it up to an average man's shoulders. A boy tended a fire and was pouring hot water from a bucket into one of the three tubs.

"Booming business for baths around here?"

"Not really, I like to be prepared." He nodded to the Gilded Lily. "Sometimes I get several of the ladies." There were nails in posts by each tub and a long bench along the fencing at the foot of the tubs.

Jack sat on the bench and began taking his boots off. "How much?"

Farnsworth smiled. "Four bits for first bath, two bits for everything else, twenty cents for towel and soap. Shave's two bits, and so's a haircut. Have them both done and it is a mere forty cents."

"I'll give you a dollar for it all, but that depends on me getting the shave and haircut as soon as I'm out of here."

Farnsworth calculated for only a moment. "You have a deal, Marshal. Come in as soon as you're done."

The bath went quickly. The feel of the hot water on his body tempted Jack to sit in the tub and soak, but he didn't have the time. He finished, got dressed, and strode into the shop.

Farnsworth was working on Casey. He dusted off his hands and followed Jack into the barbershop.

Jack watched him.

He reached for the mug and brush.

"Hold up, Farnsworth. You've been working on a dead body, right?"

"Yes, of course."

"Did you wash your hands?"

"Why?"

"If you're gonna shave me with the same hands you used to work on a dead body, you're gonna wash 'em first."

The barber-undertaker-dentist looked at Jack as if he were insane. "Wash my hands?"

"Yes."

He sighed and shook his head. "Well, alright, if you insist." He moved to a washbasin, poured water into the basin, and started to wash his hands.

"With soap."

Farnsworth's eyes rolled. His lips pursed as if he was going to reply, but he picked up the bar of soap and, with it, washed his hands. "Now?"

Jack nodded.

There was a bucket of hot water next to the barber chair. Farnsworth poured until a basin was half full. Then he took a towel and soaked it in the hot water, gingerly wrung the towel, and wrapped it around Jack's face.

"Leave the eyes uncovered," Jack said.

Farnsworth spread the towel so Jack's eyes had a tunnel to see through. When the man removed the towel, he made fast work of Jack's shave and swiftly completed the haircut, lifting the hairline above Jack's ears.

Jack felt along his cheek. The smoothest shave he'd had in a long time. He pulled a dollar from his vest pocket and dropped it into Farnsworth's waiting hand. "Good job. I feel like a new man."

Jack picked up the dirty wadded clothes and reached for his Spencer.

"If you'll leave the clothes, I'll have them washed and ironed. I don't remember what she charges, but it will be a fair price."

Jack dropped the pile of clothes back on the chair and lifted the Spencer along with his saddlebags. "Thank you. When can I pick them up?"

"They'll be ready tomorrow. Stop by anytime in the afternoon."

"Thanks." Jack pushed out the door and headed for Johnson's Stables. No time for breakfast this morning, too much of it had already been wasted. It was six fifteen, and he needed to be in the saddle.

As he neared the stable, Sully called, "'Bout time. Almost pulled the rig off your grulla. Saw you comin' up just as I reached for the cinch."

"Good thing you didn't. You'd just have to put it on again."

Sully eyed Jack. When he saw the grin, he spit. The tobacco juice sailed out into the street. "Maybe. Maybe not."

Jack stepped up to Smokey and rubbed him on the cheek. "You miss me, boy?" He reached across the saddle and dropped the Spencer into the scabbard. Flipping the reins from the door post, he swung into the saddle. Then he looked over at Sully, who had been standing by Stonewall with his arm across the mule's back, the two of them watching.

"How you doin', boy?" Sully asked.

"I'm all right. A little cantankerous since I missed breakfast, but it ain't like this is the first time."

"I heard what happened. He was on the prod. It was a fair shooting, Jack. You had to do it or you'd be the one lyin' over at Farnsworth's place."

Jack rested both hands on the saddle horn. A quail whistled from behind the stable, and several more answered. The long, early morning shadow of a buzzard traced its way across the street. Kids played, and a dog barked. "I know, Sully, but it's never easy when you have to shoot a kid and take his future away from him."

"You didn't, boy. I'm thinkin' you've seen a lot of killin' and dying. You know that when you strap on a gun, in this country, it's just a matter of time before you're shot or you shoot someone. That's just the truth of it. Now git on out of here, and go do what you have to."

Jack touched the brim of his hat and turned Smokey into the street. The gray horse walked through the street past the Rusty Bucket, the Gilded Lily, and past the Cherry Creek and the attorney's office. Jack pulled him up in front of the marshal sign. Clint stepped out, shotgun in hand.

"You expecting trouble?"

Clint nodded. "Always. How you doin'?"

"Fine. How far's your place from here?"

"Steady riding, at a walk, probably three hours southeast of here. You heading over there?"

"Yeah, thought I might. I want to look around. Get a feel for this country. Where's Mather's ranch from your place?"

"Almost due west. An hour, maybe."

"And the Carter place?"

"Not far. Less than half an hour south, along Cherry Creek. Can't miss it. Their house is built right on the shelf above the creek. I tried to tell Tobias to build farther up the slope of the hill, but he wouldn't listen. He's never seen these Texas creeks rise. Said the shelf'll be fine. Anyway, that's where it is. You gonna take her money to her?"

"Glad you mentioned it. I hadn't thought about it until now." He started to swing down.

"Hold up. I'll get it."

Clint turned back into the office as Dr. Cook walked up.

"Morning, how's Bart doing?"

The doc shook his head. "Bart amazes me. He's up and

moving around. His shoulder is hurting him, but he's doing a lot more than he should be. He's even talking about moving his equipment into his new office."

"You know him a lot better than I do, Doc. Were it me, I'd say if a man felt like doing, let him do."

"You're right, Marshal. I know him a lot better than you, and I know medicine. His body needs to heal before he starts galivanting around."

"Just my two cents, Doc."

Clint walked out with the paper money rolled and a band around it. He handed it up to Jack.

Dr. Cook watched. "That's a lot of money, Marshal."

"Yes, it is." He turned, loosened a flap on his saddlebags, and dropped the roll inside.

Clint gave Jack a questioning look and held out the change. Jack nodded toward the open bag, and Clint dropped it in. While he was closing the bag, he said, "Donations for Mrs. Carter. I'm taking it out to her."

"I'd say that is a pretty large donation."

"Yes, sir, it is. Some folks have a real kind heart."

Wade looked at Jack. The humor could only be detected by the laugh wrinkles around his eyes deepening.

The doctor reached into his gray vest, pulled out a double eagle, and handed it to Jack. "Please include this."

"Thanks, Doc, I sure will. That's mighty big of you." He slid the double eagle under the flap and let it fall into the saddlebag.

"I have some business." Dr. Cook touched his hat. "Good day to you. Oh, I almost forgot, Nancy asked me to tell you to stop by, if you're free this evening, for dinner."

"Tell her that's mighty nice, Doc, but I probably won't be back in town today. I've got a lot of ridin' to do. I'm headed out to see Mrs. Carter and checking on Clint's place and look around."

"I'll tell her." The doctor strode off toward the Cherry Creek Saloon.

Clint watched him go. "That was mighty nice."

"Yes, sir, donating a twenty-dollar gold piece isn't something to sneeze at."

"Yeah, that was nice, too, but I was talking about your dinner invite."

Jack looked at Clint. His deputy's humor wrinkles were still there.

"Yep. That was nice of her. Too bad I won't be here. I'd like to check up on Bart and see how he's doing."

"Umm-hum, yep, I'm sure he needs checkin' up on."

Jack's brow creased in a frown. "What the blazes are you drivin' at, Clint?"

"I was just thinkin' Nancy's mighty pretty."

"Are you crazy? She's a married woman."

It was Clint's turn to frown. "When'd she get married? Who'd she marry?"

"Dang it, Clint. Are you trying to pull my leg? She's married to the doctor."

Clint slapped his leg and broke out in laughter, his head shaking. "Boss, you got it so wrong. Nancy Cook ain't the doc's wife, she's his sister."

Jack's eyes widened in surprise, and then his mouth spread into a grin. He leaned forward. His right forearm rested on the saddle, and his left forefinger pushed his gray Stetson up and back. "Are you foolin' me, Clint? I'd hate to have to get down and beat some sense into you."

"No, it's the gospel truth. The two of 'em are the only family they have. It's actually kind of a sad story. Their folks were killed in the war. The doc came to Cherry Creek to make a new life, and he wasn't about to leave his sister back there all alone."

Jack shook his head and said, low, to himself, "Brother and sister, well, I'll be. Who would've thought? She ran that house just like she owned it."

Clint nodded. "She treats sick people too, helps him out in

surgeries. She's quite a woman, though I think Bart's got his hat set for her. Seems the three of them knew each other back east."

Jack straightened in the saddle. "I've got to be moving on. Thanks for filling me in. I sure thought they were hitched." He turned Smokey down the street. "Anything you need me to do at your place? I've been known to milk a cow when needed."

"Just look it over. Neighbor'll keep an eye on it." Clint paused. "What about Blaisdale?"

Jack was about to bump Smokey in the flanks, but held up.

"I don't expect Mather to be coming back any time soon, but you never know. If he does, don't fight him. You're by yourself. Just let him have Blaisdale. We'll get him back. Being by yourself ain't no time to be a hero."

"I'm wearing the same badge you are. I'm responsible to the town."

"Forget that. You're responsible to me. If they come into town before I get back, do not fight them. I'll need your help to get him back. We clear on that?"

Clint nodded. "We're clear."

"Take care. I'll be back in a couple of days, three at the most." This time he bumped Smokey in the flanks. The horse started a fast walk, passing the bank and general store, the doc's house and the old oak. The town fell away behind them.

10

J ack kept Smokey at a ground-covering walk. Distance fell away. This part of Texas was different from around Laredo. The hills were taller and more frequent, the bunch grass greener, and the prickly pear thinner. The one thing similar, cattle were scattered throughout the country. Though the brands were more varied than he'd expected.

He figured he would see mostly Lazy T and 7 Bar, but he was also seeing CP, which had to be Clint Paget; TC, which would be Tobias Carter; a Rocking S; and a Box K. All of these other brands must be from the homesteaders.

Nothing said they couldn't use open range just like the big ranchers did. The difference was in the open range they were staking out one hundred and sixty acres. If those acres were around water, the big ranchers would have a tough time watering their stock if enough homesteaders moved in.

He saw the head of a big whitetail buck just before the animal stood. It was summertime. The bucks were in velvet, and the antlers were sensitive. During this time, the animals tended to be more solitary. This old fella was by himself. He had bedded down in a dense oak thicket. Jack would never have seen him if that monster rack hadn't moved. It looked like tree limbs moving. He pulled Smokey to a stop.

The buck stood, his eyes glued to the horse and rider. Two minutes passed. The buck stomped a front foot and blew, the sound almost like a fractured whistle. Jack clucked and turned Smokey slightly away from the animal. The deer's head swiveled to follow them, and, evidently still feeling safe, it buckled its front legs and dropped back into its bed.

"Good sign, Smokey. If we found that old fella bedded down, nothing dangerous to us is near about."

He found himself crossing and recrossing Cherry Creek as the stream continued to meander southeast. He enjoyed the crossings. The creek bottom was mostly rocky, and there were waterholes all up and down the creek bed. The stream tripped musically over the rocks, never deeper than a foot or two at the crossings, and sometimes only inches.

It provided him a fresh drink whenever he wanted it, and the opportunity to keep Smokey watered. The only problem he found, besides the Lazy T bunch, was the Comanches. They weren't as bad as they had been during the war, but if you ran across a band, they were still deadly. He had seen cavalry operate around the world, and there was none better than the Comanche warrior, or more deadly.

He had been riding for about three hours when he again came upon the creek. On the other side, against a slope above the creek, he could see a combination sod and rock house. *It must be Clint's,* he thought, *if I got his directions right.*

There was a nice barn and corral. In fact, from here, the barn looked nicer than the house. He stopped in the creek bottom and allowed Smokey to drink. Once the horse had his fill, they started up the creek bank. The bank was steep, and Smokey, kicking rocks and digging for a hold, made quite a bit of noise. Tall pecan trees rose above the thick shrubs and brush along the creek. He heard the clucking before he saw them, and just as he made it up the slope and out of the creek, they flew.

There must have been fifty of the big birds. Big, dark bronze redheaded and blue-headed turkeys. "Dang, Smokey," Jack said. The noise of their wings and their clucking would be heard as much as a mile up and down the creek.

If Comanches were around, he would be in big trouble. He watched the big birds set their wings and sail like a dove in mating season. They glided almost to Clint's fenced yard, landed, and ran a short distance. Then they started pecking at the ground. *Grasshoppers. Just like a chicken, they love grasshoppers.* The turkeys appeared to have completely forgotten him in their haste to stuff themselves.

Jack rode slowly toward the grasshopper massacre. After flushing away from him and making a terrible racket, the turkeys were ignoring him in their frenzy to eat. He shook his head. Finally, as he approached, the turkeys grew skittish and ran over the hillside. He rode up to the fenced yard and stepped down from the saddle.

He led Smokey to the trough, looked, and ran his hand through the water. Still fresh. Clint must have filled it yesterday. Smokey, having just had a drink in the creek, ignored the water and turned his head so he could look south, down the creek. "Whatcha looking at, boy?" Jack followed Smokey's gaze, but saw nothing. "Don't pull my leg, fella." He patted the big horse on its shoulder and wrapped the reins around the hitching post next to the trough.

His next stop was the barn. There were four stalls, but no animals. Clint's neighbor must have moved them to his place. There was no sign of a cow either, so the neighbor must have also taken it. He found a feedbag and some oats, put a few in the bag, carried it out, and pulled it over Smokey's muzzle. He slipped the strap behind the animal's ears and listened as the horse crunched the oats.

Smokey had turned so he could watch down the creek. Both ears were pitched forward. "What are you looking at, boy?" Jack looked closely at the treeline, his head turning as he followed the creek. Nothing. He shook his head and decided to check out the house while the horse chewed on the oats. Just to be safe, he pulled his Spencer from the scabbard and carried it with him into the house.

Stepping inside, Jack looked around Clint's place. It wasn't huge, but it wasn't small either. He had put in a lot of work here. There was a large room that made up the kitchen, dining, and living room. A rock fireplace took up much of the west wall and doubled as heater and kitchen. A long iron rod extended across the front of the fireplace. Pots sat on the wide hearth to the left side, with multiple hangers pulled to the same side.

A doorway at the back off the living room opened into a bedroom. There was no door, but a curtain, hanging from a rod at the top, was pulled to one side. The room had been dug into the rocky hillside. It was lower than the rest of the house, no more than six feet high, if that much. Jack had to take his hat off and bend over as he walked in. Clint had put a rock floor throughout the house. *Pretty nice,* Jack thought, *clean.*

Nothing had been disturbed. He stepped out of the bedroom and straightened at the sound of a distant shot. There was another. He pulled the hammer back on the Spencer and moved out onto the covered porch, pulling the door closed behind him. The sound of shots was coming from down the creek in the direction Smokey had been looking. They were faint. Running to Smokey, he heard two more, coming almost together.

Jack leaped into the saddle, hit Smokey in the flanks with the spurs, and they were racing across the countryside. The patches of prickly pear flashed by as the big grulla stretched long legs through the broken land. Jack leaned forward over his horse's neck, feeling the wind in his face. His big Stetson, acting like a kite, seized the wind and sailed from his head, but his homemade loop caught around his neck, holding his hat to him. He could feel the line pulling at his neck and the hat swirling and banging against his back and shoulders. He rode hard for almost ten minutes, the shots growing closer. The race had taken him up and over several hills, passing clumps of mesquite and thickets of post oak. As he neared, the shots slowed, one or two only occasionally. They were louder now, and he could both see and smell smoke. He was getting close.

He slowed Smokey to a walk and headed for a thicket of oak on the low hilltop. The trees would break his outline so he could peer over and hopefully spot the trouble. He eased Smokey to the top, and between oak trunks, he could see eight Comanches taking turns firing both guns and arrows into a soft brown jersey cow that lay dying, still tethered to a milking post next to the sod house. Arrows protruded from her body. The post was located on a side of the house where there were no windows or shooting ports.

Why wouldn't they have ports all around the house? Jack thought. *Sodbusters come out to this country expecting it to be as safe as if their homes were with their police force.* Jack looked around to make sure there was no Indian slipping up on him. Still safe. He looked back at the house and the cow. *The damage is done,* he thought. *The folks inside are safe unless they caught a stray bullet. If killing a cow is the worst they do, I'll just sit here until they leave.*

The thought had no sooner registered than the front door flew open, and a woman stepped through the doorway. She grasped a double-barreled shotgun in her hands, and he could tell from the way she held it, she knew how to use it.

She screamed, "Leave Bossy alone, you heathens."

The instant she stepped from the door, Jack moved. He threw the Spencer to his shoulder. The big carbine bucked, sending a .56-caliber chunk of lead toward a hapless Comanche brave. He was thankful he had trained Smokey. The big horse stood solid when the rifle roared over his head. Simultaneously dropping the

Spencer into the scabbard and drawing his two Remingtons, he kicked Smokey and yelled, heading straight for the five Comanches, for the woman had fired her shotgun at the same time the Spencer blasted. With the one shot, she took two braves out of the saddle. Closing fast, Jack opened up with his Remingtons. The first shot missed, but his second one caught one of the braves in the side of the head, killing him instantly. *Lucky shot if I've ever seen one,* flashed through his mind.

The woman had fired the second barrel of her shotgun and blown another brave from the saddle. The Comanches were far from cowards, but they made a rapid assessment and realized they were outgunned. The remaining three yelled and kicked their ponies into a blur of motion. With them leaving, Jack immediately stopped firing. He dashed up and yanked Smokey to a sliding stop.

"Are you alright, ma'am?"

The lady walked over to the cow. "Our poor Bossy. She was the kindest soul." The jersey, her big brown eyes watching the woman as she approached, gave a weak moo.

Jack jumped to the ground to check the Indians who had fallen. He didn't hanker to be knifed or shot by a supposedly dead Comanche.

The woman knelt next to the cow and ran her hand over the beautiful soft fawn-colored hide. Blood was seeping from its black nose and staining the soft white hair around the nose. The cow tried to lift its head but was too weak.

The lady pulled a butcher knife from a pocket in her apron. She rubbed the animal's head. "Poor Bossy. I'm so sorry." She felt for a spot on the cow's neck, found it, and plunged the knife deep, immediately pulling it out. The blade was followed with a gush of blood pumping across the cow's long neck. The woman continued to rub the cow between its ears. It slowly relaxed and, with one final long sigh, died. She sat there, stationary, next to the cow. Then she sighed and stood.

She turned to Jack. "Yes, I and my children are fine. They are hiding inside."

"The Indians are dead, ma'am."

"Yes, thank you. I did not intend to kill anyone, but my little son managed to dig a hole through the wall with his fingers. He saw Bossy fall. I'm afraid I lost control. We brought that cow with us all the way from Illinois. The children loved her."

"Yes, ma'am," was all Jack could think to say. What he wanted to say was she had made a crazy move, stepping out like she did. If he hadn't been there, they would've all been dead or captured, which he figured would probably be worse.

She looked more closely at him. "You are a very big man."

"Yes, ma'am. So I've been told. My name's Jack Sage. I'm the marshal of Cherry Creek."

"I thought Marshal Winfreid . . ." Her voice trailed off.

"He was. I took his place."

"Oh." Her eyes grew wider with understanding. She looked around at the death in the yard. "I've never had to shoot anyone."

"Well, ma'am, for someone never having shot anyone before, you did a mighty good job."

"I only meant to shoot over them with my first shot."

Jack gave a quick twist of his head. "Next time you want to shoot over a body's head with a shotgun, you'd best point that barrel a little higher. Those two braves you shot were both shot in the head. Killed 'em on the spot. The other one took most of the load in the chest. If I were a bettin' man, I'd say you've shot that scattergun a time or two."

"Yes, Marshal Sage, I have. Occasionally I go to the creek and get us a turkey. I like to shoot them flying. I shouldn't say it, but it is more fun."

"That's a fact, ma'am. May I ask your name?"

She was holding the bloody butcher knife in one hand and the shotgun in the other. She reached up with her left hand, the one with the knife, to brush hair from in front of her eyes. Seeing the butcher knife and her hand, she changed her mind. "Oh, sorry, my name is Sarah Purcell."

The woman was not an unattractive soul. Her face was a little long, but she had wide brown eyes that seemed to balance her features. Her brown hair had been in a bun, but whatever was holding it up had lost control, and curls were hanging over her face. A young-old face. Physically, no more than twenty-seven or twenty-eight. Life years was a different matter. Her face showed Sarah Purcell's life, to this point, had been hard. Though humor still resided in those eyes, it appeared to be crushed by grief and loss. What little humor remained did not extend to her mouth. Even at her young age, her mouth was developing wrinkles usually caused by years of being stiffened and pursed, not wide with smiles.

A young male voice from inside the house called, "Can we come out now, Ma?"

Her head turned quickly from Bossy to each of the dead Indians. Then her shoulders gave a slight shrug. "Yes, Alan, but the rest of you kids stay in the house for now."

Two smaller voices said in unison, "Please," the word drawn out as if it might make a difference in the outcome.

"No," she said firmly. "Alan only."

Her stern response brought only silence from inside the cabin.

The boy stepped outside and was looking at the dead Indians. Then his eyes found Bossy. He fought back tears and ran to the cow's side.

"Why'd they have to kill Bossy, Ma? She ain't never done nothing wrong to them."

Jack watched the boy kneel and stroke the cow's soft head. His hand moved slowly from just above the cow's nose to between its horns. It followed the path over and over.

"She was a good cow, Ma. She walked all the way from the settlement with us. All the way to Texas."

"Yes, she did, son. She was a good cow."

From inside, a little girl's voice cried, "Bossy ain't dead, is she, Ma?"

Another voice, Jack thought was a boy, but could be a girl, it was so young, called out, "She ain't, is she, Ma?"

"Yes, children, Bossy is dead."

Wailing rose from inside the house.

Sarah's voice hardened. "You children stop this instant. Bossy was a good cow, but she's gone. Crying won't help her now."

The crying stopped. After a few audible sniffles, the two children called out in their tiny voices, "Yes, Ma."

Jack looked around the yard. Flies were buzzing over the Indians and the cow. "Mrs. Purcell, I know you've got to take care of your children, but I need to get these men buried. Is there a place you'd prefer nearby?"

The woman looked around the yard, up at the hill where Jack had waited, and then down at the creek.

"The creek. About a quarter of a mile south, on the other side of the cornfield, there's a nice open area. Should be fairly easy digging."

"Do you have a wagon, ma'am? That'd make it a mite easier."

She shook her head, her brown curls cascading into her face again. She stuck out her lower lip and blew, hard. The curls moved a little, sticking on her perspiration-covered skin. "William, that's my husband, took the wagon to town early this morning. He should be back this evening. He's going to feel terrible about Bossy."

"He may, ma'am, but I'm sure he'll feel real good about all of you surviving a Comanche attack."

"Yes, I'm sure," she said vacantly, "but as I was saying, our wagon is gone. We do have a mule. We could load several of them on the mule and bring them down if you'd like to start digging. I appreciate your offer. It's so hot. They would be swelling and stinking in no time."

Jack could see the woman was in shock. He walked over to her and took the shotgun. "Mrs. Purcell, why don't you get cleaned up, then lie down for a few minutes. I think that'll help a lot. Alan, can you help your ma, and we'll get started?" He turned back to the woman. "You have a handgun in the house?"

"I have two. I reloaded them both when it looked like the Indians might be resting or leaving."

"Good. You keep one."

He turned to the boy. "Alan, I'm Marshal Sage. I'm sure you've shot those guns your ma was talking about."

The boy gave a vigorous nod. "Yes, sir. Pa's let me shoot those Dragoons several times."

"Good. Does your pa have a holster for them?"

"He does, Marshal. It's supposed to hang over a saddle horn, but he's made belts for both of them."

"Good. You take one of them, put it in the holster, and sling the holster over your shoulder, but first help your ma in the house. Make sure she gets washed up. Then help her to the bed and leave one of the Dragoons with her. Take this shotgun and reload it. Is that clear?"

"Yes, sir." He took his ma by her elbow. "Come on, Ma. Let's get inside, and then I'll help Marshal Sage."

Jack walked Smokey to the watering trough near the barn and let the horse drink. "You did good, Smokey. I should've listened to you this morning and eased on down here. You were trying to tell me all the time." He rubbed the horse's neck as it drank.

Within a few minutes Alan was back outside. He came over to the barn. "You want I should get the mule, Marshal?"

"Yeah, and we need a shovel and a pick, just in case."

"Alright."

Jack followed the boy into the barn. It was a little smaller than Clint's but still in good shape. Hay was in the loft, and there were three stalls. A mule stood in one. Hanging on the wall were shovels and a pick. He grabbed the pick and a shovel and watched Alan lead out the mule. Smokey had stopped drinking. With Alan walking beside him, the big Dragoon slung over his shoulder, Jack headed for the braves.

They loaded three on the mule. Then Jack swung into the saddle, cleared his stirrup, and reached his hand down.

"You want I should ride with you, Marshal?"

"Only if you want to, boy."

Alan grinned. "Yes, sir, I sure do." He grabbed Jack's hand, and before his foot could find the stirrup, Jack had yanked him up behind him.

"Now where's this spot your ma was talking about?"

Alan pointed to an area on the creek a little south of the corn patch. "Over that way."

Jack looked the little flat over. The lady had been right. This looked like about the softest ground he'd find to dig a hole. "This'll work. Let's get these fellas unloaded, and we'll go back and get the other two."

They unloaded the three, rode back to the house, and loaded up again. In no time they were back at the burial ground with the last two Indians, shovel, and pick.

After unloading, Jack looked across the land at the house. He considered for a moment. "Mount your mule, boy. We're heading back to the house."

"I thought we was burying these Comanches, Marshal?"

"They're not in any big rush. I've got something I think is a mite more important. Let's go."

11

J ack eyed the dead cow as he rode past. The heat was oppressive, and flies were everywhere, but there was still time. The two of them dismounted at the front of the house. "Alan, go inside and ask your mom if she feels like coming out here. If not, can I come in?"

He had barely finished when Mrs. Purcell said from inside, "Come in, Marshal. You'd best duck, as you will find it a little low in here for you."

Jack removed his hat and followed Alan into the sod house. Mrs. Purcell was sitting in a rocker, facing toward the door. Two children, a girl and a boy, were playing on the dirt floor with tiny carved horses. Mrs. Purcell was sitting in a chair at the table.

"Yes, Marshal."

"Ma'am, the cow carries a lot of meat. In this heat it's gonna spoil fast, but I think I can get a couple of good meals for you if you feel like cooking it up now. Would you like me to give it a shot or just haul it off?"

The little boy, who had been staring at Jack, suddenly made a face, and his entire body shook. "Ooo, Ma, I don't want to eat

Bossy. She wouldn't eat us." He turned his round little face toward his ma. "Would she?"

"No, Jacob, she wouldn't, but I think Bossy would be very happy if she could feed us one more time. She loved us, and she would want to help this one last time."

The little girl looked up. "Really, Mama?"

"Yes, Jenifer. Really.

"If you wouldn't mind, Marshal, that would be very kind."

"Don't mind at all. Is it alright if Alan helps?"

"I'd be helpful, Ma, and I'll stay out of the marshal's way."

"Then go ahead, Alan. And Marshal?"

Jack had already turned, in a hurry to get started butchering the cow. He paused. "Ma'am?"

"Get the backstrap first, and I'll cook it up for all of us. You've certainly earned a decent meal."

"Thanks." Jack strode out the door, headed for Smokey and his saddlebags. He removed his vest, hung it on the saddle horn, and rolled up his sleeves. Opening the right side of the bags, he pulled out his knife, nestled in a leather scabbard. The scabbard had a desert scene with a camel tooled into it. He slid the blade out, exposing the seven inches of sharp steel. The handle was of polished African ebony. He stared at the knife. Had it been that long ago? After giving his head a quick shake, he checked the blade, bent over, and stropped it on his boot, felt again, and nodded. Reaching over Smokey's back, he pulled the Spencer from its scabbard and took it with him.

Alan stood by watching. "We gonna hang her at the creek on one of them big pecan tree limbs?"

"No, boy, we're not going to open her up. We'll dress her where she lies."

"But that's the milking post. It'll get all bloody and messy around it."

"No, you just watch and learn."

"First, we're going to get the backstrap. She's swelled so bad we may not be able to get the tenderloin, but we'll get plenty of meat from the two backstraps. Then if the heat and flies aren't too bad, we'll get those hams." He went to work.

At the same time Sarah started the outside cooking fire. It was sunken with large rocks surrounding it. Heavy iron braces were mounted on each side of the firepit. A long iron rod with a handle on one end stood against the house.

Jack and the boy straightened the cow so the body lay in a fairly straight line from nose to tail. Then Jack split the heavy hide along the backbone from the neck to the tail and began skinning the hide away from the meat. The sharp knife made fast work, but the hot sun pushed sweat from Jack's body. His shirt looked like he had been swimming in the creek. Flies tried to cover everything. "We'll have to get this cookin' fast," he said.

Jack had Alan busy waving away the flies while he skinned one side of the cow down about a foot from the spine. Going back to the neck, he inserted his knife blade vertically, right against the spine, and sliced along the back until he was about even with the hip bone. Once the center cut was made, Jack pointed the edge of the backstrap out to Alan. The line where the meat and sinew met was obvious. He cut perpendicular to the spine, turned the blade and started pulling and separating the backstrap from the backbone. Once he had separated half of the length, he cut it free. It was heavy.

"You think you can carry this, boy?"

"Yes, sir, I'm strong for my age."

Sarah brought out what looked like a section of an old sheet. She laid it over Alan's extended arms. Once he had the long section of cloth across his arms, she stepped back, and Jack laid the heavy strip of backstrap in his outstretched arms. Sarah waved away the flies and flipped the loose end of the sheet over the meat. "Take it to the cutting board, Alan." To Jack she said, "I'm going to roast a section of it, and, with the other, I'll cut us steaks. I'll fry up the steaks while the remainder of the backstrap roasts."

The boy disappeared into the house, his mother right behind him.

Jack bent to remove the remaining portion of the backstrap. At that moment he heard running hoofbeats, along with the sound of a wagon creaking and wheels banging across the rocky ground. "Grab your shotgun, and close the door. Someone's coming almighty fast. Don't open it until I call, and then make it quick."

He moved to the front of the house, knelt to make himself a smaller target, and raised the rifle in the direction of the rapidly approaching sound. Over the western knoll burst four men, one driving the wagon, one attempting to hold on to a rifle and his seat, and two on horseback.

"Don't shoot," one of the men on the wagon yelled. They slowed their approach and pulled up in the front yard. The same man looked between Bossy's remains and Jack. "We heard the shooting and came as fast as we could. Who are you? What happened?"

Jack had lowered the rifle when he saw the riders meant no harm, and stood. "Jack Sage, Cherry Creek marshal. What happened was a bunch of renegade Comanches. Who are you?"

"I'm Coburn Cooper. My boys, Collin, Corey, and Conner. Collin, on the bay, is the oldest, next is Corey on the pinto, and the youngest here"—he patted the boy's knee sitting next to him in the wagon—"is Conner."

The door flew open as Coburn was speaking.

"Oh, Coburn," Sarah said, "thank you so much for coming. The Comanches attacked us, and I had to kill one."

Coburn's eyes widened. "You shot a Comanche?"

"She's being modest," Jack said. "She shot three. Killed two with one shot from her shotgun."

All of the Coopers stared at her. Jack couldn't tell if it was with dismay or admiration. But they were wasting time. "I'm glad you showed up. Alan and I were trying to butcher Bossy as best we could before the heat ruins the meat. I've still got to strip half of one tenderloin plus the other side, and there are five Comanches who need burying down past the cornfield."

Coburn looked at the cow. "I see what you're doing. I'm thinking we can get the other tenderloin and the hams off and take care of the Comanches pretty quickly with all of us here." He turned to his sons. "Boys, go down to the creek and bury the Indians." Concerned, he looked at Jack. "How many were there?"

"Eight. Five were killed. I don't expect the three to come back, but I'd still be on the alert."

Coburn nodded his head. "You boys heard the marshal. Keep your rifles handy, but get those Comanches buried deep so they don't come floating out should the creek rise.

"Ma'am, you have another shovel? That would sure speed things up. We brought both of ours, just in case."

Sarah Purcell's face momentarily showed a look of horror, then went right back to the stoic face Jack had seen most of his time there.

Coburn saw it too. "I'm right sorry, Sarah. We just didn't know."

She shook her head. "It's alright, Coburn. The thought shocked me. But you were doing what you should. That's the same thing William would do."

Coburn's brow furrowed. "Sarah, speaking of William, where might he be?"

"He left for town early this morning, long before the Indians showed up. It was hours later when they attacked. If it hadn't been for Marshal Sage, you would've needed those extra shovels you brought. I just hope he made it safely."

"I'm sure he did, Sarah," Coburn replied.

Jack was growing impatient. "If we're going to save the rest of the meat, we'd better get started." The two men worked feverishly in the blazing sun, hoping to save as much as possible. Once they had removed all of the backstrap and the two hams, Jack shook his head. "I think that's the best we can do."

"Yeah," Coburn said, "too bad it ain't winter. We could've saved all of it."

"Can't be helped. This is a lot more that I thought we'd get. It's a good thing you and your boys came along."

"Reckon it is. We heard the shootin', but we had to make sure our womenfolk were put away before coming down here."

Jack could smell the thick steaks frying in the pan. Backstrap steaks were mighty good, and he suspected that since they were off the milk cow, they were gonna be especially good. The boys were back from their burial detail and were helping Sarah slice up meat. She had a bag of salt out and was salting down everything she couldn't get cooked from the one hindquarter. The kids were out now, playing in the dirt and smelling the cooking meat.

"I'm hungry, Mama," the little girl said.

"I know, Jenifer. We'll eat in a while."

The little boy sniffed audibly. "Bossy smells really good, Ma."

"She does, doesn't she, Jacob."

Everyone was silent following the kids' short conversation, wrapped in their own thoughts.

Jack had slipped his gloves on, and now he grasped the end of the hot iron rod and rotated it a half turn. The melting fat from the brisket was dripping into the coals, sizzling for a second, releasing a tantalizing aroma.

"Mr. Cooper," Jack began, "are you taking care of Clint Paget's place?"

"Call me Coburn. Yes. I was in town yesterday when you hired him. I've moved his stock to my place. They'll be fine."

"Good. That's where I was this morning, when the attack started. I figured you had picked up his animals, since there weren't any around. He'll be pleased."

"Glad to do it." Coburn turned to his oldest son, Collin. "Why don't you get Corey to give you a hand, and you two pull that carcass out of here. Get it out of the yard."

"Sure, Pa," the boys responded. They washed their knives, stabbed them into the washboard stand to let them dry, and mounted up. Moments later they dropped loops over the cow's head and dragged her over a shallow ridgeline to the south.

Jack watched their progress. "They don't need to take her far. The buzzards and coyotes will have her pretty well cleaned by morning."

Sarah, removing steaks from two big frying pans, shook her head. "Shh, Marshal. Don't say that around these children. They're extremely broken up over the loss of Bossy. That doesn't make it any easier."

Jack was mortified. "Sorry, ma'am. I didn't think. Just making a comment. Since you're in good hands, I'll be moving on."

She moved the steaks to more plates and dropped fresh steaks into the pan, placing the pan on coals at the edge of the fire. "Boys, come eat." Wiping her hands on her apron, she stood and turned to Jack. "Nonsense. You're not going anywhere until you at least have a steak." She handed him a plate with a thick steak, a large potato, and a fresh ear of corn. "I guess you could say we grew all of this."

Jack touched his hat, still filled with remorse for not considering the kids' feelings. "Thanks, ma'am. Do you know when your husband is expected back?"

"Of course I do. He should be back before dark. He's going to be devastated over the loss of our milk cow."

Coburn spoke up. "Sarah, why don't you and the kids come over to our place until William gets back. You can leave him a note."

She thought a moment. "Only if your family will take half of the remaining backstrap and the other hindquarter."

"We can't take your meat supply."

Impatiently she shook her head. "Look at the amount of meat,

Coburn. There is no way we can preserve it in this hot weather. We'll salt it down and stick it back in the root cellar, but even with that, it won't last long. It will mildew, mold. We'll be eating meat until it's running out of our ears, so please take it."

Coburn gave Sarah a bow of his head. "Thank you, Sarah. The family will enjoy it." But he was speaking to vacant space, for she had wheeled back toward the fire to take care of the cooking steaks and roast.

Jack, chewing on his tender and tasty backstrap, swallowed and looked at Coburn. "Mather giving you any trouble?"

"Not if you don't count cut fences, a trampled corn patch, and shot-out windows. He came by with his men, and while I had my whole family standing around me, he threatened to drag me across the prairie. Even laughed about how funny it would be to see my head bouncing off the rocks. He is not a nice man."

"Have you heard if he's threatened anyone else?"

"Everyone else. Of course, you've got his man locked up for killing Tobias, and right in front of the man's wife."

"Blaisdale."

"Blaisdale doesn't do anything Mather hasn't told him to do. He may be a killer, but the man has no initiative. Mather tells him everything."

Jack only nodded and said, "Interesting." After a time of silence while both men ate, Jack said, "Where's Carter's place?"

"On the other side of Clint's. We came home with them last night and buried Tobias. As hot as the weather is, they have to be buried quick." He looked at Jack. "Tobias and Clint were good friends. I think they both fought in the war."

Jack nodded. "Most men did."

"I think they fought together."

Jack said nothing. Finished, he placed the knife and fork on the plate and headed over to Mrs. Purcell. "Reckon I'll be going."

She looked up, and the unruly shock of hair fell into her face. She blew it with her lower lip protruding. When that didn't work, she brushed it back out of her way. Her face softened. "Thank you for today, Marshal Sage. You saved our lives and gave us several meals to remember Bossy by." She thrust out a hard calloused hand.

Jack took it, feeling a strong grip. "Glad I could help, ma'am. You folks be careful, and I don't just mean the Indians."

"I know. Mather's also been by here. He seems to be a determined man. I also believe, an evil man."

"Don't know about evil, ma'am, but I do think he's dangerous. So like I said, be careful. If you need anything, send word to me."

"But as I understand it, you don't have any jurisdiction out here."

"I think that'll be changing, ma'am."

He nodded to everyone, and a tired Alan Purcell walked over. "Thank you for your help, Marshal."

Jack extended his hand, and the boy took it. "Thank you, Alan. You were a big help today. You did a man's job. I'm mighty proud working with you. Your pa will be proud, too."

The boy's face brightened. Jack watched as Alan's shoulders stiffened and eyes glowed. "See you soon?"

Jack turned back to Smokey, tightened the horse's cinches, and swung into the saddle. "Could be. Take care now." Nodding to the folks in the yard, Jack walked Smokey around the congestion and turned his horse back north. He still needed to see Mrs. Carter.

12

J ack kept a sharp lookout on his ride north. The sun was lowering in the west, and he had yet to find Mather's place. That would have to wait until tomorrow. He pulled his watch from his lower vest pocket and, before opening the cover, ran his thumb over the rough bump on the external cover of the pocket watch. It was an emerald, set in the body of the exploding grenade engraved on the otherwise smooth silver surface. For an instant his thoughts traveled thousands of miles.

Annoyed, he snapped the top open and stared at the hands of the watch. *Three o'clock,* he thought. He carefully closed the silver timepiece and dropped it back into its resting place. *I'd sure like to get this behind me as soon as possible. It's gettin' tired out, and I bet I can find me a nice deep hole in that creek to take a swim in.* As he'd ridden north, weaving in and out of oak and mesquite thickets, Cherry Creek, twisting and turning through the countryside had remained to his right, sometimes close, sometimes far.

He could see the rock house ahead. *Why not. There's plenty of rock around, and it makes the inside cooler in the summer and warmer in the winter.*

There was no activity in the yard or around the house. When

he was fifty yards from the structure, he pulled Smokey up, fingered his hat to the back of his head, and called, "Hello, the house. It's Marshal Sage."

The door opened, and he recognized Mrs. Carter. She stepped out and stood by one of the two rocking chairs. He clucked, and Smokey resumed his walking pace. There was a low wooden fence around the yard. It appeared to be built more to keep the little kids in than to keep anything out. Jack pulled up by the trough and hitching post and touched his hat. "Howdy, Mrs. Carter. Would you mind if I join you on the porch?"

"Please, Marshal, come on up. Would you like a cup of coffee?"

I'd love a cup of coffee, Jack thought. *I don't think I've had a cup since leaving this morning.* "No, ma'am. Thank you anyway. I have something for you. It won't take but a moment."

He wrapped the reins around the post, and Smokey took advantage of the trough. The gate squeaked both when he pushed it open and closed it. Four strides took him to the porch. He removed his hat and took a folded piece of paper trapped inside the lining. "Hold your hand out, ma'am."

She cast a questioning gaze at Jack, but extended her right hand, cupped, palm up. He tilted the paper, and several coins rolled out. The double eagle was the last to fall into her palm. She looked up in surprise. "What's this, Marshal?"

"We took up a collection, ma'am."

Her eyes widened.

"That's the change we got. By the way, that twenty-dollar gold piece came from Doc Cook."

She uttered a soft, "Oh." Tears began to flow.

"Mrs. Carter, if you're gonna cry, wait just a second. There's three more blessings to cry over." He opened the sheet of paper and, one at a time, laid the banknotes in her hand. "That's three hundred dollars. All yours to do with as you want."

He could see she was working hard to keep her emotions in

check, but her lips were trembling, and tears flowed freely down her cheeks. She fondled the money in her hand. "Who? Why?"

"Just some folks who care, ma'am. Even Mr. Mather saw fit to include a little something. Also, Clint Paget said that since you folks have proved your claim, if you have a mind to go back east somewhere, he'll buy your place for two hundred dollars. That'd give you five hundred dollars and a chance to start a new life."

She dropped into the rocker and began to sob. Crying women made Jack extremely uncomfortable. He could handle just about any situation, but for this, he had no answer. He stood looking out across the pasture at the cows grazing. A lone coyote chose that moment to meander across the clearing no more than fifty yards from him. It stopped and momentarily looked at the crying woman. Almost immediately it broke into a trot, disappearing into the thicket of mesquites on the northwest side of the clearing. Jack watched the animal, thinking, *I'd like to be right there with you, fella.* He felt more awkward the longer he stood.

Finally Mrs. Carter gave a long sigh, pulled a cloth from a pocket and wiped her nose and eyes. She stood, and gripping the coins and folding money tight, she flung her arms around his shoulders. "Oh, Marshal Sage, you are an answer to a prayer. I have been praying so hard for a way to leave this wretched land, and here you ride up. God bless you."

Jack couldn't believe what was happening. He patted her lightly on her back with his fingers. "Now, now, Mrs. Carter. I ain't no answer to anyone's prayers. I'm just bringing what everyone else donated."

She dropped her arms, looked up at him, and smiled. "Whether you want to believe it or not, you are. And please tell that wonderful Clint Paget I will accept his offer. We'll load up and be in town tomorrow." She stopped and stared up at Jack. "You don't think that's too soon for Mr. Paget, do you?"

"No. I think he'll be fine with that. You may beat me there, because I still have some riding to do. He's my deputy now, so you'll find him at the marshal's office. He'll be glad to see you. You oughta be sure to bring your deed."

"I will, Marshal." Her face was beaming. "Won't you stay for supper?"

"No, ma'am. I'll be making camp down by the creek, so I won't be far. There's been some Comanche business over at the Purcells', so keep an eye out. Ain't much sense in worrying. I don't think they'll be headin' this way."

The smile dropped from her face. "Comanches?"

"Mrs. Carter, I don't think it's likely you'll be havin' any trouble from Comanches. We killed a few of them, and it didn't leave many. Plus, last I seen of them, they were hightailing it south, so don't you worry. Like I said, I'll be down by the creek."

"Oh, please, Marshal Sage. We're leaving tomorrow. Can't you wait until we're loaded? My children. I can't even imagine what I would do if something happened to them."

Jack stood looking down at the distraught woman. *What am I thinking? I don't believe there's even the slightest chance of those Comanches doubling back this way, but she is upset.* "I'd be glad to wait here, ma'am. In fact, I'll ride back into town with you tomorrow."

"Oh, bless you, Marshal. Bless you. I'll fix you a fine meal tonight. A big man like you needs his food."

"It's not necessary you do that. I've food enough with me. I'll take care of my horse and just bed down alongside him in your barn if that's alright with you."

"I won't hear of you sleeping in the barn. I'll make a nice pallet for you on the porch. It'll be much more comfortable and not near as scratchy as that straw. That way when you're finished eating, you can sit on the porch and let your food digest." She indicated the rockers. "Tobias and I do that after supper every night." She caught herself, and tears again filled her eyes. With the cloth, she wiped away the tears and sniffed. "I'm sorry. It's just so hard to realize he's gone." She straightened. "Enough of that. I won't take no, Marshal. It's the least I can do, changing up your plans and all. Won't you?"

Jack could see the pleading in her eyes. This poor woman had just lost her husband to a killer, and she was begging for a means to show her thanks. "Sure, ma'am, I'd be happy to. I'm just gonna ride down to the creek and take a quick swim, maybe wash some of this dirt off. I'll be right back."

"Yes, you do that. When you get back, it'll almost be suppertime. The children will enjoy having you here to eat with us."

Jack stepped off the porch, passed through the gate, and flipped the reins from around the post. Mrs. Carter stood watching him, still clutching the money in her hand. He waved and swung Smokey toward the creek. It was less than a hundred yards from the house. He scoured the countryside to ensure there were no hostiles in sight and rode into the thick trees along the creek. Smokey twisted and turned through the pecan grove until Jack guided him to a trail that dropped over the edge of the cutbank and into the creek.

In the bottom, Jack checked in both directions. There was a long expanse of water, like a miniature lake, on each side of the crossing. He chose the left and rode to the edge of the water. Dismounting, he sat on the rocks and pulled his boots and socks from his feet. After removing his extra Remington and gun belt, he stripped out of his clothes, laid the additional revolver on the garments, straightened, and swung the gun belt back around his naked waist. After fastening it, he stripped the saddle, blanket, and bags from Smokey and led him into the water.

The horse seemed to know what was happening. He high-stepped until reaching the deeper water. Once the water reached Jack's mid thighs, he halted Smokey and took a deep breath. The water was cold, but it felt good. He had been hot and sweaty all day. He splashed water on the horse's sides and neck. Smokey pulled his gums back and snapped his teeth together, then whinnied.

"You like that, boy? Feels good, doesn't it?" Jack splashed water on himself, taking care to keep it away from his revolver. He tossed more water on Smokey's back and began washing the sweat from the horse's back and sides with his hands. When he had finished with the horse, he washed himself. He had no soap. His arms and hands still carried remnants of the butchering of Bossy. Jack carefully washed away the blood from around his cuticles. Once it was removed, he leaned over and shook both hands in the water.

A whiny nasal voice sounded from the opposite creek bank. "Well, boys, ain't this here the ugliest thing you ever did see? Why, I ain't never seen fish-belly white stacked so high."

Jack slowly straightened. Above him, on horseback on the edge of the opposite bank, were three characters who looked more like drifters than cowhands. But he recognized one from Mather's bunch last night.

The cowhand he recognized spoke in a deep gritty voice, like he had been hit in the throat in the past, and it never healed. "You getting all clean for the widow, Marshal? Too bad she ain't goin' to have a chance to get to know you better."

Jack realized that the cowhands or gunfighters, whatever they were, couldn't see his gun belt from where they sat. The angle was perfect for Smokey's body to block the gun from their sight. Jack moved closer to Smokey.

The gritty-voiced man spoke. "Here now, Marshal, don't think about leapin' on that there horse. You try it, and we'll just have to fill that pasty-white body of yores with a bunch of holes."

"Yeah," the whiny-voiced rider said, "I bet Mr. Mather would like that a whole bunch."

Two talkers, Jack thought. *The third man's holding his peace, and he looks a lot more salty than the other two. He's first if I have to shoot.*

"Move that horse back to the bank, Marshal," Gritty said.

Jack eyed the three of them. "This is your lucky day, boys. You turn around and ride out of here and I won't throw you in jail."

"Throw us in jail?" Whiny said. "Why, Marshal, you ain't even got any clothes on. How you think you're gonna throw us in jail?"

"I don't need clothes to arrest the likes of you. Last chance."

"No chance," Gritty said. "You either come out of there, or we'll kill you and the horse."

Jack could feel his anger rising. There was no telling how many people, how many homesteaders, these three had run roughshod over, even killed. His hand moved slowly to the Remington. This was a time for stealth not speed. He slipped the leather loop from over the hammer and eased the Remington from its holster. At the same time, with his left hand, he gathered Smokey's reins. The horse had been trained to gunfire, but this would be a surprise. Plus, his left hand would be a distraction for the riders.

"What you doin' there, Marshal?" Gritty asked.

"You can see. I'm just getting ready." At that point he brought the revolver over Smokey's back and leveled it at the surprised men. "I'm just getting ready to blow you out of the saddle if you don't drop your guns right now."

The three men sat their horses in silence, stunned at the sight of the Remington's muzzle pointing at them. The quiet man was the first to recover. "You can't get us all three."

Jack smiled at them. "You think not? There's only one way to find out. Maybe you're feeling lucky. Try me out." Jack's anger was boiling. "You can't let a man take a bath in peace? I should kill you where you sit. Either draw or drop your gun belts. Do it now!"

"All right, Marshal," the quiet man said. He unfastened the gun belt and let it drop to the ground.

The other two sat there like lumps on a log.

The quiet man turned to the others. "Drop your gun belts, boys. The man's dangerous. He'll kill you."

Jack watched the weapons fall. "You have any hideout guns you think it might be smart to part with? Now's the time to do it."

The quiet man pulled a Colt pocket pistol from behind his back and let it fall to the ground.

"Anybody else? Your friend there is right. I'll kill you if you draw on me. You'd best drop it if you've got it."

The gritty-voiced man raised his left leg from the stirrup, pulled out a Deringer with his thumb and forefinger, and let it fall.

"Now your scabbard guns. Nice and slow. I swear, you just jerk, and I'll put a bullet right between your eyes."

Three rifles fell to the ground.

"Dismount!"

The men swung to the ground and stood holding the reins of their horses.

"Good, now I want you to come down that trail right in front of you, single file. Take it nice and slow. Don't even think about slipping behind your horse."

The three of them, in single file, eased their horses down the bank, making sure they remained in front of the animals. After a few minutes, they were all standing on the rocky creek bed.

Jack nodded at the rocks. "Sit down."

The three sat, and Jack led Smokey out of the water, ensuring the grulla did not come between him and the gunfighters. "Alright, I'm going to get dressed. I'm edgy about this, so I'd suggest you sit very still, and you need to know I can shoot just as good with my left hand as my right."

Jack had laid out clean clothes before leading Smokey into the water. Carefully holding his revolver, he removed his gun belt with his left hand. He laid it on the ground and pulled his pants on, leaving his suspenders hanging. Then he moved his gun to his left hand and thrust his right arm through the sleeve of his shirt. After moving the gun back to his right, he slipped his left arm into the sleeve. Now came the challenge. The shirt needed to go over his head. He brought the neck opening as close as he could, staring through it at the gunmen.

Before he shoved his head into it, he said, "Think about how sure you are you can get to me before I get this shirt past my eyes. Think real hard." With that, he snapped his head through the neck hole of the shirt, and it was done. The men hadn't moved. He pulled the shirt down, tucked it into his trousers, and picked up his gun belt, fastening it with one hand.

"Good, I feel much better." He moved to his other clothes and picked up the additional Remington, slipping it behind his waistband. He slipped his socks on and stepped into his boots one at a time, wiggling and pushing until each foot slipped into a boot.

"So start talking. What were you doing on Carter land?"

Whiny snorted. "It ain't Carter land. It's Mather land. These squatters are messing with our cattle business."

"Your business? I didn't realize Mather had made you a partner."

"I ain't no partner, but I ride for the brand."

The man's voice grated on Jack's nerves. He pointed the revolver at Whiny. "I'm tired of listening to you whine. Keep your mouth shut. You"—he pointed the muzzle at the quiet one—"what's your name?"

"Reno Hawk."

"Alright, Reno Hawk, what were you doing over here?"

"We came to run the widow and her kids off her place."

This is a dangerous man, Jack thought. *To him, he was only stating a fact.* "After her husband was killed yesterday?"

Hawk looked at Jack with cold blue eyes. "Is there a better time?"

Jack made up his mind. These men would have given the woman and her children no mercy. "I've heard enough." He shifted his revolver from his right to left hand and, with his right hand, drew the other from his waistband.

13

Whiny's eyes opened so wide it looked like there was only a dot floating in a sea of white. "Now, wait, mister? You cain't shoot us down like dogs. We wasn't gonna do you no harm."

The gritty-voiced man looked at his partner with contempt. "Shut up. He's either gonna kill us or he ain't. All yore whining ain't gonna do a bit of good."

Hawk said nothing, just stared at Jack.

Jack let the time click by, one minute, two. "I'm not going to kill you. You may wish I had if you make it back to your ranch. Strip."

Hawk began removing his clothing while the other two stared, mouths open.

Gritty said, "What do you mean, strip?"

Jack pointed at Hawk with the muzzle of the revolver in his left hand. "He got the idea. Are you slow? You have a mental problem?" He started to fire at their feet and then thought of the family in the house. The sound of gunfire would scare them to death. No shooting unless necessary.

The other two began the process of removing their clothing.

Boots came off first and then trousers and shirts. In a few minutes the three men stood in front of Jack in stocking feet and union suits.

Jack waggled the two revolvers at the three men. "You boys ain't done yet. I said strip, and I mean strip. All of it. I don't want to see anything but skin."

Hawk spoke up. "Marshal, this ain't necessary."

"I think it's necessary. Now get those clothes off."

The three of them stripped down until they were fully dressed in birthday suits only.

Whiny, who probably couldn't remember the last time his scrawny body had seen a bathtub, had stayed quiet, but Jack could see the man couldn't hold it in. "Marshal, we can't ride back to the ranch like this. We'll be a laughingstock. Those fellers will never let us forget it."

"You were about to run a woman and her kids off the only home she knows, and you didn't give it a second thought. Maybe you will now.

"But, boys, who said anything about you riding back to your ranch? I never even mentioned you riding. How about you cat-foot your way back to the Lazy T. That should give you plenty of time to think about what's going on here. Maybe it'll give you enough time to decide this isn't the place to be."

If it was possible, Hawk's face had turned harder. "Marshal, you've had your fun. Let us get dressed and ride out of here. We'll leave the woman alone."

"Too late. By the way, look out for Comanches. A bunch of them attacked the Purcell place. They may have been headed this way."

"Please, Marshal," Whiny begged. "There ain't nothing but rocks and cactus and scorpions and them big red ants all the way to the ranch. It's way too far to have to walk. Could you at least let us have our boots? Maybe one rifle so we can defend ourselves should those Comanches come around?"

"No boots, no rifles, and you'd best move fast. I think you'll have a hard time hiding those *pasty white* bodies." Jack thought for a moment. It was a long way to the Lazy T, and he wasn't trying to kill them. "I will let you take your canteens, but that's it. Get them from this side of your horses and don't try anything."

Without a word, Hawk grabbed his canteen and started up the cutbank.

"Whoa up there, Hawk," Jack said. "You boys go up the side you were on. That way Mrs. Carter won't be seeing you. We don't want her or the kids to see any naked gunfighters. It might embarrass them."

Hawk turned, stopped, and stared at Jack. "You didn't need to do this, Sage. I'll be lookin' for you."

Jack returned the look. "You see, *Mr. Hawk*, I did need to do this, and you'll be able to find me in Cherry Creek when you pick up your horses and gear at Mr. Johnson's stable. Be ready to pay for the storage."

Hawk walked by Jack, heading to the opposite bank. "We don't use Johnson's place. We use Bryant's. Leave 'em there."

"Johnson's is where they'll be. Now git."

Jack watched the three men place their feet carefully on the rocks. He knew cowhands didn't care much for walking. He also knew they wouldn't be putting boots or anything else on those feet, except salve, for quite a while. He listened as the sound of their hesitant steps diminished with the distance until he could hear nothing. He gathered his clothing and stuffed it into his saddlebags. Then he walked up the bank where the men had dropped their guns. It took him two trips, but he secured them all, dropping the handguns in the first saddlebags he came to. He slid the long guns into their scabbards.

Using piggin' strings from the men's gear, Jack slipped them through the pull straps of their boots. He tied it short and swung the boots over the saddle so the two boots straddled the saddle and hung against the fenders. Finished, he mounted Smokey and gathered the reins of the other horses.

The three horses trotted close as he rode into the yard. The older boy was standing on the porch with Mrs. Carter and one of his sisters. She must have said something to him, for he jumped down and ran to the barn, opening the door.

Jack rode into the barn, nodded to the boy, and dismounted. "Much obliged."

"It's nothing, Marshal Sage. Ma sent me out to help."

"I can sure use it. What's your name?"

"My name's Weston, sir, but everyone calls me Wes."

"Wes it is, then. I'll start with Smokey here, if you'll start on the others."

"Glad to, Marshal."

"The name's Jack, boy. Just call me Jack."

Wes shook his head. "No, sir. If Ma heard me do that, I'd get a lickin'."

"Whatever you like, Wes."

While he had been talking, Jack had led Smokey into a stall and was stripping the gear. Mr. Carter had built a nice barn. He'd even built a fine tack area. Multiple rails for saddles and blankets, wooden pegs for bridles and ropes. He was a good planner and builder. Jack settled the saddle across a rail and hung the bridle. He moved on to the next horse.

Wes looked over the three horses. "Marshal, when you rode up, you only had your horse."

"That's a fact, Wes." Jack dropped the second saddle on the rail.

The boy's confusion bothered Jack. He was normally a close-mouthed kind of person, but after thinking about the boy while he uncinched the next saddle, he decided to explain a short version. "Mather's men came up on me while I was cleaning up and washing Smokey. I got the drop on them. They're walking back to the Lazy T."

The boy, hands full of saddle, stopped and looked at Jack. "Walking? It's at least five miles to their ranch headquarters."

Jack continued to work with the horses. "Mmm, guess they'll get them a little exercise tonight."

Wes had hung a saddle and now had a pair of boots in his hands, holding them as far as he could from his face. "Marshal, there are three pairs of boots here. Are they just in their stockin' feet?"

Jack shook his head. "Nope." Then he looked over the horse's back and grinned at Wes. "They're barefooted."

The boy's eyes opened wide. He had already noticed how stuffed their saddlebags were, and he saw an off-white sleeve sticking out from under the flap. Jack watched him open the saddlebag and pull out the shirt. Like the boots, he held it out from his face.

"It's a dirty union suit. Why would anyone carry a dirty union suit in their saddlebags?"

"That's a mighty good question, Wes. I'm gonna let you puzzle on that for a while. Let's get these animals fed and watered. It'll be dark soon, and you don't want to keep your ma's supper waiting."

The boy went back to work, but while he was working, a wide grin began to spread across his face. It lasted all evening.

THEY HAD PULLED out at daylight. Jack had enjoyed the supper. At first the younger kids were a little subdued, but later they loosened up. Wes blurted to his ma what he had figured out about Mather's gunhands. She was aghast at first, but like her son, a shy grin spread across her lips. For a while there was a little twinkle in her eyes.

It was midmorning when they rolled into town. The eastbound stage was sitting at the hotel. Jack pulled the wagon to a stop alongside the stage. The driver was on top, positioning the luggage. "Howdy, you have room for six?"

The stage driver looked down. "I count seven."

"I'm not going."

"Yep. We can make 'em fit. If he likes, that young feller"—he indicated Wes—"can sit up here with Rocky and me. Make it a little more comfortable inside."

Wes leaned forward to his ma. "Can I, Ma?"

"Yes, of course. Just stay out of the men's way."

"Good," Jack said, "you've got six more customers. Tickets?"

"Inside. See the hotel clerk. You need to make it quick. We leave at nine sharp."

"What time is it?"

"Eight fifty-five."

Jack shook his head. "That's not gonna work. This lady needs to go to the marshal's office and then probably the bank. It'll take at least fifteen maybe twenty minutes."

It was the driver's turn to shake his head. "Sorry, we leave at nine sharp. We got another stage next week, same day, same time, nine sharp."

Jack's face hardened. "Driver, listen real close. This lady and her family are going to be on your stage when she finishes her business. Clear?"

The driver straightened. He was not as tall as Jack but was a husky man. It was obvious not too many people told him what he could or couldn't do. "Mister, I don't know who you think you are, but there ain't a soul within five hundred miles who can keep Jackson Hewitt from pulling out on time. If that lady and her family want to leave with me, they'd best be gettin' tickets and gettin' on board."

Jack turned to Wes. "Boy, get the kids on the stage. Then you hop up on top. Mrs. Carter, you go on down to the office and close your deal with Clint. Am I right, you're headed for Nashville?"

"Yes, Nashville. My brother and his family live there."

He secured the reins, stepped down, and helped her down.

"What about the tickets?" she asked.

"Don't worry about that. You go on and get your business done, but try to make it fast. We want this stage to leave on time." He left the wagon and horses in the street next to the stage and strode in to the hotel, quickly bought the tickets, and walked out to the stage. He pulled a piece of paper and a pencil nub from his vest pocket, scribbled a note, and signed it. He got back outside just in time to lift the youngest child, Kent, into the stage.

The driver stepped up, giving him a severe look. "Time to go."

His face the picture of innocence, Jack said, "What's your name?"

"Names Jackson Hewitt, and the fella up there"—pointing to the driver's box—"is my shotgun, Smokey."

"Smokey, that is a fine name. That's what I named my horse."

Hewitt's frown grew darker. "It's time to leave. Where's your missus?"

Jack leaned close as if he wanted to keep his conversation confidential. "She's not my wife. I'm the new marshal. Her husband was murdered by a Mather gunslinger yesterday. She's leaving town. That's what's happening right now. A neighbor offered to buy her place to give her a little traveling money."

Hewitt's dark face changed instantly. "Who did it?"

"A no-good by the name of Blaisdale."

The driver spit a stream of tobacco juice and wiped his mouth with his hand. "Heard of him. How'd it happen?"

"He shot her husband down right in front of her and the children."

The driver cursed softly. "You gonna hang him?"

"Try him first. Then depending on the jury, we'll hang him."

"Good luck. I've heard of him. He's a coldblooded killer if there ever was one."

Jack pulled his watch from his vest pocket, popped it open and checked the time, ten minutes after nine. He closed it up.

Hewitt looked away. "Not nine yet."

Jack nodded. "I noticed."

Wes stepped up to Jack and stuck out his hand. "Thanks for your help, Marshal Sage. It's been real fine meeting you."

Jack took the small calloused hand. "You too, Wes. Your pa would be proud of you. You keep on taking care of your ma. You'll have to work, but figure out a way to study. Education is the ticket to freedom."

The boy's eyes brimmed, but he held the tears back.

Smokey was watching. "Come on up here, boy. I'll show you around."

Jack squeezed and released the boy's hand, grabbed him under the armpits, and tossed him up to the top of the box. He watched Smokey grab Wes's hand. Jack turned back to Hewitt. The two of them stood at the side of the stage, waiting. At least fifteen minutes later, Mrs. Carter came running out of the bank with Clint right beside her.

Breathless upon reaching the stage, she tossed her small valise inside and turned to Jack. Before she could say anything, Jack shoved the piece of paper and pencil into her hands. "Ma'am, this is for your horses and wagon. I figured two twenty-five for the whole shebang. If that's fair, just sign it." She did, and he handed her another two hundred and twenty-five dollars. Her eyes overflowed. She flung her arms around his neck and pulled his head down so she could whisper in his ear. "You have been our guardian angel." She released him, still looking up into his eyes. "Thank you."

A faint pink could be seen through the burned brown skin of Jack's cheeks.

Then she turned to Clint. "Tobias had a great friend in you. Now I have one. Thank you so much."

Hewitt cleared his throat. "Ma'am, it's gettin' close to leavin' time. You need to get aboard."

"Yes, and thank you, Mr. Hewitt."

The big driver nodded and swung up onto the box. Clint helped her into the stage and latched the door. "Have a safe trip."

She smiled through her tears. The children waved and called, "Bye," at the top of their voices. Wes waved from up top.

Hewitt pulled out his watch, looked at it, and announced, "Nine o'clock. On time again." He dropped the watch back into its pocket, picked up the reins to the six horses, and popped them, hollering, "Hi-yah." The horses jerked the stage, and the family was off, everyone waving.

Jack waved until they disappeared around the first turn. They were gone. Only the dust cloud remained. He pulled out his watch, opened it, and checked the time. Nine thirty. He thought, *I could grow to like Jackson Hewitt,* and turned to his deputy. "How are things?"

Clint shook his head. "Nothing going on. Nobody showed up, no shooting last night. It's been mighty quiet. Even Blaisdale's been quiet and really nice to Amy when she brings his meal, but you've only been gone a day. I thought you were planning on at least three."

Jack looked around and saw Nate across the street washing windows again. "Does his pa have him wash the windows every day?"

Clint nodded. "Pretty much. The old man's not keen on dusty windows. Figures folks can't see his wares." He looked at the three additional horses behind the wagon, which was now sitting in the middle of the street. "Those brands look suspiciously like Lazy T to me. Something you wanta tell me?"

"Maybe." Jack pursed his lips and let out an earsplitting whistle. Clint grabbed his ears and looked at Jack like he was crazy. "Sorry, I needed to get his attention."

"You got the attention of the whole county. My ears'll be ringin' for a month."

When Nate turned, Jack waved him over, and the boy came running. "Hi, Marshal. What can I do for you?"

"You feel like earning another four bits?"

Nate's face lit up at the mention of the silver coin. "Sure, Marshal. What do you need?"

Jack nodded toward the wagon and horses. "See all those horses and the wagon?"

Nate nodded.

"I'd like you to take them down to Mr. Johnson. First, I want to make sure Smokey is watered and fed with some oats. Now let me explain about the others. I've bought the wagon and the two horses pulling it. I don't need it or those horses. Tell Mr. Johnson to make me a good price and they're his. Now, the other three are Mather horses. I'd like for him to take good care of them and run a tab on them. Tell him to be sure to collect when Mather or his men come in to pick up the horses." Jack thought for a minute. "I think that's it. Any questions?"

"No, sir. I can repeat it back for you if you like."

Jack laughed. "No, that won't be necessary. If you'll give him a hand with unharnessing, rubbing down, and feeding the horses, I'd be obliged."

"Glad to, Marshal."

Jack fished another quarter eagle out of his pocket and flipped it to Nate. "Thanks, Nate."

Nate caught it, said, "Thank you, Marshal," jogged to the wagon, jumped in, and drove off.

"Now," Clint said, "tell me about those Mather horses and speak up. My ears are still ringing."

"How's about stopping at the Cherry Creek," Clint said. "I think Doc Cook is there, and we can get a cup of coffee. She's got good coffee."

Jack nodded, and the two of them headed for the Cherry Creek Saloon. As he always did, Jack paused inside the swinging doors to allow his eyes to adjust from the bright sunlight to the darkened saloon. He saw Doc Cook at a table and started over.

Clint followed. Gabriella spotted them, and it looked like she planned her intercept so that she'd reach them just before they made it to Doc's table.

"Hi, Clint, Marshal." Her beauty was almost breathtaking in a strong but sultry way. Long dark eyelashes covered striking golden eyes, and the purple gown she wore emphasized her alluring figure.

"Miss Gabriella," Clint said.

Jack watched. His deputy was obviously caught in this beautiful woman's spell. He didn't recognize the perfume she was wearing, but it was exotic, bringing back memories of better times. He glanced at Doc Cook. *Yep,* he thought, *he's another of her admirers.* "Howdy, looks like you have quite a few admirers in here."

"Oh, are you saying you're not one?"

Jack thought the question came out a little harder than she might have planned. "No, ma'am. I'm not saying that at all. I admire all folks who run an honest business and please their customers." He grinned at her and winked.

She looked back as if she was trying to figure him out.

Clint said, "If you've got time, we'd love to have you join us."

The batwing doors squeaked, and Wade stepped in.

Gabriella, her business face back on, said, "I've got to get those doors fixed." Then in a sweeter tone to Clint, "Thank you so much, but I have work to do."

Jack watched both Clint and Doc follow her departure, as did he. The thought drifted across his mind. *Quite a nice-looking woman, but I don't think I'd want to cross her.*

14

W ade made it to the table as Jack and Clint were pulling out chairs on the side offering a good view of the door. "Lunchtime."

Doc said, "That's why I'm here."

Jack looked at the doctor with a half-smile.

"What?" The doc's eyes narrowed as he gazed at Jack.

"Nothing. What's good today?"

Wade looked at Jack and then nodded first at Clint and then the doc. "Whatever they're serving. For those two it's always good."

Clint frowned. "What's that supposed to mean?"

Wade looked up at the ceiling and rubbed his chin thoughtfully. "Well, I think you two are more interested in the scenery than the food."

Doc immediately took umbrage, was about to speak when the sound of racing hooves stopped him. They all listened.

Multiple horses, Jack thought. *Could be three, but no more than four.*

The horses stopped in front of the Cherry Creek, and moments later three men rushed in. Jack recognized two of them as having ridden with Mather when he came into town. He reached under the table and eased the Remington from behind his waistband. It felt more comfortable in his hand than his waistband.

The men looked around the room, spotted Doc Cook and rushed over. Halfway to the table, one of them jerked to a halt, causing the others to stop and look at him. The man nodded to Jack. "It's him."

The three of them shuffled around so they could face him.

"You boys looking for something?" Jack asked.

The one who had recognized him spoke. "We need the doc. Thanks to you."

The piano had stopped. So had the chatter from the gambling and the tables. The saloon was silent. A quail could be heard making its bobwhite call. The sound of a wagon rolling through the street filled the saloon.

Jack nodded. "He's sitting right there. If you have anything to say to him, speak up."

"You're in big trouble, Marshal. Hawk's a killer, and you've made him real mad. In fact, he said he's goin' to kill you the first time he sees you."

Jack nodded. "Thank you, boys. I appreciate you warning me. Now did you want to talk to Doc Cook?"

The men closed the distance to the table, at the same time trying to keep their eyes on Jack and Clint. The one who had previously spoken said, "Doc, you need to come out to the ranch, now. We've got three cowhands in a real bad way."

Doc Cook jerked up and out of his chair. It flew back, hitting the wall. "Anything broken, gunshot, axe?"

"Ain't nothing like that."

The doctor stopped. "Talk straight, Huck. What's wrong with them?"

In a laconic tone, Jack said, "Sunburn."

"Sunburn?" Doc said.

Jack nodded. "Among other things. You might take something for lacerations."

Doc turned fully toward Jack. "What do you know about this?"

"Pretty much everything, unless they ran into Indians." He turned to the cowhands. "Did they run into Indians?"

All three men shook their heads.

"Tell me if I'm wrong, boys. They can't lie on their bellies because of sunburn, and they can't lie on their backs for the same reason. Is that about right?"

This time they nodded.

"But they can't stand because their feet are all cut up. Am I still right?"

They nodded again and turned to Doc Cook. Huck, who evidently was the spokesman, said, "He's right, Doc. That spells it out, so bring the stuff you need for a really, I mean really bad sunburn and cut-up feet, but we got to go. Mr. Mather said to hurry."

Jack spoke up again. "Hold up, Doc." He looked at the riders. "If he isn't returned, not sent back, but brought back safely, I'll hold you three responsible, along with Mather. All three of you understand?"

The three nodded, and the doctor started to leave.

"Hold up, Doc."

"I want the three of you to swear to me, out loud, that he will be returned safely. Not just sent back. There are Comanches ranging out there, and he'll need protection. Let's hear it."

All three men glared at Jack, but one after another, each man said, "I swear."

Jack nodded to Doc Cook. "Alright, Doc. You can go, but make sure you have plenty of whatever you use for sunburn. Those boys are gonna need it."

The doc started out of the saloon, but Huck held his place,

staring at Jack. "You shouldn't have made them strip and walk back to the ranch without their boots. That ain't even human."

Jack, expressionless, watched Huck. "Maybe they shouldn't have ridden to the Carter place with the intent of running her and her kids off. To compound it, there were Comanches roaming. By the way, Huck, you tell the three of them they are posted from this town. If I see them, I'll throw them in jail and lose the key. You got that?"

Huck nodded.

"Now get out of here, and take care of Doc Cook."

As they passed out the door, Jack heard the doc saying, "I must stop by the house to pick up more supplies."

Huck replied, "You can ride double with me down to your house, Doc."

Moments later the sound of retreating horses was heard through the swinging doors, and dust sparkled in the sunlight as it drifted into the saloon.

Clint, sitting next to Jack, turned so he could see him. "You made them strip down? All the way?"

One of the young women sidled up and bumped Jack with her hip and giggled. "Made 'em strip, huh? In that Texas sun? Ouch!" She looked around the table. "What would you boys like?"

"Dinner," Jack said. The other two nodded.

"Coming right up. Chicken and dumplin's and biscuits. If you're real nice, I might bring you a piece of peach pie. I think that's the cook's special recipe. Mighty good, anyway."

Jack looked up at her. "Add coffee to that."

"Us too," Clint and Wade said in unison.

She whipped around, waggled her hips, and headed for the kitchen.

Laughter was rippling through the saloon.

Wade, joining in the laughter, shook his head. "Made 'em strip. I'd like to have seen that. You've got to tell us about it."

Clint looked over at Wade. "It's not so funny. Have you heard of Reno Hawk?"

"Can't say as I have."

"He's faster than lightning. I saw him in action in Santa Fe. He killed two men before either one could clear leather. He's a cold one. He was just standing there while they yelled at him. Don't remember what about. They were yellin' and then, for some reason, decided to draw. He was leaning on the bar with his right elbow. He had to push himself off the bar and draw his gun. He still killed them both before their guns ever cleared their holsters. I've never seen the like."

The woman had brought their coffee and placed it on the table while Clint was talking. Jack picked up the pot, reached across, poured Clint a cup, then Wade, and then himself. "Mather must be paying a pretty penny for Hawk. Wonder what he wants out of all this."

Wade poured some of his coffee into his saucer and blew on it. He looked up at Jack. "Everything. Mather wants it all. He wants all the homesteaders' land and Birch's also. I've seen his type before. He thinks he's better than everyone else and believes he deserves it."

Clint let out a long whistle. "Birch? Now that's a feller who was born with the bark on. Mather may be chewing on too big a hunk."

Jack took a sip of his coffee, blew on it, and took another. He gazed out the nearest window and said, "I've seen folks like Mather. They seem to always do like you said, Clint, bite off more than they can chew. You boys know where he came from?"

"Back east," Clint said. "Like most of us. Other than that, I don't really know."

Wade just shook his head.

Jack contemplated their response and then said, "I swear I detect a foreign accent in there, but I can't put my finger on it."

The saloon girl brought their food out on a huge tray.

She bent over, giving everyone a view that left little to the imagination, and placed three large plates of chicken and dumplings in front of them, then three big slices of peach pie, and finally a huge stack of biscuits.

Clint looked at all the food. "You carried all of that?"

She pulled her short sleeve farther up and made a muscle. "Honey, you have no idea how strong I am."

Clint laughed, and she bent over and gave him a stiff pinch on the cheek. He grabbed at her hand, but missed. "You be careful. I might have to arrest you for assaulting an officer of the law."

She straightened and smiled. "You mean you'd have to cart me off to jail?"

"Never can tell."

"In that case, you'd better get the name right." She smiled at him. "It's Eileen."

"I'll remember that."

Her smile widened. "You make sure you do." She flounced off to another table, where she took an order and headed for the bar.

The three men ate quickly. When they were finished, Jack pushed back, tossed a half eagle on the table, and stood. "Clint, I'll be by later. I'll take the night watch tonight. You can get a room in the hotel."

Clint looked up. "Thanks, boss."

Jack nodded. "If you need me, give a shout. I'll be around. See you, Wade."

He caught Gabby watching him as he walked out, gave her a relaxed salute, and pushed through the batwing doors. He needed to get his things. He turned left and headed for Sully's stables. It'd be good to see Stonewall.

Passing the Rusty Bucket, someone called, "Marshal!"

He stopped and turned toward the doors as the owner, Brian Sullivan, stepped out.

"Afternoon, Marshal."

"How are you, Mr. Sullivan?"

"I'd not be offended if you called me by my given name, Brian."

"Brian it is. What can I do for you?"

"'Tis a hot day, Marshal. I have a cool sarsaparilla sitting inside, and I'm believing it's your name that's on it."

Jack gave a single shake of his head. "Just ate dinner, and I'm headed to the stables. How about I make it another time."

"Fine it is, Marshal. May I walk with you to the livery?"

"You're more than welcome, but it's only a few steps."

The two men started for the wide door of Johnson's Stables.

"It's only a moment I'll be needing from you. Were you aware there are a couple of Mather men in town?"

"You're speaking of the three who came in to get the doc?"

"No, there were more. By the by, I hear it was you who made three of Mather's boys take an afternoon stroll under our fine Texas sun."

Jack said nothing.

Brian grew serious. "A very bad man is Reno Hawk. He is not a man I'd be wanting for an enemy. Once he's healed, it's a sharp lookout you'd best be keeping, but that's not what I need to tell. It's word I've heard that Mather's men are planning to ambush you in the street tonight."

They had reached the stables, and Sully was sitting in his rocker, smoking a corncob pipe that had to be at least eight inches long.

Brian stopped and waved to Sully. "I'd best be getting back before they rob me blind. Just a warning for you."

"Thank you, Brian. I owe you."

"Never you think of it." The owner of the Rusty Bucket turned and walked back to his saloon.

Sully waved Jack to come in. With his long strides, he covered the short distance quickly.

"You drumming up business for me, boy?"

"Best I can. Does it meet your approval?"

The old man let loose a high-pitched chuckle. "Heh-heh-heh. I reckon Mather is some kind of mad." He pointed to the stables across the street. "That's his stable. He could keep his horses in there for free. Now he's stuck payin' me room and board for three of his nags. Yes, sir. I bet he's fit to be tied."

Jack took off his Stetson and wiped the moisture from the sweatband. He pulled his neckerchief from his neck and mopped the sweat from his face. "Hot today."

"Summertime in Texas. Sit down." Sully pointed to the other rocker.

Jack lowered himself into the chair. "You be sure to charge Mather for those horses and for the storage of his men's gear, and I'd make it stiff. He may not be around much longer."

The old man squinted at him through smoky-looking eyes. "You know something I don't?"

Jack leaned back in the rocker, pushed and released. It felt good on his back. "I'm guessing there's not a chance I know anything you don't."

"You know there's a couple of Mather's boys stayed in town?"

"Brian Sullivan just told me. Said their goal is to blow a few holes in me tonight."

Sully nodded vigorously, causing his rocker, which had stopped while he was listening to Jack, to start moving again. "He's right. He's a good man. You listen to him and me. We'll keep you safe. Yes, sir, we sure will. Now tell me what happened with this here Reno Hawk." Sully leaned closer to Jack, his voice lower. "Between you and me, I don't think he's near as fast as everyone says he is."

Jack didn't know why, but he liked talking to this old man. Sully was smart. He had way more experience than Jack did, and best of all, he could tell a good story. Through the afternoon, they sat and talked. Jack helped when a couple of horse returns came in, after which they went back to their rockers.

Normally Jack wasn't much of a talker, but Sully could draw

him out. He told Sully about everything that had happened the day before. The Comanches, the Mather crew, and Mrs. Carter's decision to leave the country.

The sun continued its trek west, drifting low on the horizon. "Listen, boy, that lady made herself a fine decision. She wasn't fit for this country. Now don't get me wrong. She's a fine woman and strong, but it takes a different breed out here. This country either grows on you or eats on you. There ain't no in between."

Jack took out his watch to check the time.

Sully saw it. "My, my, that is a fine watch. Looks like an emerald set in an exploding grenade." He examined Jack more closely. "I figured you for more than just a westerner. How many wars you fought in?"

Jack looked down at the watch. Memories flooded back. The perfume. The feel of soft skin. The smile. He stopped, flipped the watch open and checked the time. Almost three hours had gone by since he arrived at Sully's. He stood. "I'd better say hi to Stonewall. I don't want to make him mad." He walked straight over to the stall where Smokey and Stonewall were stabled.

Stonewall turned his head, gave Jack an evil glare, and turned back to the hay. "Now don't get yourself all upset," Jack said. He ran his hand along the mule's spine as he walked forward. As he neared the mule's head, Stonewall suddenly swung around, pulled his lips back, and took a nip at Jack, catching his hand between the big teeth. But he didn't bite down. Jack could feel the rough tongue feeling around his hand. Then the mule opened his mouth and faced forward again.

"No, I didn't bring any apples. Maybe next time." Jack stood there rubbing between the animal's ears and scratching his neck. He heard shuffling footsteps in the straw behind him.

Sully moved closer. "I know what that emblem means, Jack. The one on your watch. It's the French Foreign Legion, Légion étrangère."

Jack turned and looked at the old man. "You?"

Sully shook his head. "No, not me. My brother. Many years ago. He was only two years older than me. When he came back, he told wild and breathtaking stories.

"I couldn't go with him. I had already married. Of course, he hadn't. He died soon after he returned. Some disease he had brought back, maybe picked up in the desert. He never married. Like you, when he would talk about it, he'd get this faraway look in his eyes."

Jack rubbed Stonewall. "Légion étrangère. I haven't heard that for quite a few years."

"Can you tell me about it, Jack? I'd sure like to hear what you've got to say."

Jack looked down at the old man, who had somehow become a solid friend. "Maybe. Someday." He took a deep breath and let it out slowly. "But for now, I need to make my rounds before I relieve Clint. See you later."

Jack walked away from Sully's stables toward Carmen's Cantina. It was hot, even this late in the day. There were only two couples sitting on the covered veranda. He walked to the front, considered going in, and decided against it. Arguing wasn't on his agenda for today. He turned to go down the other side of the street, and a melodic feminine voice called, "Hello, Marshal. Do you have a few minutes?"

He turned and touched his hat. "Afternoon, Miss Belinda."

"Good afternoon, Marshal. You were not coming in? I feel slighted." She softened the comment with a smile.

"Still have rounds to make. It looked pretty peaceable around your place."

"That's because it is, but won't you come in for *un pequeño momento*?"

"Alright, just for a moment."

Inside the cantina, Belinda motioned to a small table with three chairs. He held hers as she sat. She smiled up at him while he studied the spindly chair that was supposed to support his weight. Carefully, he lowered himself onto it, bringing only a few creaks of complaint.

She nodded to the bartender and motioned to one of the girls, who hurried to the bar and picked up the two drinks. Reaching their table, she gave Jack a wide smile as she placed the glass in front of him and, in a businesslike manner, set Belinda's in front of her.

Jack gave a slight bow of his head to the girl. "*Gracias.*"

With a small curtsey, she replied, "*De nada*," and whisked away.

Belinda smiled. "I think you both intrigue and frighten my girls."

"Don't know why for either one." He pushed the purple drink away. "I appreciate the thought, but I'm not much of a drinker."

"There is no alcohol, I promise." Her lovely hand slid the glass toward him. "Just try it."

Jack picked up the small glass and took a sip. It was cool and sweet and tart. He smiled at the taste, surprise in his tone when he said, "A grape juice. It's delicious."

"Yes, it is from my own vineyard. Vines that have been handed down for several generations. I also make my own wine."

The taste pleased him, and he found it cooling. "Thank you, but you wanted to talk to me."

She reached across the small table and placed her hand on the back of his. "I must apologize. I attacked you viciously last night with accusations against the Americanos. I should also apologize to Señor Pierce. After saying what I said last night, I did some more investigating and found they were untrue, brought only by troublemakers. Please accept my apology."

Jack waved his hand. "Don't worry about it. I haven't had time to do any investigation anyway. Like I said, it would be a while."

"Yes." She sat straighter in her chair. "However, Mr. Franklin is another story. I also double-checked on him. He is not a good man. He takes advantage of not only our people but also yours."

Jack sighed. "You realize I'm your marshal just as I am for all the whites, don't you?"

She waved her hands in front of her. "Sorry. I have trouble with English."

"Well," Jack said as he began speaking in Spanish, "why don't you switch to Spanish. I'm pretty good at it, as you might have noticed last night."

"Thank you. I can speak English, but as I mentioned, it is difficult for me. Mr. Franklin is calling loans as they come due."

"That's not against the law."

"Yes, but he's giving no leeway and setting short periods for the loans to be paid. The people are desperate and accept the note in hopes they can pay it off, but it never happens, and his properties continue to grow. I believe he also carries a note on some of Mr. Mather's land."

Jack's eyebrows lifted at the last statement. "That's interesting. Is it possible Mather isn't the only one who wants to own all this land?"

She nodded her head, the shiny jet-black hair reflecting the sun's light as her head moved.

"When I get things calmed down, I'll look into it." He tilted the glass and drained it. "Thank you. The grape juice is delicious." He stood. "I've got to be going."

She smiled. "Thank you for hearing my apology."

Jack nodded and strode from the cantina.

15

Scott Mather paced the floor in his office. He was livid with the circumstances facing him. Before yesterday, he basically owned this country if you didn't count Birch's 7 Bar. He had the squatters buffaloed, and many of them were starting to leave before they proved on their land titles. It was falling into place just like he and Franklin had planned. Now this do-gooder marshal was butting in. And Blaisdale. What was wrong with that man, shooting a sodbuster in the general store. Was he absolutely crazy?

Hoofbeats brought Mather out of his pacing trance. He marched from his office to the front door and, still in a huff, threw it open. Huck was arriving with Dr. Cook. Impatiently he waved them toward the bunkhouse and followed. He hadn't seen his men since they were brought in, and wasn't looking forward to the sight awaiting him, but he had to make sure Reno Hawk was still alive. He cared very little about the other two, but he was paying Hawk a sizeable chunk of money.

The doc jumped from his horse and tossed the reins to Huck. Mather followed Cook through the door, asking, "What took so long?"

Dr. Cook stopped and looked at the three men stretched out on their bunks. The other men had left. Mather knew the others were having a hard time holding in their laughter, and no one wanted Hawk upset with them. That could mean a bullet.

While the doctor moved to the nearest man, Mather stood back and watched. He had never seen skin on any man this red. Now, all three were swollen with big, nasty blisters forming across their bodies. Two suffered in silence, but Arlo was constantly whining and moaning. His high-pitched voice filled the bunkhouse. Mather had heard several of the men threatening to take him out back and shoot him. If it weren't for his friendship with Hawk, Mather felt sure the whining would have already been silenced. He watched Cook move to Arlo first.

Arlo was lying facedown, a sheet over his body, with his bloody feet sticking out from under the edge. The doctor pulled the sheet from Arlo's back, and the man let out a loud moan. "I'm gonna die anyway, someone shoot me. Shoot me, please."

Hawk, in the other bunk, muttered, "Arlo, if you don't shut up, I'll be glad to."

Arlo whined, "But I'm hurtin' bad, Reno," and fell silent until the doc touched his back. He let out a yelp.

"I am Dr. Cook, sir. I must examine you. Please lie still."

Arlo gave a low moan, and the doctor continued to examine the man. When he reached the bloody feet, he stopped and pulled out a pair of tweezers. Before starting, he straightened and spoke to the three men. "I am a doctor. I am here to help you. Though your body hurts, I must take care of your feet first. If they are all like this man's, they are in very bad shape. This is going to require cleaning, and there is quite a large amount of debris embedded in your feet. I will need to pick it out with tweezers. It will be painful, but if I don't, you could lose your feet." He paused. "Or even your life."

He turned to Mather. "See that someone keeps me supplied with warm water. Understand, I need warm, not hot, and plenty of towels. Also a lamp, either held or on a stand, so that I have sufficient light."

Mather turned to one of his hands. "You heard the man. Go tell Cookie to start heating up water, but not too hot. Also get some towels."

The man pushed through the grinning mass of cowhands who had followed them into the bunkhouse, and headed for the kitchen.

Mather turned back to inform the doctor, but he had already begun his work on Arlo's feet. The first thorn came out easily, but the next was driven deep into the man's heel.

Arlo jerked his foot away and groaned even louder. "That hurts bad, Doc. You've gotta stop."

In a stern impatient voice, Doc Cook said, "I told you what will happen if I stop."

Sounding similar to a novice pulling a bow across a fiddle, Arlo repeated, "But it hurts bad."

Doc Cook turned to the men watching. He pointed at two of them. "Get over here and hold both of his ankles. I have no desire to get kicked in the head with one of those things."

He reached to the floor, pulled a tongue depressor from his bag, and put it in Arlo's hand. "Bite on this."

Arlo lifted his head, looked at it, and looked at the other cowhands and gunfighters watching him. He stuck it in his mouth and bit down.

Mather watched the man writhe in the grip of his companions as the doctor dug into his foot. Having seen enough, he turned his scowl toward the cowhands watching. "I'm not paying you men to stand around."

With his pronouncement they quickly cleared from the bunkhouse and headed for their separate duties. Mather strode back to his office. Hawk's injury could cause a delay. The marshal was exactly the reason he had hired Blaisdale and Hawk. Not that he knew Sage was coming, but he had received information that the town was getting fed up with his actions and were liable to do something, something damaging to his plans, and so they had.

The fact Blaisdale had turned into a good foreman had been a bonus. However, with him in jail and looking at a hanging and Hawk laid up for goodness knows how long, he might need someone else to take care of Sage. Hopefully his plan for tonight would work out, and his immediate worries could be over.

He stopped at the front door. Huck and two other hands were walking to the barn. "Huck," he called, "come into my office. I need to talk to you."

Huck had stopped at the call of his name and turned toward the house. Mather didn't wait for him. He left the door open and walked into his office. He could hear Huck's boots on the porch and the door close. He motioned Huck to one of the chairs in front of his desk and sat in his tall-backed leather chair.

Huck dropped into the chair. "You wanted to see me, boss?"

"I did. Tell me about how it went in town."

Huck removed his hat and wiped the sweatband with his hand. "Smooth as silk. The doc was at the Cherry Creek Saloon, just like you said he would be. He wasn't drinking. Looked like he was just there to eat dinner."

Mather held up his hand to stop Huck. "I don't mean that part. How did it go dropping the other boys off?"

"Same way. Afore we came into town, Milo and Oby peeled off. They circled the town. I seen 'em just pullin' up to Bryant's Livery when we pulled out with Doc. Tonight will be the last time *Marshal Sage* ever walks that street."

Mather nodded. "Good. Now I want to talk to you about the other situation. This is a two-pronged problem. First, if the boys aren't able to take care of Sage, we'll need someone to do it. In the open, maybe."

"What about Hawk, boss? I don't think there's a soul faster with a handgun than him."

Mather stared past Huck, his mind churning. "Did you see

Hawk's feet?" Without waiting for his gunfighter to respond, he continued, "What if he can't get back on those feet for weeks, even months? We'll be in a pinch. I need Sage out of here now, so back to my first thought. Who can we get to take care of Sage if the boys aren't able to get it done tonight?"

Huck leaned back in the chair and stared at the ceiling. Mather was growing impatient. The gunfighter suddenly snapped his fingers. The calloused thumb and forefinger sounded so loud it was almost like the popping of a whip. "I've got it."

One of Huck's bushy eyebrows lifted. "But he don't come cheap. He's a cold-blooded kind of feller. He can take a man up front or from way off—dead shot with his Sharps. Got one of those fancy glass sights on it. 'Pre-cise' is what he calls it. Feller riding the grub line told me he was in Waco. The ole boy likes to gamble. He usually hangs around when he's got a winning streak going. If he's still winning, he'll still be there unless the law's run him out." Huck grinned, showing a missing front tooth. "Most of the time, they leave him alone, not a good man to rile."

Mather grew impatient. "Who the blazes is he?"

"Chance Doughtry."

"Never heard of him."

Huck nodded his head knowingly. "That's the way he likes it. Makes his living killin', and he ain't got any desire for a reputation. He don't dress different than a regular ole cowhand. At least not out here. I hear he goes back east once in a while. But though I know him, I don't know much more than what I've told you."

"Any idea what he'd cost?"

"Pretty much know exact. I helped him once. He won't move out of his chair for less than a thousand dollars." He thought through his statement. "For a marshal, maybe fifteen hundred, up front."

Mather had been leaning back in his chair. At Huck's pronouncement, the chair slammed forward. With one hand he grabbed the edge of the desk, and the other came crashing down flat on the surface. It cracked like a forty-four. He thrust his head toward Huck. "Fifteen hundred dollars? I can buy out most of these sodbusters for that much. And what's this up front? I don't pay a cent until the job's done."

Mather's reaction hadn't fazed the gunfighter. He just sat there staring at his boss. "That's the only way he'll do business. There's something else, too."

"More?"

"Yes, sir, he won't deal with you. He says he doesn't want to be seen talking to any of the people who hire him. He always uses a middleman. Makes it safer for him that way."

Mather hadn't moved. He still sat frozen, gripping the desk's edge until his knuckles were white, and leaned forward across the wide desk. "I don't deal like that."

"Most people don't, boss, but some do. Those are the ones he works for, 'cause he won't do it differently."

Mather's grip relaxed on the desk, and he leaned back in his chair, pensive. He raised his right hand to his face. His thumb slid under his chin while his thick forefinger massaged the dark hairs of his mustache. "Fifteen hundred dollars. That's a lot of money." He stared at Huck. "You say you know him? Is he worth it?"

Huck turned his head slightly to the left, straightened, and made a slow single nod. In a low voice, he said, "Boss, as long as I've knowed him, he ain't missed. That's at least three or four times, and he was doing this afore I met him, and I guarantee he's been doin' it since I left."

"So if he won't meet with me, how do I get money to him?"

"He don't take cash. As far as I know, he never has. A go-between arranges it. The person takes the money to the bank and either opens an account with more than he's paying or has an account at that bank."

"Why more?"

"Says it makes fewer questions from the bank when he moves

his payment. Anyway, then the go-between gives him a signed check for the amount agreed on. He moves it to his account or has it sent somewhere or something. I don't really know the details after that."

A faint scream reached the house. Huck shook his head. "Guess he's still working on Arlo. Doc's gonna be workin' a long time."

Mather nodded, ignoring the scream, thinking, *Fifteen hundred dollars? Would his partners go along with him? That was a lot of money, but the last herd he'd taken north had brought in way more than enough to take care of Doughtry. Why, it would take care of fifty like him. They'll have to go along with me.*

"How do I hire him?"

"Me."

"You?"

"Yeah, boss. He knows me. In fact, he's worked with me before."

Mather saw Huck with fresh eyes. *If he's telling me the truth, then Huck may be more useful than I thought, but what if this is just a way for him to steal fifteen hundred dollars?* "How would you do it?"

"Just like I told you. Waco ain't that far, maybe a three-day ride. You give me the money, I'd go set it up, and you'd be done with Sage. Just that easy."

Using his right hand, Mather aimed his pointer finger at Huck. "But what if you decided to make yourself a little richer and ride on out of this country with my money?"

Huck grinned. "That ain't happening, boss. You see, Doughtry would find out. It might take a month, a year, maybe two, but when he did, he'd hunt me down. The minute I rode out of here with the intention of double-crossing him, I'd be a dead man. That'd be cut and dried."

Mather nodded. "You think you could find him?"

"Oh yeah. He'll still be in Waco. Like I said, winning streaks keep him in one place. The rider said he was winning, and he's a smart man. With the Comanches out and about, that'll probably help keep him staying close."

"I have an account in the Waco Bank."

"That'd be even better. You wouldn't have to give me no more than the fifteen hundred dollars, unless you've got that much and more in your account."

Mather moved around in his chair, finally coming to a stop leaning slightly forward and resting his weight on his right forearm and the arm of the chair. "You think he might take less?"

"I don't think so, but you could give me the full amount and tell me where to start."

Mather nodded. "I could, couldn't I."

He leaned back in the chair again, this time more talking to himself than to Huck, kind of mumbling through his problem. "We'd save some money if he took less. That'd be good. They'll be more apt to agree to pay me back." His eyes examined Huck. "I'll be putting a lot of trust in you."

Huck said nothing.

"When could you leave?"

"When you tell me. Right now if that suits you."

"When you think he'll be here?"

Huck shook his head. "He won't be coming here. He may come into town, or he may never be seen by anyone. Sage will just show up dead, if he isn't killed tonight."

"That's right. He'll probably be killed tonight. Why don't you send a couple of the hands into town early in the morning. If Sage is dead, we'll forget about Doughtry."

"If he's not?"

"I'll give you the fifteen hundred dollars and a check for that amount. You can deposit it in my account in Waco and give the check to Doughtry."

Huck stood. "Alright, boss. Anything else?"

"Yes, tell Cookie Dr. Cook will be staying tonight. I don't think he'll finish before dark, and we need to keep our only doctor safe.

Also tell Cookie to have his wife fix up an extra room in the house. Dr. Cook will be staying here. I'd like to talk to him."

"I'll do it."

As the gunfighter rose, Mather turned cold eyes on him and said, "If you steal from me, I never forget either."

Huck grinned at Mather, flashing the wide gap where his top front tooth was missing. He touched his hat brim and left the office.

Moments later Mather heard conversation. It stopped, the door closed, and he went back to his thoughts. *We are so close. Killing the marshal is imperative. After Hawk killed that worthless Winfreid, I thought the trail was clear, but, no, they had to go and hire Sage. But hopefully, tonight will end his time as marshal of Cherry Creek. He'll be dead and down the creek.*

Mather smiled at his little joke. Before long it would all be his, the land, the cattle. He could easily take care of his partners. Maybe pay Doughtry another three thousand. That would do it.

16

J ack looked at the hand-scrawled name across the wide front window, The Cherry Creek Gazette. With a smaller brush and lower on the window, Editor Bart Stanton Lawrence III was written. He reached out to the lettering and wiped his thumb across the edge of the first letter C. It came away white.

The door opened, and Bart stood in the open space, one foot in the newspaper office and one foot on the boardwalk. "Whitewash. That's all I had, and Mr. Farnsworth said it would take several days for him to make the sign and the brackets for it to hang on." With his good hand, Bart pointed to above the front door. "That's where it will hang."

"Very nice. Looks like you're anxious to get the first edition of the paper printed."

"Jack, I can't wait. The first story is going to call out Mather. It'll blow this town wide open. It's time people started standing up to that scoundrel. He thinks he's going to run those settlers off their land? When this paper is finished printing all of his evil and corruption, the rangers will be here to throw him under the Huntsville Prison!"

Jack watched Bart's face turn pale as he was speaking, his breathing sped up, and his hands began to shake. "Whoa, pardner, let's get you inside."

He took the newspaperman by his good arm and helped him past the boxes Jack had seen in his wagon and into his office. He helped him sit in the only chair currently available.

Between breaths, Bart said, "Thank you, Jack. I guess I'm not completely healed."

Jack shook his head. "Not completely healed? Bart, you ought to be in bed resting. This equipment will get set up in due time." He looked around the room. "You didn't have all these boxes in your wagon when I found you."

"No, that was my second trip." He first pointed at a stack of boxes against the wall and then to several large boxes on the other side of the room. "All those are books. The other stack is type, typesetting equipment, ink and part of the press."

"Who helped you move it?"

"Some of the boys in the Cherry Creek Saloon. They've been real helpful. I think this whole town is excited about the newspaper, except Mather." He laughed. "I don't think he's very happy at all."

Bart wobbled in his chair, put out a hand, and braced himself against a stack of boxes.

"You need to be in bed. You look like you're about to pass out."

"I am feeling a little light-headed."

Worried, Jack watched his new friend. "I'm going to Sully's and get a buggy to take you back to Doc's."

"No, no, no," Bart said, shaking his head. "I don't need a buggy. I can walk." He looked up at the big marshal standing in front of him. "Jack, I won't ride a buggy back. I can walk if you'll help me."

Jack examined his friend, wishing Doc Cook were here. Bart's face did look like it had a tad more color in it, but the heat of the sun would be brutal. "Alright, but if you pass out, I'm gonna carry you over my shoulder like a sack of oats."

"I hear you. I won't pass out."

He placed a hand under Bart's good arm and lifted. The man rose and rested his hand on Jack's shoulder. They went out the door. Jack waited while Bart fumbled for a key, found it, and locked the office door.

Late in the afternoon the town was surprisingly busy. Several wagons coursed the town street in opposite directions. Two packed prairie schooners entered Cherry Creek from the north. The boardwalk was still crowded with men and women.

Jack felt Bart's weight increase as they progressed. There were concerned looks from passersby, and several voiced their solicitudes.

Nate and his father stepped from their store to greet the marshal and the printer. The senior Pierce spoke first. "Mr. Lawrence, I'm surprised to see you out in the heat so soon after your attack. I do hope you're doing better."

Bart smiled and nodded. "Much better, Mr. Pierce, thank you for asking. I think I merely overestimated my strength."

Nate spoke up. "Glad to see you're feeling better, Mr. Lawrence. Anytime you need any help, you just let me know."

"I will keep you in mind, Nate. Thank you."

They continued their trek along the boardwalk.

Jack watched as Joseph Franklin exited the bank across the street, waited for a wagon to pass, and hurried in their direction. "Here comes Franklin," he said softly to Bart. He could feel Bart leaning heavily on his arm, but he said nothing.

Franklin jumped up onto the boardwalk in front of them, blocking their passage. He gave a dismissive nod to Jack and said, "Bart, I'm glad to see you up and about, though I must say you look a little drained. Getting your paper started is not so important it damages your health."

Bart nodded. "You're right, Mr. Franklin. I'm on my way back to Doc Cook's. He has me resting up there until I get better. I probably shouldn't have pushed myself."

"I fear you speak the truth. I have known men die from lesser wounds than yours. I'm sure if you only relax, Miss Cook will be more than happy to satisfy your every need."

Jack picked up on the suggestive tone of Franklin's comment, his eyebrows pulled together, and his brow wrinkled, but his hat was sitting low over his forehead, and his reaction couldn't be seen.

The banker continued, "And I hear that Dr. Cook has gone out to Mr. Mather's ranch to see to several of his cowhands." After dropping his comment, the banker raised his eyebrows and pursed his lips.

Jack felt Bart's grip on his arm tighten, but before the newspaperman could respond, he replied in a brusque tone, "Miss Cook is nursing our good printer, nothing else, Mr. Franklin. I'd hate to hear someone start a rumor suggesting anything different."

Franklin wrung his hands, perhaps sensing he had gone too far. "Oh my. You have misunderstood me. I was just concerned about Mr. Lawrence's health. Please forgive me if I've offended."

He jumped off the boardwalk and hurried back to his bank.

Bart, his grip tight on Jack's shoulder, said, "Did you hear what I heard? I cannot believe he suggested that. If I weren't about to fall on my face, and he weren't so much older, I'd probably knock him flat on his butt."

Jack said nothing, but seethed inside. He hated rumormongers. It was all he could do to keep from grabbing the old man by the throat. It surprised him. Here the banker was supposed to be one of the town leaders and he was making such off-color suggestions and about the doctor's sister? He had also noticed the man hardly acknowledged his presence, like he didn't exist. He thought about it for a moment longer and shrugged it off. He had more important things to deal with, like getting Bart to the doc's and watching for Mather's two men, certainly in town and planning to do him no good.

They were at least fifty yards from the doctor's house when the front door flew open, and Nancy came running down the front steps, her blonde hair bouncing from side to side. She continued running until she fell into step beside them with her arm around Bart's waist. Her wide smile was gone. Now her lips were pursed and narrow, protruding slightly. "I told you not to go. You are not ready to be doing anything but resting. Alex is going to be so angry with you, and me for letting you." She stomped a foot in the dust. "You can be so stubborn. You've been that way since we were little. I would think you would have grown out of it."

Nearing the porch, she sighed. "I am sorry, Marshal. I may have mentioned earlier, Bart is a childhood friend and as such can be extremely frustrating."

"No apologies needed, ma'am. I'd say he needed that dressing-down and more."

Bart was exhausted from the walk, but turned his head up to look at Jack and, with sarcasm dripping from both words, said, "Thanks, friend."

Jack grinned and nodded. "Any time. Now let's get you inside and in bed."

Nancy ran up the steps. Jack couldn't help but notice her slim waist emphasized by her dress flowing from side to side with her rapid movement. She pushed the door open. "Bring him in to our first bedroom. It is for *invalids*."

She stood close to the bedroom door as he helped Bart through. The light fragrance of her lilac perfume lingered in her wake. Her smile had returned, but he saw it disappear when she helped Bart onto the bed.

"I'll get you some water. You've lost blood, and you need to replace your fluids."

While she was gone, Jack eased Bart's boots and socks off.

"Whew. You might think about washing those things every couple of months or so."

"I didn't ask you to take my boots off."

"Yeah, you're right. I won't be making that mistake again."

Bart loosened his suspenders and unbuttoned his pants. Jack grabbed the cuffs and yanked them off.

"Make yourself useful, newspaperman, and get under the covers. I don't want to have to smell those feet any longer than necessary."

Bart rose, slid the sheet out from under him, and swung it across his waist and legs. "You don't have to stay, you know, and Jack?"

"Yeah?"

"Thanks. I don't think I woulda made it."

"You wouldn't have, but I'm glad to do it. Now get some rest."

Nancy returned with a glass of water. "Not before you drink this.

"Marshal, would you have a seat in the parlor? I'll be there shortly."

"Sure, ma'am."

She tossed him another smile. "Nancy."

"Nancy it is." He turned back to the parlor and sat on the same sofa he had used only two days ago. It seemed longer. He heard Nancy scolding Bart into drinking all of the water.

Moments later she was in the room, sitting next to him.

"Thank you for helping Bart. I wasn't being a shrew. He truly is the most stubborn man I think I've ever met, but enough about him. I hear you've had an interesting two days."

Jack, holding the Stetson in his hands, tried to brush away a dirt spot on the crown. "You could call it interesting. Certainly it wasn't boring."

She looked directly at him with a worried face. "Do you think Alex will be safe? He'll take care of anyone. If they need help, he's there. It doesn't matter how bad or mean they might be. I worry about him so when he takes off like this. With the Indians around, it is doubly dangerous. And then you add Mather. I hope he doesn't hurt him. Do you think he will be alright?"

With his right hand, Jack combed his hair back to where it ended on his neck. His neck was sore, and he gave it a couple of rubs. "Nancy, don't you worry. Your brother's the only doctor around for at least a hundred miles. No one, not even Mather, wants any harm to come to him. As far as Indians, Mather will send some of his men with him both ways, and I don't think those Comanches will be attacking anyone, especially two or three armed men. There just isn't enough of 'em. Now don't you go expecting him back tonight either. I'm almost certain he'll be staying until tomorrow to make sure those fellas are alright."

The wrinkles disappeared from her forehead, and her shoulders relaxed with relief. "Oh, thank you. I feel so much better." She suddenly clapped her hands. "Why don't you stay for supper. It's almost time, and I fixed fried chicken. I think you'll like it."

"Thanks so much, but I've got to get back to the office. Clint's been stuck in there with Blaisdale, and I promised him a night off tonight. I'll be going back on my word if I don't give him a chance for a sit-down supper for himself." At his last word, he stood.

She extended her slim hand to him. "Thank you so much, Marshal. When Alex gets back and things are more settled, I want you to plan for supper with us."

"I will, Nancy, thanks."

He released her hand and stepped out into the evening. Her smell traveled with him on his clothes. Being around all these women lately was intoxicating. He looked up into the big oak. That old tree had been here for a long time. A lot longer than the white man had been around, maybe longer than the Indian. He stood looking up into the heavy branches, wondering what all it had seen, then turned, and headed for his office.

He heard the harmonica before he reached the door. Opening it, he saw Clint reared back in the desk chair, feet up on the desk, and playing away on the harmonica. His deputy stopped, looked up, and said, "Howdy, boss. Welcome back." He removed his feet from the desk and started to get up.

"Keep your seat." Jack pulled one of the other chairs near the desk and propped his feet on it. "Didn't know you played the mouth harp. Don't stop because of me. I like it."

Clint leaned back, put his feet back up, and continued to play. Time passed while the two lawmen, one playing, one listening, took a few carefree moments, boot toes tapping air in time with the music.

Jack finally raised his hand. "You need to get out of here and go enjoy a good meal and a good night's sleep."

Clint pointed to the made-up cot with the harmonica. "It ain't bad. I slept pretty good, but it'll be nice to settle in to a real bed." He shook out the harmonica against his palm, dropped it into a vest pocket, and stood. "You need any help, give me a holler or fire a shot. Either way, I'll be there."

Jack nodded. "Good to know. How's Blaisdale doing?"

"Quiet as a church mouse. He eats and sleeps. I swear, you'd never know he's got it in him to be such an ornery cuss."

"Any word on the judge?"

"Mr. Jessup, the lawyer, said he'd gotten word on the last stage the judge'll be here the first day of next month."

Jack shook his head. "I was hoping for sooner."

"Never know. Maybe tomorrow you can tell me about all of your excitement while you were gone. Right now I need to wrap myself around a nice big meal. Oh, Blaisdale has already eaten, and Amy picked up the remains."

Jack raised his hand. "See you tomorrow. By the way, I've heard a rumor there's a couple of Mather boys in town to take me down a notch. Better take a shotgun with you."

Clint's face broke into a frown. "You want me to hang around? I won't mind a bit."

"Naw. Just a rumor. Anyway, if it's true, there's only two of 'em."

Clint looked at his boss and grinned. "Guess that puts them at a big disadvantage." He grabbed some shells along with one of the scatterguns from the rack and disappeared out the door.

Jack started to shift to the desk, but stopped. *I should at least look in on the prisoner.* He moved to the wall, removed the keys from their hanger, and unlocked the cell door. When it opened, Blaisdale was sitting on his bunk, staring at him.

Jack said nothing.

He closed the door, locked it, and took a seat behind his desk. Normally he'd make his rounds around midnight, but tonight, he was going to make them an hour earlier, see if he could surprise someone.

He heard boots on the walk. His hand slipped to the Remington. He pulled it out and laid it across the desk, the muzzle pointing toward the door.

The door swung open, and Wade Garrett stood framed in the doorway. He glanced down at the .36-caliber Remington and shook his head. "Now I'd be mighty concerned if you had a real gun out and pointin' toward me, but that little peashooter probably wouldn't even break my skin."

Jack turned the Remington so the muzzle wouldn't be pointing toward his friend. "I've found it does a pretty good job of penetrating tough hombres' skin anytime I want it to."

Wade moved to one of the chairs and sat. "Just the same, you ought to consider carrying a real gun. You might stop by and take a look at my assortment. I can fix 'em up where the hammers and triggers will be smooth and light and crisp as a green peach."

Jack looked his friend over and shook his head. "You oughta give up gunsmithin'. You'd make a fine drummer. Yes, sir, maybe selling ladies' unmentionables might suit you real well."

Wade held his palms up toward Jack. "Uncle. I didn't come over here to be ridiculed."

Jack said nothing, just raised his eyebrows.

"Alright, you're right, I started it. But seriously, you've got some trouble on your hands. I wandered into the Gilded Lily this afternoon ..."

Wade responded to Jack's look. "It's right next to my shop, and being close gives me an excuse for stoppin' in there once in a while. It's a good place to pick up information. You know that's where most of Mather's crew hang out?"

Jack nodded but said nothing.

"There's two of Mather's men in town. It felt a little tense when I was in there. I think they're up to no good."

"Thanks," Jack said.

"You don't look too excited."

"Two of Mather's men aren't much call for excitement, but Sully told me earlier today, right after I got back. I figure they're here to put an end to Mather's problem, namely me."

"Aren't you a little worried? It's dark, and they'll try to ambush you."

"No. To tell you the truth, I do my best work at night. Don't know if it's a gift or not, but seems I can see better than most in the dark. Course, for a pair of Mather's men, I won't need an edge. I just hope I can capture one of them in the act. That way he'll have a chance to implicate Mather."

Wade looked at the marshal. "You know neither of those boys'll talk. They won't spill the beans on their boss. They ride for the brand."

"Wrong, Wade. The cowhands ride for the brand. We're talking about gunfighters, killers supposedly. They ride for nobody but themselves. Either one of them will sing like a canary to save his skin. You watch."

"How are you gonna do it?"

Jack pulled a pair of moccasins from a desk drawer. "These'll help. I'll turn the lights out, go out the side door, and find them. Nice and easy. Then they'll talk."

"I saw Clint leave with a shotgun. Is he a backup plan?"

"Only if I need him. Hopefully he'll get a good night's sleep. He probably needs it, sleeping on that thing." Jack nodded toward the cot on the other side of the room. "Wade?"

"Yeah?"

"Thanks for the recommendation. Clint's a good man, and he plays a fine mouth harp."

Wade nodded and stood. "I thought I was bringing you hot news, but I'm still glad you already knew it. I have a little work remaining, so I'm gonna get back to work. Let out a shout if you need help."

Jack nodded. "If I do, make sure you and Clint don't shoot each other."

Wade walked out shaking his head.

17

The wall clock across from his desk chimed. He pulled his watch from his pocket, opened the cover, and confirmed it was eleven sharp. Knowing he didn't need it for just two guys, but opting to err on the side of safety, Jack took the shotgun from the gun rack and broke it open to confirm it was still loaded. Seeing the bases of the two shells in the chambers, he snapped it shut. He took out two additional shells from his desk, closed it, and dropped them into his lower right vest pocket.

He checked both of his revolvers and returned one to its holster, and the other he slipped behind his waistband. He looked around the room one last time, leaned over and blew the lamp out. Darkness filled his office. While he was waiting for eleven, he had changed from boots to moccasins. His feet always felt more comfortable in the moccasins, but they just didn't give the foot protection of the hard leather boots. In the faint light from outside, he grasped the keys, removed them from the rack, and inserted the door key into the jail room door. It opened silently. He glanced at the hinges in appreciation. Clint must have oiled them.

Blaisdale was lying on his bunk with his eyes closed. At first they opened, and, when he saw the shotgun, they opened wider. He sat up on the bunk, careful not to bang his head on the one above him. "What's goin' on?"

"Keep quiet," Jack said, and blew out the wall lamp. He stepped to the door, opened it, and was gone.

He leaned against the closed door, listening. Three pianos were competing. There was laughter and conversation coming from all three saloons. Footsteps staggered along the boardwalk, passed, and continued on their journey. He waited until his eyes had completely adjusted, then stepped into the alley. He had planned his route. It entailed moving to the back of the buildings and only far enough into each alley to make sure there was no one waiting. When he knew it was clear, he'd back out and move to the next one. He remembered his training, slow is fast. Take your time.

He began his search. The night wasn't pitch black, but it wasn't far from it. The street was lighted only by the lights from the three saloons. Everything else was dark. There was no moon yet, and only occasionally could the stars be seen through the clouds. The aroma of roasted meat drifted from the Cherry Creek Saloon. It had his mouth watering.

He went to work. After clearing several alleys, he had found nothing. He moved on to the north side of the Rusty Bucket. As he had done with each alley, before peering around the corner, he stood motionless, inhaled deeply, and listened. This time he picked up a scent of tobacco, different from the smell of the saloons. This was fresh. A single scent, drifting on the breeze. After removing his hat, as he had done at each building, he peered around the edge of the wall. The glow of the cigarette stood out clearly, followed by the faint outline of the man waiting for him. The man held a rifle in his hands. *Good,* Jack thought, *he'll try to swing that around to bring it into play, but he'll never make it.*

Jack checked to make sure there was no one else in the alley or behind him. Once he was confident he and his would-be attacker were alone in the night, he began his stalk. His moccasins allowed him to feel everything he stepped on. When his foot recognized a dry twig, he was able to stop the descent, lift it up, and move it to the side without breaking the twig, which would have caused an audible crack. He did all of it with a calm self-assurance. He was close enough to the guy he could smell the sweat of fear from the man. *Not as confident as he should be,* Jack thought. *Probably hasn't done this sort of thing before. Just a few more feet and we'll be having a heart-to-heart.*

Suddenly the side door from the Rusty Bucket jerked open. The cook froze in the open doorway with a box of trash. Jack was still fifteen feet from the guy with the rifle. He could see his stalk falling apart.

The man spun around, his rifle swinging up on the cook. He still hadn't seen Jack. The cook, stunned at the sight of Jack with a shotgun and the other man turning to aim a rifle at him, thrust the box forward as if it would be an effective shield.

Jack had only an instant to save the innocent man. He yelled, "Drop the rifle!" hoping the guy would drop his Winchester but knowing it would be either the cook dead or the guy with the rifle. As he saw the rifle stop its swing, he knew it was decision time. The shotgun roared in the alleyway. Only a man the size of Jack and with his training could fire the big scattergun the way he did—one-handed.

For an average man, the force of the recoil would have driven the weapon back into the shooter's face or at best out of his hand. At worst, it could have broken his wrist, trigger finger, or thumb, or all three. For Jack, with his massive wrists and hands, the recoil drove the muzzle up only a fraction higher than if he had fired it from his shoulder.

In the short distance the buckshot traveled, even with the open-bore scattergun, the shot spread only four inches with all nine of the 54-grain lead pellets arriving at the man's chest simultaneously. They drove the would-be killer back on his heels. The muzzle of his Winchester swung skyward as his finger reflexively jerked the trigger and fired the waiting round in the chamber. The .44-caliber bullet sailed harmlessly into the night sky. However, the buckshot tore a ragged four-inch hole in the gunman's heart and left no chance he would ever answer anyone's questions in this life.

The cook stared first at the dead man and then at Jack. "He, he, he was going to kill me."

"He would've," Jack said. "You came out at the wrong time. Come over here."

Jack reached out and grabbed the reluctant man by the arm. "Come on. He's not going to hurt anyone now." He pulled the cook nearer to the man, and with the light from the Rusty Bucket's open door falling across the dead man's face, Jack asked, "You recognize him?"

The cook stared at the bloody hole in the man's chest.

"Don't look at his chest. Look at his face."

By this time, all three saloons had emptied, and people were gathering in the alley. "No, sir, I ain't never seen him before."

"Alright. You can go." The man stood looking down at the dead man as if he were in a trance. Jack gave him a gentle shove. "Go. Go on, get away from here."

The cook nodded, walked only a couple of feet, and threw up every single piece of food he had eaten that evening. It seemed he would never stop, but finally it came to an end, and he staggered out to the boardwalk and disappeared.

Brian Sullivan, owner of the Rusty Bucket, pushed his way through the growing crowd and stared down at the dead man.

Seeing him, Jack asked, "You know him?"

Sullivan called for a lamp from inside. It was rushed out to him. He held it to the side of the man's face and gazed at him. He knelt, moved the chin left and then right. Finally he stood, shaking his head. "No. He's not a one I'll be knowing. He looks on the familiar side, but after examining him closely, I cannot say I do. Sorry."

A horse came racing through the street, heading south toward Mather's place. People were gathered all around, and Jack had no chance to try to stop the horse or get a look at the rider.

He saw Farnsworth hurrying toward the gathering. At the same time he heard a distant whack. A heavy object struck the ground. "Take care of that body, Farnsworth," he called as he raced down the street. *Good,* he thought, *I'll at least have one to question.*

Passing the hotel, a white apparition raced up beside him, Clint. A grin escaped Jack as he recognized his deputy. Clint was wearing only his hat, boots, and union suit with his gun belt around his waist and the scattergun in his hands. Two shotgun shells protruded, gripped between his fingers. In the dust of the street, the two men ran toward where they had heard the commotion. Growing closer, Jack saw a man standing with a motionless form at his feet.

Jack drew closer and recognized Wade. He also saw the form on the ground was not moving. Nearing the gunsmith, he slowed to a walk. "What happened?"

Wade shrugged. "Heard the commotion. I grabbed my Winchester and dashed out. I no sooner got into the street than this feller came racing like his tail was on fire. I figured it might be better if he stayed around and answered a few questions. So I just switched business ends on my rifle and swiped him right off his horse."

"You did good, Wade," Jack said as he knelt to examine the man. "Looks like this guy is out cold." He motioned toward Wade's shop. "Would you bring a light?"

Wade turned and jogged back to his shop. Moments later, he returned with a lamp.

Jack and Clint were looking at the man as Wade and the lamp

grew closer. Most of the people who had gathered in the alley had followed the marshal and were now surrounding the unconscious man.

"Boss," Clint said, "his neck don't look right."

Jack leaned closer, laid the shotgun on the ground, and began feeling the man's neck. Halfway between head and shoulders he felt it. The backbone was completely separated. He leaned over the man's face and listened for breathing, nothing. He struck a lucifer and, cupping it in his hand, held it up to first the prone man's mouth and then his nose. The flame didn't move.

He stood. "The man's dead. Must've broke his neck in the fall." He looked around the crowd. "Anybody recognize either one of these two men?"

He saw Bull at the edge of the crowd, a slight smirk on his face, and addressed him. "Do you recognize him?"

"You talkin' to me, Marshal?" the big bartender asked.

"I am. Do you recognize this man?"

"Can't say as I do. Must've just been passin' through. I'd say that gunsmith killed an innocent man right here in the middle of town. Whatcha gonna do about that, Marshal? You gonna throw him in jail like you did Flint?" Bull turned and addressed his remarks to the crowd. "Course, Wade Garrett's a friend of our marshal's. He'll probably just let him go."

"That's enough, Bull!" Jack ordered.

"You tellin' me to shut up, Marshal? You tryin' to silence a law-abidin' citizen?"

A murmur traveled around the crowd. A woman in the crowd shouted, "He had no right to knock that poor man off his horse. He attacked him for no reason."

Bull spoke up again. "I asked you a question, Mr. Marshal? You plannin' on shutting me up, too?"

Wade eased next to Jack and whispered, "He's looking for a fight. Don't give it to him over me. The best thing you can do is put me in jail for tonight. We can work this out in the morning."

Jack could feel the cold fury slowly flooding his body. If he released it, it could become a terrible thing, but over the years he had learned to recognize it, control it, use it. This was neither the time nor the place. Bull's time would come, but that time was not now. Jack needed to maintain control of the crowd and find out if these two men were affiliated with Mather. He knew they were, but right now he couldn't prove it. He opted to ignore Bull, for now. "Alright, folks, get back to your homes or whatever you were doing. The excitement is over for tonight."

The same woman yelled from the crowd, "Ain't you gonna arrest Wade Garrett, Marshal? He killed that poor man."

Jack shook his head. "Mr. Garrett was acting as a good citizen. He believed this man was involved in the attempt to kill me. That's why he stopped him."

A man's voice from the crowd said, "He stopped him alright. He killed him."

Jack stepped toward the crowd. "I said go home. Do it. This will look different in the morning."

The crowd continued to murmur, but began to drift apart. Farnsworth came up with a long board to put the dead rider on. "Can I take him now, Marshal?"

Jack nodded. "Sure."

Though the crowd was thinning, Bull was still standing in the street. He had shoved his sleeves up to his elbows, exposing massive forearms. Legs spread, he stood with both fists braced on his hips. "I haven't shut up, Mr. Marshal. You still need to arrest Garrett."

Clint stepped to his side. "He's baiting you. Look at him. No telling how many men he's killed with those fists. Let it be."

Jack stared at Bull and smiled at the man. "No, Clint. I need to shut him up for tonight," and began to walk toward Bull.

He could tell his smile puzzled the brawler. He glanced to the boardwalk behind Bull. Korkeran was standing in front of the

Gilded Lily, leaning against the tie rail with his arms crossed and a smile on his face.

Setup, Jack thought. He looked around, but could spot no one. He continued to walk toward Bull. He watched the big man swell his chest and bow his arms out like he was going to hug a keg. A big grin was across the scarred face. Jack stepped close, never said a word, switched the shotgun around so the butt was facing Bull and drove it deep into his belly. The stench of breath gusting from the fighter's body was almost overpowering.

Jack continued toward Korkeran, reversing the direction of the shotgun. The saloon owner was cool. He never made a move when his man was driven to the ground. His arms remained crossed and his body relaxed.

"You know he'll kill you for that."

Jack shook his head. "Better men than Bull have tried, and I'm still here. You keep your dogs on leash, or you might get bit."

Korkeran was a gambler. Jack had seen his kind in the east, across Europe, and Northern Africa. They might dress differently, or they might be poor or wealthy, but they all looked the same. Jack smiled at him. "Don't mess up, Korkeran, or you'll be moving to another town. I've got your number." With his last statement, Jack poked Korkeran in the center of his brocaded vest with a stiff finger. It was hard enough to hurt.

Korkeran's veneer cracked. He came off the hitching rail, his green eyes blazing, right arm dropping close to the butt of his .44-Colt. "Don't ever touch me, Sage, or you'll never do it again."

Jack grinned down at him. "Naughty, naughty, Korkeran. As many times as I figure you've been run out of towns, you should know by now threatening an officer of the law can be detrimental to your livelihood." Then his face turned coldly serious. "Trust me. You're on thin ice."

Jack watched the veil of control drop back over the gambler's eyes and his posture relax. "You have a good evening, Marshal."

The man turned and strolled back into the Gilded Lily, leaving his bartender staggering to his feet.

Jack turned back toward his office. As he walked by Bull, the big man croaked, "This ain't over, Sage."

Jack said nothing. The spectators had disappeared as quickly as they had turned out. Shootings were nothing new for the citizens of Cherry Creek, and he felt sure they would have the opportunity to see many more.

Wade still stood in the middle of the street, covering him and waiting. When Jack reached him, he asked, "You going to stick me in jail?"

"Not a chance. Those two were together, and the guy you knocked out of the saddle was trying to get out of town before I found him. There may be a little complaining, but as far as I'm concerned, you did the right thing. Now why don't you go grab some sleep. That's what I'm planning on doing."

"You won't be sleepin' yet. Mr. Johnson came down from his stable and said he needed to talk to you. He headed for your office."

"Thanks." Jack started for his office and could make out Sully sitting in one of the chairs by the office door. He had locked the front door before he left. He didn't want someone slipping in and releasing Blaisdale while he was hunting the two who were now dead.

"Howdy, boy. Glad you made it through all that. Course, there'll be more. You can bet on it," Sully said as Jack approached.

"Evening, Sully. You're up mighty late." He pulled the key from his pocket and unlocked the door. "Come on in." Reaching his desk through the darkened room, he pulled a lucifer from his pocket, struck it, and lifted the lamp globe. Immediately upon sliding the match near the wick, it caught, and while he lowered the globe, light filled the room.

Sully grabbed a chair and slid it next to Jack's desk. He pulled a long pipe from the hole in his shirt where it hung and held it up. "Mind?"

Jack raised his hand in consent and waited. Holding his pipe by the bowl, Sully retrieved a bag from his ragged vest pocket. While grasping both his pipe bowl and the bag in one hand, he inserted a finger into the mouth of the bag and wiggled it, extending the string closure and widening the opening. When it was wide enough, he slipped his thumb and forefinger into it, spread it more, and then pinched out some tobacco. He placed the tobacco in the pipe bowl and packed it down with his thumb until he was satisfied. He turned the bowl so he could clearly see the tobacco, and reached back into the bag for more. He repeated the process, checked the bowl, made a confirming nod, closed and stowed the bag.

Jack tossed a couple of lucifers across the table. They rolled and stopped within Sully's reach. He grasped one, held it up in salute, and struck it across the desk corner. He placed the match above the mouth of the bowl and began drawing on the pipe. Each inhalation sucked the flame into the bowl and tobacco.

Jack could hear a barely audible crackle as the tobacco lit.

Sully inhaled several times, blowing the smoke into the office as he exhaled. Finally satisfied, he popped out the match and spit on the lighted end. With calloused fingers he rubbed the end and tossed it into the trash can next to Jack's desk. Satisfied, he looked up at Jack.

"So you ventilated one of them hombres." It was no question.

Jack nodded. "Shotgun."

"Guess he won't be tellin' you who sent him."

Jack said nothing.

"Sounds like folks think Wade is in trouble for killin' that poor innocent cowhand."

"That's what some are saying. I know he's not innocent."

Sully's pipe was being stubborn. He thumped it on the side of the bowl, looked into it, and took another long draw. After he exhaled, he looked at Jack and let a sly smile pull at one corner of his mouth. "I know it too."

Jack leaned forward, placing forearms on his desk. "Really."

"Yep, for sure I do. If you head on down to Bryant's place, you'll find the horse for the one you shot still in there, but it might be gone before morning. I'd be careful, though. That's Mather's stables. Bryant just runs it for him. Bryant may not appreciate you snoopin' around. He might shoot you and claim you was a horse thief trying to steal his horseflesh." Sully took a couple of puffs and blew them out toward the ceilin'. "Yes sirree, I'd be mighty careful. I also wouldn't want to shoot a business owner neither."

Jack nodded. "I take your point, Sully. You're just tryin' to make sure I don't get any sleep tonight, aren't you."

"Heh-heh-heh." Sully chuckled. "At my age, I don't sleep much anymore. Can't see any reason why a young feller like you should."

The door opened, and Clint walked in shaking his head. "That horse just plain disappeared. I searched all around town, but there's not a sign of it. It's too dark to trail it, and if it's headed home, it'll be there before there's light enough to catch it."

"Pshaw, boy. That horse ain't gone nowhere except back to Bryant's. That's where it watered and ate last. It's familiar with it. That's where it'll be."

Clint shook his head. "I don't think so, Mr. Johnson. If it was going back to Bryant's, it would've just trotted straight down main street. That's the shortest distance."

Sully shook his head. "No such thing. I don't know what's happenin' to the younger generation. They just ain't got the ability to think for themselves. Let me tell you what happened. Wade swatted that feller off that little horse, and he just rightly ran on for a ways, maybe turning right or left, don't matter. Then when he realized there weren't nothing after him, he decided to go back where he had been sleepin' so fine before he was yanked awake. Problem is, only now the main street is filled with people yelling and milling about. So he just trotted the shortest way he knew, which weren't noway near that crowded street."

Jack stood. "Let's go have a look. We're not getting any sleep tonight, anyway."

He stood, leaned down, and blew the lamp out as Clint opened the door. Once through, he locked the door and said to his companions, "Let's go talk to Bryant."

18

T he three men stepped into the street, Sully in the middle. The saloons were still open, rowdy and noisy as ever. *I'll have to do something about that*, Jack thought. *They can't run all night. Honest folks need their sleep.*

They strode quietly, their steps muffled. Sully wasn't armed, so he angled to the left when they neared his stables. He waved and softly eased his door open, disappearing inside.

Bryant's Livery, as it was named, was located on the opposite side of the street from Sully's place and one building north, just past the newspaper office. Jack waved Clint to the back while he walked straight to the front door and knocked.

The front was made up of a wide sliding door with a loft above. Cut into the sliding door was a normal-sized entry. No one answered. Jack knocked louder and called, "This is Marshal Sage. Open up."

Time ticked by, and he thought he heard movement inside. He knocked again, louder. Another minute passed, and the door jerked open. Jack examined the man at the door, middle to late forties, bald on the top. He could tell because he was looking almost straight down on shiny scalp, with untidy clumps of hair around the sides, and the man was at least fifty pounds over-weight. He was dressed in a pair of pants he must have just pulled on quickly, stocking feet, wearing the top of his union suit. He just stood there looking at Jack.

"Are you Bryant?"

The man scratched his belly where his union suit bulged and hung over his pants. "Yeah, why?"

"You have any Mather horses here?"

"Nope."

"What's your name?"

The fat man pointed straight up to the lettering on the outside of the sliding door. "Just like it says, Bryant."

"Mister," Jack said, "I should apologize. I made the rounds the other night, introducing myself. It was late, and I was tired, so I missed meeting you. I'm your new marshal, Jack Sage. I need to know all of the business owners so I can be available should you need me. Does that make sense?"

Bryant nodded. "Makes sense."

"Good. I understand you don't know me well since I'm new. What you should know is I'm not a patient man. I've been known to lay one of these upside someone's head if they give me a hard time." When he spoke, he held up his massive right fist.

"Now let me ask you again. What is your full name?"

As he talked, the sneer gradually fell away from Bryant's face to be replaced with concern. Bryant couldn't take his eyes from Jack's fist. "Your name?"

"It's Lem Bryant, Marshal. What can I do for you?"

"I asked you if you had any Mather horses here. You want to reconsider your answer?"

The man scratched a thin scraggly beard. "I might, Marshal. I don't rightly remember."

"How about if I take a look?"

"Why, shore. Come on in, and don't you worry about not stoppin' by. I'm just pleased as punch to meet you now."

He backed up, clearing the doorway and allowing Jack to enter. The entryway was short, even for a normal person, and Jack had to remove his hat and bend way over to get through. It was dark, but he could make out the outline of two horses, led by a man walking back into the barn.

"Look what I found," Clint called from behind what, as they neared, Jack recognized as not a man but a boy, maybe fifteen or sixteen. "He was slipping out of here leading these two horses. Now where do you suppose he might've been going this time of night?"

"Come on over here, boy," Jack said.

The boy brought the horses to Jack, and he examined their brands. Both had Lazy T on their hips. "Where are you headed with these horses, boy?"

The boy looked at Lem Bryant and said, "Pa?"

Jack turned to Bryant. "Whose horses are these?"

The fat man scuffed his toe in the straw on the floor of the barn and mumbled, "Looks like Mather horses."

"Speak up, man. I know these are Mather horses. Who was riding them? Was it the two men dead in the street? Were these their horses?"

The man's voice was quivering. "Please, Marshal, don't let Mather know I told you. He'll kill me and my family. He's a bloody man."

"You're saying that those horses were ridden by the two dead men?"

"Yes," Bryant said, almost in a whisper.

"Alright. Here's what we're going to do. You're going to say nothing to anyone about telling me." Jack brought his face down close to Bryant's. "You understand me, Lem?"

The man said nothing, only nodded.

"Good. Can you write?"

Bryant shook his head, and Jack turned to the boy, raising his thick eyebrows in a question.

"Yes, sir, I can read and write."

"Good. Here's what I want you to do. You write out what your pa tells you." Next he pointed to Lem. "Then you'll make your mark on it in front of me. Then I'll sign it. Once that's done, it will be our secret until the judge comes to town. At that point, we'll make it public, I'll arrest Mather, and we'll send him to prison for conspiracy to kill a law enforcement officer."

Bryant was shaking his head vigorously. "No, Marshal. He'll kill my whole family. I just can't do that."

Jack put his hand on Bryant's shoulder. "Don't you worry, Lem. I'll protect you. Nobody is going to harm your family."

Bryant looked doubtful but finally agreed. They put the horses back in the stalls, and everyone went into the office.

Once inside, Jack looked at the boy and pointed to the desk. "What's your name, son?"

"It's Otis, Marshal."

"Alright, Otis. Your pa is going to dictate, and you'll write down exactly what he says. Once he completes it, you sign it, and then he can make his mark."

Otis nodded.

"Lem, start talking."

Bryant looked at his son and then at Jack. He explained what the horses looked like, and that they belonged to Mather. He added they were ridden by the two men who were planning on murdering Marshal Sage.

It was a slow process. While the dictating was taking place, Jack had checked his watch, one in the morning. He listened to the pen scrape as Otis wrote his pa's words. Finally they were finished.

Jack took the paper and read it. He looked at the sleepy lad. "Otis, you did a fine job. Thank you."

"Thanks, Marshal."

He handed the paper over to Bryan and tapped the pen where he wanted the man to make his mark. It left a small dot of ink.

Bryant took the pen and leaned over the table. With his left hand, he protected the paper so no one would be able to see him sign. Laboriously he made two strokes with the pen, forming a wobbly, lopsided *x*. Jack took it and signed it. "Clint, how about you also signing."

"Sure, Jack." Once he signed, Clint looked up to Jack. "What about the horses?"

"I have a plan for the horses. They're going to stay right here." He turned to Bryant. "If someone comes for them, you send Otis for me. If I'm not here, get Clint, but let one of us know. We'll take it from there."

Bryant nodded his agreement.

"That takes care of everything. Mr. Bryant, you have a good rest of your evening. Otis, thanks again." He looked at his deputy. "You ready to get some sleep, Clint?"

"Won't be much."

Jack slapped his deputy on the back. "No, but I think I'm going to enjoy it." They walked out of the Bryant Livery, waved to Sully, who was standing in the doorway of his stables with a long single-barreled shotgun, and headed up the street. *I don't care if I'm sleeping on that cot in the office. It's going to feel mighty good.*

THREE DAYS HAD PASSED with no trouble, and Jack was beginning to believe things had smoothed out in Cherry Creek. He still needed to speak to the Mexican folks who were claiming Franklin was cheating them out of their land, but there had been no shootings. Clint had taken a couple of days to ride home and do some work around his place. Blaisdale was being a model prisoner. It seemed he had no desire for another cold-water bath.

Jack was in his office, going over wanted circulars, when a commotion arose from up the street. He grabbed his shotgun and charged out of his office. A circle of onlookers was gathered in the middle of the street, and he could see the top of Bull's head. Even from where he was, he could hear the whack of big fists on a body. He knew Bull could kill a person with one blow, and that could happen before he was there to stop the fight. He eared a hammer back on the shotgun, pointed it into the air, and pulled the trigger.

Everyone jumped and cleared a way for him straight to a staggering cowhand. The cowhand had both fists up to fight, but his eyes were so full of blood he could see nothing.

Bull looked back. Their eyes met. The big man grinned, turned back to the cowboy, and drew back his big right fist. Jack knew a blow like Bull was planning could kill the cowhand. He yelled, "You let fly with another blow, and I'll load you up with buckshot. Drop your hands!"

The bartender lowered his hands and glared at Jack. "He started it, Sage."

The cowhand, who had managed to wipe one eye clear, spotted the star on Jack's vest. "He's a liar, and so is that fancy-dressed cheat by the door."

Korkeran had been leaning against the outside wall of his saloon, watching Bull take the smaller man apart, but when the cowhand called him a cheater, he jerked off the wall and stepped forward. His hand shot down to his Colt.

Jack said, "I've got one load left in this shotgun, Korkeran. I can use it on Bull or on you, makes me no difference."

Korkeran's hand hesitated. His face swiveled toward Jack. "No one calls me a cheat and lives."

"Drop your gun belt."

Korkeran stared at Jack. "I haven't done anything."

Jack's voice, loud enough to be heard, but cool and relaxed, slapped at Korkeran. "And I'm keeping it that way. Unfasten that belt and let those ivory-handled Colts fall to the boardwalk."

Korkeran stared at Jack for a long moment before unfastening the buckle and letting the belt drop. The two guns thumped on the hollow walk. "Now what, Marshal?"

"Don't move." Jack broke the scattergun open, flipped out the fired shell, dropped another one into the empty chamber, and clicked the action closed. While keeping Bull and Korkeran covered, he said to the cowhand, "I don't think I've seen you before."

"Name's Miles Delaney. Just passin' through. You've got a mighty unfriendly town here, Marshal. All I wanted was to wash the dust down and a friendly game, but this here feller tried to cheat me"—he pointed at Korkeran—"and I do believe this big ox was goin' to knock my lights out."

Winchester in hand, Wade came trotting up. "Need some help, Marshal?"

"Keep Bull honest and keep your eyes on Korkeran's bunch." He turned to the cowhand. "What were you playing?"

"Roulette, I like that game. I mostly lose, but I've played it long enough to know when a ball drops out naturally or when it's tripped out. He let me get a little ahead, but then I started losing. When I started losing, I started watching the ball. Almost all of my losing rounds had the ball shooting off the track early. I've seen it before. I know when it's happening."

"That's a serious charge, Delaney."

"I work hard for my money, Marshal. If I want to throw it away on the wheel, it's my business, but ain't no man stealin' it from me without getting called out." He wiped his face and pointed at Korkeran again. "Like I said, that man's a cheat."

Korkeran had regained his self-control. Coolly, he said, "Marshal, this man's just a bad loser. I did not cheat him, but I will give him his money back. However, he can't come back inside the Gilded Lily, and I'd appreciate it if you would post him out of town."

Korkeran's almost believable, Jack thought, *almost.* He motioned the muzzle of his shotgun toward the door of the Gilded Lily.

"Inside, Korkeran. How about we take a look at your roulette table."

Banker Franklin stepped out of the crowd and moved close to Jack. He leaned toward him and spoke in a conspiratorial tone. "Marshal Sage, do you really want to do this? Mr. Korkeran is a respected businessman and a depositor of the town's bank. His word should be taken over a ne'er-do-well such as him." He made a small nod toward the cowhand with his head.

Jack looked down at the little man. He was beginning to believe what he had heard from Belinda. Maybe it was time he looked into it. "Step away, Mr. Franklin. This is marshal business." He saw the immediate flush of the man's face, the anger in his eyes.

Franklin spun around and, with his short legs, hurried himself back to his sanctuary.

Jack saw the doctor hurry past Franklin. He was almost running toward them. "Doc, take care of this fella."

"No, sir," Delaney said, "I ain't dying. I want to be there when you expose that wheel."

"Alright, stay out of my way." He turned back to Korkeran. "You heard what I told you. Inside." Jack could see the gambler wasn't happy with the order. He watched him move slowly to the door, then turn as Jack stepped on the boardwalk.

"You don't need to do this. I'm sure a little extra money would come in handy. I can make you very wealthy."

Korkeran's offer made him angry. He had never taken a bribe, even in Laredo when it would have been so easy. He knew his father would roll over in his grave if he even considered it. He kicked the man's gun belt aside and shoved the muzzle of the shotgun hard into his back. "You offer me a bribe again, and you'll be sitting in jail with Blaisdale. Now get inside."

The man grabbed the batwing doors to maintain his balance, caught himself, and stepped into his place of business. The roulette wheel, surrounded by poker tables and a faro table, was located near the back. When Bull had thrown Delaney through the door, the patrons had bailed out to watch. The saloon was empty except for Jack, Korkeran, and Delaney. Wade remained outside, protecting Jack's back.

The marshal called past the door, "Wade, get someone to bring Pierce, Franklin, Jessup, Gabriella, Sullivan, Farnsworth, and Belinda."

"I'm on it," Wade called back.

"Doc, why don't you come on in. You can watch and keep an eye on your patient."

Jack could hear him giving orders to collect those who weren't already outside, which were only Belinda and Franklin the banker.

He nudged Korkeran through his silk vest. The gambler wore no coat. Expensive silk garters wrapped around his biceps, holding pristine white shirtsleeves close. "Keep moving."

Korkeran stepped between tables, sliding chairs out of his way as he walked slowly to the back. Footsteps of others followed, and he moved sideways, in the direction of the bar, so he could see those who were entering. Doc was first, followed by Pierce, Gabriella, Farnsworth, Sullivan, and Jessup. They stood waiting.

Franklin came in, breaking the silence. "Marshal, I don't need to be here. The bank doesn't run by itself."

Jack said nothing.

Belinda stepped through the door. *She is a beautiful woman,* Jack thought. He watched her as she examined the bar, the mirror, the gambling area, and the stairs. *She's never been here.* He had noticed for everyone else, the sight was Korkeran, not the interior of the Gilded Lily. Belinda was the last to arrive.

Jessup was standing close. Jack handed the shotgun to the lawyer.

"What am I supposed to do with this?" the man asked.

"Just hang onto it. I have a feeling I'm going to be busy."

To Korkeran he said, "Move behind your roulette table." The

gambler walked around the table, stopped at the back, and placed steady, relaxed hands on the surface.

"Good, now spin and start the ball in the track. Keep both hands above the table after you release the ball."

Korkeran did as he was told. The wheel spun. The ball raced around the track and eventually dropped into the black ten slot. The next spin, it dropped into the slot for red three. Jack had him spin several more times.

"That's good. Step to the front of the table."

Korkeran moved to the front and waited. Jack traded places with the gambler, started the wheel, then the ball, and waited for it to drop, black seventeen. Then he started feeling around under the table. He checked the edge first, but didn't expect anything there, it was too obvious. It had to be within easy finger distance.

"Nothing, Marshal?" Korkeran asked. "I told you. I run honest games in the Gilded Lily."

Jack gave Korkeran a cold smile. "I'm not through yet." He continued to search.

After five minutes of searching, Delaney said, "Marshal, I promise you, I saw that ball jump. I know it's rigged."

Jack said nothing, just kept searching. Two minutes passed, and he was rewarded. It looked and felt like a splinter. He had felt it several times. In fact he had stuck his finger on it once in his search. He had almost broken it off out of a habit of removing splinters. But it wasn't a splinter. It was a little wider. It was located on the flat portion of the table, just on the opposite side of the table frame brace from the dealer, almost too far. It would take a man with a big hand or long fingers to reach it. He knelt down and examined it. It looked like a splinter. From his position, he looked at Korkeran.

He could see the man was resigned to whatever happened, but Jack could also see the hate in the man's face. It radiated from his entire body. Though to the unpracticed eye he looked relaxed, every muscle in the man's body was on high alert for action.

Jack smiled at him.

He stood and spun the wheel, quickly followed by the ball, and just as quickly pressed the splinter button. The ball leaped from the track. Before it could fall into a number slot, he picked it up and repeated the process. He picked up the ball again and did it one more time. This time he let it fall. It fell in the zero slot.

Jack looked around at the witnesses he had brought in. "Do all of you see what is happening with this table?"

Nods traveled around the circle.

"Thank you for that, but I would like a verbal answer individually, beginning with Dr. Cook."

The doctor stood at the far right and answered a resounding, "Yes. I saw it." He turned so he could see Korkeran and addressed him directly. "Sir, you are a member of our community, and you have been cheating the very people you depend on for your success. I will not set foot in your establishment again."

Each person answered with a positive answer, even a dejected Mr. Franklin.

Jack looked at the storekeeper. "Mr. Pierce, would you bring me an axe, and ask Wade to bring Bull in, please."

The tall sober-faced man turned and disappeared through the batwing doors. He could be heard speaking to Wade. Moments later Bull pushed through the doors, followed by Wade.

Jack waved Bull to the front of the bar. "Korkeran, go join your lapdog."

Bull glared back at Jack. His face looked like that of a charging mad dog. "If I ever git my hands on you, Sage, I'll rip your arms off your body." He looked like he could do it.

Jack said nothing but kept an eye on the crazed man.

Pierce returned, pushing his way through the door. He carried a large axe, which, upon reaching Jack, he handed to him and stood back.

19

Jack hefted the axe, waited until Pierce was clear, swung it high and drove the heavy head through the wheel. The weight of the axe continued through the table and crashed to the floor. Splinters banged against the back wall. The table buckled. The center rested on the floor, tilted down from the unbroken legs. They still held the ends erect. Jack walked to one end and again drove the axe into the table, splitting it longitudinally, each half dropping to the floor. He walked around to the remaining end and repeated his actions. Next, he let the handle of the axe slide through his hand until the axehead hit the floor.

He looked at the remaining gaming tables and moved to the faro table, repeating his actions. He didn't stop until the last gaming table was demolished. Jack turned to Pierce and handed him the axe. "Thanks."

He stepped in front of Korkeran, whose face looked drawn and white, but turned to the others, singling Sullivan, Gabriella, and Belinda out with his gaze. "When I came to town, I gave everyone warning that there would be no cheating of patrons, either by gambling or by watering down their drinks. As you can see, I'm serious." To all in attendance, he said, "I wanted you here today so there would be no rumors claiming I set up Korkeran. When you're asked, feel free to share what you've seen. Thank you for being here." No one moved.

He addressed Korkeran. "How much money did you bring to Cherry Creek?"

Jack could see Korkeran had figured out what was coming. "Now wait, Sage. I've got a lot of money tied up in this place. I have money in the bank that's mine. You can't be doing this."

"What you have is money you cheated honest people out of. I asked you a question. If you can't come up with a reasonable answer, you're going to leave here with little more than the horse you rode in on. Now how much did you bring to Cherry Creek?"

"I'm going to kill you, Sage. I'm going to gun you down in the street. You're a coward. You only draw on kids. You won't draw against a *man*, much less me."

Jack ignored the challenge. "Last chance, Korkeran, give me a number or ride out broke."

Korkeran's anger was causing his body to shake, but reason took over. He took a deep breath. "I rode in here with three thousand dollars."

"Do you have that much in your safe?"

The gambler nodded.

Jack turned to Wade. "Have someone saddle his horse and bring it to the front. Discharge his revolvers carefully, that's the quickest way to empty them. Then sling his gun belt, with the weapons, on his saddle horn."

One of the men watching over the batwing doors said, "I know which horse is his. I'll do it."

"Don't shoot anybody," Wade said.

The man disappeared from the door. Shortly a forty-four could be heard blasting outside the saloon, five shots and then another five shots.

"Alright, get your money." Jack followed Korkeran through his office door. They continued to his desk at the back of the room. The gambler sat, turned around in his chair, and opened his wall safe. Jack had moved to the side and could see into the safe. A .44-caliber two-shot Deringer was atop several stacks of banknotes.

Conversationally, Jack said, "That would be your last move. As it stands now, you have the opportunity to start over somewhere else. But if you go for the Deringer, I'll kill you before you get turned around."

Korkeran sat still, his hand on the safe door. "I think I can beat you."

"Let's say you manage to shoot me. Do you think you're going to kill me? No two shots are going to stop me unless you manage to put one of them in my head, and then there's Wade just outside the door. You're the gambler, but I make that bad odds."

Korkeran thought for a few more seconds. "It's on top of the money. I need to move it."

"Two fingers, by the barrel."

The gambler gingerly gripped the barrels of the Deringer with his thumb and forefinger, turned, and dropped it on his desk. Jack, keeping his eyes on Korkeran, picked it up and slipped it into a vest pocket.

Korkeran pulled a heavy bag from the back of the safe. "There's a little more than three thousand in gold in this. I've got paper money, but I know gold will spend, wherever I end up."

"Take it, and leave the safe open. How much do you have in the bank?"

Korkeran stood, the bag of gold coins clutched in his left hand. "A little over twenty-five thousand. There's at least six thousand in the safe. Don't let that money-grubbing snake Franklin get it. He will if he gets half a chance."

"He won't. Out the door."

Korkeran walked through his office and into the Gilded Lily. He looked around as if soaking it all in. "I had a good deal here."

"You'd still have it if you ran an honest game and didn't attempt to kill off your customers. Keep walking."

They passed Bull. "What about me, boss?"

Korkeran shook his head. "I guess Sage has something else planned for you. See you around, Bull." He stopped to pick up his coat hanging at the end of the bar, slipped it on, straightened it, and pulled at the ends of his vest.

Jack spoke first to Franklin. "How much money does Korkeran have in your bank?"

"Twenty-six thousand. Why?" Jack could see the expression on the banker's face. He had answered reflexively, and now he regretted his statement. "I . . . uh . . . think. It may not be quite that much. I'll have to check."

Jack shook his head. "We'll call it twenty-six thousand. I need you to empty Korkeran's safe, total the amount in it, and add it to his bank account."

A smile broke out on the banker's face. "I'll be glad to help, Marshal."

Jack looked over at Jessup, the attorney. "Mr. Jessup, would you assist Mr. Franklin in the count? Two sets of eyes are always better than one."

"I'd be glad to," Jessup replied.

As he turned to Wade, Jack caught Franklin's frown. "Keep an eye on Bull. I'll be back." He followed Korkeran through the doors and out to the horse.

"I could use my rifle."

"Where is it?"

"In my office. Saddlebags are in there too, change of clothes, powder, lead, molds, plus some ammunition for the rifle."

Nate had been standing around outside. Jack turned to him. "Did you hear?"

"Yes, sir. I'll get it."

While they waited, Jack asked, "Where do you think you'll head?"

"Maybe up Abilene way. Lots of cowhands with money up there that's burning holes in their pockets, and the turnover's high. I'm thinking it's time I left Texas in my dust. I've had nothing but bad luck since I arrived in Galveston."

Nate came back with the rifle and saddlebags. He handed the saddlebags to Korkeran, waited until the gambler had them tied behind his saddle, and started to pass the rifle to him.

"Hold on." Jack took it and worked the lever, loaded. He jacked fifteen rounds out of the weapon. Korkeran watched, lips pursed and forehead wrinkled. Jack rammed it into the scabbard, picked up the fifteen cartridges, and dropped them into Korkeran's saddlebags. "You'd be smart to leave them there till you're well down the road."

Korkeran looked down at Jack. "You really messed up a good thing."

Jack said nothing.

"Next time I see you, I'm going to kill you."

"Hit the road, Korkeran." Jack yanked off his Stetson and slapped the bay on the rump. The surprised horse jumped forward, almost unseating its rider, but the gambler regained his balance and kicked the horse in the flanks, riding north until he disappeared in the mesquites.

Jack watched the dust float stationary in the air. *No breeze,* he thought, *this is going to be hot work.*

Most of the citizenry had disappeared back where they had come from. The sun was hot, and no one wanted to be outside in its burning rays. Nate stood next to him, watching the dust. "Nate, could you do something for me?"

Nate grinned. "Why, sure, Marshal, you're my best-payin' customer."

Jack chuckled. "No pay for this one." He took off his gun belt and handed it and the extra Remington to the boy. "Would you take care of these, also my shotgun. Mr. Jessup still has it. If I'm not able to get them to my room, would you be sure they end up there?"

Puzzled, Nate took the belt and weapons. "I guess. Sure, Marshal, but why wouldn't you be able to take them up to your own room?"

Jack called, "Wade, bring Bull out here." He removed his vest and hat, handed them to Nate, and rolled up his sleeves. "I've got a little heavy lifting to do. Now get out of here, boy."

Nate slowly took three steps back, and urgently Jack said, "Go on, make room." Nate took off for the hotel, but stopped halfway and turned to watch.

The batwing doors swung open, and Bull stepped outside, blinking at first in the bright sunlight. He looked around, confirming Korkeran was gone. His glare stopped at Jack. He saw the marshal's guns and vest were gone, his sleeves rolled up. Without a second thought, he swung, his big fist catching Jack on the left temple. The power and surprise of the blow drove him back against the wall of the Gilded Lily. He bounced off, got his hands up just in time to partially deflect the bruiser's left, which struck at the hairline on the right side of his head. He staggered out into the street, groggy, but still on his feet.

The brawler backed off a few steps and looked him up and down. "You surprise me, big fella. Maybe you'll last longer than I expected." Then he grinned. "More time for me to give you the lickin' you deserve."

Jack said a quick thank you. Bull wanted to talk instead of fight. Those few seconds gave him time for his head to clear. He was ready when Bull moved in.

The overconfident bruiser stepped in closer and swung a roundhouse right. If it had hit him, the fight would have been over, but Jack moved his head just enough to allow the blow to sail past his ear. He came off the balls of his feet, leveraging forward, with all the power he could muster, and landed the blow perfectly on Bull's chin. He watched as Bull backpedaled as fast as his feet could take him, until he overcame the momentum of the blow and stopped.

Bull spit blood and grinned from a bloody mouth. "If that's all you got, Mr. Marshal, this here fight ain't gonna be near as long as I thought it would be."

Jack was stunned the man was still on his feet. He had hit him with all he had, and the guy was still standing. He'd never had anyone survive a blow like that. In fact, he'd killed a big Frenchman in Algiers with that one blow. He had been much younger, and he hadn't known his own strength. That was really his introduction to what he could do with his fists. Was this an introduction to his waning strength? He shook his head to chase the idea from his mind.

"Bull, are you gonna brag or fight?"

The man charged Jack, his thick arms spread wide to snare him and crush his spine. Unfortunately for Bull, Jack had seen this maneuver many times before. He let him come in, slipped under his wide left, and drove a smashing left into the man's heart as he went by, and then two quick rights into his left kidney. The three blows made Bull stagger, but he kept his feet under him, spun around, and closed, more cautiously this time.

Jack's eyes were busy. He watched Bull's feet, his ham fists as they described ovals in the air in front of him, and his eyes.

He shot a quick jab, smashing Bull's mouth, and crossed it with a right to the man's left eye. But out of nowhere came a freight train that collided with the left side of his head just above his jaw. He felt his legs go numb. Everything turned gray. He could see Bull, dim and moving slow. He felt the breeze of a massive fist pass over his head. *He missed.* Jack's mind registered the thought just before he hit the ground. He had the sense to roll and keep rolling.

His vision came back. He saw Bull recovering from the last

stomp attempt, which had missed, but now he was jumping high to bring a huge booted foot down on Jack's chest. Jack, still in a fog, grabbed the descending foot and twisted as hard as he could. Bull grunted, crashing to the ground only inches away.

Jack, feeling his senses returning, levered up and threw a blow at the man's throat. It missed. He felt chunky fingers clawing at his eyes. He brought his arm up and across, trapping the hands, flexed his hips, and threw a smashing kick into Bull's thigh. The grasping hands momentarily ceased their relentless search, but turned into claws dragging across his left cheek. Jack scrambled to his feet, so filled with adrenaline he registered no pain from the gouges across his cheek. He backpedaled to stay out of the reach of Bull's swinging leg.

He was having a hard time focusing out of his left eye. He wiped at it, and his hand came away covered in blood. He took another swipe to clear his eye. The thought flashed through his mind, *Forget his face, work on his belly. The belly is where a man lives. The face and head are there only for breaking hands.* But it did feel good to see blood flowing from Bull's smashed lips.

Bull gave him a grotesque grin. "Come on, big feller, I'm gonna tear down yore meat house. I've done it to bigger men than you."

They moved together, and Jack said, "Bull, you talk way too much," and hit him a smashing blow in the nose and mouth. Bull took the blow and slammed Jack in the head again, deepening the cut over his left eye. Blood was flowing steadily now, making it almost impossible for Jack to see out of that eye. But he had caught something. Every time he had used the jab on Bull's mouth, his opponent had followed up with a right to his head. His fault, but Bull's, too. They moved back together, and Bull threw a roundhouse right. Jack slipped the blow, grabbed Bull's arm and kept him moving over Jack's right leg, tossing him to the ground.

Jack could feel the ground shake when Bull smashed into it. The wind was knocked out of his opponent, but he didn't stay on the ground. He leaped up, still gasping for air, and charged Jack again. The charge came as a surprise. There were few men who could land that hard and not lie gasping for minutes.

Though Jack was surprised, it didn't catch him off guard. He slipped Bull's blow and drove a hard left-right combination into the man's solar plexus. Bull's arms lowered. He hadn't recovered from the previous throw, and the precious air he had managed to drag back into his lungs was smashed out.

Jack watched Bull's eyes fly wide, and pounded him relentlessly in the belly. *I've got him*, Jack thought. *Now's the time to end this.* He rained incessant powerful blows into Bull's midsection. He could hear the man gasping. He stepped in closer.

Wrong move.

He felt huge arms encircle him, and tried to duck out, too late.

Through gasping, painful breaths, but with a triumphant tone in his voice, Bull said, "I've got you now. I'm gonna break your back."

Jack felt the vise grip of the arms clinch around his body. Pain coursed through his spine. Back muscles screamed as he was bent backwards. Desperately, he threw his arms straight up and, using every ounce of his two hundred pounds, tried to drop down and out of the man's arms, only to feel them tighten and crush him closer.

He felt the air relentlessly squeezed from his lungs. The pain was excruciating. His choices were grim, death by asphyxiation or separated spine.

He cupped both hands and clapped them hard over Bull's ears. The man staggered, his grip loosened, but before Jack could take advantage of the looser grip, it tightened again. He drove his spurs into the man's legs and ran them up and down his calves. Bull let out a scream of pain, but his grip didn't relent.

Because of the lack of oxygen from his lungs being crushed,

Jack began to feel light-headed, the onset of unconsciousness and, ultimately, death, but he also felt his toes touch the ground. As strong as Bull was, he couldn't keep the almost six feet and four inches of Jack Sage bent back and lifted clear of the ground. He was growing tired. A glow of hope burned through Jack's fading mind.

Almost the full length of Jack's feet were now touching the ground. If he waited any longer, he would die. He reached as far over and down Bull's back as he could, grabbed two handfuls of shirt, union suit, and skin, and lifted. His opponent's feet came off the ground, and Jack threw himself to the back, landing with the full weight of both men on Bull's forearms and clenched fists. The grip relaxed instantly. He was free.

He grabbed a handful of Bull's hair and yanked his head to his left and slammed his fist into the big man's left eye. Bull rolled off Jack and staggered to his feet. He was rubbing his arms and flexing his fists. Blood was streaming from both ears.

Jack slowly rose to his feet, eyes locked on Bull, watching for the attack he was sure to come. Deep breaths filled his empty lungs. His body and mind responded to the fresh oxygen that poured in.

He looked Bull over. He was a huge man. His shirt had been torn from his body, exposing a massive chest and arms to fit. The man was bleeding from several cuts above his eyes, forehead, mouth, and nose. *So much for not hitting him in the head,* Jack thought. His legs were bleeding where Jack had given him a good dose of spurs, and his ears were bleeding.

Jack shook his head. *Any other man would be out of the fight,* he thought as he recovered. But he felt himself getting his second wind. He felt the cold edge of rage. There was no telling how many men this animal had coaxed into a fight only to beat them to death. That wasn't ever going to happen again.

Bull looked up, and it was almost like he could read Jack's mind. His bravado was gone. He looked like a cornered, injured bear. He was going to create as much pain as he could before he was put down.

Bull's hand dropped to his boot top and pulled out a knife. The blade, edged on both sides, was about eight inches and looked deadly. "He stared at Jack. I'm gonna kill you, Mr. Marshal."

20

"Jack!"

Jack glanced toward the voice. It was Clint. He was back, and he had tossed a knife, now sailing toward him in a smooth arc. Jack plucked it from the air, returning his full attention to Bull.

Bull smiled a bloody smile through smashed lips and broken teeth. "I'm gonna open yore guts to let everyone see you ain't got any."

Jack smiled back. "You still talk too much."

The bartender held his knife low and started circling cautiously. Jack heard women hustling children away from the fight. A confused rooster crowed, and he smelled Nancy's perfume. *That's crazy,* he thought. *She wouldn't be watching this,* but he knew better than to take his eyes from his opponent.

Bull made a feint. Jack moved to block it, and Bull slashed him across the belly. He jerked his hand to the wound and moved his head, as if to look down at his stomach, but kept his eyes on his opponent. Bull fell for it. He stepped close to make another slash, and Jack drove the point of his knife toward the wrist that held the knife. Bull was quicker than one would expect of a man that size. He was able to yank his arm out of the way and, with his opposite hand, slap Jack's knife hand up and out.

But Bull hadn't been completely successful. The point of Jack's knife entered Bull's arm just behind the wrist and traveled past his elbow before it moved up and away. It wasn't a debilitating cut, for it wasn't deep enough, but, like the cut across Jack's belly, it brought blood. Enough cuts, and a man would lose too much blood, becoming weaker and slower and susceptible to his opponent's attack.

Jack could tell Bull was an experienced knife fighter. He parried Jack's thrusts, flicking his blade and causing a slice here and a slice there. But Jack was accomplishing the same thing, and Bull carried more of Jack's marks than Jack did of Bull's. This was a game of patience, only the loser of this game would die.

A thrust came in low again, and Jack parried, following it up with a move that took his blade close to Bull's throat, but only sliced across his jawbone. Bull had thought he was pulling a knife on a cowboy who had only used a knife to whittle with, but he couldn't be more wrong.

Jack's training had begun in Virginia, at his father's bidding, when he was only twelve. It had been the whiplike foil, and his teacher was an experienced master. As he'd grown in stature, which happened early, he learned the saber. His father had insisted he also learn fighting with a knife. Jack took to all fighting with an excitement and hunger. His master's continuous criticism was that he was too aggressive.

Jack waited, circling with his opponent. He could tell the man was becoming desperate. Bull must have placed his hope of disemboweling Jack in his first thrust. It had been close, but he had failed, and they both knew time was running out for Bull. Jack had shallow slashes across his body and arms and facial bleeding from his opponent's blows, but Bull was bleeding from his entire body. Cuts and gashes covered his upper torso, and the damage from Jack's blows and spurs was causing much bleeding.

The end was near, but Jack knew overconfidence and complacency kill. He and Bull continued to circle in the street. Through most of the fight the crowd had been cheering and yelling, but in the last ten minutes, it was as if they too could sense the end was near. Quiet had settled over the town.

The sun was low in the west and, through the alleyway between the Cherry Creek Saloon and the hotel, alternated striking Bull and then Jack in the face as they circled. Each man made feints, but in the last couple of minutes neither had drawn blood.

Jack's anger had cooled. He'd beaten this man. He'd forced him to pull a knife, admitting he couldn't best Jack with his fists. Jack stepped back. "Listen, Bull. I'm satisfied. It's been a good fight. You ride out of here, and I'll let you go. I'm willing to call it quits."

Bull looked at Jack like he was listening to a being from another planet. "What're you talkin' about? You think this is some kind of sport? I don't need your permission to leave town. I can go when I want, and I'm going when I'm done. You don't realize it, but you're a dead man." Bull spit a wad of blood into the dirt. "All your highfalutin talk about letting me ride out of here ain't worth a plugged nickel to me." He took two steps toward Jack and began circling again, the sun gradually shifting.

He's waiting for the sun, Jack thought. *Could he be any more obvious?*

Jack went back into his fighting stance, but declined to circle with Bull. He just stood there watching him, refusing to allow him to position the sun behind him.

There was a big rock in the street. Not so big you had to go around it, but large enough to trip an unsuspecting person. Bull's right foot struck the rock. He began to fall. He tried to catch himself by windmilling his arms, and staggered toward Jack. At the last moment, abandoning the ruse, he regained his balance and lunged at Jack. This time, he committed. Driving a thrust straight for Jack's belly, his arm stiff and solid behind the knife.

The only problem with his move was that Jack's belly was not there. He knocked the arm away with his left hand and stepped straight into Bull, face-to-face. Jack's knife entered the man's belly and ranged upward, the blade doing massive damage before slicing into the heart. Jack immediately yanked out the knife and stepped back, allowing Bull to slowly collapse to his knees and, after several short gasps, fall forward on his face.

Jack looked down on the dead man, thinking, *I should feel something.* But he didn't. He was numb. Except, all of a sudden, he wasn't numb. His whole body hurt. The cuts, the blows, his back, he was tired and needed to sit down. He looked around for Clint to return the knife to his deputy but couldn't find him. He felt dizzy. The knife dropped from his hand, and he looked down at it. *That's about the craziest thing I've ever seen, letting a knife slip from my hand.* Jack watched the knife get farther away. It was like he was looking at it through the wrong end of a spyglass. Puzzled, he leaned over to pick it up, and followed the knife.

HE AWOKE to the smell of sun-dried sheets and lavender, darkness, and coyotes howling. He tried to figure out the strange combination and decided it wasn't really important, thought about his sore hands, and promptly went back to sleep.

Jack opened his eyes and stared at the ceiling. Where was the thick spiderweb built in the left corner by the industrious spider? It wasn't there, and this ceiling didn't look like his hotel room ceiling. It was much cleaner. He raised his head to see a man in a chair reading a newspaper. The newspaper blocked the man's face.

"Hey!" Jack said.

The newspaper came down, and there sat Bart with a big smile on his face.

"Where am I?"

"You, my good fellow, are the reason I am no longer able to reside at the Cook residence. Nancy kicked me out and replaced me with you. I think she likes playing nurse."

Jack frowned, raised the sheets, and looked down his naked body. "What the devil?"

"What the devil indeed. You almost bit off more than you could chew, my good fellow, but that's behind us. I'm glad you're awake. I'd like to interview you for our paper, the *Cherry Creek Gazette*. You'll be able to make it into the second issue. You are becoming quite the news hog. You also made it into the first issue."

Jack's brow was wrinkled. His eyes were pulled so tight together his eyebrows looked like one long thick mass of hair. "Can you tell me why I'm here, why I have no clothes on, and what is going on?"

Bart seemed to be enjoying Jack's consternation. He turned his head to the side, gazed up at the ceiling, and asked, "Which one of those would you like for me to answer first?"

At that instant, Nancy opened the door and stepped into the room. Her face spread in a smile, blonde hair floated around her, and her blue eyes were brilliant with light. She made a half-turn, held the door handle with one slim hand, while the other braced on the door facing, and called, "Alex? Our patient is awake."

Jack had noticed the trim ankle slipping out toward him from under the light blue skirt, but he was in a mood. "This is the last time I'm asking. What is going on? Why am I here, and most important, where are my clothes?"

Bart looked at Nancy. "I think you might be more qualified to answer than I."

Nancy smiled at Jack. "Do you remember your fight?"

Jack scowled back at her. "Of course I do. Where are my clothes?"

"You lost a lot of blood. Do you remember fainting?"

Jack's scowl grew darker. "I do not remember anything of the like. Where are my clothes?"

Jack watched Nancy's smile fade. Her voice became icy, and small wrinkles coursed across her forehead. "Mr. Sage, you do not have to be a bear. No one stole your precious clothes."

Doc Cook stepped to the door, and Nancy stepped back so he could enter the room. "Good afternoon, Jack. How are you feeling?"

Nancy cut in. "I don't know how he's feeling, but he is acting like a bear." She spun around and moments later returned with strips and rags of clothing. All of it covered in blood. "Since you are so concerned about your clothes, there you are!" She threw what remained of Jack's clothes at him, whipped around, and left the room. Her shoes could be heard clicking on the floor as she charged from his bedroom. Moments later a door slammed.

Doc Cook looked at Jack and then Bart. "Can someone tell me what just happened?"

Bart nodded toward Jack. "Your patient was a little too concerned about his lack of clothing and showed a little too much of his pleasing personality toward your sister."

The doc nodded. "Big mistake. She is a very nice person, but I find she doesn't act well with an overbearing attitude turned toward her. She can become a bit aggressive."

Jack sprang to his defense. "I wasn't being overbearing. I just wanted to know where my pants were. I kept asking, and he wouldn't answer me." Jack threw a hand toward Bart. "Then your sister came in, and I asked her." The excitement had taken Jack's mind off his injuries. Since things were calming down, the pains were beginning to override his concern for his clothes. His entire body registered pain.

The doctor moved close and took his wrist. Jack waited

quietly. This was nothing new for him. He had been in hospitals before and knew about checking the pulse or the beats of the heart. "So how am I doing, Doc?"

"Where do I start?"

The three men heard the door open and close.

The doctor continued, "Nothing is broken. Your back will be sore for a while. I'm surprised Bull didn't break it, but I think his problem was you are so big, and the thickness of your backbone is commensurate with your size."

Jack held up his hand. "Just get to the point, Doc. I need to get back to work."

Doc Cook, unfazed, continued his explanation. "Not only are you big, but your backbone is also big, making it harder to break. But it will be sore. You've also lost a lot of blood. You'll need to drink plenty of fluids. That will help build your blood back, along with the necessary rest." He held up three fingers. "How many fingers do you see?"

Jack was starting to get frustrated again. "Doc, I see exactly the number you held up, three. What kind of question is that?"

"You received several severe blows to your head. We don't know exactly why, but blows like that can cause vision problems, nausea, and dizziness, just to name a few. Are you feeling any of those symptoms?"

Jack shook his head.

"Good. You have contusions all over your body." He stopped at Jack's raised eyebrows.

"Bruises. You have bruises from Bull's heavy blows. You're going to be extremely sore for a while. I have to say, you are very lucky. The first cut Bull made across your abdomen was deeper than you thought. We put in twenty-five stitches across your belly. If he had gone another eighth of an inch, or if he had hit you in the wound, you wouldn't be here. It would have opened, and you've been around long enough to know what would have followed."

Jack had pulled a couple of the bed pillows behind his back and was sitting up as the doctor explained his wounds. He leaned back and thought, *An eighth of an inch, and my guts would've been all over the ground. I let him get too close. That was my fault.* "How long am I supposed to remain here, Doc?"

"Jack, this is very important. Your body has gone through more than the average man could survive. I would like for you to stay with us for two more weeks. That will allow your head to clear and your wounds to heal, especially the belly wound. We definitely don't want anything to go wrong with that. We are fortunate there appears to be no infection, but I couldn't say what might happen if it breaks open. In a couple of days, you'll be able to get up and move around. You'll find it difficult to straighten with those stitches, among all the others we had to make on the cuts. But it won't take long for you to be back to your old self, assuming you follow orders."

Jack stared at the doctor like the man was crazy.

"Doc, I can't stay here for two weeks. Besides, I feel fine." Forgetting his state of dress, he swung his legs out from under the sheet and stood. Two things shocked him. The first was his nakedness, which was exposed just as Nancy stepped back to the open door. The second was the failure of his strength. He fell back onto the bed, dizzy and faint, but desperately attempting to pull the sheet out from under his weight and spread it across his body.

Nancy rushed in, grasped the edge of the exposed sheet and yanked hard. It jerked out from under Jack and settled protectively across his body. With all of his travels and experience, he was not a man who blushed at anything, but under the sun- and windburned dark of his skin could be seen a bright red glow.

Doc Cook assisted Nancy straightening the sheet while Bart tried to hold in his laughter. His entire body shook. His face was almost as red as Jack's from straining to contain himself.

Jack glared at him. "I've never run a newspaperman out of a town before, but you may be the first."

Bart shook his head, still unable to speak for fear he would break into laughter.

Jack stole a glance at Nancy. Her face, protected from the sun, was rosy red.

Doc Cook had maintained his professional demeanor, though the wrinkles at the corners of his eyes were more pronounced. He cleared his throat. "Well, that was unfortunate, but now you see, Jack, you are too weak to try moving around by yourself. The weakness will disappear within a couple of days, but you'll still not be able to exert yourself. If you do, you'll again find yourself faint."

Resigned, Jack nodded his head. "Alright, Doc, I understand, but could someone please go to my hotel room and get me some clothes? If this place should burn down, I don't feel like running outside in my birthday suit."

Bart couldn't resist. "Yes, that would be quite a sight, as I can attest."

Nancy giggled and turned from the room.

Doc Cook smiled. "Yes, well, Marshal, your deputy has been waiting in the parlor. Should I bring him in?"

Jack gave a single emphatic nod and said, with equal emphasis, "Please, and get that laughing hyena out of here." He pointed at Bart.

Bart stood. "I'm leaving, but I'll be back. You still owe me an interview for my next issue."

Jack heard the newspaperman laughing as the front door closed behind him. "Doc, I hate to be a bother, but I'm almighty hungry. You think you could send up to the hotel for a steak and about six eggs and biscuits? Tell 'em to send plenty of butter, too."

The doc shook his head. "Not necessary. I believe Nancy has whipped up something."

As he spoke, Nancy walked in with a tray. On it sat a bowl of soup and several homemade crackers.

Jack looked at it and didn't try to hide his aversion to such slim fare. "Soup? I don't want soup. I want something that'll stick to a man's ribs."

Ignoring him, Nancy placed the tray gently across his lap, taking care to remain clear of the stitches. Once the tray was in place, she straightened and placed her hands on her hips. "You listen to me, mister. You are in my house. I am a nurse, and that soup is by the doctor's orders." Her lids were tightened around her pretty blue eyes so she looked as if she was squinting at him. "If you want your steak and eggs, you're going to have to eat this first." She took a deep breath and softened a bit. "Try it, Jack. I think you'll like it."

Jack had been staring at the soup and crackers. When her voice softened and she called him by name, he looked up at her. Her blonde hair shone in the light from the window, and her blue eyes had gone from angry to almost pleading. Feeling guilty for his outbursts and his display, Jack also took a deep breath. His wide exposed chest with the numerous cuts and stitches across it rose and fell.

"Sorry. I guess you were right. I've been nothing but an old ungrateful bear. It's just that I was so surprised my clothes were gone." He picked up the soup spoon, dipped it into the soup, and brought the spoon to his mouth. The soup was good. It was a beef soup. He took another spoonful. It tasted real good. It wasn't too hot. He looked up at Nancy again. "Thanks, this is really good."

"Try a cracker. I made them myself."

He did, and it was delicious. The salty taste, the crisp snap of the cracker when he bit into it caused his mind to flash back to his home in Virginia. The cook had made the very same kind of crackers, and, as a boy, he had loved them. He looked back up at Nancy. "These are the best crackers I've had since I was a boy."

Her face lit in a brilliant smile. Wide red lips spread to show perfectly aligned white teeth. *She is a mighty pretty woman,* Jack thought. *She has spirit, too. Nobody's going to run over her.*

"Jack, that's the nicest thing I've heard in a long time. Thank you." Her smile diminished, and she switched to earnest concern. "Now, eat the rest of your soup. If you feel fine later, we might find something a little more substantial for you. Nate brought you a couple of changes of clothes. I'll bring you a set."

21

F inally having fallen asleep, Mather was rudely yanked back to consciousness by the sound of racing hoofbeats. He was up and dressed by the time he heard boots hit the porch. There were multiple fast, hard knocks.

"On my way," he called, marched to the door, and yanked it open. It was Layton Selby, one of the hands he had sent to town early in the afternoon to find out what was happening. "Well?"

The man blurted, "Korkeran's gone."

Shocked, Mather stared uncomprehendingly at the cowhand. "Gone? Gone where?"

"Just gone. Run out of town by Sage."

Brow wrinkled and lips pursed, Mather shouted, "Cookie, get up and fix coffee. We'll be in the office. Roust out Huck Munson and tell him to join us." Huck had arrived earlier in the afternoon from Waco. To Selby, he said, "Come on in," turned right and strode to his office. Once inside, he moved quickly to the big leather chair behind his desk and dropped into it. He pointed to one of the chairs in front of his desk. "Now tell me how it happened."

"Understand, boss, I'm gettin' this secondhand, but what I

was told was that Bull started beating up on a cowhand, and Sage was unhappy about it." Selby looked up at Huck Munson as he stumbled in. The man was bleary-eyed and looked like he hadn't slept for three days.

Mather pointed at the vacant chair. "You look like the devil."

"I ain't slept for danged near four days. What's goin' on?"

"Selby here was just telling me that Korkeran is gone."

Huck put one hand on the wooden arm of the chair and turned to look at Selby. "Gone?"

Selby nodded. "Clean. Sage ran him out for rigged gambling tables."

"Wait a minute," Mather said. "You just told me that he ran him out because Bull was beating up a cowhand."

Selby shook his head. "No, boss. That's just what got Sage interested. The fight had gone out into the street, and the cowhand, the one what was getting beat up by Bull, told the marshal he had been cheated at the roulette table. He called Korkeran a cheat. If Sage hadn't been there, Korkeran would've ventilated that feller, but the marshal stopped him."

Impatient, Mather waved his hand back and forth like he was chasing off a fly. "Alright, alright, get on with it."

Selby took a deep breath. "Well, Sage checked out Korkeran's roulette table, found it was rigged, and chopped it to pieces with an axe. He went on to do the same with all the other tables."

Huck stared at Selby with a disbelieving expression. "Korkeran just stood there?"

"The gun doctor had a Winchester on him and Bull, and the attorney had a scattergun. Wasn't much he could do."

"Go on," Mather said.

"When Sage finished, he dragged Korkeran into his own office and made him open his safe. He let him take three grand with him and ran him right out of town."

Mather looked hard at Selby. "I know Korkeran had more money in his safe than that, and there's no tellin' what he has deposited over in the bank. He wouldn't have left with that little bit."

"He did, boss, least that's what I was told."

Amazed, Mather sat and shook his head. Then another thought came to him. "Korkeran didn't draw? I've heard he's mighty fast."

"Didn't draw, and from what I was told, he had the chance to. Kept telling Sage he was gonna kill him but never made a move."

As they thought about it, all three men sat silent, shaking their heads. Mather let out a long breath. "So Bull has the Gilded Lily now?"

Selby shook his head. "No sirree. The Lily is shut down. Just a big vacant building."

Huck asked, "Where's Bull, in jail?"

Selby shook his head again. "You ain't gonna believe this. I know I didn't. Bull is dead."

Huck nodded. "It figures. Sage runs Korkeran out of town and then shoots Bull. That makes sense."

Even as Mather was nodding in agreement, Selby said, "Nope, it weren't anything like that. Bull and Sage had them a good old-fashioned fistfight. Feller I was talking to said it lasted for maybe a couple of hours, up and down the street. Both men were supposedly beat to a pulp, but the marshal whipped Bull."

Huck shook his head. "Now I ain't believin' that. There's not a man in these parts who could whip Bull with fists."

Selby held up his right hand. "I swear. I didn't believe the feller I was talkin' to either, but he called over two others who witnessed it to back him up. Sage beat Bull down."

Mather leaned back in his chair and steepled his fingers. "So Marshal Sage beat Bull to death. I would never have believed that could happen. It's still hard to believe, Bull beat to death."

Selby shook his head again. "No, boss, Sage didn't beat Bull to death. He beat him, but when Bull saw he was done for, he drew his knife. That was the end of Bull."

Selby stopped and took a long sip of his cooling coffee, waited, and took another. "They fought with them knives for over thirty minutes. Feller said it was bloody something awful. Both of them got cut up bad. But he said Bull must've been getting tired or something, because he struck straight at Sage. He said it was so fast nobody could follow it, but Sage made this fancy move and then stuck that knife hilt deep into Bull. Bull just dropped to his knees and fell on his face, dead with blood everywhere."

All three of the men sat silent, lost in their own thoughts. Mather's mind was racing. *Who is this Jack Sage? Rumor is, he cleaned up Laredo, but who was he before that? Can we beat him? What can we do? Hopefully this Chance Doughtry will be the answer.* He looked at Huck, who was staring back at him, and cleared his throat. "So that's it?"

"Pretty much, boss. That feller I was talking to did say it was a good thing Sage got Bull when he did. Said Sage stood there lookin' at Bull like he couldn't believe it. Then his knife slipped right out of his hand. He bent over to pick it up and passed out cold. Said it figured. It looked like his whole body was bleeding, so he must have lost a lot of blood. He's at the Doc's. Rumor says he might be laid up a couple of weeks. Who knows, we may get lucky. He could die."

Mather nodded. "He could, but I wouldn't bet on it. Not a man like this Sage appears to be. Alright, Selby. Why don't you have Cookie whip you up something to eat and get some sleep, and close the door behind you."

The cowhand nodded, rose, and walked out of the room, pulling the door closed. Mather took a long sip of his coffee and returned the cup to his desk. "You have any idea when Doughtry might get here?"

Now it was Huck's turn to shake his head. "Nope. It's like I was tellin' you this afternoon. He comes and goes on his own schedule. He's paid. He'll get it done. With Sage laid up, it might be even easier. I'm thinkin' he's cut and beat up pretty bad."

"Maybe. Did Doughtry say anything about how he might handle it? If he'll stop by the ranch?"

"Like I said, boss, he don't talk about his work, his comings and goings, nothing. If you start questioning him, he gets all quiet and threatening. He don't want us or anybody to know his doings, and it's best not to ask him."

Huck let out a long yawn. "By the way, boss, the boys are gettin' restless. They're ready to go burn something or somebody. A couple have even mentioned riding into town."

"No, I don't want anyone attacked or harmed, especially the squatters and the townspeople. Now that Korkeran is gone, we want Cherry Creek to be the quietest and the most peaceful place in Texas. We want it so quiet a single killing of a town marshal will cause little investigation."

"Alright, but the boys need something. Maybe I could let them raid and shoot up those Mexicans? That wouldn't cause much ruckus."

"Huck, don't make me say it again. I want peace around here until Doughtry takes care of Sage. Then, after a few weeks, when things settle down, we'll tear this place apart, the squatters and the town."

Huck stood. "I don't know how long we can control the boys. They're feelin' bloody, and when they get like this, somebody usually dies."

"How's Hawk and the others doing?"

"Healing, but slow. Way their feet look, they won't be puttin' any boots on for at least a couple of weeks, and Hawk is fit to be tied. Even though they're friends, he's threatened to kill Arlo several times. That whiny feller won't shut up."

"Alright. I need to ride in pretty soon for a meeting. I'll let you know when." Mather slid his chair back and stood.

Huck followed. "If you don't need me anymore, I'm gonna go hit the sack."

Mather nodded and watched Huck disappear out the front

door. He stopped by the kitchen. Selby was finishing his late supper, and Cookie was washing dishes. To the cook's back, Mather said, "I'm heading to bed. You can put out the lamps." He turned for the bedroom, pleased. He was feeling sleepy.

CHANCE DOUGHTRY LAY RELAXED against his saddle, eating a piece of beef jerky. He had a plentiful supply. Two weeks before leaving Waco, he'd killed an unbranded calf, considered a maverick nowadays, dressed it out, and made a batch of jerky. He liked it well seasoned, spicy enough to make his head sweat, so it wasn't bothered much with flies.

An armadillo was rooting around the edge of his camp, totally oblivious to Doughtry. He watched the little hard-shelled animal snuff, dig, and eat. He liked animals. In fact, he had almost cried when he killed the calf. It was such a pretty little thing, but he needed meat. He needed meat for his long trip. He had planned his trip out completely. He would take care of business in Cherry Creek, then ride on to Galveston, and take a ship to New York City. He was ready to go back east and enjoy the benefits available, if a man had money, and he had money.

A doe with two fawns walked into his camp. The fawns had almost lost their spots. The doe was browsing, and the fawns were bothering her for food. She bumped first one and then the other with her back legs, but they were unrelenting.

Doughtry grinned watching the two fawns. They were so cute. He thought of his little sister and brother. They were twins. They were so playful. Finally the doe relented and allowed them to suck. It seemed they'd never get full, but at last they stepped back, their mouths white and foamy. They each came forward and stood beside the doe with their little heads up and alert. The doe licked the neck of one and then the other. Doughtry thought how lucky he was to watch this and be so close. The deer were no more than twenty feet from him on the other side of his camp. Finally the doe lifted one leg and laid it softly across one fawn's neck and laid her neck across the other. The fawns stood stationary as if they were enjoying the moment. Then the little male jerked away and trotted into the mesquites, the mother and his sibling following.

Doughtry had been sitting frozen in position while the deer were close, but once they were gone, he took another bite of jerky. He had no fire. He wouldn't have one until the job was finished and he was well away from this part of the country. He wanted no sign around to mark his passage. While he leaned against the saddle, in no hurry to get moving, he thought back to the twins.

He had been much older, so had Ma. He'd overheard her telling his sister she never expected the twins, but they seemed to just show up. His family didn't associate much with people. Pa kept to himself. He'd hunt and fish and sell the game to folks, but mostly nobody came around.

He had followed Pa into the woods when he was no more than five or six, and started learning about hunting and fishing and trapping and all the stuff a man needs to survive. Then the war came. He was maybe fifteen. He never kept up with numbers too well.

With the war, Pa went away to fight, and it was left up to him to provide for the family, and he did a fair job until that day. The day that Reb artillery started firing. The big shells were blowing up close to the homeplace, and everyone ran into the house for protection, which was a bad idea.

It wasn't long before one of those shells hit right on the house and blew it all to smithereens, no more Ma, no more twins, and no more sister. That was the day he crawled toward the Reb artillery and picked off all six of the men shooting those two guns. Then he ran away, joined the Union Army, and had the best job in the whole army—sniper.

He liked killing men. He wouldn't shoot a woman or a kid,

but he'd kill the daylights out of men. But the war ended, and all of a sudden it was against the law to kill other men. But he figured out how to keep on doing it and get paid for it, and he got smarter. Now it didn't make any difference to him if a man fought for the Union or the Rebs, he'd kill him if he was paid enough. But it was always on his terms. Pa always said, "Trust yourself or trust your family, but don't trust nobody else." That's what he did.

Now he was going to a place called Cherry Creek, and he was going to kill the marshal. He preferred the rifle, but he'd killed several men with his .36-caliber Navy Colt revolver. He'd had the barrel shortened and could get it out of his holster pretty quick.

Doughtry pulled his legs up, stood and stretched. He walked to his horse, a little bay mustang. He was a quick little horse and was a real stayer. He grasped the rope and pulled the stake from the ground, looped the rope, drawing the bay nearer. With the tension, the bay trotted to Doughtry and nuzzled his jacket. The man pulled an apple from his pocket, and gripping it with a thumb on each side of the stem, he twisted and broke it in half and held out one of the halves to the horse. The bay pulled back his lips and delicately lifted the apple from Doughtry's hand, crunchy it enthusiastically. Doughtry ate the other half while he led the horse to the small creek.

Tall pecan trees lined the narrow creek. He waited for his horse to drink his fill. While he waited, he could hear pecan cuttings raining into the creek. A squirrel was working on the pecan with his sharp, efficient teeth.

He led his horse back to camp and thought about the description he had been given of his subject. The man's name was Jack Sage. He was described as a big man, near six and a half feet tall. He grinned at the thought of the size of the casket it would take for Sage.

Doughtry liked killing big men. He was only five feet six inches. A man like Sage would tower a foot over him. He'd killed a lot of big men in the war. They'd given him medals for it. He killed a lot of big men after the war. He actually liked that better. They gave him money for those killings.

Once he had saddled the bay, with his saddlebags and bedroll tied, he swung into the saddle. He liked sitting in the saddle, it made him feel bigger, but he knew he wasn't. He also knew that his Sharps and his two Colts made up for the size of any big man. He smiled at that thought. Pa would have agreed with him. He wondered if his pa had ever made it back to the homeplace. He would sure be surprised. Would Pa be proud of him, of what he was doing now? He nodded. Sure he would. He would say you have to provide for your family, and since he was the only one left, he was his own family. He nodded again, eased out to the edge of the pecan trees and briars. He searched for movement, examining every bunch of mesquites and oaks. He looked at the bigger individual trees, letting his eyes run along the edges of the bark and limbs, looking for anything smooth, anything that didn't fit. It was all clear. *Another hot day,* he thought, scratched the bay between his ears, and clucked. The horse stepped away from the pecan thicket and moved on toward Doughtry's destination.

22

Jack rechecked his Remington revolver. He was bored out of his mind. The doc was nice, Nancy was nice, and he was going nuts. *What is happening in town?* Jack thought. *How is Clint doing? What about Mather? Especially what about Mather. It's been way too quiet.* He had been confined to the house for a week and two days. Nancy was visiting someone, the doc was out on a call, and here he sat, alone with nothing to do.

Reading wasn't in the plan when so much was at stake. He needed to be off his rear and taking care of his town. He suddenly stood, jerking up to his full height. The stitches in his stomach and several other sewn slashes on his chest protested, sending pain signals to his brain. He ignored them. He slid the revolver behind his back, inside his gun belt. He didn't like carrying it there. Number one, it was more uncomfortable, especially with his back sore, but he couldn't carry it pressed against his belly. With it stuck between his waistband and the stitches, the hard metal made his belly hurt like the dickens, so he selected the lesser of two evils. He never knew when he might need those extra five rounds.

One of the hardest things for him to do was pull his boots

on. Nancy helped him do that. She had finally let him out of bed on the third day. He'd had to threaten her with his leaving before she gave in, but he won that one. He looked around the parlor with a sense of regret. He had to admit, Doc Cook and Nancy had provided him with great care, and he did enjoy her company. However, he also noticed how much Bart enjoyed Nancy's company, and he had known her much longer than Jack.

He picked up his hat. He'd get the remainder of his things when he felt better. *Actually,* he admitted to himself, *I need to get out of here before she gets back, or I'll be in deep trouble.* He chuckled in disbelief. He was afraid of a slip of a girl who couldn't weigh over one hundred pounds. *No,* he thought, *I only hate to disappoint her.*

The shotgun was standing next to the bed. He picked it up, looked around again, and opened the door. Safe so far. He slapped his hat on, not taking time to level it, and made his way toward the office.

He passed several people, who nodded and spoke. He responded in a like manner, reaching his office without being stopped. He opened the door and stepped inside. It was neat and clean. Everything was put up. He heard Clint call from the back, "Hold on a second. I'll be right there."

Within moments Clint emerged, a broom in his hand and his face red from effort. "Oh. Hi, Marshal."

Jack looked the man over. He was carrying a bucket full of soapy water in one hand and the shotgun and a broom in the other. "Getting in a little summertime spring cleaning, Clint?"

His deputy grinned. "Yeah, boss, kinda. It had gotten a little messy around here, and I thought I'd clean things up."

Jack nodded. "Good. I won't disrupt your cleaning by sitting at my desk, will I?"

"Nope, sit. I've just finished. Soon as I dump out this water and rinse the bucket and mop, I'll be done."

Jack waved as he sat. "Don't let me hold you up. When you get done, come on back in. I'd like you to bring me up to snuff."

"Sure thing. I'll just be a minute."

Jacked picked up the new wanted circulars and began going through them. He had got to the third one when Clint stepped back into the office and closed the door.

"Boss, you may have some trouble on the way."

"Why's that, Clint?"

"Town council. They're headed for your office. Be here any second."

Jack nodded his thanks as the door opened, and Franklin stepped into the office, followed by Farnsworth, Pierce, Wade, Gabriella, Jessup, and Dr. Cook. Cook looked both surprised and concerned, but closed the door. It was immediately pushed open, and Sullivan, Sully, and Belinda stepped in, accompanied by Bart.

Franklin swelled up like a toad and said to the new arrivals, "This is town council business. You were not invited."

Brian Sullivan leaned toward the older man. "You listen to me, you pompous money changer. No way we the people of this town will allow you to railroad a marshal who gets the job done. You had best put that in your wee little brain and think on it. We are a-staying."

Jack looked at each of the arrivals. "Thank you for being here, but I was hired by the town council, and they do have the authority to fire me, although there is a substantial cost to them should they elect to do so. Let me take care of this, and I'll stop by to see each one of you later, except for you, Bart. Since you represent the paper, you can stay."

Franklin's frown grew deeper, but he said nothing.

"You sure, Marshal?" Sully asked.

"I am, and thank you, Sully, and you, Belinda, and thank you, Brian. I appreciate you coming here."

The three nodded and left the office, backs stiff and chins high.

Jack looked to the remaining group. "Who's the spokesman?"

Franklin spoke. "I shall speak for the group."

Wade chimed in, "He's not speaking for me, Jack."

"Nor me," Cook said.

"Definitely not me," Farnsworth said. "Since you arrived, the burying business has dramatically improved."

"Alright, Mr. Franklin, what do you have to say?"

"I . . . we are greatly concerned about the mayhem you have caused since your arrival."

From the jail in back, Blaisdale chimed in, "That's a fact."

Jack called, "You getting dry back there, Blaisdale?"

Blaisdale remained silent.

Franklin continued, "You ran out of town a man who brought a large amount of business to Cherry Creek, and then you brutally murdered—"

"Stop right there. I did not murder Bull. If I hadn't defended myself, he would have killed me, so, yes, I killed him, but I did not murder him."

"Well," Franklin continued, "you conducted a brutal battle in the street like any ruffian, in front of wives and children. You are the town marshal. You are above such things."

Jack said nothing.

"You had no right to throw Mr. Korkeran out of this town. You acted like a dictator, and we'll have none of that."

Jack sat relaxed behind his desk. His elbows resting on the arms of his chair, he brought his hands together and steepled his fingers. "You firing me, Mr. Franklin?"

The man hesitated, took a quick glance at the other town council members, and shook his head. "No. I am not, but I'm putting you on notice. Either act like a gentleman, or we will fire you."

Jack smiled, but there was no humor in it. "Just in case you may have forgotten, I'll refresh your memory. You can fire me, but you can't tell me how to do my job. So, from now on, unless you have useful information on thieves and robbers, I expect you'll be better off sticking to running your bank. Anything else you'd like to say to me?"

Jack watched Franklin's face turn red, and his little eyes blinked at him like a confused owl.

"Consider this a warning," Franklin said, reached for the door latch, and opened it, exiting abruptly.

Doc Cook, Wade, and Bart stayed while the other visitors followed Franklin out the door.

Clint grabbed the door latch. "Need to finish cleaning the mop. I'll be right back."

The doctor's brow wrinkled. He said, "We went to the house first. You weren't there. I thought you might be leaving, but this is far too soon. You should still be relaxing at home."

Jack flexed his sore hands. Both were still puffy around the knuckles, but he could hold a gun. He didn't much look forward to firing one, but at least they weren't forty-fours. "I thank you and Nancy for your concern, but I was going crazy. I had to get out and move around. Find out what was happening in town. Seems I got out just in time."

Wade shook his head. "I don't know what's going on with Franklin. He's been upset since you ran Korkeran out of town. Keeps saying a businessman's not safe in town with you here." Wade scuffed his boot against a knot in the floor. "That's plain stupid. Before you got here, a man or woman couldn't walk the street without fear of getting roped or shot or trampled. I don't know what's got into him."

The doctor said, "I fear our banker may be more worried about his money than his town. That's just a suspicion, but I've heard he's called notes on several of our Mexican friends. They, similar to some of the homesteaders, are also losing their land."

Perplexed, Wade frowned. "He's a strange one. He came over and offered to loan me money to grow my business. He said he'd give me a reasonable note and could make it even better if I'd throw in with him as a partner."

Jack's eyebrows moved up in surprise. "He wanted part of your business? I wonder if he's made that offer to anyone else. Maybe I'll check around." He turned to Bart, who was jotting notes on his pad. "You heard of anything like that going on?"

"Nope, I have not, but I too will do some investigating. One thing I do know is that he's had some dealings with Mather, but that really isn't unusual. Ranchers, just like farmers, sometimes need money until they can get stock sold."

Bart turned to the doctor. "Alex, since Jack left, you think I'm still invited for supper tonight?"

Doc Cook grinned and nodded. "I think you'd better be there, or my sister will be upset at two people instead of just one."

Bart flipped his tablet closed. "Good, I've got to get started setting type for tomorrow's edition, but I'll be there on time."

"And I have a family to check on," Doc Cook said. He stepped toward the door, stopped, and turned back to Jack. "Be sure to continue soaking your hands in warm salty water twice a day, and for goodness' sake, don't go riding or lift anything for another week."

Wade raised his hand in a wave, and the three men left the office. Jack flexed his hands again. They were still stiff and sore, but better than he expected they would be by now. Bull's head had done real damage to both of Jack's hands, but nothing permanent, as long as he didn't have to shoot a handgun anytime soon.

Through the front window of his office, he watched the shadows lengthen. *I need to look around town,* he thought.

Clint came inside as Jack started to stand. He dropped back into his chair and pointed at one of the other chairs. "Tell me what's been going on around town and if you've heard anything new."

"Everything's quiet. Nothing has been happening with the

homesteaders. They're keeping watch, but there's not been a peep from Mather or any of his bunch. No Indians either, and since your little dustup with Korkeran and Bull, the town has been near as quiet as a cemetery. A few cowhands come and go, some of them Mather's hands, but there's been no trouble."

Jack shook his head. "I don't like it. It's like the quiet before a storm. From my take on Mather, he's a grudge holder, and he's got men to do the fighting for him. I know we have his main man in jail, but Hawk should be recovered or close to it. I'd bet he's spoiling for a fight. Keep your eyes and ears open. It'll be coming, I guarantee it. If it doesn't happen within the next few days, I think the lid will blow off when the judge arrives. That's next week."

"All I can tell you, boss, is that it's been quiet, but I'll keep a lookout."

"Good. Hang around until Amy brings Blaisdale his supper. I'm gonna take a stroll around town. I'll be back and take over."

"You up to it?"

Jack just looked at his deputy and stood.

He took his shotgun and left the office. He stood on the small porch and looked right toward the end of the street. Next door was the bank. It was closed. He stepped over and checked the door handle. Locked. He waited for a wagon to pass, and crossed the street to Pierce's General Store. Parked in front was a buckboard pulled by two horses. He stepped to the door, pulled the latch, and walked in.

Mrs. Pierce was assisting a lady at a table where bolts of material lay. He recognized the Coburn boys, Collin and Conner. He had met them at the Purcells' homestead after the Indian attack. Everyone looked up when he walked in.

"Hi, Marshal," Conner said.

Collin joined in. "Afternoon, Marshal."

"Howdy, boys. Good to see you. You know if Mr. Purcell made it back home alright?"

The lady spoke up. "I am Cathy Cooper, Marshal Sage. These two are my sons. They speak very highly of you, and, yes, to answer your question, William Purcell made it home fine. I must tell you, he is a very grateful man."

Jack removed his Stetson. "Ma'am, it's nice to meet you, and I appreciate your kind words. I'm glad Mr. Purcell made it home alright.

"Mrs. Pierce, nice to see you."

"It's so very good to see you out and about, Marshal."

Jack nodded his thanks and addressed Cathy Cooper. "Mrs. Cooper, you and your boys aren't planning on heading back home tonight, are you?" He glanced out the big store window. "It's getting dark fast."

Mrs. Pierce shook her head. "Oh, no, Cathy and the boys are staying with us tonight. They'll go back in the morning."

Jack nodded. "Good to hear. I'm off for a little stroll. You folks have a good evening."

Multiple good evenings and good nights followed him as he closed the door. Through the thin walls, he heard Mrs. Cooper say, "He is so big and such a handsome man."

Her statement was immediately followed by her youngest son Conner's exasperated voice. "Ma!"

Jack grinned to himself and, leveling his hat on his head, stepped along the boardwalk to his next stop, Wade's Gun Shop.

He made his way round the town. For those stores closed, he would check the doors to make sure they were locked. The open ones he would enter and discuss the day with them. By the time he made it to Johnson's Stables, darkness covered the land. Independent shafts of light escaped from homes and buildings, illuminating swatches of street and boardwalk.

The large stable door was open, and light flooded the darkness from the stable's interior. Sully relaxed in his rocker inside, close to the hay bales and his office.

"Howdy, young feller," Sully called as Jack walked into the light, headed for Smokey and Stonewall.

Jack nodded and walked into the stall with his two animals. Both had turned their heads so they could watch him approach. He came up between them so he could scratch each at the same time. "How you boys doing?"

Smokey leaned his neck toward Jack and lowered it just a bit, trying to position Jack's hand on a particular itch. Stonewall nosed at his vest pockets. "Nothing there for you, Stonewall. No apples tonight." The mule smelled his vest pockets and turned his head slightly so he could watch Jack.

Sully creaked in his rocker. "That mule's disappointed with you. He's looking for whatever you usually bring."

"Apple," Jack said. He patted both animals on the backs and then walked over to Sully, who had pulled up the other rocker. "I usually split an apple between them."

Stonewall chose that moment to raise his tail and deposit a fresh load of horse apples, or in this case, mule.

Both men laughed.

"Guess he's made his comment about no apple," Sully said.

"Pretty definite, I'd say." Jack sat rocking and grinning. "That mule has a mind of his own."

"Most do." Sully said nothing for a few moments, the only sound that of the two creaking rockers, then said, "So how you feeling, boy?"

"Like I've been beat up by the best and sliced up for good riddance."

Sully chuckled. "Heh-heh-heh, you shore took a lot of whomping. Course, not near as much as Bull did. He shoulda known not to tangle with you. I knew he'd made a big mistake when he slugged you."

"Darned near knocked me into next week."

"Yeah, but you got over it and pert near whipped him senseless. You would've too if he hadn't of drawn that pig sticker."

A bullbat dove low in front of the stable door, then turned almost straight up and swooped out of the light.

Sully had stopped talking to watch the bird. "They get their bellies full out there. Every night I watch them perform all sorts of tricks chasing them danged bugs. Hope they eat every single one of 'em." He stared into the blackness, then turned to Jack. "Where was I?"

Jack's rocker was moving slowly back and forth. He felt relaxed in the warm evening air. "Pig sticker."

"Oh yeah. I sure thought you was in trouble, until Clint tossed you his knife. When I saw you catch it and turn it in your hand, I remembered you was in the Legion. I figured then Bull had leaped from the skillet right into the fire."

Jack shook his head. "Almost didn't. He came very near laying me open with his first slash. Caught me off guard."

Sully's head nodded with his rocking. "Yep. I thought you was hurt bad, but when no guts rolled out, I figured he didn't get quite close enough."

Jack stopped rocking and turned to Sully. "I had made up my mind to turn him loose, until he pulled that knife. At that point I decided it was either him or me."

Sully shook his head. "'Tweren't nothin' else you could've done. He was plumb bad. He woulda gone on hurting folks as long as he lived. No telling how many people you saved by ending him. I say good riddance to bad trash." Sully let out a long stream of tobacco juice, hitting a June bug crawling across the straw-laden floor.

"Thanks for the conversation, Sully," Jack said, pushing himself out of the rocking chair. "I'd best get on back so Clint can take a break."

Sully turned a concerned face up to the marshal. "How you doin', boy?"

"I'm fine. I'll be as good as new in just a few more days. Have a good evening." He patted Smokey and Stonewall on his way out and stepped out of the barn. He turned right, moved across the dirt until he came to the northern edge of the boardwalk. He eased his two hundred pounds softly onto the dry boards. They emitted a loud creak. He thought he saw a furtive movement in the entrance to the alleyway a few stores down. It was there, and then it was gone, but his eyes hadn't yet adjusted to the darkness, so he wasn't sure. He berated himself for not being more cautious.

23

There was no way to walk quietly on the boardwalk. The dried boards squeaked and groaned with his steps no matter how carefully he tried to move. He passed the batwing doors of the Rusty Bucket and looked in. Sullivan was behind the bar. He saw Jack and waved him in. He shook his head, waved back, and moved into the darkness.

He gave up trying to see into the deep alleyways, some of which opened out into the countryside. He examined what he could across the street and kept moving. He passed the hotel without looking inside, trying to shelter his eyes as much as possible. His peripheral vision showed him several people eating at the hotel restaurant, which reminded him how hungry he was, which reminded him of Clint. The Cherry Creek Saloon would be next, followed by the attorney's office, and finally his. Then he could release Clint for a well-deserved rest.

The boardwalk ran only in front of the buildings, leaving the alleyways free for horses, mules, or wagons. He decided to pick up his pace just as he stepped off the south edge of the boardwalk in front of the hotel. Due to his impaired night vision, he miscalculated the end of the wooden walk at the alleyway. His right boot heel caught on the edge, and his six-foot, four-inch body lurched down and out toward the ground.

He caught himself before sprawling face-first into the dirt, but his stumbling brought his head down and forward just far enough. A gun roared from the alleyway, and if his night vision had been hampered before the blast, it was totally gone after the muzzle blast of flaming powder almost in his face. Another shot followed immediately after the first, and he felt a bullet shift the position of his hat on his head. Jack had the crazy thought, *Dang it, there goes another hat,* race through his mind while his muscles were functioning automatically. His right hand filled with his Remington New Model Police, and three .36-caliber balls raced down the alley, toward the muzzle blast he had just seen. They were fired so quickly, the blasts almost sounded like one continuous roar.

On the heels of his shots came a woman's scream. He held his fire, crouched in the street, and listened for any sign of his attacker. All he could hear was the loud, constant ringing in his ears. The stinging sweet acrid smell of the gunpowder lingered around him and in the alley. He heard a woman crying and moved toward the sound. He holstered the Remington he had fired and drew the one behind his back. It gave him five rounds, where he only had two left in the other.

Jack could make out a form lying on the ground behind two barrels sitting side by side. She was more moaning than crying. The side door of the saloon burst open. Light shot out into the alley. It was followed by several customers. With the light, Jack recognized Gabriela Campbell lying on the ground. He shoved the revolver back into its place and knelt beside her, lifting her gently into a sitting position supported by his arm.

She looked up at him. "Oh, thank goodness it's you, Jack. I thought he had killed you."

"Did you get a look at him?"

"No. I came outside for a breath of fresh air just as you fired. He was turning to run, and knocked me down."

In the light, Jack could see a bruise forming on her right cheek. "Are you hurt anywhere else?"

"No, no, I don't think so. Help me up."

"Are you sure?"

"Please, Jack, everyone is looking."

He helped her to her feet, holding her arm until he was sure she was steady. He looked back down the alley. There was no way he'd find whoever did this, not as dark as it was. In the morning, he'd come back and check the tracks.

He placed his arm around her waist and carried her inside. Clint was right behind him. Jack turned to Clint. "Go on back to the office just in case this is a ruse. We don't want to lose Blaisdale."

Clint nodded and dashed up the alley to the boardwalk. His running steps could be heard. A door opened and slammed closed.

Jack listened. No other sounds came from the marshal's office. *Good,* he thought, *at least Blaisdale is still in jail.* "Do you want to go to your room or just sit at a table?" He could see she was visibly shaken. Other than the darkening bruise, she was as white as a newborn calf's belly.

In a low husky voice, she said, "Table, please."

"Get her a brandy," Jack ordered.

In seconds it arrived. He handed it to her. "Drink this."

She took it in shaking hands and lifted it to her lips. She took a sip and said, "Oh, thank you, Jack. I don't know what might have happened if you hadn't rushed back to help me. He could've killed me."

He shook his head. "I don't think so. I'm guessing he was as surprised as you. He only hit you to get you out of his way. You must've walked out right on top of him."

Something was bothering him, but he couldn't quite picture

it. It was like he was looking down a long tunnel full of fog, and the picture was at the end. He could almost make it out, but the details were obscure. *Forget it. I'll never remember if I keep straining. It will eventually come to me.*

"Gabby, do you remember anything about him, height, size, smell, anything?"

She took a few seconds to consider his question but finally shook her head. "I don't. It all happened so quickly. I am so glad he missed you."

Her statement reminded him of his hat. He pulled it from his head, and sure enough, there was a burn along the underside of the hat brim just behind his head. "He didn't completely miss, but at least I don't have to buy a new hat." He showed it to her.

Her eyes brimmed. "Oh, Jack, that was so close. What would I do if he had killed you?"

Jack gazed into her golden eyes. She was definitely a beautiful woman. He noticed above the blow to the side of her face there was a scratch along the edge of her scalp. "What did the man hit you with?" He watched her gorgeous eyes, and there was a flicker in them before she answered.

"Why, I believe it was his fist." She thought for a moment. "Yes, I'm sure it was his fist."

"Let me through. I'm a doctor. Let me through."

Doc Cook arrived at Jack's side, pushed him out of the way, and bent over Gabriella. "How are you feeling?"

Jack stepped back and said, "Gabriella, I have a few more questions, but they can wait until tomorrow. I'll see you then."

She looked past the doctor up at the marshal. "Thank you, Jack. I know you saved me. I don't know how I'll ever be able to repay you."

Doc Cook turned to look up at Jack. "Make it later tomorrow." Then almost as an afterthought. "Are you alright? You aren't hit? Nothing tore loose?"

"I'm fine, Doc. I'll make it later tomorrow." He turned for the batwing doors. Passing the bartender, he said, "Make sure no one uses that door or goes into the alley tonight or tomorrow, not until I get a chance to look at the tracks."

"But we've got garbage that needs to go out."

Jack's face turned hard. "Not until I get a chance to look at it. Understand?"

The bartender nodded. "Sure, Marshal. Whatever you say."

Jack knew the bartender was trying to do his job. He relented slightly. "I'll check it early and give you an all clear."

"Thanks, Marshal."

Jack walked back into the night. Once outside, he moved to his right and sat on a bench in front of the saloon. After a few minutes his eyes adjusted, and he carefully walked to his office, pausing to check the attorney's door. It was locked.

THOUGH HE ONLY HAD THE cot, Jack had gotten a good night's sleep. He awoke to daylight slipping into the front window of the jail. He sat up, took his watch from his vest pocket, rubbed the emerald for good luck, and opened it. Ten minutes past five. He'd get a shave from Farnsworth, maybe even a bath. He looked at himself in the mirror. His eyes were clearing up, and the cuts on his face were healing. The swelling had almost disappeared. A few more days, and he would look human again.

He put his hat on and dressed, swung the gun belt around him, fastened it, and checked both guns. Five loads in each. He had reloaded as soon as he got to the office last night.

Daylight was coming fast. He wanted to check the alleyway before anyone else had time to walk through it. Hopefully no drunks had made it out the side door last night. He quickly looked in on Blaisdale, who was still sawing logs. The man slept like he didn't have a worry in the world. Jack relocked the jail door, stepped out the front door, and locked it. He turned to face the new day.

Another beautiful one in Texas. He could smell the sweet aroma of the honeysuckle Nancy grew around her and Doc's house. Two scissortails, he had known a birder in Laredo who called them scissor-tailed flycatchers, danced in the sky above the main street, chasing and catching bugs. They were amazing birds, able to split their tails and turn on a dime and leave nine cents change. He heard several bobwhite quail calling to the early morning. He thought, *If it weren't for people, this would be great country,* and then laughed to himself. *No people would mean no me.* He headed for the alley.

Arriving at the alley between the hotel and Cherry Creek Saloon, he started making his way slowly toward the two barrels. He was looking for anything the shooter might have dropped or left as sign, a nick in a boot heel, run-over boots, anything.

He was gratified to see the bartender had stayed out of the alley. Just before reaching the side door from the saloon, he came to the barrels. This would probably be where the shooter had stood. He examined the ground as much as he could without moving around. He didn't want to inadvertently destroy something of interest. Slowly he stepped around the barrels, placing his feet carefully so as to mar nothing.

On the rim of the barrel nearest the saloon, he found something. He examined it, leaned close, and moved his head so as to allow more light against the barrel edge. Removing his bandana and holding it between thumb and forefinger, he pinched his discovery off into the cloth. Then he carefully folded it and shoved it into an inside vest pocket. Moving to the hotel side of the alley, he examined every inch of ground, working his way to the far end past the back wall and into the brush. What he found confirmed his suspicion from last night. He had finally grasped what had been floating on the edge of consciousness, but he couldn't put the why to it.

Jack walked back to the saloon's side door, examined the tracks around the door and walked in. The morning bartender looked up when the side door opened, and Jack signaled him it was alright to use the door and alleyway. The bartender waved his acknowledgment, and Jack walked out the front door and back to his office. Clint was sitting on the bench, waiting for him.

"Morning. You get the feeling there are folks around here who don't like you?"

Jack grinned. "More than once." He took the keys from where they were hanging around the butt of his revolver and tossed them to Clint. "See Blaisdale eats and gets a little exercise. I'm getting a shave and a bath, then some breakfast. Meet you in about an hour at Ma McGinty's for breakfast."

"What about Cherry Creek Saloon?"

"Not today. See you in an hour."

An hour later, cleaned and shaved, carefully around the scabs, Jack walked into a crowded Ma McGinty's. Clint had managed to grab a table and was guarding it at the back of the cafe. Jack made his way back and seated himself facing the door, his revolver loose in its holster.

A lady of indeterminate years walked up with a pot of coffee. Cups were upside down on the table. Jack turned his cup right side up. "Yes, ma'am, I could sure use some of that."

The woman poured coffee into first Jack's cup and then Clint's.

While pouring, she said, "I'm a blessed woman. It's only taken the marshal two weeks to find my poor place of business. Why would you say that is, Marshal?"

Jack, surprised at being put on the spot, said, "Mrs. McGinty, I have been a little busy."

She nodded. "I'll give you that, Marshal, but I know you've eaten several times at the Cherry Creek and also at the hotel, and I'll tell you, there isn't a better cook in all of Cherry Creek than here in Ma McGinty's."

She slapped Clint on the back of the head with the dish towel she carried stuck in her apron. "And you, Clint Paget, why haven't you been in here?" Before he could answer, she said, "I know, it's that golden-eyed hussy at the saloon."

Clint grinned at Ma. "Yes, ma'am. Guilty as charged."

She slapped him again, leaned back, and roared. "At least you are an honest man, Clint Paget. Now what can I get you boys?"

"Ma," Jack said, "I'm a hungry man. I need eggs, bacon, biscuits, and whatever kind of sweet you have back there to go with the biscuits."

Clint nodded his head. "Sounds good to me."

"Alright, boys, it'll be just a minute."

Ma had no sooner disappeared into the back than six horses pulled up out front. Clint stiffened. "Trouble. Gideon Birch."

A big man walked in with five cowhands behind him. A full head of white hair slipped from under his black hat, and he was clean shaven. Thick white eyebrows separated his forehead from the rest of his face, but it was his eyes that were striking.

Jack stared straight at the man's eyes. They were lapis blue, hard like the stone, but deep. The eyes and face of a frank man.

The talking and laughter stopped with the entry of the rancher and his men. The leader looked the room over, spotted the badges, and marched straight to Jack.

"You Sage?"

"I am, but you have me at a loss."

"Gideon Birch. I own the 7 Bar. I come to talk to you."

Jack examined each of the new arrivals. He'd been around men all of his adult life. These men weren't killers. They'd ride for the brand, they'd even kill for the brand if it came to that, but they weren't killers. They were cowhands who were rough and tumble and backed up from no one, but they didn't kill men for profit.

Jack waved his hand toward the two empty chairs. "Room for two. The rest will have to wait their turn."

Birch motioned one man to sit and turned to the others. "Hang around till a table opens, boys. Then breakfast is on me."

One of the cowhands said, "Boss, I hope you brought plenty of money 'cause that ride has worked me into quite an appetite."

Birch pulled out a chair and sat. Without turning toward the cowhand, he said, "Eat all you can, Jody, 'cause I'm gonna work it off of you before the day's over."

The other cowhands laughed. One of them said, "That's for danged sure."

Birch pointed to the older man seated next to him. "This is my foreman, Levi Eldridge."

The man removed his hat, hung it on the back of his chair, and nodded. He was smaller than Birch, with wide shoulders and narrow hips. His dark hair was salted with gray, and he wore a full mustache that drooped around the corners of his mouth almost to his jawline. He had the look of a man born to the saddle. Jack had noticed his gun before he sat. It wasn't flashy. An old forty-four Remington that had a dull sheen to the butt and sat comfortably in the holster, molded over time to its shape.

Birch leaned forward, elbows on the table. "I hear you're a paid killer come to run me out of this country."

Sage stared straight into the lapis blue eyes. "And I hear you're running the homesteaders off their land."

The two men sat silent, examining the other. Finally Birch spoke. "You don't look like most killers I've seen."

Jack responded, "After talking to Sully and a few others, I don't think you're trying to run the homesteaders off. So where does that leave us?"

Birch leaned back and crossed his arms. "It leaves me questioning my information source." He turned around and looked directly at the cowhand who had popped off.

"Boss, I swear that's what I was told. Feller told me Sage was a killer from Laredo. That's a fact."

Jack leaned out from the edge of the table so he could look

directly at the rider. "Mister, you should know your sources before you start labeling a man a killer."

The younger man bridled. "I'm just saying what I heard, truthful like. I ain't adding nothing."

Jack ignored him. To Birch he said, "I'm thinking someone didn't want us getting together. Any idea who that might be?"

The rancher's lips pursed. "Maybe, but I'm hungry." He called to the back, "Ma, you gonna take my order or let me and my men starve to death?"

24

Ma took their orders and returned to the back. The other customers relaxed, and the hum of conversation returned. Birch leaned forward again, his voice lower. "Tell me about yourself first. I want to make sure you're a man I can trust and not just another crook with a badge."

Jack started in Laredo. Gave him a brief description of what had taken place there and described his finding Bart and the happenings since his arrival, glossing over his running Korkeran out of town and his fight with Bull. He finished with, "I'm marshal here. My job is to keep peace in this town, but I'm also going to make sure those homesteaders aren't chased from legally titled land."

Birch listened and watched Jack intently. When the marshal finished, Birch nodded at Clint. "You hired a homesteader as deputy?"

Clint kept his eyes leveled on Birch.

Jack nodded. "I did. Wade Garrett recommended him, and I interviewed him. He's a good man. He'll be staying. Any other questions."

"I hear you have Blaisdale in jail."

"I do, and I aim for him to get a fair trial, after which, if a jury rules the way I suspect it will, I'll hang him. He deserves hanging. He shot a man in front of his family and then laughed at him. If I'd been there, I would've taken care of Blaisdale then, but I wasn't."

Birch shook his head. "I don't hold with killing. In fact, as much problem as they are, I don't hold with running legitimate homesteaders off their land."

Jack's eyebrows rose at Birch's remark. "That's a refreshing statement coming from a Texas rancher."

"I said if they're legitimate. Someone comes along and sees a nice piece of my land and decides to try to take it, I'll run 'em off. No questions asked. But, Marshal, you've got to understand something. I've got most of the water on my land locked up. I own it, so I'm not afraid of some squatter filing on a piece of water, building around it, and blocking my stock from getting to it. I did the filing a long time ago. Most of these ranchers are still trying to figure out what they're doing. I'm not like some of these shady outfits, or bankers."

The food arrived, and conversation stopped. After they had eaten, Jack leaned back in his chair. "That was mighty good."

Birch nodded. "This is where I mostly eat when I'm in town."

Jack stared at the white-haired rancher. "You think something's shady's going on in town?"

Birch turned to look at his foreman. Eldridge gave an almost imperceptible nod, and Birch said, "What do you know about Franklin?"

Surprised, Jack shook his head. "I know he runs the bank. I know he's on the town council and isn't too happy with me running Korkeran out of town. Other than that, I don't know much. Didn't figure it was necessary."

Birch continued, "I knew him from Austin. He was a bank teller there. The bank had a lot of money disappear. He was suspected, but even the Rangers couldn't prove anything. They let him go, and he disappeared for a while. Then, lo and behold, he shows up in my backyard and starts his own bank."

"You said there was never anything proven?"

Birch nodded. "But he left town under heavy suspicion."

Jack shook his head. "Suspicion doesn't cut it. With no proof, he could be an innocent man."

Birch shook his head. "Last label you can slap on him is an innocent. Another interesting detail, he dealt with a fella in Austin. Some say quite a bit. The man's name was Scott Mather. What do you think of that?"

That was exactly what Jack was doing, thinking. *Mather and Franklin have a history? What could that mean? Maybe Mather just told Franklin this was a good town for a bank? Even I don't believe that.* While he was thinking, Jack watched a tiny mouse run across the room and disappear into a hole in the corner.

He looked back up at Birch. "I think it's pretty suspicious, though for now, I can't figure what they might be up to. Other than Franklin being upset I shut down Korkeran and ran him out of town, he has left me alone. In fact, he was one of the folks who hired me."

Levi Eldridge leaned forward. "Marshal, you need to also keep an eye on Gabriella Campbell. She's not all she puts up to be. She's mighty pretty, but she's as shifty as any two-bit gambler and more deadly than a coral snake."

Clint shifted in his chair. "Now look here. You cain't be talking about a kind and considerate woman like Miss Gabriella. She's a mighty fine person."

Jack watched Birch and Eldridge eye his deputy. He said to Clint, "We're just listening. We'll make our own decisions when the time comes."

Birch slid his chair back and extended his hand. "Good talk, Marshal. You need any help with Mather, send a rider our way. We'll come a-running."

Jack took the strong hand. "Thanks. I'll keep it in mind."

Eldridge nodded and followed his boss. The remaining cowhands trailed behind them. Once they were gone, Jack sat back down and motioned for Clint to join him.

"What'd you think of their comments?"

Clint shook his head. "I don't know about Franklin, for some reason, he seems awful upset about Korkeran leaving town, but I'm sure Miss Gabriella doesn't deserve that type of vicious talk. She's been too kind to everyone."

The breakfast rush had ended for Ma's place. It was empty except for Jack and Clint. Jack lowered his voice. "You may have to reconsider your opinion of her."

His deputy's face turned red, and he started to reply. Jack held up his hand. "Hear me out. Those two shots last night would have gotten me if I hadn't stumbled. As it was, the second burned my hat right behind my head."

Impatiently Clint nodded his head. "Yeah, I know, but anyone—"

Jack held up his hand again. His voice hardened. "Clint, if you can't listen to me with an open mind, then you're no good to me."

Clint sat for a moment. "Alright, tell me what you have."

"Good. This morning early, I went back to examine the alley. When I was jumped last night, I got off three shots at the muzzle flash. All three shots ended up in the barrel nearest the middle of the alley. I saw where someone had thrown themselves down behind the barrels. There were blurred impressions of knees, small ones. They were blurred and dim because the knees had to press through so much material, like a bunch of petticoats under a dress."

Jack watched Clint's eyes widen in dismay, but he continued, "There's more. When she dove down to get away from my shooting, she hit her cheek on the sidewall of the barrel closest to the saloon, but she also struck her head on the edge of the barrel and scratched herself."

Jack pulled out the handkerchief from his vest pocket and

spread it out. In the center was a piece of skin with three long black hairs. Clint looked at the hairs, up at Jack, and back down at the hairs. He shook his head in disbelief. "It shore looks like her hair, but there's no way to prove it. It could belong to any woman, or man for that matter, with long hair."

Jack nodded. "I agree, except she lied to me. Last night she said she came out the side door as the shooting was taking place, and the man knocked her down. If she had come outside when the shooting was taking place, I would have seen the light from inside the saloon when she opened the door. There was no light until after the shooting when people inside thought it safe to come out. There was never any light during the shooting, only darkness, and the gun that fired sounded just like my Remingtons."

Clint immediately looked up at Jack. "Did you see a gun on her?"

Jack shook his head. "Nope, but she could've put it in a pocket, or might well have been holding it in the folds of her skirt.

"Clint, do you know if she has a .36-caliber Colt or Remington?"

Clint shook his head. "I don't, but we might check with Wade. He works on everybody's guns. If he's worked on hers, he'd know."

"Let's go talk to him."

Jack stood, tossed money on the table, and headed for the door, Clint right behind him. They hurried to Wade's Gun Shop and walked in. Wade was wiping down a Sharps. "Morning. What are you fellers doin' here?"

Jack stepped up to the counter. "We need your help. Does Gabriella Campbell own a .36-caliber anything?"

"How'd you know? Did she show it to you? She's got a Colt almost exactly like your Remingtons, except it has only a two-and-a-half-inch barrel. Stubby little rascal, but it'll sure get the job done up close. I wouldn't want to try to hit a barn door more'n about fifteen feet away."

Jack looked at Clint. His deputy looked like someone had stolen his favorite horse. "Jack, it's really hard for me to believe."

At his boss's expression, he held up one hand. "I know, I know, the proof is there, but I sure hate to believe it. What are you gonna do?"

"Come with me and find out." He turned to Wade. "You mind joining us? If you're there, she can't deny owning the Colt."

A puzzled expression on his face, Wade said, "Sure. Let me lock the place up."

Jack and Clint waited on the boardwalk while Wade put the Sharps away and locked up. The three of them threaded their way through the wagon and horse traffic as they crossed the street diagonally to get to the Cherry Creek Saloon.

Jack pushed through the batwing doors and stepped inside, Clint on his left and Wade his right. Gabriella waved to them and made her way to meet them.

She gave each of them a brilliant smile, allowing her lovely eyes to focus on each. "You're late for breakfast and early for dinner, but for you, I can make an exception."

Jack didn't smile. "Can we go to your office?"

"My, Marshal, you seem awfully serious. We can't take care of whatever's on your mind right here?"

"I believe, Miss Campbell, you'd prefer your office."

The dazzling smile disappeared. She said, "Follow me." and whirled around, stepping quickly away. The rapid click of her shoes could be heard over the din of the saloon's midmorning business. Jack stepped aside, allowing Wade and Clint to precede him. He followed, pulling the office door closed behind him. Gabriella seated herself behind her desk and folded her hands together on the surface of the shiny cypress wood.

"What can I do for you, Marshal?"

"I'd like to see your .36-caliber Colt."

She feigned surprise, looked at Clint, then back at Jack, and batted her lashes toward him. "My Colt? What in the world for?"

"Don't make me ask again, Gabriella. Get it out and do it slowly, thumb and forefinger."

"I don't understand, Jack. I thought we were friends."

"So did I, until last night. Now get the Colt, or we'll shut this place down and tear it apart until we find it."

Her face hardened, and she glared at Jack, eyes narrowed, but she recovered quickly and forced a smile to her lips. "Whatever you like, Marshal." She leaned to her right, pulled the top right drawer open, and reached inside.

Jack's Remington seemed to leap into his hand, muzzle pointed straight at her. "Thumb and forefinger, *Gabby*."

She lifted the Colt from the drawer with her thumb and forefinger gripping the cylinder. Her hand showed a light tremor.

"Now lay it on your desk and move your hands away."

"I'm not going to shoot you, Jack." She tried to make it sound light and sweet, but the words fell into the silence like shards of ice.

Jack holstered his revolver and picked up the Colt, handing it to Wade. "Can you tell how long it's been since it was fired?"

As he was reaching for it, Wade said, "If it hasn't been cleaned, I can get a pretty good idea." He took it and wiped his fingers along the front edge of the five loaded chambers. "I can tell you it hasn't been fired recently." His fingers came away with a light greasy film, and he held them up, his head shaking. "There ain't no burned powder on this here weapon. It ain't been fired, and that's a fact."

Jack was puzzled. *She has the right caliber,* he thought. *I found her tracks outside. There was no light from the door until the shooting was over. It has to be her.*

She leaned toward Jack, her slim forearms on her desk, and her face honest and sincere, pleading for him to understand. "I would never shoot at you, Jack. You're a friend. I don't know why you would think I'd do something like that."

Clint turned to Jack. "Maybe you made a mistake. It happens to all of us. She sure looks innocent to me."

Gabriella smiled at Clint. "Oh, thank you. It's so good to have trusting friends."

Jack leaned back in his chair. The pressure of his additional Remington behind his back sent a quick burst of pain from his injuries. He leaped up. "Wait a minute. Get away from your desk."

Gabriella's eyes were wide. "What? Don't hurt me, Jack." She held up her hands in front of her face.

He charged around her desk and yanked her up and out of the chair, thrusting her toward Wade. "Keep an eye on her." Then he bent over and started going through the other desk drawers. The top left, nothing. The bottom left, nothing. The only remaining drawer was the bottom right.

Gabriella yelled at him, "You have no right to treat me like this. Stay out of my personal things!"

He yanked open the bottom right drawer. A bottle of wine stood in the deep drawer, beside it a wineglass. Nothing there but a pile of rags at the back of the drawer. He reached in and yanked the rags out.

There it lay. The matching .36-caliber Colt Police. He picked it up, bumping the wineglass. It tinkled in the shocked silence. Jack held the revolver sideways to his nose. The smell of burned powder was strong. He checked the chambers. Two were empty and black. Still holding the weapon, he moved away from the desk and pointed to the chair. "Sit down."

Head down, Gabriella moved behind her desk and sat. Jack handed the revolver to Wade. "Now what do you say?"

The gunsmith checked it. Stunned, his eyes remained on Gabriella. "Fired within the past twenty-four hours."

Jack knew the answer, but asked anyway. "How many chambers?"

"Two. Two shots." Wade held on to the weapon.

Jack looked at Gabriella. "Why did you do it?"

Her eyes wide, she said, "Do what, Jack?"

"Take a shot at me, a marshal. You know what that'll get you. You'll be spending your next ten to twenty years behind bars in Huntsville." He nodded toward the door. "Get up. I'm taking you to jail."

Gabriella shook her head. "Isn't there any way I can persuade you not to? If I go to prison for twenty years, I'll be old and wrinkled by the time I get out. No man will want me. My life will be over."

"Your life was over when you decided to pull that trigger. Now get up and walk out of here, or I'll drag you out."

The golden, beautiful eyes Jack had admired were wide with fear and pleading. "Please, Jack, Clint, isn't there anything I can do to persuade you to let me go? Just let me go. Give me a horse, and I'll ride out of here right now. You can have my place and money." She pointed to her office safe. "I have thousands of dollars in there. It's all yours. Do for me what you did for Korkeran. Give me three thousand dollars and let me go."

Jack gave a hard quick shake of his head. "Korkeran didn't try to kill me. You did." He reached out his long arm and started for her. "I said let's go." His big hand closed around her small upper arm.

She cried out. "I can tell you something. Something you don't know. Please."

Jack stopped. "It would have to be good."

In a small little-girl voice, she said, "It is." She hesitated only for a moment. "My real name's Grace Mather."

Aghast, Jack stared back at her. "Mather?"

She nodded and said nothing.

Jack turned to Clint. "Go get Doc Cook. I want him to be a witness."

Tears started flowing down Grace's cheeks. "Please, not Dr. Cook. He's such a nice man, and he likes me."

Clint had made it to the door. He stopped, his hand on the latch, and turned toward her. His face was grim. "I liked you, too, Gab . . . Grace."

She turned sad eyes toward him. "I know, Clint. I like you, too."

He turned his back on her and charged from the room, slamming the door behind him. The three of them waited in silence. Jack watched the tears flow down Grace's cheeks. There was no sobbing, no sound, just tears down those lovely cheeks. Dismayed, Jack thought, *She tried to kill me. That's the first time a woman has ever tried to kill me.* He mulled it over for a few minutes and then put it from his mind. They continued to wait.

The door opened, and Clint walked in, followed by Doc Cook. There were two chairs in the room. Jack stepped into the saloon and grabbed two more, closing the door behind him. The men sat.

Dr. Cook looked at the tearstained face of Grace and then at Jack. "Jack, what's going on here? Why am I here? Is someone hurt?"

Jack shook his head and said to Grace, "Tell him."

Eyes pleading, she gazed back at Jack. "Where do you want me to begin?"

"How about with what happened last night and your name."

Still puzzled, the doctor looked around the room, eyes questioning. The men said nothing. Grace was silent.

Jack leaned forward, his hands on his knees. "Tell him right now, or I'm taking you in, your choice."

She turned to the doctor. "My name isn't Gabriella Campbell. It's Grace Mather."

The doc's eyes grew large. He looked at Jack, who just pointed back to Grace. The doc shook his head. "Grace Mather? I don't understand. Are you married to Scott Mather?"

It was Grace's turn to shake her head. "No, Alex, I'm his sister."

"I still don't understand."

Jack was getting mad. He wanted answers, and this was drawing out too long. He stood. "That's it. If you're not going to talk, I'm taking you to jail. You can tell your story to the judge in a few days. He's going to have a busy day."

She spit out quickly, her eyes locked with the doctor's, "I shot at Jack last night. I was desperate. Our plan was in jeopardy of falling apart, all because of an inquisitive marshal. I didn't want to. I like Jack, but I had to do it. We have worked so hard, and we are so close." She turned her eyes on Jack. "But you kept asking questions." She balled her hands into tiny fists and yelled at him, "Why couldn't you leave well enough alone?"

The door was jerked open by the bartender, and Reno Hawk's voice filled the room. "I know you're in there, Sage. Come out and take your medicine!"

Jack rose, surprised but frustrated from not yet getting the full story from Grace. He looked at Clint. "Keep an eye on her. I'll be right back." He stepped from the office into the saloon.

Hawk was standing at the bar. He had ordered a drink, and as Jack moved into sight, he picked it up, brought it to his lips, and tossed it back. He slammed the glass back on the bar. "Give me another. I'll drink it after I'm finished the marshal."

25

The sound of scraping and falling chairs filled the saloon as men jumped to get out of the way of the gunfighter and the marshal. No one wanted to be near the line of fire. They all knew that too often stray bullets found bystanders. Several made a dash toward both the side and front doors, leaving the batwings swinging and the side door open. Dust rose from the floor and drifted, sparkling through the shafts of light streaming above the batwing doors.

Jack could feel the cold calm settle over him. He had no desire to kill Hawk, but he would not back down. He was the law. "Mather send you?"

"Ain't nobody sends me, Sage. Fact is, Mather told everyone to leave you, the town, and the sodbusters be. Said he has a big surprise coming." Hawk's lips pulled back, showing even white teeth, what must have been a grin in his mind. "But I thought I'd bring *you* a real special surprise."

"I don't have any paper on you, Hawk. You're free to ride out of here. I'll forget this, and we can call it quits. You called me. People will know. That'll make us even."

Hawk's laugh sounded like that of a mad coyote, harsh, high, and sharp. "We'll be even when you're beggin' on the floor with a bullet in your gut, not before."

I gave him a chance, Jack thought. *If he's going to go through with it, I might as well get him riled.* "You have a nice walk in the country, Hawk? How are your feet feeling? I figure Doc Cook must be pretty good if you're up and around this soon."

"Keep talkin', big man. I told you not to make us walk. You went too far. Now I'm gonna show you what happens to folks who don't listen."

Hawk's hand moved, and Jack drew. He didn't know Hawk, had never heard of him, but he knew someday there would be someone faster than him. He didn't think today was the day.

It was much like being outside his body watching the action. He didn't feel any fear or even excitement. He just felt steely cold. He watched Hawk's forty-four clear his holster. He saw the gunman thrust the weapon toward him as the muzzle was swinging up, and thought, *Bad move, Hawk. You should rotate at the hip. That'll cost you time.*

Jack's Remington reverberated against the saloon walls. His first shot struck Hawk dead center in the chest.

Jack's big hands almost swallowed the Remingtons. The size of his hands made a fast follow-up shot possible. His thumb wrapped around the hammer even as it fell, struck the cap, and ignited the powder. He drew the hammer back so fast it was a blur and followed with his second shot. The two could be covered by a silver dollar. Jack saw the surprise in the gunman's eyes, followed almost immediately with the light going out. He was dead before the second ball hit him.

Hawk's first and only shot struck a table leg behind Jack before burying itself in the saloon's floor. He had felt it burn along the inside of his left knee as it flew past. A quick jolt of relief flooded his body. Good thing the shot hadn't been higher, but it was quickly gone from his mind as he watched Hawk for signs of life. There was none. He did a border shift and yanked the unfired Remington from behind his back with his right hand and scanned the saloon. There were no guns being drawn, only the wide eyes of those behind tables they had pulled over for protection.

"It's over," he said. "Someone get Farnsworth. Tell him he's got more business." He looked at each man in the room. "Clint will be taking statements from everyone here. Don't leave before he talks to you."

The bartender placed a sarsaparilla on the bar. "Drink up, Marshal. It was a good shoot."

"Thanks, Tom," Jack said, and lifted the glass to his mouth.

He heard the batwings swing and a demanding voice. "What's going on here?"

Jack turned back to see a man of average height, older, with thinning white hair pushing out from under his wide black Stetson. He was a little paunchy, dressed in a suit of black broadcloth. Gripped in both hands and ready to use was a ten-gauge double-barreled shotgun.

Jack said, "I'm Marshal Jack Sage. Who are you?"

"I'm Judge Nagle." He stepped past Hawk's body, took out a pair of spectacles and slipped the hooks over his ears, one at a time. After carefully laying the shotgun across the bar, he leaned over to examine the dead man. "Well, well," he said softly. He reached into a vest pocket and pulled out a silver dollar and laid it on the man's chest. "Um-huh." While still bent over, he picked it up and dropped it back into the same pocket.

The judge continued to carefully study Hawk's face. Satisfied, he rose, removed the spectacles, one side at a time, folded them, and dropped them into an inside coat pocket. He turned to Jack. "You know who you just killed?" Without waiting, he continued, "That man is Reno Hawk. You made yourself a little money there, Marshal. I've got a new circular in my saddlebags from Arkansas, offering a two-thousand-dollar reward, dead or alive. Seems he killed himself a wealthy man in Little Rock. The family will be pleased to know you've finished off this killer. I understand you have someone awaiting trial."

"You're early, Judge, but I'm glad you're here. We may have more than one."

The judge turned to the bartender. "Whiskey. You know what I drink, Tom." Then he turned back to Jack and smiled. "The more the merrier as long as I'm out of here in three days. There's more folks waiting on me down the trail."

"If you'll excuse me, Judge, I'm interviewing one of them in the back office."

"You go right ahead. I'll finish my drink and head over to the hotel. I can get set up in the hotel lobby, and we can start this afternoon."

Jack had started to turn toward the office, but stopped. "Judge, you think we could start in the morning? This situation is coming together even as we're speaking, and I don't have all the principals in custody."

Judge Nagle frowned. "Marshal, I'm on a tight schedule. I need to be out of here no later than Saturday. Can you make that work if we start in the morning?"

Jack nodded. "I'll make it work. Now I've got to get back to it." He turned away from the judge and headed to Grace's office.

"The judge is early," Clint said as Jack walked back in.

"Yeah, we're going to have to work fast."

Jack looked at Grace Mather. Her face was bone white. She looked like she might pass out at any moment. Her eyes were wide and glued on him. "You killed Reno Hawk." It was a statement not a question. A statement of surprise. "I saw him shoot another gunfighter down in the streets of Austin. He was fast."

Jack knew that if looks could kill, those once lovely eyes would have him dead on the floor. "Alright, Mather, I want to know everything. You still have a chance to get out of prison while you're young. But if you sit there and clam up, I'll do my best to ensure you never see the light of day again."

She kept her eyes locked on Jack, refusing to look at either Dr. Cook or Clint, and began. She told them the whole story, and Jack was amazed at their plan. They hadn't cared who might get hurt. Greed was their driving force.

When she finished, there was silence in the room. It was hard for Jack to believe the cold and methodical nature of the woman who sat before him. Finally, he stood and said to Clint, "Can I trust you to keep her here?"

Clint gave him a slow nod. "Oh yeah, this woman had me fooled right from the beginning, but I guarantee she'll be sitting right there when you get back."

"Good, we shouldn't take long. Then we'll move her to the jail. That's where she belongs, with the rest of her crowd.

"Doc? Would you go get what's left of the town council and bring them all to the bank? Also Belinda, I think she'll especially want to be there."

Jack, Wade, and Dr. Cook left the Cherry Creek Saloon. Dr. Cook headed up the street toward Carmen's. Jack and Wade turned toward the bank. Passing his office, Jack stopped. Wade pulled up and looked at him.

"Wade, I need you as a deputy." When the man started to object, Jack held up his hand. "Hear me out. It won't last long, just until Judge Nagle tries these folks and we can get 'em moved to prison. The judge says he's got to be out of here no later than Saturday, so I'd say the end of next week."

"Can I still work? I've got customers."

"Sure. Clint and I will need you to spell us, but that's it. Maybe help out if we have a problem with Mather's people."

"Alright, just until they're out of here."

"Fine, raise your right hand."

Wade raised his hand.

"You gonna help me enforce the law?"

"Yep."

"Good. Put your hand down. You're a deputy."

They crossed the alley to the bank. As Jack reached for the door, Wade grinned and asked, "I don't get a badge?"

"I don't have any more badges. You want mine?"

"Not on your life."

The two men stepped inside the bank. This was only the second time Jack had been inside this one, but they all looked the same. Eight feet from the front door, there was a half-wall erected. The wall extended across the width of the room. An eight-inch header ran across three-quarters of the length, and set between the low wall and header were vertical iron bars. There were two cutouts, each had Cashier across the top just below the header in large letters. An additional set of shorter vertical bars were set in the cutouts. They stopped about two feet above a counter that extended in front of and behind the wall. The counter provided a writing and counting area for the cashier and, on the entrance side, for the customer.

At the open end of the room, behind the wall, were offices. The only access to the offices was through a swinging door built into the low wall. It was through this door that Jack strode, followed by Wade.

"Just a minute," a cashier called. "Marshal, you can't be back here unless you have an appointment with Mr. Franklin."

"I do."

Jack tried the latch to Franklin's office door, locked. He turned to the cashier. "Is he in?"

"Yes, but—"

Jack made a short jab with his shoulder. The lock gave way, and he pushed the door open. Inside, Franklin had his safe open and was filling saddlebags with gold and bills. He was caught with one hand inside the bags and the other gripping the edge of the desk. Surprise and fear covered his flushed face.

Jack looked at the bags and then at Franklin. "Going somewhere?"

Franklin took a moment, gathered himself, and shouted,

"What do you mean crashing into my office. You are fired. Do you hear me? You are fired as of right now. Hand over your badge."

Jack kept his eyes on Franklin. "We've just spent an interesting couple of hours with Grace Mather."

At Jack's mentioning the name, Franklin blanched. His bluster disappeared like fog burned off by a summer sun, and the man seemed to wither into his overstuffed chair. "How much did she tell you?"

"What do you think? She told us her real name and that she's Scott Mather's sister, plus a whole lot more. Your banking days are over. The question now is whether you're going to prison or the hangman's noose."

"No, that's not fair. It's all their fault. It was their idea, not mine. I wasn't going to go along with them, but they threatened to kill me. I had to."

"Whoa up, Franklin." Jack heard the front door open. "I want plenty of witnesses for your confession. I thought the town council might be suitable. Don't you?"

Franklin watched the people squeeze into his office. Wade slid one of the extra chairs over for Belinda, who sat directly across the desk from Franklin. Jack watched the young woman. She was a beauty, and she was smart.

When everyone was in, Jack said, "Tell it from the beginning. Grace has told us everything, so we'll see how well your story matches. I have one question before you start. Was Korkeran involved in your scheme?"

Franklin shook his head. "No. Korkeran was just a good businessman. He made a lot of money, and I kept his books for him."

Jack interrupted. "I can read between the lines on that statement. You were skimming profits."

Franklin looked around the room, desperate to find a friendly face. There was none. Angry stares greeted him.

"Yes, I diverted some of his profits. He trusted me. It was easy for me to do."

"Alright," Jack said. "Lay it out. Your associates haven't heard the story."

Franklin cleared his throat and began. "We met in Austin. I met Grace Mather first. She was working as a dance hall girl." He paused to emphasize his meaning.

"We understand your implied meaning, Franklin. Go on."

"She had opened a savings account. I was quite impressed with the amount she was depositing. Her brother was a gambler, and he was putting his money with hers." He paused again for emphasis and said, "In her account."

Jack leaned across the table with both of his big hands flat on the surface and his face inches away from Franklin. "We know how smart Grace Mather is, Franklin. I'm not going to tell you again. Tell your side of this and get it done."

Joseph Franklin was sweating profusely. He pulled out a handkerchief and wiped his face. Clutching the handkerchief tight in his left hand, he continued, "I met Scott Mather one day when the two of them came in. He was talking about getting a ranch out west and building it into the biggest ranch in Texas, but they were having problems. He thought someone might be onto his cheating, and they needed to get their money out of the bank. You know, just in case they had to leave suddenly."

Everyone nodded impatiently.

He wiped his face again, leaned back in his chair, and took several deep breaths. He continued, "I too saw the handwriting on the wall as far as my tenure with the bank in Austin."

The attorney, Val Jessup, spoke up. "You mean you had been embezzling money from the bank, and they were about to catch you."

The banker looked down at the handkerchief in his hand. "Yes."

Jessup asked, "How much?"

"Twenty-five thousand dollars."

There were several whistles around the room.

"When did you throw in with the Mathers?" Jack asked.

"A couple of days after that meeting. Over a relatively short time, they had been able to save five thousand dollars. Mather wanted a ranch, and I had a plan."

Jack noted that Franklin couldn't help but let pride take over. If he had any sense at all, he would be laying it all at the feet of the Mathers, but instead he was dead set on showing how smart he was.

"I had heard about this Cherry Creek country. A lot of wild cattle and plenty of water. There was a problem with the land grants the Mexicans had, but I knew people. During tight times they have to borrow money, and they knew very little English. I loaned them money on short terms, and when they couldn't pay it back, the land was mine." He shrugged. "Easy."

It happened so fast, no one could stop her. Belinda leaped to her feet and, leaning across the desk, slapped Franklin with every ounce of strength her petite, but strong, body could muster. It almost knocked him out of his chair. She shouted in Spanish, "You are a monster. Hell will be waiting for you."

Wade grabbed her by both arms. She struggled momentarily, then stopped. She looked around at the others watching her. "I am sorry. It is just that my people have been hurt, and some have died because of this man."

"Ma'am," Jack said, "I imagine everyone in here is sorry for what has happened to your people at the hands of this man. But I've got to tell you. You can stay in here if you remain calm, but you can't be having those kinds of outbursts."

"Yes, I will be fine."

Jack nodded to Franklin. "Go ahead."

Franklin's already red face was glowing with Belinda's handprint. He continued to rub it. "You've got to get her out of here. There's no telling what she might do. I'm not safe."

Jack's day had been hard. He'd killed a man today, and he was tired of trying to coax subjects into talking. He walked over to

Franklin and knelt down beside him. Leaning close to the man's ear, he whispered, "Listen real good, you piece of dirt, if you don't tell me everything, I'm going to personally take you to the Mexican folks and let them have their own court just for you. Nod your head if you understand and will tell everything."

Jack stood, towering over the man, and watched Franklin's head bob up and down.

race came out first. She bought the building and started a saloon. She made sure she brought a faro table. Cowhands love that game even though they rarely win. She was profitable immediately. Next, I came out as if I were scouting the area for a new bank. Every town wants a bank. I explained my wife had died and I was starting a new life. I was welcomed with open arms. Business boomed."

Franklin fidgeted in his chair, glancing up at the big marshal, who towered over him. He cleared his throat and continued, "Then Scott arrived with several riders he had picked up on the way, gunfighters of course. One of them was Blaisdale. He was unique. He knew cattle, made a big difference. Scott needed money right away to pay the men, but we had it, so we still had no problem. He bought out one of the ranchers here, after a little persuasion, and we were in business. Hired a trail boss last year to take a herd north. It was a big herd, and we lost a few, but they got there with three thousand head. After paying off the hands and all of the expenses, we netted twenty dollars a head, which came out to sixty thousand dollars of pure profit."

Jack shook his head. "Why didn't the three of you stick to cattle and become legitimate? You had the opportunity."

"No, we didn't," Franklin said. "We wanted to be the biggest ranch in Texas. To put together big herds, we needed a lot of land, a lot of *water*. The Mexicans had the grants, and homesteaders were filing on the open land faster than we could. So I made short loans to the Mexicans, and Scott ran off the homesteaders. It was working, too"—Franklin glared at Jack—"until you came into town. Scott could depend on Blaisdale to kill anyone he wanted him to, including every marshal we've had, except the ones who ran with their tail between their legs."

Jack rubbed his chin. "But there was always Gideon Birch. He wasn't going to deal with you. What were your plans for him?"

For the first time, a smile played around the corners of Franklin's lips. "He drove a herd to market last year just like we did. Only he wasn't so lucky. He started late, got caught up behind other herds. The grass turned brown, and most of the water dried up. Add the Indians on top of that, and he lost every head of cattle he started with. He's hurting financially. I tried to give him a loan, but he ran me off his ranch. He's banking out of Waco. I know he's had to let some men go. It's only a matter of time before I was going to be able to buy him out. I won't now, but he'll still go under. Pity, all that land."

Jack shoved his hat to the back of his head. "Franklin, I've got one more question. If everything was working so well, why did you hire me?"

The banker lowered his head and shook it. "You have no idea how much I wish we hadn't, but you showed up when we needed a marshal. Blaisdale had just killed Marshal Winfreid. If we didn't get one soon, we would have had Texas Rangers here. You were handy. You were a stranger. How was I to know you had just cleaned up Laredo?" He put his head in his hands and stared at the desk, his voice low. "The worst decision I've ever made."

Jack had noticed Jessup, the attorney, writing continuously while Franklin talked. "What are you writing, Mr. Jessup?"

"Marshal, I've written, word for word, a copy of Franklin's statement. All you have to do is have him sign and date it, and it's yours. You can give it to Judge Nagle."

"Great idea. Slide it across the desk. Franklin, sign it and date it."

"Can I read it?"

"Sure," Jack said, "help yourself, and then sign and date it."

Jessup slid the pad across to Franklin. "Initial each page, then sign the last."

Jack turned to the others. "Alright, folks, you've gotten an earful. Franklin, along with Grace Mather, will be going away for a long time. Depending on what Judge Nagle thinks, Scott Mather may get his neck stretched right along with Blaisdale. The trials will start tomorrow, beginning with Blaisdale. Thank you for being witnesses. You'll probably be asked to testify. You folks have a good evening."

Belinda rose and turned to Jack. "Thank you, Jack. I can't tell you how much I appreciate you helping my people. Stop by my cantina anytime." She gave him a subdued smile. "I will always have grape juice available, and maybe, if you stay around, something a little more exciting."

Jack grinned and touched his hat. "Thanks. I just might take you up on it."

Everyone left the bank except Jack, Wade, Jessup, and Franklin. Jack motioned for Jessup to stay. He closed the office door. "How much is left in the Korkeran account?"

Jessup didn't even glance at Franklin. "The final total came to thirty-two thousand two hundred and a few cents. That includes the money in his account and what came out of his safe."

Franklin nodded, but no one cared.

"That money is confiscated money for the city to do with as it sees fit, right?"

Jessup nodded slowly. "I suppose so."

"I've got a couple of suggestions. First, I need to know how much total debt the homesteaders and the Mexicans are carrying on those short-term notes."

Jessup said, "Ask the cashier. He knows what's on the books."

Jack opened the door, called the cashier, and explained what he wanted. Moments later the cashier was back with a slip of paper. He handed it to Jack, who looked at it and handed it to Jessup.

Jessup said, "Five thousand three hundred and fifty dollars. So what do you want to do? Pay this off?"

Jack shook his head. "No, I'm just the marshal of this town. I suggest the town council get together and figure out how they can help those folks. Extend the loans, do whatever they think is right, but come up with something to make up for Franklin's theft. By the way, you're going to need some more town council members. I'd suggest Belinda and Brian Sullivan. I think they're both outstanding people. I'd add Sully Johnson, but he'd have nothing to do with it. He doesn't have a very high opinion of government of any size."

"But what about the bank?" Jessup asked.

"Like I said, I'm just the marshal, but, for now, I appoint you to be in charge of it until another arrangement can be made." Jack turned to Franklin. "Stand up."

Jessup picked up the pad, tore the pages of Franklin's testimony out of it, and handed them to Jack. He took them in his left hand and pointed to the door. "Move it, Franklin. It's time you enjoyed a bed compliments of the town."

Both cashiers stood silent as the bank owner was pushed out the front door and toward the jail. Jack heard Jessup say, "Alright, new day, let's get busy." People in the street stopped and stared at the banker who had held so much control over many of their lives. Franklin gazed straight ahead, his face still red.

Jack gave Wade the keys. "Open the office. We'll drop Franklin off and head back to the saloon. Blaisdale's going to have more company than he ever thought possible."

They dropped Franklin in the cell next to Blaisdale's. The killer had jumped to his feet and stared, silent, watching as they pushed the banker past the steel door and locked it. Franklin stumbled to the bunk and sat, staring at the floor. Jack and Wade said nothing, moving quickly out of the jail.

The saloon was packed, but no gambling was taking place. There was no laughter, no yelling when Jack and Wade walked through the door. In fact, what talking there was ceased the moment they were recognized. A voice from the back yelled out, "Is it true, Marshal? Are you gonna arrest Miss Gabriella?"

Jack stopped. His eyes searched the back until they found the man who had spoken. Jack nodded at him. "That's a fact. Only you might ought to start calling her by her real name, Grace, Grace Mather."

The room broke into a loud buzz, everyone talking over one another. Jack held up his long arms. "If you boys are interested in seeing and hearing what's been going on in your town, the trials will be starting tomorrow. Those who would like to serve on the jury should be at the hotel early for jury selection. Those on trial will be Flint Blaisdale, Grace Mather, Joseph Franklin, and Scott Mather. At least those four, and maybe more."

The room exploded with noise at the mention of Franklin. Somebody yelled, "You ain't got Scott Mather yet, do you, Marshal?"

Jack shook his head. "No, we don't, but we'll get him before the judge leaves." Jack marched on to the office and let himself in. Wade followed. Moments after Wade closed the door, someone was pounding on it. Jack motioned to it, and Wade pulled the door open. It was Bart.

"What's going on? Someone said you had arrested Gabriella . . ." He saw the saloon owner's dejected tear-streaked face. "Jack, what are you doing?"

"With the help of Clint and Wade and Dr. Cook and more, I am cleaning up your town."

Bart, originally stunned, came to his senses. He yanked a pad and a pencil from inside his vest. "Is it true you have also arrested Joseph Franklin, esteemed banker of Cherry Creek?"

Jack grinned at Bart. "I don't know how esteemed he's going to be when the folks of this town find out what he's been doing, but yes, he has been arrested."

Bart started another question, and Jack held his hand up. "It's been a hard day, Bart, and we still have a lot to do. Wade, would you buy Bart a drink and fill him in on all the happenings. When you're through, meet us at the office."

"Sure, boss."

Jack looked at Grace. "Stand up. You're going to jail."

She stood and glared at Jack. "Scott is still out there. He will break me out and see you dead in the process."

"Yes, ma'am," Jack said, "I'm counting on it."

He and Clint walked Grace through her saloon. She stopped and turned to the bartender. "Tom, keep operating. I'll be back soon."

Jack took her arm and pulled her forward while at the same time he said, "Tom, she's right on one count. Keep operating, but she ain't coming back. She'll be sitting in Huntsville for at least ten and maybe twenty years."

He led her through the batwing doors, Clint following. They turned right, past the alley where she had attempted to kill Jack, and past Jessup's office. Jack tossed the keys back to Wade. "Unlock it, and then the jail. We'll put her in the remaining cell."

Though the Texas summer sun was hot, a crowd had gathered in front of the marshal's office. The people flowed into the street, almost blocking it. "Go ahead and take her in," Jack said.

Clint unlocked the front door of the office, grasped Grace's upper arm, and pulled her in. He closed the door.

Jack turned to the crowd. A voice called, "What's going on,

Marshal?" The crowd created a substantial commotion difficult to talk over. Jack barely heard the man's question. He held up his hands.

"Quiet down, folks." The rumble slowly died. "That's better. I know you're curious."

Somebody yelled, "You've got our banker in there. What about our money?"

"Just hold on," Jack replied, "and I'll explain everything. First, relax about your money. Yes, Franklin is in jail, but your money is safe."

The same voice called again, "Are we going to lose our bank?"

This time Jack recognized the questioner. It was the husband of one of the families who lived in town. "Reese, hold up on the questions. I'll probably answer all of them if you'll just give me a minute."

The man, his brow knitted in worry, nodded.

"Alright, the town council will be taking over the bank for now. The judge will give us a ruling over the next couple of days, but I think that'll be fine until we locate someone to manage or buy the bank. They'll be looking at the loans Franklin has made and the repossessions. There might be some changes made."

The people started buzzing again. Jack raised his hands. When they quieted down, he continued, "We've also arrested Gabriella Campbell for the attempted murder of an officer of the law. She's the one who tried to shoot me last night."

The buzz started again. Jack waited until everyone quieted. "Her real name isn't Gabriella Campbell. It's Grace Mather. She's Scott Mather's sister."

This time bedlam broke out. Jack waited, and it didn't seem to be dying. He turned to go inside. Everyone started quieting down, and someone else yelled, "What about Blaisdale and Tobias Carter?"

With the question, silence returned. Jack looked at the sea of faces. "The death of Tobias Carter is the reason I hired on here. I

wanted his murderer and the instigator brought to justice. Blaisdale will be tried tomorrow, and if he's found guilty, and the judge
rules like I think he will, I'll see to his hanging the next morning."

Reese asked another question. "Marshal, Blaisdale was
working for Scott Mather. You gonna hang Mather, too?"

"If the court finds him guilty, I'll subject him to whatever is
ordered by the court. That's the best I can tell you. I will tell you,
he'll be tried before the judge leaves, and he's leaving Saturday."

"That ain't but three days, Marshal."

"You're right, Reese." Jack looked around. "Any more
questions?"

A feminine voice spoke from the crowd. "Thank you for
cleaning up our town, Marshal."

Jack nodded to the lady and touched his hat. "Ma'am, it hasn't
just been me. Several good citizens have come to my assistance,
but I thank you. One more thing. I announced it in the Cherry
Creek Saloon, but everyone here also needs to know. The trials
start tomorrow. If you'd like to be on the jury, show up early." He
nodded, waved to the crowd, and stepped through the office door.

Clint had pulled a chair up next to his desk. He had reversed
it and was sitting with his arms on the back. The chair was positioned so he could watch out the front window. "Whoo-we, I'm
glad you're the marshal. That'd be more talkin' than I've done in
the past year."

Jack grinned at his deputy, shoved his hat to the back of his
head with his right forefinger, and sat in his chair behind the
desk. "Comes with the job. Maybe next time, I'll let you do the
talking."

Clint's eyes widened, and his head shook. "No, sir. I'd rather
face a passel of Comanches than stand out there and talk to all
them folks."

The door opened. Wade and Bart walked in.

Jack looked at Bart. "You get all the information you need for
your paper?"

Bart shook his head. He was concentrating on something he had written on his pad. He slashed his pencil across an entry and jotted something in its place, then looked up. "You know as soon as Mather finds out, he's going to be on his way here."

Jack said nothing, only nodded.

Bart watched him. The big clock on the wall ticked. Time slowly slipped by. The office was quiet. A dog could be heard barking, and a mockingbird continuously trilled its tunes while sitting on the eave of the office.

Bart spoke again. "You expect him here, don't you."

Jack nodded. "Let's just say it'll make it easier if he comes to us rather than if we have to go after him."

"So you expect him to try to rescue his sister."

"I'd expect that from a normal person. Maybe that's what he has in mind."

"What else do you think he might have in mind?"

"Of course, I can't read his mind, but there is the old adage, dead men tell no tales."

Bart had stopped writing. He leaned forward, his forehead wrinkled. "You don't think he'd try to kill his sister, do you?"

Jack shook his head. "I don't really know, but what if he was planning on killing all three witnesses against him? That would pretty much leave him as an innocent rancher just trying to defend himself against encroachers."

Clint's chin had been resting on his forearms on the back of his chair. He rose and looked at Jack. "I ain't no encroacher. I filed on my property fair and square. I prove it out, and it's mine."

Jack turned to his deputy. "Of course you did. But you've ridden for ranches. How did they feel about homesteaders?"

Clint thought for a moment. "Yeah, I guess from the free-range standpoint, they might see me as an encroacher, but they'd be dead wrong."

"But if Mather's jury was made up of ranchers and ranch hands, how do you think they'd rule?"

Clint nodded. "Yep, they'd probably set him on the road to freedom."

"Exactly," Bart said. "So his goal will be to kill everyone and to not be tried here, but where the jury panel will be made up of ranchers and ranch hands."

"Unfortunately for him, I don't think Judge Nagle will allow a change of venue. If we can catch him and get him tried within the next few days, he'll be up the creek." Jack looked pointedly at Bart's shoulder. "How's your shoulder feeling?"

Bart moved it around and swung his arm. "Pretty good. Still some soreness, but not bad. Why?"

"You think you can use a rifle?"

"Certainly. Rifle or handgun, I wouldn't care. I'd be fine. Why?"

"How would you like to be a deputy?"

"Sure."

Jack swore him in. "I'd like to have a couple more. I'm thinking maybe Pierce, Jessup and Sully Johnson." He looked around the room. "Anybody have a problem with those three?"

Clint and Wade shook their heads, but Bart said, "You don't think Mr. Johnson might be a little old?"

"No, I think Sully would surprise anyone who thought he might be past his prime. He's sharp as a tack, and I just imagine he can outshoot most people in this town. He's also a man who won't have a problem pulling the trigger should he have to."

"So what's the plan?" Wade asked.

Jack leaned forward. "Here's what I'm thinking. Mather's getting a double dose of bad news. The first is that the judge is early. He wasn't supposed to be here until next month. He hasn't planned for that.

"Next, he's going to find out Franklin and his sister have been arrested. That pile of information is going to affect him at least two ways. He'll have to decide if he needs to light out and disappear. If he decides on that, he'll have to forget most of his money.

I figure they decided to keep it in the bank, and if he leaves his money, he'll have to leave his sister. So I figure he'll be coming into town as soon as he hears about what's going on. The only other question remaining is whether he plans to kill everyone and take his money, or take his money and rescue his sister."

No one responded. Jack wondered, *How do I play this? I know he's going to try to hit the bank. He wants his money, but will he try to rescue or kill everyone in the jail? That's the question.* He considered it a little longer, then said, "Any ideas?"

Bart said, "I can't imagine he would kill his sister. That would take a cold individual."

Jack nodded. "That's true, but when I met him and persuaded him to contribute to Mrs. Carter, he kept his cool. For a moment, I could see the anger, but he controlled it. Maybe he can exercise the same control over his feelings for his sister." He paused. "Does anyone know of a place in town where we could keep the prisoners for tonight? I expect Mather to hit us tonight, before Blaisdale or Grace have a chance to take the stand tomorrow."

Wade spoke up when no one else answered. "I have a possible place. It would mean all three of them would have to be together. There's not a lot of room, but there's enough for them and at least two guards. It's where I keep all my new weapons, also powder and lead and other ammunition."

"Alright," Jack said, "can you move your other weapons out of there? I don't care about the powder and lead, as long as there's nothing for them to fire it in, we'll be fine."

"Sure. I can move them into my living quarters."

"Bart, can you guard them, along with Sully?"

"If that's what you want."

Jack could tell he was disappointed, but someone had to do it. "Good, I'll get Sully to join you." He turned to Wade. "Can you make sure he's armed with something other than that single-barrel shotgun?" He tossed a thumb toward the gun rack. "Any of these rifles or shotguns will be fine."

Wade nodded his assent.

"Good. As soon as it's full dark, we'll move the prisoners." He turned to Clint. "I want you to go to Sully and tell him what we need. You deputize him. On the way, stop in the hotel and tell the judge. Tell him to make sure he keeps his head down. He's the most important person here. Without him, we're out of luck. Everybody move out, grab something to eat, and meet back here at six o'clock. The earliest Mather could make it here will be eight if he kills his horses getting here. I suspect it'll be more like nine. I'll pass the word around town and see Jessup and Pierce."

27

Mather heard the horse coming at a dead run. He grabbed a rifle from his office gun rack and raced to the door. He swung it to his shoulder. His body was outlined from the light inside the ranch house.

"Don't shoot!" came the call from the incoming rider. "I've got news."

Mather recognized the voice, lowered his rifle. In the dark, it was impossible to see others, but he shouted, "Put your guns down. Don't shoot. It's Dusty." He could hear movement and the click of hammers being lowered.

Dusty pulled up at the hitching rail in front of the house and leaped from the horse. The animal was gasping for precious air. Mather had heard that sound before. His cowhand had ridden the horse so hard, the animal might not survive. A loss of a horse was a loss of money. He called to one of his men trotting up from the bunkhouse. "Walk Dusty's horse and cool him down. Once he's back to breathing normal, give him a good rubdown. Keep an eye on him." He turned to Dusty. "What's the big hurry?"

"The judge is in town. It's Nagle."

"Come on in. Let's talk." He saw Huck jogging up. "Huck, get up here. We've got news."

Huck had been filling in as ramrod while Blaisdale was in jail, and he was doing a pretty good job. Huck trotted up the stairs. He was the last through the front door and closed it behind him.

"Cookie," Mather yelled, "bring us coffee for three."

He led the way into the office and dropped into his chair. His large desk separated him from whoever else might be in his office. Plus, he had the desk on a wide stand that allowed him to roll it around, but also guaranteed he would be above anyone sitting on the other side of his desk. He pointed to a chair, and Dusty dropped into it.

"Well?"

"Reno Hawk is dead."

Mather jerked forward in his chair. "What do you mean?" He snapped a look at Huck. "Isn't he still getting those feet healed?"

Huck shook his head. "No, while I was looking at stock this morning, he slipped out of here. One of the boys said he was going into Cherry Creek to kill Jack Sage."

Mather turned his head and looked at the darkness on the other side of his office windows. He was furious, but he didn't want any of his men to see it in his eyes. Once he regained control, he turned back to Dusty. "What happened?"

"I saw it all. I stopped into the Cherry Creek Saloon. Now that the Gilded Lily is closed, it's the next best."

"Yeah, yeah, get on with it," Mather said.

"Well, I get there, and Hawk comes in and starts yellin' for Sage. Finally the bartender knocks on Gabriella's office door. It opens, and he says something to someone inside. You could have blown me over when Jack Sage walks out."

Mather's eyes narrowed. "What was Sage doing in Gabriella's office?"

Before Dusty could answer, Cookie brought the coffee in. He poured a cup for everyone and left.

Dusty put sugar and cream in his coffee, stirred it, took a sip, and continued, "I'm getting there, boss. Anyway, this here Sage come walking out." Dusty looked at Mather and then Huck, then back to Mather. "Sage is huge. I'd hate for him to hit me. So he walks to the bar and tells Hawk to move along. He didn't want to kill him. Reno just laughed at him, took a drink, and drew." Dusty shook his head. "He should've listened. Sage killed Hawk dead with one shot. He put another right there with the first, but the first did all the business what was needed." He shook his head again, dismay written all over his face. "Never thought I'd see it, as fast as Hawk was, but Sage beat him clear with time to spare. Two shots you could cover up with a silver dollar. I've never seen the like."

"Is that all?" Mather asked.

"What, uh, no. There's more. Then the judge walked in. Said the trials would start tomorrow and he was leaving Saturday."

Mather stared out the window again. *I've got to get Blaisdale out of there. I can't have him talking. If he thinks he's gonna hang, he'll spill his guts, and he knows way too much—not everything but too much.*

Dusty was saying something else. "What'd you say, Dusty?"

"The marshal arrested Gabriella. Somebody tried to shoot him last night, and he said it was her."

Mather watched his cowhand. "Is that all? Do you have something else to tell me?"

"Boss, I ain't knowin' how to tell you this."

"Just spit it out."

He watched Dusty take a deep breath. He could see him make up his mind.

"Alright. The marshal said Gabriella ain't Gabriella at all. Said her name's Grace. Grace Mather. Said she's yore sister."

It was Mather's turn to be shocked. His mind raced. *Nobody's supposed to know that. If the marshal knows she's my sister, he knows everything. I was worried about Blaisdale, but it's Grace who's stabbed me in the back.* He could see the shock on Huck's face. All of his men would know.

"Yes," Mather said, "Grace is my sister. We had a plan, and it was working very nicely until she evidently spilled her guts. Now the whole town will know. Huck, we're headed for town."

Huck, eyes wide with surprise, said, "Tonight? You don't think we oughta wait until morning?"

"No, I don't."

"Boss?" Dusty said.

Mather looked at the rider gripping a cup of coffee. "What is it? We've got to ride."

"I heard the marshal telling a bunch of folks in front of his office he'd arrested the banker, too. You know, Franklin?"

This time Mather leaned toward Dusty. "Is there anything else?"

The cowhand shook his head.

"Then go tell Cookie to get you something to eat, and get ready to ride. We'll be heading back into town."

Without another word, Dusty, coffee cup in hand, charged out of the room, closing the door behind him.

"Alright, you men have been drawing fighting wages, now's the time to earn 'em. We'll ride into town. I want every man here, except Cookie, on a horse. We're going to hit the town hard. There'll be two objectives. We hit the bank and the jail. I want every dime out of that bank, and we'll kill every person in the jail."

"What about your sister?" Huck said.

"She's been a liability since we were kids. Now she's gone and implicated me. With her testimony, she'll either send me to prison for the rest of my life or to a hangman's noose."

Huck shook his head. "They'll be expecting us. There's no way we'll make it into that jail."

Mather shook his head. "We don't go in. The jail has windows. We ride up from the creek, slip in behind the jail, and shoot through the windows. Anyone in the jail is a sitting duck. They can't hide. Put three men on that, and tell them not to stop shooting until their guns are empty. I want everyone in that jail to be shot to doll rags. The rest of us will hit the bank. I know the combination of the safe. We'll be in and out of there before anyone knows we're around, and Huck?"

"Yeah, boss."

"When we're done, we ride. We can't come back here, but you tell the men a message for me. After we hit that jail, they'll have more money than they'll need for a long, long time." He winked at Huck. "You stick with me and you'll be able to do anything, anywhere you want."

Huck grinned back. "I'll get 'em moving, boss." He jumped up and strode out of the office. A man on a mission.

Mather watched him pass through the front door and into the darkness. He could hear him yelling at the bunkhouse. Mather grinned to himself. *Enjoy your money now, Huck, because you're never going to see a dime. It's all mine. It always has been. Now I'll have no one to take care of but me.* His grin changed to a satisfied smile. Tomorrow was going to be a better day.

JACK HAD MOVED the women and children into the old Gilded Lily. It was in the middle of town and should be more protected from bullets. He had been pleasantly surprised that most of the males had volunteered to fight. Even the judge had stepped for to fight, but Jack and the town council had insisted Judge Nagle defend the women and children. He understood their reasoning, but was not happy.

Under Jack's direction, they worked quickly. They strung a rope about chest high to a man on a horse. The rope ran from the big oak in front of the doc's house to another oak across the street that wasn't as large, but was big enough to take the abuse.

Other men were working on torches. Once Mather's men were past the doc's house, the torches would be thrown into the street to light the night. A separate group were placed inside the bank. They were led by Jack and included Sully, Clint, Bart, and two others.

Sully had flatly refused to be a guard. He said this could be his last fight, and he was going to be in it. Mr. Pierce had taken Sully's place inside Wade's Gun Shop with the prisoners. Lastly, three men were waiting behind the jail. They would attempt to arrest those who tried to shoot the prisoners. Jack expected them to do it through the windows. He had three bundles of blankets made up like people on the bunks in the jail. They were ready.

JACK'S first indication was the pounding of hooves. Horses were racing toward Cherry Creek, coming up the road just as he had predicted. "Here they come. Don't fire unless they start shooting. Is everyone set?" He looked around in the semi-darkness of the bank. They were waiting in the area behind the cashier's windows. He saw heads nod. "Good luck." He waited, listening to the pounding rhythm grow closer. Then the rhythm disappeared into a jumble of hooves and men yelling in surprise and pain.

He wasn't sure which happened first, the light from the torches in the street or the blast of guns from behind the jail, for they both happened almost simultaneously. Then the front door crashed in, and men appeared in the door. "Throw your guns down!" Jack yelled. He could see Mather in the lead, the man's surprise at the demand, his angry twisted face in the light from the torches in the street. He could see Mather spot him and the other men with guns facing him. One of his men, surprised, yanked his gun up.

Mather yelled, "Nooo—"

The room erupted in smoke and flame. Guns blasted on both

sides. Jack felt a tug in his shirt on the right side. He had a Remington in his right hand. He fired three times toward Mather and switched to the man to Mather's left. After firing twice more, he dropped the revolver into its holster and yanked his other Remington from behind his waistband and fired once. It was over. The bank was filled with smoke and moaning. He looked around to his men. "Is everyone alright?"

Bart said, "Clint's hit."

Jack could see his deputy and friend struggling to get up. Blood was flowing from his chest. Jack rushed to him, pushed him back on the floor, and ripped his shirt open. He could see what looked like a massive hole in his deputy's chest. He stopped and listened. All the firing in his town had stopped. He said to the man nearest, "Get me a light."

A lamp flared and steadied, then came nearer. As the lamp drew closer, Jack could see Clint's eyes watching him.

"Am I dead?"

"Where you're hit, you oughta be." He turned to the man with the lamp. "Hold that lamp right over his chest."

The lamp moved closer until Jack could make out a glint in the blood and gore. "This might hurt." He reached into the hole with a finger. It wasn't deep. He could feel something. He managed to get a finger under an edge and pried up. The badge popped out of Clint's chest. Jack held it up to the lamp, looked at it, then looked down at the star indentation in Clint's chest. He shook his head. "You're about the luckiest cuss I think I've ever seen."

Clint wasn't smiling. "I don't feel lucky. My chest hurts like the dickens."

"You're lucky you can feel it hurting. The bullet hit you dead center in your badge, drove it through your vest, your shirt, your union suit, and about a quarter inch into your chest. You're branded with a star." Jack started laughing. "You're gonna have to be a lawman for the rest of your life."

Everyone was laughing except Clint, when Doc Cook hurried into the bank, stepping over several bodies. "I heard Clint was shot. Let me back there."

Jack stood. "Hurry up, Doc. This man needs your immediate assistance. Seems he's been branded with a star."

The laughter increased.

Puzzled, the doctor made his way through the men to Jack, who dropped the dented and bloody star into his hand. He knelt next to Clint, examined the ugly wound, and shook his head. "You are one lucky man."

Clint looked at the doc. "The next person who tells me that is liable to get shot. I've got a hole the size of a badge in my chest." He started to get up, and the doc pushed him back. "Let me get this cleaned up and bandaged first. Stay still."

Bart, standing over Clint and Doc Cook, had pulled out his notebook and was scribbling in the dim light.

"What you writing?" Clint demanded.

"I'm making you a hero. This'll run here, but I bet they pick it up all over Texas. The name Clint Paget will be famous."

Clint stared up at Bart. "Dang, Bart, I ain't no hero. I just happened to get shot."

"That'll do it. Why, I'll put your name in the headline. Folks in New York City might even read it."

Jack left the squabble and walked over to the bodies near the door. Mather sat with his back against the wall, blood coming from several wounds in his belly. He looked up at Jack and cursed him. "I wish I'd never seen your face."

Jack looked down on the dying man. "You were just too smart for your own good. You could've had a nice life out here if you hadn't been so greedy. Now you're gonna die on the floor of a bank, shot up and bleeding to death. Was it worth it?"

Mather stared up at Jack and cursed him again. Jack stepped past the dying man into the night air, out of the acrid smell of burned gunpowder mixed with blood and sweat. He took a deep breath and looked around. The light from the torches was growing dim as they burned out. Several were being carried by men who were examining bodies in the street. He walked over to the big oak. Three men were twisted grotesquely on the ground, lying as they fell, necks or backs broken. Two more were sitting up but groggy, townsfolk looking after them. He shook his head. "What a mess. All because a lazy man wanted what a working man earned."

One of the men helping with the wounded looked up. "What was that?"

Jack just shook his head and turned back toward the jail.

"Marshal!"

He turned toward the call. It was Wade running toward him. "Jack, you'd better come with me. Grace and Franklin are shot."

The two men trotted toward the gun shop and charged through the front door. In the back room, Grace and Franklin were bloody. Grace was dead from a gunshot wound to the head, and Franklin had a sucking chest wound. Blaisdale had blood on his head, but it looked like he would survive.

"What the devil happened?" Jack asked.

Pierce, who had been holding a revolver on Blaisdale, made a half-turn. "It was all my fault, Marshal. Wade moved to check the door when the shooting started, and I turned to see what he was doing. Blaisdale grabbed my gun away from me."

Wade spoke up. "I shouldn't have worried about the door. My job was to help guard the prisoners, not check doors, but I did. You should have seen Pierce. He went after Blaisdale like a wild man. He never slowed down. While they were wrestling, Blaisdale got off three shots. One of them killed Grace, and one caught Franklin in the chest. He's dying. I think the last one caught some of Mr. Pierce's hand, but he held on. He got the gun away from Blaisdale and smashed him a good one across the head with it."

The doc pushed his way into the room and knelt beside Franklin. He ripped the man's shirt open to expose the frothy pink blood blowing out of his chest. He looked to Jack and shook his head.

Franklin lifted his eyes to Jack and gasped, "Marshal."

Jack knelt down beside Doc Cook. "Don't talk, Franklin."

The man gave a weak shake of his head. "No matter." He coughed. Pink froth covered his chin. "I'm dying. Tell the town I'm sorry."

Jack's face was hard. "I'll tell them." He stood and walked out of Wade's Gun Shop and headed to the back of the jail. The men he had assigned to keep watch on the back had three men in custody.

One Jack recognized. "Hello, Arlo."

One of the citizens he had deputized stepped up. He had a big grin on his face. "You should've seen it, Marshal. They came sneaking out of the creek. Rode up to the edge of the brush and eased, Indian like, up to the jail windows. All of a sudden, it sounded like a young war taking place. Each one of them emptied his gun into a blanket. It was just like you said, easy as pie."

"Good, why don't you boys throw them into those cells they just shot up. Maybe there's enough of the blankets left to keep them warm tonight."

He tossed the keys to one of the deputies and turned toward the Gilded Lily. *I hope none of those kids are hurt,* Jack thought. He ran into an irate Nate Pierce sitting outside the saloon. "How are you doing, Nate?"

"Not worth a cow pie, Marshal. I had to stay in here with my ma and the little kids instead of being out with the men."

"It'll come soon, Nate, way too soon." He patted the boy on the shoulder and proceeded into the Gilded Lily.

Inside, the judge was having a cup of coffee one of the ladies had poured for him. "Any of that left, Judge? I could sure use a cup."

Even as he spoke, Nancy Cook was pouring him a cup. "Here you are, Jack. How are you feeling?"

"Actually, Nancy, I'm feeling mighty fine. It looks like we got through all of this with only a few scratches. The only folks killed were in Mather's bunch. They just rode right into our town like they owned it."

Judge Nagle joined in. "Guess they found out different. You get Mather?"

"He's dead, along with several of his men who tried the bank with him. Also, Joseph Franklin and Grace Mather are dead."

The judge looked up from his coffee. "How they'd get killed?"

Jack explained what had happened.

"Guess that's gonna cut my stay shorter than we expected."

"It could," Jack said, "but remember, we've got all those cowhands and hired guns we caught."

"Check to see if you've got paper on any of them. If you do, I'll give them a trial. If you don't, run those turkeys into me in a bunch. I'll sentence them to thirty days or until they're finished repairing the damage to the town. They'll remain in jail and be under your supervision. When you figure they're done, you can turn them loose."

"Sounds good to me. Jail's gonna be a little tight for a while."

The judge took a sip of coffee. "It'll be a lesson, especially for those cowhands. Nothing comes free." He set his cup down. "Long day for an old man. I'm heading to the sack."

"Good night, Judge," Nancy called to his back. She turned to Jack. "You look tired."

"We all are. As soon as I get Mather's bunch corralled in the jail, I'm heading for the hotel. I may just lock 'em up and throw away the key."

She smiled. "How's Bart?"

"He's fine. I imagine he'll be along to see you as soon as he can. That poor boy can't seem to stay away from you."

Nancy blushed. "We've known each other for a long time."

"Well, I think if he can't get his nerve up to ask you, you need to prod him. The two of you are wasting time."

Her face turned a deeper red. "Jack Sage, a woman can't ask a man to marry her. That's unseemly."

"Then let him go. Do something. Either put him out of his misery or marry him."

Jack set his cup down and strode out the door. His mind was busy cataloging everything he had to do. It looked like problems were straightening out in Cherry Creek, and he was feeling itchy. Soon it would be time to move on.

28

F ebruary came in like a lion. Freezing rain stopped all movement. No stage had been through for three days. It was even treacherous to walk from one end of town to the other. The wind had blown the rain up under the roofs over the boardwalk, and it was frozen solid on both sides of the street. Jack had spent the last two nights sleeping in the jail. It was a lot safer than trying to get back to the hotel.

He was reading Bart's *Cherry Creek Gazette*, his feet propped up on the desk, when he heard cussing coming down the board-walk. Steps banged on the portion in front of his office, and the door flew open.

Sully stomped in. He was a sight to see. He looked like he must weigh over two hundred pounds. He slammed the door against the north wind, and Jack laughed. Sully gave him a dirty look from under a hat that was tied on with a wool scarf to keep it on the man's head and to keep his ears from freezing. Sully marched up to the glowing potbellied stove and thrust his hands out.

"You're a sight, Sully. You have any clothes that you're not wearing?"

"Don't mouth me, boy. I swear I ain't been this cold since the winter of eighteen sixteen. That whole year was bad. I weren't but ten or eleven. Can't remember exact, but we had a stranger come through our part of Virginia. He said a volcany erupted somewhere and plumb blocked out the sun. That was mighty cold, but weren't near as cold as it is here and now. I swear this must be the coldest place and the hottest place on this here earth."

He stopped talking long enough to grab a chair and pull it close to the stove. Before he sat, he took a cup from a hook on the wall and looked at Jack. "You want a fill-up?"

Jack shook his head, then took a sip.

Sully poured a cup and sat sideways in the chair, facing Jack, his left shoulder almost touching the hot stove. He took a sip and made a face. "Boy, ain't you ever learned how to fix coffee? This'll rot yore guts." Then he took another sip.

"Sully, it's not polite to drink a man's coffee and complain."

"I ain't complainin', Jack, just tellin' the truth." He took another sip. His coat began to steam. "When you leavin', boy?"

Jack had put the paper down and was staring at his coffee. The mention of leaving brought his head up and his eyes wide. "I haven't said anything about leaving."

"I can tell. You been checking on Smokey and Stonewall a lot more than you usually do. I heard you got your ree-ward the other day for shootin' that Hawk feller. You've talked a lot about buying cows with that money and taking 'em to the railroads up north. Spring roundup'll be starting pretty soon, so you'll have to get busy. I ain't stupid, boy. I've had that itch before myself."

Jack took another sip of his coffee. "You're right, Sully, but I'd like to keep it quiet for a while longer."

Sully nodded. "I knew it. Yessirree, I sure did. You know you could stay here, Jack. The people of this town like you. They like you a lot." He stood, pulled his gloves off and then his coat. After shoving the gloves in the coat's left pocket, he dropped it over the back of the other chair. Once he was seated, he shook a finger at Jack.

"You listen to what I tell you. You could have a home here. There's the Mather place. It's still up for grabs. If you didn't want that, you could homestead yourself a piece of land. There's all sorts of possibilities. This town owes you, and they all know it. Come on, boy, sink some roots. That little Mexican gal's sweet on you. She'd make you a fine wife."

Jack leaned back in his chair and stared out the front window. The sun came out and shone through the glass and ice. It would start warming soon. The ice would melt, and the trails would dry. He shook his head. "Not ready, Sully. I still have some country to see."

The door flew open again. Bart stood in the doorway, bundled similarly to Sully.

"Close that danged door, boy. That's a cold wind on a pore old man's neck."

Bart pushed it shut.

Jack held up his copy of the *Gazette*. "Just reading your handiwork."

"Good. I need all the subscribers I can get." He turned to Sully. "You should subscribe to my paper, Mr. Johnson."

"Why do that when I can buy a copy just as easy?"

"It'd save you money, plus it would give me a little more operating funds."

"Well, shoot, boy, why didn't you say so. Course I will. Stop by my place when things thaw out, and I'll take care of it."

"Thanks, Mr. Johnson." He turned to Jack. "I've been meaning to tell you. With the last stage run, I received a letter from the *Chicago Tribune*. They want me to write a story about you. They'll pay me two hundred dollars."

Jack shook his head. "Who would read it?"

Bart pulled up the extra chair and sat so he could see Jack and

Sully. "Jack, those articles I wrote about you and Clint were carried in papers on the east coast. They even made it to Europe. People are hungry for news of the West. That story will be read by people all over the world."

Jack shook his head. "They must live some pretty dreary lives if they're willing to read about me."

Sully laughed. "Ain't that the truth, boy. Here we are in this little nowhere, out-of-the-way town, and people want to read about it? Bart, you'd better go see Doc Cook. He might have something for what ails you."

"Listen, you two. What happened here excites readers. Jack, you stopped a war and hanged a bloodthirsty killer who, besides other people, killed the banker and a woman. You did that. And Blaisdale. He's the kind of bad guy folks want to read about being caught and hanged. Shoot, he was cussing people so badly when you led him to Doc's oak tree, you gagged him with his own neckerchief. And what about Mather's bunch, why, Mather himself, and his sister, Grace? Jack, I'm excited. I want to write the story."

Jack looked at the excitement in his friend's face. "Will it help you, Bart?"

Bart stopped. "Jack, don't say yes for me. I want to write the story, but I also want you to see the importance of it. It's big."

"What does your wife think?"

Bart grinned. "It's been six months, and I'm still not used to thinking of Nancy as my wife."

Sully let out a snort. "Humph. In another few months that filly of yores will be ready to foal. I reckon you'd better get used to it. You're gonna be called pa pretty blamed soon."

Bart's grin got wider. "I can see the wisdom in what you say, Mr. Johnson. I believe I shall."

Jack nodded to his friend. "Alright. Just don't blow things out of proportion. There really wasn't much to it. Why don't you give Clint the credit? That'll work even better."

As they sat around talking, Jack realized he hadn't had friends like this for a long time. *I could make Cherry Creek my home. It's a fine little town.* He continued to listen to his friends and gaze out the window. He could see Nate scraping ice from the boardwalk in front of their store. The boy looked up and saw him watching and waved. From inside his office Jack waved back and thought, *But I'd sure like to see that Colorado or maybe even Montana country. Maybe have my own ranch up there.*

JACK SAT EASY ON SMOKEY, turned and looked back at Cherry Creek. Everyone had come out to tell him goodbye, but now the streets were back to normal. The homesteaders were in town buying seed. They didn't have to worry about early foreclosures thanks to Jessup taking over the bank. It looked like he was turning into quite a good banker. Clint had become marshal. He still carried the damaged badge, said it was a good luck charm. He was a good man. He'd make a fine marshal.

He thought of memories. There were a few bad, but a great number of good memories from Cherry Creek. He turned back to the front and urged Smokey forward. The lead rope tightened, and Stonewall gradually picked up his pace. Jack thought, *That mule hates to leave Sully. Come to think of it, so do I.*

Jack rode north. He knew of several folks who were interested in selling their stock, and with his pay and the reward on Hawk, at five dollars a head he'd have enough for three hundred head plus expenses. He felt another twinge of sadness at leaving his friends. They had been good friends and were there when he needed them.

He rode on. Miles passed. He remembered he hadn't checked his Remingtons before leaving. There'd been too much excitement and talking. He pulled Smokey to a stop, flipped the leather thong from his holstered revolver, and slipped the Remington out of his holster. He checked it and dropped it back in.

Just as he turned it loose, a jackrabbit dashed out from beside a patch of bunchgrass and spooked Smokey. The grulla jumped and started crow-hopping. It caught Jack by surprise, and he tightened his grip on the reins. "Settle down, boy. It was just a blamed rabbit. You've been in the barn way too long."

At the sound of his voice, Smokey calmed down. Jack guided the grulla to Stonewall, picked up the lead rope, and they continued their travels.

They had ridden another mile and were winding their way among an area of massive red boulders. Jack pulled Smokey to a stop when they rounded a boulder. In the middle of the road sat a mounted rider, his Winchester pointing down the trail toward them. He was no more than twenty feet in front of them.

Jack started to drop his hand to his hip, and the man's rifle tilted just enough to where Jack could look straight down the muzzle. The man said, "Easy. Move your hand away from that six-gun."

Jack moved his right hand to rest on his thigh. "What can I do for you, Mister . . . ?"

"Name's Chance Doughtry. You'd be Jack Sage, the marshal of Cherry Creek?"

Jack nodded to the man. "Mr. Doughtry, you're mostly right. I'm Jack Sage, but I'm no longer a marshal. I quit, and I'm headed north."

"Now ain't that something. No longer a marshal. Here I've been hired to kill Marshal Jack Sage, and you ain't no marshal. That sure creates a question, don't it?"

"I'd say it does. Who hired you, Mr. Doughtry, if you don't mind my asking?"

"I can't see where it makes any difference now. A Scott Mather hired me through a feller named Huck that I knew. He was pretty set on me killing you."

Jack adjusted his posture and watched the rifle track him. "Mather's dead. Whether you kill me or not won't amount to a hill of beans to him.

"I'm no longer a marshal, and Mather's dead. I don't see where it makes a bit of sense to kill me now. It just gives you kind of a windfall."

"I reckon it does. Kind of makes me breaking my leg a good thing."

"When did you break your leg?" Jack thought, *I need to keep him talking. He won't shoot while he's talking, and maybe I can persuade him not to. That'll be a plus for both of us.*

"Shortly after getting out here. I was plumb clumsy. I slipped on a deadfall, and my leg went all the way through it. My weight went in the other direction, and it broke between my knee and my hip." He patted his left leg.

"How'd you survive the winter? It's been pretty hard."

"I managed to drag myself to my horse. Couldn't mount him, but just hung on. He took me to an abandoned homesteader's place. They had food and everything. It was like they just up and walked away from it."

"Was it within a rock chunk of Cherry Creek?"

"It was, for sure. You know it?"

"I think I do. Belonged to a woman whose husband was murdered. She decided to go back east and left everything."

The man looked genuinely sorry. "I surely hate to hear that, but her bad fortune was my good. By the time winter came on, I was mending pretty well. I shot a few deer and managed right nice."

The man took a deep breath.

Jack thought, *Here it comes, one way or the other.*

"Mr. Sage, I think I've made up my mind. I've enjoyed our little talk, and I can't see a reason in this world to kill you."

Doughtry lowered his rifle. "You go right on by, and have yourself a good day."

Jack nodded. "I thank you, Mr. Doughtry. I'll be seeing you." He bumped Smokey, and with Stonewall following along, he rode past Doughtry. As he passed, he looked the man in his eyes. They were cold and empty. *Those are the emptiest eyes I've ever seen,* Jack thought. *He's planning on shooting me in the back.* The instant the thought hit Jack's mind, he threw himself to the right, launching his body into the air while his right hand shot down to pull the Remington. He turned in midair and watched Doughtry, while he thanked his lucky stars he had forgotten to dog his revolver down when Smokey started crow-hopping.

Jack's move had taken the killer by surprise, but his rifle was coming up fast. Doughtry fired. The shot snapped past Jack's head. He hit the ground and rolled as another shot from the rifle kicked dirt in his eyes. But luckily for him, Stonewall trotted away from the first shot and between Doughtry and Jack.

Jack's immediate thought was, *Don't shoot my mule.* He rolled out from behind Stonewall, and there sat Doughtry, bringing his rifle to bear. Jack fired, and again, and again. Three times the Remington spoke. The grouping wasn't as good as it had been on Hawk, but it was good enough.

The first shot had taken Doughtry in the right shoulder, causing him to lose his sighting on Jack. The second had tracked right and struck the man in the right collarbone, while the third one had tracked farther right and struck the killer right between his cold empty eyes. Doughtry dropped from his saddle.

Jack rose to his feet and moved to the killer's side, still covering him with his revolver. He stared down at the man's eyes. The only difference between now and when he'd ridden by him was they were starting to dry and turn lifeless, still just as empty.

Smokey was cropping grass, and Stonewall was stamping his front foot. Jack picked up the rifle and shoved it into the boot, then threw the man over his saddle and tied him. He removed the bridle from Doughtry's horse, looped the man's rope over the horse's neck, and mounted Smokey.

Stonewall waited until Jack had picked up his lead, and then led off, anxious to be on his way. Jack bumped Smokey and said, "Come on, boy, let's follow Stonewall."

Stonewall, Smokey, and Jack headed north.

AUTHOR'S NOTE

I hope you've enjoyed reading *Stranger With A Star,* the first book in the Jack Sage Western Series.

Thanks for buying and reading my books. Your hard-earned income provides the funds necessary to hire the artists who design the book covers, the editors who edit the books, and the advertising to allow other readers to find out about them. It is a true privilege to be able to share these stories with you.

If you have any comments, what you like or what you don't, please let me know. You can email me at: Don@DonaldLRobertson.com, or fill in the contact form on my website.

www.DonaldLRobertson.com

I'm looking forward to hearing from you.

If you'd like to follow Jack Sage into his next adventures, you can find Book 2 of the Jack Sage Western Series, *Without The Star*, available on Amazon.

Thanks for reading my books.

BOOKS
A Jack Sage Western Series
STRANGER WITH A STAR
WITHOUT THE STAR

Logan Mountain Man Series
(Prequel to Logan Family Series)

SOUL OF A MOUNTAIN MAN
TRIALS OF A MOUNTAIN MAN
METTLE OF A MOUNTAIN MAN

Logan Family Series

LOGAN'S WORD
THE SAVAGE VALLEY
CALLUM'S MISSION
FORGOTTEN SEASON
TROUBLED SEASON
TORTURED SEASON

Clay Barlow - Texas Ranger Justice Series

FORTY-FOUR CALIBER JUSTICE
LAW AND JUSTICE
LONESOME JUSTICE

NOVELLAS AND SHORT STORIES

RUSTLERS IN THE SAGE
BECAUSE OF A DOG
THE OLD RANGER

Made in the USA
Las Vegas, NV
30 November 2024

13011473R00177